Maeve Haran

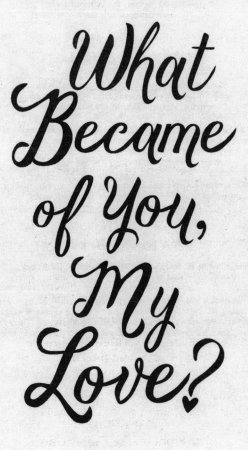

What Became of You, My Love?

PAN BOOKS

First published 2016 by Pan Books
an imprint of Pan Macmillan
20 New Wharf Road, London N1 9RR
Associated companies throughout the world
www.panmacmillan.com

ISBN 978-1-4472-9189-3

1 3 5 7 9 8 6 4 2

A CIP catalogue record for this book is available from the British Library.

Typeset in Albertina MT by Palimpsest Book Production Ltd, Falkirk, Stirlingshire
Printed and bound by CPI Group (UK) Ltd, Croydon, CR0 4YY

Visit **www.panmacmillan.com** to read more about all our books
and to buy them. You will also find features, author interviews and news
of any author events, and you can sign up for e-newsletters
so that you're always first to hear about our new releases.

For my musical heroes
(who my husband says were all popular before 1972).

As Bruce Springsteen wrote in 'Glory Days', he hoped that
when he was old he wouldn't sit around thinking about how
great life had been when we were all young.

But he probably would.

Prologue

The thing Stella was most aware of was the strange atmosphere in the manor house, even on this bright, cold day. The Glebe must have been beautiful once, before it got so run down, but now it seemed slightly forbidding.

Of course it might just be in her own guilty mind.

'That's because it's supposed to be haunted,' Duncan commented, not looking at her. 'We're renting it because it's cheap and it's been used by other bands, so we know it's OK.'

Ever since that night last week, neither of them had looked at the other. How she had ever gone to bed with Dull Duncan, Cameron's shy and awkward friend, she found it hard to imagine. But she'd been really upset at the time and he'd offered temporary comfort and understanding.

Cameron, on the other hand, was oddly jolly. He'd come back from his sudden dash to America rather crestfallen, but ever since he'd produced this new song, he'd been his old cocky

1

self. In fact, he was so exuberant that she wondered if he was on something.

The record company had been brutal and had told him they weren't interested unless he could come up with something new and stronger.

And he had.

It was amazing. Cameron and his musicians were here at The Glebe to rehearse and improve some of their old stuff and then record the new song and mix it in the mobile van outside. Then they'd see if the record company would change its mind.

Inside, the house was freezing. The heating obviously didn't work and though there were a couple of large fireplaces, no one had laid them ready for the touch of a welcoming match. Pulling the tattered red brocade curtains wouldn't achieve much because, though they had once been beautiful, they were moth-eaten and falling apart. Stella slightly dreaded to think what the five bedrooms would be like, and tried to tell herself that being here was a big and very cool adventure.

Laurie, the roadie, kept his beanie hat on and recommended that everyone else did the same.

Stella wished she'd worn something warmer than the floaty floor-length dress in paisley silk that she'd bought at Kensington Market, and was now wearing with just a camisole underneath. She'd been delighted when she'd found it because it looked exotic and Bohemian and just right for a rock star's girlfriend; she'd even wondered whether to wear a flowery headband with it, but now they were inside she was shivering.

'Can I borrow your jacket?' she'd asked Cameron, indicating his usual black Levi's bomber.

'This isn't some fucking Oxford ball,' had been Cameron's pithy reply.

Still not looking at her, Duncan had given her his.

'Where shall I set up the drums, Dunc?' asked the session musician they'd booked to play with them. Duncan had somehow morphed into their manager, she noted.

Duncan looked around the sitting room with the Indian bedspreads thrown across the sofas, sniffing the scent of patchouli joss sticks.

'Probably to mask the damp,' Laurie had moaned.

'There.' He pointed to a space in the large hall, right under a chandelier that looked like it needed polishing.

'What, on the tiles?'

'There's no room in here.'

With Laurie's help he assembled some acoustic screens in each corner of the once-grand drawing room to separate the instruments from each other. The lead and bass guitars took up their positions with Cameron in the centre.

Cameron stood at the mic and brushed back his thick shoulder-length hair, the hair his mum kept telling him looked like a girl's. But there was nothing remotely girly about Cameron Keene.

'I'll have to start just to keep bloody warm.' He grinned and began to sing the new song.

Don't leave me in the morning,
Baby, I don't want to let you go;
Don't leave me in the morning,
Baby, I know our love could grow . . .

Stella forgot the cold as she listened. There was so much vulnerability, so much raw pain and longing in his voice, that she wanted to get up and hold him, she felt so unbearably moved.

If the recording company couldn't see that this new song was a hit in the making, then they were deluded.

'Just add a bit of echo from the echo unit,' Duncan advised. 'The drums sounded incredible with that reverb from the wood panelling and your voice was amazing, Cam, like Leonard Cohen with a dash of Frank Sinatra.'

Everyone laughed. Cameron reached for Stella. 'I need a half-hour nap,' he announced, dragging Stella towards the dilapidated stairs as the others looked on in varying degrees of envy and lecherousness.

'Well, don't make it any longer,' Duncan still wasn't looking in her direction, 'we've only got this place for three days.'

Stella examined her tangled emotions. A certain exultancy at being a rock singer's girlfriend who was behaving outrageously, laced with a sprinkling of suburban discomfort for exactly the same reason, together with a definite dash of relief that obviously Duncan had not mentioned her slip of the other night to Cameron, along with a healthy dab of irritation that their lovemaking was being allotted only half an hour.

She'd have to see about that.

Afterwards, he leaned across her and lit a joint.

'That song . . .' she began, eager to know more about it. 'There's so much pain and loss in it . . .'

'You think it's about you!' Cameron was suddenly laughing at her. 'Why do all women think they're the centre of a bloke's universe? It's a song, Stell. A work of art. Like a Picasso but with the ears in the right place.' He patted her on the hand. 'Here, come on, sorry, love. We'd better get back down or Duncan'll be up reminding us how much we're wasting of his rental fee.'

Stella turned away to hide the tears welling up in her eyes at his brutal tone. There were some aspects of being the lead singer's girlfriend that, frankly, she could do without.

One

2016

Stella laid out the ingredients for spaghetti Bolognese on the wooden worktop of her Arts and Crafts kitchen: beef mince, onions, garlic, tinned tomatoes, puree, salt and pepper, dried oregano and basil. She also added her mystery ingredients: red wine and a Parmesan rind which some TV chef maintained would transform the dish and which actually did. How many times, Stella wondered, had she made spaghetti Bolognese? T. S. Eliot's Prufrock might have measured out his life in coffee spoons, but Stella's was definitely measured out by batches of spag Bol.

It might be humble but it was the perfect dish for a day when her daughter Emma and son-in-law Stuart plus beloved grandchildren, as well as her over-reliable husband Matthew and unreliable best friend Suze, would all turn up at different moments.

Besides, she had a meeting this afternoon with a particularly petulant pug owner. Stella's career as a pet painter had flourished with the arrival of social media, rather to her surprise. It had all started when she decided a blog might be good for business, and started one under the endearing persona of a Jack Russell called Frank whose portrait she had painted a couple of years back. She then added some of Frank's friends, who happened to be other pets she had painted, and the whole thing took off.

And she had to admit, the outcome had been extremely satisfying: a whole succession of pets to paint. Of course it was hard to make them as winning as Frank, but then as every successful portrait painter knows, whether of humans, pets or probably, for all she knew, Martians, a little flattery never went amiss. It might mean you didn't get into the National Portrait Gallery, but you could make a reasonable living. And ever since Matthew had stopped working Stella had found it more and more essential to get out of the house. She didn't want to think too much about that, especially since the statistics about long life meant that they might have another thirty years together.

The thought almost made Stella burn the onions. She was saved by the arrival of Suze, the friend she'd had right through childhood and then art college, bearing a Marks and Spencer's cheesecake. Suze, as usual, presented a colourful picture, reminiscent of Vivienne Westwood with a dash of Grayson Perry. Even at her age she delighted in scouring charity shops for old velvet curtains and scraps of lampshade brocade which, with surprising deftness, she transformed into astonishing outfits on her ancient Singer sewing machine.

'It's just out of the freezer so it needs defrosting,' Suze announced. 'That's why I popped round now. You don't mind, do you? If I wasn't so busy watching re-runs of *The Wire*, I could have whisked up a fatless chocolate with ganache filling but, as you know, I'm post-domestic.'

Stella refrained from asking when her friend had ever been anything else and gratefully accepted the cake. 'Fancy a coffee?'

'Fabulous. Have you got any chocolate biscuits? Only I'm trying to push my cholesterol level up. My bloody GP won't give me statins unless it's higher so I'm doing my best to oblige her.' Suze was convinced statins were the answer to every problem faced by their generation and had been furious when refused this basic right on such unreasonable grounds as her obvious fitness. Amazingly, Suze managed to maintain this despite lounging in a dressing gown watching endless box sets. 'If you haven't got a man in your life,' she was wont to argue, 'they make a passable substitute. And at least you don't have to spend hours arguing about who the killer will turn out to be.'

'I thought that was the whole point of box sets,' Stella responded. 'Giving long-term couples something to talk about when the children have left home. Marriages saved by sadistic murder.'

Actually Stella and Matthew enjoyed them as well. In fact, sometimes Stella thought it was the only thing they did enjoy. Maybe that was what this stage in life should be called. Falling in love. Settling down. Having children. Paying off the mortgage. Retiring. And, after that, box sets.

Stella rooted out the chocolate biscuits from the larder. Naturally they were in an Arts and Crafts tin. This one featured the famous strawberry thief.

'Matthew still as William Morris-obsessed as ever?' asked Suze. 'Where is he, anyway? Trying to discover the last roll of the great man's wallpaper at a car-boot sale?'

They both laughed.

It had all started harmlessly enough. Thirty years ago, while most of their contemporaries headed for the big city, Matthew had seen the advantages of staying in Camley, on London's southernmost fringes, which had both cheap housing and a pleasant high street somewhat influenced by his architectural heroes, so they had remained here and found a house with a turret and an oriel window. Matthew had proceeded to fill it with Arts and Crafts treasures – fireplaces with chased copper surrounds, simple wooden chairs with rush seats, Moroccan-style coffee tables from Liberty, the great specialists in the style, round brass mirrors with turquoise enamel insets. Nothing that was not in period had been allowed house room. The star attraction was a vast embroidered panel that proclaimed William Morris's most famous saying:

HAVE NOTHING IN YOUR HOUSES THAT YOU
DO NOT KNOW TO BE USEFUL OR BELIEVE
TO BE BEAUTIFUL.

Looking at it sometimes, Stella had to repress the thought that these days Matthew himself might not fit into either category.

'Why don't you just move into a museum so you can relax?' Suze teased from time to time and Stella knew exactly what she meant. The house reflected Matthew far more than her. Stella was embarrassed to admit how unconfident she'd been about her own style when they were first married (what a thing for a woman to admit!) and how oddly confident Matthew had been. She had her own domains, though. The kitchen and their bedroom. The rest she'd abandoned to the Arts and Crafts movement. They'd certainly feel at home if they ever came here. Except that they were dead.

Of course, it hadn't always been like this. When they'd

first met, Matthew hadn't been eccentrically obsessed but interestingly different. His degree might have been in chemistry but his major interest had been with Matisse and old saxophones, which he quietly collected. Maybe she should have noted the signs. He had been dark and intriguing, given to wearing black and occasionally a beret and sunglasses like his sax-playing heroes. It had certainly made him stand out in a hippie era of long hair and loon pants. And he'd wanted more than anything to play sax in a band.

To give him his due, as soon as they'd married and had Emma, he abandoned his dream of making it as a musician and trained as an accountant instead. It had been Matthew's earnings, Stella reminded herself sternly, which had kept them all afloat. However, she had compromised too. She had put the idea of becoming an architect on hold in exchange for full-time motherhood. Had she given up too easily, telling herself that there was no way they could afford the childcare during Matthew's training?

But then she'd adored looking after Emma. Her own mother had found it difficult to show affection, but Stella loved nothing more than lying on a rug with her delightful baby under the apple tree in their large suburban garden. Her high-flying friends who'd moved on from Camley to greater things might widen their eyes at the idea of staying in suburbia and looking after your own child, but Stella had made new ones and Suze, as eccentric then as now, a round peg in a square suburban hole if ever there was one, had formed a bridge between the two worlds, caring so little what people thought that they didn't dare think anything.

After a lifetime of buckling down, she supposed Matthew deserved to be as eccentric as he wanted. She just wished it was golf rather than car-boot sales feeding his Morris-mania.

And the idea, the merest suggestion, that they might downsize to a nice flat with deep cosy sofas, carpets you could sink into and underfloor heating instead of aesthetically accurate bare rooms with polished boards and carefully placed pieces was, to Matthew, somewhere between disputing the discovery of DNA and denying the existence of free will. A total affront to everything he believed in.

'Come on,' Suze insisted, 'you'd better get on with the cordon bleu. At least let's have some decent music.' She twiddled the dial on the retro Roberts radio which Matthew had grudgingly allowed into the kitchen.

'Radio 2!' protested Stella, a diehard 4 fan.

'Haven't you heard? Radio 2 plays our sort of music now.'

Stella looked scandalized. The last time she'd listened to Radio 2 had been thirty years ago at her mother-in-law's when Jimmy Young dominated the airwaves telling you a thousand things to do with a discarded pair of tights.

As if in endorsement, DJ Mike Willan's cheery tones filled the room. 'Hello, Flower Children! Hands up anyone who can remember those crazy hippie days?'

Stella and Suze both put their hands up, laughing. 'I see what you mean!'

'Do I have a surprise for you later in the show!' Mike enthused. 'A mega-famous mystery guest who will make all you ladies get your caftans in a twist! So get your matches ready to light!'

'It can't be Bob Dylan?' Suze speculated. 'Remember those Dylan concerts where we all lit a match and held it up?'

'Emma says they use the light on their iPhones now.' They both shook their heads in silent disapproval.

'How old is Dylan anyway?'

'About a hundred and two.' Stella shrugged.

Suze consulted her phone. 'Seventy-five. Bloody hell, Stell, how did that happen?'

'You know what Chrissie Hynde says? All our heroes are going to die in the next ten years.'

'That's cheery! Though they do have a rock-star death a day on the *Today* programme,' Suze conceded gloomily. 'They should start calling it Death of the Day instead of Thought for the Day! But we're still here. What did they say in that Small Faces song? "Mustn't grumble"!'

Fortunately, they were distracted from their gloomy thoughts by the next choice of music. 'It's Steppenwolf!' shouted Suze, turning the radio up so loud that the pictures rattled on the walls. '"Born to Be Wild"! God, I loved this song! I remember staying up all night sitting on my sleeping bag at some festival till they came on at dawn!'

Abandoning the spag Bol to its fate they skipped across the kitchen, revving up their imaginary Harley Davidsons and singing 'Born to Be Wild' at the tops of their voices.

'And here he is, our mystery guest – Cameron Keene!'

'It can't be!' Stella blurted. 'He hasn't been on tour for years.'

'Maybe he needs the cash, like Leonard Cohen when his manager ran off with all the dosh.'

Stella had to sit down at her dresser, glancing up at the photo Matthew had dug out of her when she was a first-year student. All big eyes and blonde Marianne Faithfull hair, wearing the tiniest miniskirt and knee-length suede boots.

Going to art college had seemed such a huge adventure. Wonderful and terrifying. She had been the first in her family to opt for further education, and when they'd dropped her off on her first day, her parents had dressed up as if for a wedding, her dad in his only suit and her mum in a flowery hat. They had been appalled and embarrassed when they'd seen the casual clothes the other parents wore and had never set foot near the place again. Maybe they had been right in their fear and suspicion that their only child was leaving them for an alien world that would change her forever, that she would, as Bob Dylan prophesied, very soon be beyond their command. They certainly watched, baffled and slightly hurt, as she shortened her skirts, went on protest marches, and mixed with young men who, to them, looked like girls. When she got home she would disappear to her tiny bedroom, carting huge volumes with titles they couldn't comprehend, and turn up the equally incomprehensible music. Could that really be a lifetime ago?

'But before we hear from Cameron himself,' Mike Willan continued, 'let's listen to *that* song. It's still one of the most famous tracks of all time. Ladies, does it make your hearts beat faster? How many years ago was it, Cameron?'

'I never was any good at adding up,' replied a grating, guttural voice that made you think of smoky rooms and all-night drinking sessions.

'God, it really is him!'

Suze's arm went out to Stella and they stood, as if frozen by some hippie fairy, listening to the words of Cameron Keene's iconic song 'Don't Leave Me in the Morning'.

'To think we knew him,' Suze whispered reverently. 'And you more than knew him, Stell.'

Stella didn't even hear what her friend said. Instead she listened, transfixed by the words of the song that had become a worldwide lovers' anthem. How many people had gone to bed with someone hoping passionately that it could be the start of love, yet fearing the other person already knew it was a mistake and couldn't wait to get dressed and leave?

Cameron Keene's rasping tones conveyed such passionate

longing, scored with a visceral fear of being abandoned, even more powerful in this song because it was so often the woman who felt used and discarded but this time it was the man. And as she listened she felt the years fall away until she was her eighteen-year-old self once again, listening to the demo being recorded all those years ago at The Glebe.

'I wonder how many people have sat in their bedrooms playing that song over and over again?' Mike Willan asked his audience as the music faded. 'I know I did. And if you're listening, Janet Morgan, I'd like you to know that I'm finally over you.' He turned to his guest. 'I've got a description of your voice here, Cameron. I think you're going to like this.' The DJ lowered his voice to a sexy whisper: *'It speaks of smoky forlorn concupiscence that comes from the heart where love and loss live.'*

'What's concupiscence mean?' demanded Cameron disingenuously.

'I think it means really, really fancying someone.'

Cameron Keene laughed. 'Pretty bloody accurate, then. I did really, really fancy the woman I wrote that song about.'

'And did she abandon you?'

Cameron laughed again. 'She married a chartered accountant.' They could almost picture him shaking his head in disbelief even after all these years. 'Oh, Stella, how could you do it to me?'

Suze gripped her friend. 'Shit, Stella, did you hear that? He really did write it about you!'

Stella shook her head. She could remember how he'd told her the song wasn't about her at all, even accused her of being a typical woman who needed to feel the world revolved round her. How like Cameron to hide his true feelings. Maybe he'd felt she'd got too close, or wanted to hurt her as a punishment because she'd said she wouldn't go to America with him?

13

Stella told herself to be sensible, not to get carried away. 'He probably just said that for effect. After all, it's a pretty good line.'

Mike Willan was clearly intrigued. 'Have you ever seen her since?' he asked, sensing a tale of long-lost love.

'No.' Cameron sounded surprisingly modest and humble. 'But maybe I will now I'm back. She had this extraordinary glowing innocence. Maybe she'll give me some more inspiration.' Cameron laughed in a sexy, self-deprecating way. 'After all, I could do with it. I've made ten albums and that was still my biggest hit.'

'And you've had quite an eventful life . . .'

'Do you mean the drink, the drugs or the divorces?'

Suze laughed. 'You have to like the man.'

'Yes. Very Keith Richards.' Stella was trying to hold on to reality.

'Of course by now she must be . . .' They both paused. It felt like the whole of England, if not the world, paused. 'Over sixty. She could be a grey-haired granny.'

Cameron Keene, raddled rock god, seemed lost for words. Eventually he answered. 'My God, I hadn't thought of that. In fact, I don't think I *want* to think about that. Maybe I'd better not look her up after all.'

'The cheek of the man!' Suze protested. 'I bet you he's no bloody oil painting!'

'And you're playing concerts while you're here?' Mike Willan prompted.

His guest seemed grateful at the change of subject. 'Yes. Thanks for reminding me. My manager will be grateful. Starting in two weeks at the Roundhouse, then Cardiff, Manchester, Leeds, Glasgow, and ending up in Brighton.'

'Fabulous. Thank you, Cameron Keene, and good luck in finding your early inspiration.'

Stella and Suze stood lost in awe as the spaghetti sauce quietly burned on the hob behind them. It was almost too much to take in. One moment she was a suburban grand-mother, the next, the inspiration of a world-famous love song, oozing with pain and passion. She'd sometimes wondered what it would feel like to be Pattie Boyd when she heard 'Layla', or Chris de Burgh's wife when they played 'Lady in Red'. Had it become a burden or did it make them smile a small secret smile – rather like the one on Stella's lips at the moment? *I'm an inspiration*, she told herself, still amazed. *If I haven't done anything else in my life, I've been immortalized. How fantastic is that?*

Suze spoke first. 'Did you have any idea? That the song was really about you?'

Stella shook her head. 'He told me it wasn't. Don't you remember? He wanted to leave art college and go to America. He begged me to go with him but I was terrified. I was eighteen, for God's sake! I didn't know which pants to put on in the morning, let alone whether I wanted to drop everything and be with Cameron. He was so angry with me it was awful. So we split up and I never heard from him again, from that day to this.'

'Get you, though. Stella Ainsworth, muse.'

'Actually, I was Stella Scott in those days.'

'OK, then, Stella Scott, muse. Think about it: "Wonderful Tonight", "My Sharona", "Don't Leave Me in the Morning" – you've inspired an anthem! Isn't that rather fan-bloody-tastic?'

'Except that it's weird too,' Stella had to admit as she thought about it more rationally. 'That song has real pain in it, that's why so many people play it in their bedrooms. I think I might even have played it in mine when Charlie Maynard threw me over for that Daphne, the blonde one, remember? Big boobs, size six.'

'Well, that's ironic!'

15

'Yes, I suppose it is.' They both laughed. 'Fancy me inspiring an anthem at my age!'

'Well, not at your age, precisely. When you were young with all that – what was it – extraordinary glowing innocence? I think this calls for a drink. What've you got?'

'At ten-thirty?'

'*De rigueur* for muses, dahling. Look at Marianne Faithfull before she gave it up.'

'And Anita Pallenberg. Actually, I think I look quite young compared to them.'

'They chose sex, drugs and rock 'n' roll. You chose Matthew and Camley.'

Much struck by this, Stella looked in the round brass mirror, with its decorative turquoise roundels, that Matthew had delightedly found in a junk shop. A still-elfin face looked back at her. Her hair was the same ash blonde, courtesy of L'Oréal now, of course, and cut to shoulder length in that style so beloved of women who don't want to look their age. It suddenly struck her that, despite the years, she had tried to keep the same look. How sad was that? Especially as, on close inspection, those little lipstick-lines had appeared above her mouth, the ones you saw on older sales ladies in Selfridges, and there were ever-deeper lines at either side.

'You know what this means?' Suze looked in the mirror over her shoulder and grimaced.

'That he's going to die of disappointment I'm not still eighteen wearing a minidress and Biba boots?'

'Every bloody journo in the country will want to track down the girl who inspired "Don't Leave Me in the Morning".'

'Of course they won't.' Stella took in the blackened Bolognese. 'This sauce is ruined.'

'Open a jar, then.'

Stella's daughter, Emma, was borderline fanatical about what she fed her baby daughter. 'Ruby's only allowed home-made. With organic ingredients.'

'Lie, then. You're a muse. Break a few rules.'

Stella opened the fridge. 'Do muses drink already-opened Chardonnay?'

'When the vintage Krug's finished I think they drink anything that's available.'

Stella poured them a large glass each and went to look for a jar of shop-bought ragu. 'Probably tastes better than mine anyway.' Stella suddenly sat down. 'I can't believe all this. This morning I was a grandmother who paints pugs. Now I find I've inspired a song I probably paid good money to listen to. I feel like Alice down the rabbit hole.'

'Who else is down there? What about Dull Duncan, Cameron's boring friend, didn't he go to America with him?'

'Yes, I think he did. God, this is all so strange.'

The years peeled suddenly away to the mad and wonderful days when she and Suze and Cameron and Duncan had all been at art college together. It had been an amazing adventure full of music, dressing up in weird and wonderful clothes, dabbling – rather nervously – in drugs and sex and feeling the world belonged to them. Then Cameron had signed with the record company and everything changed.

They had just finished their wine when Matthew barged into the kitchen, hair awry, bursting with familiar fervour. 'You'll never guess what they're planning to do now!'

They were nearly always Camley Council, long-term enemies, in Matthew's view, of all things either useful or beautiful.

'What?' enquired Suze, perfectly used to being ignored by Matthew.

17

'Knock down the corner of the high street!' He turned to Stella, shaking his head at the short-sighted stupidity of modern bureaucrats. 'You know, those red-brick buildings with the gables and oriel windows! They're unique to Camley! And now they want to turn them into another bloody shopping precinct.' His voice shook with indignation.

'Sounds like raising Paradise to put up a parking lot,' teased Suze.

'What are you on about, Susannah?' Matthew enquired wearily.

'Joni Mitchell. "Big Yellow Taxi". Were you even awake in the Sixties and Seventies, Matthew?'

At last he took in their glasses. 'I loathed Joni Mitchell. Anyway, what are you two doing drinking already? Isn't morning coffee more conventional at eleven? And what's that awful smell?'

'I burnt the spaghetti sauce,' admitted Stella, who quite liked the idea of a Little Waitrose or Sainsbury's Local on her doorstep, even if it did have to be half-timbered to fit in with the local architecture.

'Oh for God's sake, Stella, can't you even cook the simplest thing?'

Stella glared back at him. How had it happened that two people, who once had loved each other, now seemed only to find the other one irritating?

'Get over it, Matthew,' Suze replied, grateful she was single. 'She had provocation. And it isn't a conventional morning. Shall I tell him or will you?'

'Go ahead.' Stella shrugged.

'Matthew, you are married to an inspiration.'

Matthew shook his head. This was clearly not a view he shared.

'We have just listened to Cameron Keene interviewed on Radio 2 about the tour he's starting next week at the Roundhouse.'

'But we never listen to Radio 2. It's for overweight plebs addicted to AOR.'

'What's AOR, for goodness' sake?' Suze demanded.

Matthew sighed. 'Adult-Orientated Rock, though it should really be MOR, Moron-Orientated Rock.'

'Gosh, Matthew, you really are a little ray of sunshine. I assume you mean the Eagles, Crosby, Stills and Nash, James Taylor? Then I'm certainly a moron.'

'There you are, then; Radio 2 is right up your street.'

'Well, we listened to it today. And Cameron Keene was being interviewed by Mike Willan.'

'Cameron Keene?' Matthew enquired, interested at last. 'You-thought-he-was-dead Cameron Keene?'

'Nonsense, he's just been a bit quiet lately.' Despite her irritation with Matthew, Suze couldn't contain her excitement any longer. 'Anyway, he revealed that he wrote "Don't Leave Me in the Morning" about Stella!'

'Good heavens!' Matthew turned to his wife. 'I thought you hardly knew the man.'

'We went out for about a year,' Stella admitted. 'He left college and I met you.'

'As a matter of fact, he said he's never forgotten Stella's glowing innocence and hopes he might meet her again so that she can re-inspire him,' Suze announced with a satisfied swagger.

'Stella's far too old for that sort of nonsense,' Matthew asserted, failing to notice the distinctly resentful spark in his wife's eye. 'He's imagining her then not now. He'll be in for a nasty shock if he does come and find her.' Matthew became thoughtful for a moment. 'Isn't he originally from Camley?'

'Acacia Avenue off Brighton Road. Though I don't think he'd want that to get out.' Suze could feel her friend's annoyance and greatly sympathized. If she'd been married to Matthew, she'd have long ago hit him over the head with one of his Arts and Crafts treasures, the heavier the better. 'Camley is far too suburban for his rock-god image.'

'Brighton Road,' Matthew persisted, 'but that's just next to the buildings they want to demolish. Maybe I could get him interested. He could write a song like that Irish bloke . . . you know the one I mean?'

'Bob Geldof?'

Suze and Stella exchanged glances. Either Matthew's tunnel vision was getting worse or he put on this old fogeyish act just to annoy her.

'I don't know, Matthew,' Suze replied, trying to suppress a giggle. 'It isn't exactly world famine, is it?'

'You haven't forgotten Stuart and Emma and the children are coming round tonight?' reminded Stella, changing the subject.

Matthew shrugged. 'I hope it isn't during the athletics.' Athletics were Matthew's new passion.

'These are your grandchildren, remember. You can record the bloody athletics,' Stella pointed out. 'She's got something to tell us.'

'Not pregnant again, I hope. She can hardly afford the children she's got.'

'Matthew,' Suze shook her head disbelievingly, 'you should listen to yourself sometimes.'

Matthew ignored her and changed the subject. 'What's for lunch?'

'How should I know?' Stella replied, goaded. 'I've got an appointment with a pug owner so you'll just have to forage.'

'I'd better be off.' Suze winked. 'See you about seven?'

'She's not coming back, is she?' demanded Matthew as soon as Suze was out of the door. 'I don't know why she hasn't just moved in.'

'Probably because you live here,' Stella muttered under her breath as she got her stuff together to visit the owner who had commissioned her to paint her newest pug. Even pugs would be preferable to her husband sometimes. Stella sighed. She wondered if he'd created this persona as a defence of some sort. After all, when they'd met, he'd loved music as much as she did, including Joni Mitchell. She hoped it wasn't their marriage that had done this to him. What a depressing thought.

'See you later. Don't forget about Emma and Stuart.'

Her mind wandered back to the past for a moment, to those wild and heady days when anything had seemed possible and they were going to change the world.

Cameron had wanted to break free more than anyone, to get away, to shake off his suburban shackles and live.

And now he was back.

Stella found herself smiling as she wondered if he really would manage to track her down. And what she would feel if he did. And, just as important, what would *he* feel to find that his blonde-haired Sixties icon was still living in Camley and had three grandchildren? But, of course, he wouldn't do it. That had been for the benefit of the radio.

Prue Watson, a high-flying businesswoman, lived in a bijou house in a modern development not far from the centre of Camley, handy for the station and Gatwick airport. Despite her busy lifestyle she owned three pugs.

'How on earth do you manage?' Stella asked, fascinated.

'They go to Doggy Day Care.'

Stella burst out laughing. 'Is there really such a thing?'

'Oh yes. It's right next to the station. Lots of people drop their dogs off on their way into town. And if I'm late, I have a nice lady who picks them up and moves in when I'm away.'

The pugs all snapped at each other at Prue's feet, vying for their mistress's attention.

'Aren't they gorgeous? I couldn't choose which one I wanted when they were puppies so I got them all. One fawn. One apricot. One black.'

Stella hadn't known pugs came in different colourways and wondered, since Prue seemed to be some kind of interior designer, if you got them to match your décor. She almost asked if they also came in cappuccino, but decided that might be going too far. Personally, she loathed pugs; their sad, bulgy eyes always looked so anxious, as if inside that wrinkly skin and snuffly breathing a normal dog was wishing it could get out. Yet people seemed devoted to them.

It always amused Stella how people matched their breeds. Yummy mummies pretending to be country ladies opted for chocolate Labradors that went with their Hunter wellies; silly ladies who lunched chose fluffy white Bichon Frises that were never allowed to get dirty; tall rangy people went for tall rangy lurchers, and only the most confident and fearless opted for the dog with the strongest will of all, the Jack Russell. Another thing she'd noticed about dog owners: as soon as their dog died, and they'd finally got the children off their hands and were free to do whatever they wanted, go anywhere they desired, what did they actually do? They acquired a really difficult rescue dog, preferably with separation anxiety, that needed immense input, total stability and consistent training and hey presto, like gardeners who can't go away in the summer, they were no longer free and able to do what they wanted. And somehow this made them very happy.

Stella tried to ignore the faint pong of multiple dog occupation which, to her amazement, even stylish owners like Prue never seemed to notice.

Today her hopefully simple task was to photograph the fawn one. Even dog-hardened Stella had to admit that this particular pug was quite endearing. Of course they all had names beginning with 'P': Pugwash (naturally), Peaches and Pudding. She held out a doggy treat towards Pudding, the candidate for photography, and was steamrollered by Peaches and Pugwash. 'Could they possibly go in the other room? It should only take five or ten minutes.'

'Oh, but I'd like to dress him in various costumes, so we can see which is the cutest.' Prue produced a tiny Venetian opera mask, a nurse's apron and cap and – the pièce de résistance – a Santa costume. 'If I really like the painting, I'm going to make it my Christmas card.'

'But won't the others be jealous?' enquired Stella, straight-faced, as she snapped away with her beloved Fujifilm X-M1. Moments later she could have eaten her words when Prue brought the other two heavy breathers back into the room, produced two more Santa hats and expected Stella to capture all three dogs in one shot.

An hour later, exhausted, one step from committing a doggy massacre, Stella had what she wanted.

'How long will it take you?' Prue enquired eagerly.

'Now I have three to paint, it will take a little longer and I will have to up the price I quoted.'

'Then I hope you'll capture their characters. They're all completely different, you know.'

'Absolutely,' Stella replied, surveying the row of fish-eyed wheezy animals and trying to remember which one was which.

As she opened the front door at six-thirty, she had a brief fantasy that Matthew might have at least laid the table or unloaded the dishwasher. She'd seen how, when they retired, some of her friends' husbands had taken over most of the shopping and quite a lot of the cooking. Some of them, to their wives' amused but grateful astonishment, had become mini cordon bleu chefs, producing prawns with saffron rice or venison with juniper berries for weekday suppers which had previously consisted, when their wives were in charge, of shepherd's pie or pork chops. Unfortunately, Matthew wasn't one of them, though Stella was honest enough to admit she wasn't sure how she'd take it if all her domestic duties were suddenly lifted from her shoulders. On the other hand, occasionally laying the table or making the bed wouldn't go amiss.

Their daughter Emma arrived at seven on the dot with her children in tow. Jesse, at just sixteen, was pale and slender with a curtain of long black hair. In Stella's view he was worryingly withdrawn, though when she had attempted to raise this with Emma she was soon put in her place. All boys his age were like that, had been the tart reply. A grandmother's role, she'd soon discovered, was to keep her wallet open and her mouth shut.

Jesse had grown his hair even longer since she'd last seen him and almost looked like a child of the Sixties himself. He was a good-looking boy when he didn't hide behind his luxuriant locks. Emma had had him in her mid-twenties, earlier than her peer group, and the pregnancy had, Stella suspected, taken her husband Stuart by surprise, if not rendered him speechless with shock. Stuart had only been working for a couple of years, with a well-known firm of radical lawyers who had, it seemed, a rather un-radical attitude to employees taking extended paternity leave. Not that Stuart had really tried.

Stella had sometimes wondered if Jesse's withdrawal was partly due to not seeing enough of his father, and hearing his mother moan endlessly about this fact. The irony of it all was that Stuart was absent because he was helping other people, throwing himself into miscarriages of justice, giving a voice to the voiceless, as his boss liked to put it, and being altogether admirable. Unless you were his family.

Izzy was an exuberant eleven, as much 'Look at me!' as Jesse was silent and detached. She would burst into rooms, twirl around and bow, as if an eager audience constantly awaited her. She was a bright girl, supposed to be studying hard for entrance exams, but keener on capturing her life in selfies and sharing it with her two best friends, Freya and Bianca. Their world fascinated Stella, who had grown up when waiting by the phone was the only hope of communication, but it irritated Emma who was forever threatening to confiscate her smartphone, a sanction so deadly serious, that no one, least of all Izzy, believed her.

And then there was baby Ruby. Stella had been stunned when Emma broke the news that after a gap of ten years she was pregnant again. The first thought that had flown into Stella's mind was that Emma was doing just what those dog owners did when their children left home – volunteering to be tied down again.

Of course, Emma had said that it had all been an accident.

'I thought you'd be thrilled!' accused Emma when she'd told her mother the news.

Stella hadn't asked what Stuart thought because she suspected she already knew. Izzy, who Stella was babysitting one night when Emma and Stuart went out to dinner 'for a chat', disclosed that they had actually gone to see someone to talk about the situation. 'Dad's livid and told Mum she'd done it on purpose and they've gone off to talk to some lady called a Couplers' Therapist in Croydon. They think I don't know, but I overheard them shouting. What's a Couplers' Therapist, Gran?'

Stella tried not to smile at the misnomer, though coupling might be as good an answer as any. It usually was. 'Someone who helps people sort out tangles that happen in all families. A kind person who listens and helps people see the other's point of view so they come away happy again.'

'Like Jeremy Kyle when a dad comes on who's been to bed with the mum's sister?'

'No! The opposite of Jeremy Kyle! He makes people crosser!'

'So they'll be happy when they get back, then?'

'The lady may need to see them a few times, but yes, I'm sure they will.' At least, she fervently hoped so.

The solution had turned out to be Ruby herself. She was an irresistible baby, smiling, happy and sleeping through the night, enchanted by everything, especially the dogs that came to the house to be photographed or painted by Stella. Even the snappiest Jack Russell seemed to calm down when Ruby cooed at it, though Stella was always standing by to scoop her up, just in case. Stuart and Emma, to Stella's relief, seemed to settle down again.

'Hello, darling.' Stella embraced her daughter. She had been about to add, 'Stuart coming later?' but decided even that might sound loaded. 'How lovely to see you all.' She wondered if she should tell Emma about Cameron Keene but it might sound a bit show-offy when Emma was probably feeling stressed. 'Glass of wine?'

'I can't tell you how much I need it,' Emma sighed.

Jesse, silent as usual, went into the garden to kick a football about with his headphones on, so that he was beyond any attempt at communication.

'Can I play on your iPad, Gran?' Izzy asked.

'What does your mother say?' Stella asked diplomatically, but Emma seemed eager for Izzy to leave them. 'Go and find Pappy upstairs. Tell him I said you could use his PC.'

For some reason Matthew didn't like being called 'Granddad'. He said it reminded him of that song by Clive Dunn pretending to be an old geezer.

As soon as Izzy had skipped out of the room, Emma turned to her mother. 'Stuart'll be here later. He's saving the world as usual. I've come to hate the words pro bono.'

'Why, what do they mean?' Stella asked.

'For the public good, i.e., for free. It means it's some worthy case of a deprived person, an asylum seeker from Ethiopia or someone on death row in God knows where, who can't possibly pay but Stuart will have to spend his entire life fighting for them and because it's a good cause I'm not entitled to complain.' She seemed to catch her carping tone. 'God, Mum, I sound like a bitch. It's just that we hardly ever get to see him.'

Stella could see how trying that might be.

'And I'm stuck at home all the time with the kids.'

'But I thought . . .' Stella attempted, confused about why she'd had Ruby if she felt like this.

'Anyway, I've finally come up with a solution . . .'

On these ominous words the doorbell rang, and since no one else, Matthew for instance, appeared to answer it, Stella had to get up and do so.

Suze burst in, clutching flowers and a bottle of Prosecco. 'For my friend the rock chick!' she announced fulsomely.

'Not now,' Stella shook her head discouragingly, 'come in and help set the table. Emma and the children are here.' The last thing Emma in her current state would want to hear was about her mother the muse.

'Shall we wait for Stuart or go ahead and save him some?'

'His dinner can be in the dog for all I care.' This did not bode well for the progress of the Couplers' Therapy. 'Do you know, he accused me of sitting around all day just because I suggested he try and come home a bit earlier to help with bath time. He actually suggested that I'd only had Ruby so that I didn't have to go back to work!'

'Right, let's put the spaghetti on,' Stella responded, feeling herself getting into deep waters. The truth was, whatever she said would be wrong, especially on the subject of Ruby. She had been as surprised as anyone at Emma's sudden pregnancy. On the other hand, she fully supported her daughter's decision to go ahead if it was what she really wanted. A termination would have seemed somehow wrong in a settled, middle-class family, though she knew Suze, and any of her feminist friends, would have bitterly disagreed. 'What did we fight for if not a woman's right to control her own fertility?' they would have demanded. But that didn't really cover Emma's complicated motivation.

Instead, she put her arms round her daughter. 'That must be incredibly galling for you.'

Emma softened a little. She had put on weight with Ruby, but she was someone who looked good carrying a few extra pounds. Her hair was blonde like Stella's but her skin had a kind of golden glow that must have come from Matthew's side of the family. Stella's own skin was pale with a tendency to freckles and so was Stuart's. Maybe one of Matthew's rather repressed relations had once had an affair with an Italian

countess in generations past. If so, Emma was the lucky bene-
ficiary. Jesse had the same pale, almost translucent skin that
Stella had. Lucky Ruby and Izzy, like their mother, went brown
like little walnuts in summer.

'OK, well, if I'm not going to get sympathy I'll have tea
instead, or rather wine.' She held out her glass.

'You were getting sympathy,' Suze commented.

'Anyway,' Emma banged down her glass, 'I've got a little
surprise for Stuart.'

This sounded so portentous that Suze and Stella got up, as
one, and went to sort out the spaghetti sauce and lay the table.

Two

'Where's Pappy?' Stella enquired of her granddaughter, who had suddenly reappeared.

'He's working on some incredibly important document to do with the council. He gave me his phone instead, which wasn't much use, actually, as I wanted to start a test paper for my exams,' Izzy announced, enjoying being holier-than-thou at the adults' expense for once.

'Goodness, it must be important. He can't work his phone but he guards it like a terrier with a bone. Won't even lend it to me when my battery's flat. Matthew! Supper!' Stella yelled up the stairs.

Stella began ladling out the spaghetti sauce, courtesy of Loyd Grossman.

'Mmm,' sniffed Emma, 'you can always tell a homemade sauce.'

Catching Suze's eye, Stella let this pass, given the general air of tense anticipation, and decided not to admit to the sauce's provenance. Ruby would survive something in a jar for once.

'Right!' Matthew appeared, beaming and clutching a sheaf

of papers. 'I am just about to launch my Save Our High Street campaign. Let's see what the bastards in the planning department make of that!' He flourished the document with the same air of self-satisfaction she imagined on the face of Sir Walter Raleigh throwing down his cloak for Queen Elizabeth I. Of course, poor old Walter ended up minus his head in the end. She hoped Matthew's old enemies at the council would be less barbaric.

'Nice sauce, Gran.' Jesse grinned. His pale face came alive when he smiled. 'Can I have some Parmesan?'

'Run out of it; you can have mature cheddar instead.' She passed the block of cheddar over – rather inelegant, she had to admit – and as she did so she caught Emma's raised eyebrow. Maybe baby Ruby wasn't allowed English cheddar.

Ruby, meanwhile, liked the sauce so much she was plastering it all over her head until she looked like the victim of a particularly gruesome baby killer. She picked up the bowl and flicked the contents, with consummate aim, so that they landed on the pristine document that hoped to save Camley High Street from the wicked developers.

'She doesn't approve,' laughed Jesse. 'She's probably a Tory. Hey, Tory Baby!'

Ruby cooed with delight at her new nickname.

At that moment the doorbell rang.

Jesse jumped up, the pleasure draining from his face. 'It's probably Dad. I'll go.'

There was no need to ask if Jesse was aware of the rift between his parents.

Stuart came in bearing a large bunch of flowers and a bottle of red wine. He wore a pin-striped suit that was cut differently from the banker's version and gave him a crumpled, radical charm. Like Jesse's, his hair was dark, but Stuart's curled over his collar. He wore black-framed specs that made Stella think of a young Elvis Costello. They even shared the same intensity. Stella was delighted to see that he handed the flowers not to her but to Emma, who put them down carelessly on the table behind her. They were even from a proper florist, not picked up in a garage or convenience supermarket.

'Lilies, how lovely! I'll get you a vase, Em. They do smell gorgeous. Now, Stuart, some spaghetti for you?'

Matthew, meanwhile, was dabbing his document with a washing-up sponge and trying to pretend he didn't mind, which he obviously did.

She heaped the rest of the spaghetti and sauce in a bowl and handed it to her son-in-law. 'Interesting case?'

'Well, if I didn't do it, no one else would.'

'Stu isn't of the "*wretches hang that jury-men may dine*" school of thought,' Emma commented caustically.

Her parents looked bewildered, though her tone was unmistakeable.

'Pope, *Rape of the Lock*,' she enlightened them. 'I've got an English degree, remember, though obviously I don't use it while I'm lying around watching daytime TV.'

'So,' Stella suggested brightly, 'tell us about your Save the High Street plan, Matthew.'

'I've been reading up on planning,' he replied enthusiastically. 'It seems we need them to declare the high street a LASC.'

'Sounds great,' Jesse threw in, obviously desperate to lighten the atmosphere between his parents, 'as in I'm going out on the LASC.'

Matthew looked at him as if he were speaking Swahili.

'It's a pun on LASH, Matthew,' Suze pointed out. 'The young talk of going out on the lash when they mean getting drunk.'

'Oh. Oh I see. Actually, it means Local Area of Special

Character. What we need to show is that Camley doesn't need another late-night supermarket that doesn't even pay staff the minimum wage, but that there are other ways of bringing the area back to life.'

'Goodness, how on earth will you do that?'

'Yes, Dad, if Mary Portas struggled with it, I'm not sure I'd put my money on you,' Emma commented.

'I rather hoped your mother would help. She's the creative one, after all.'

Stella blinked, stunned but also touched that Matthew appreciated her artistic side.

'Will you come down there with me and have a look?'

'Of course.'

'Maybe Matthew's right.' Suze couldn't resist sharing the revelation of earlier in the day, whether Stella liked it or not. 'Maybe you should try and get your famous friend involved. After all, Camley can't boast too many rock gods, can it?'

'What's she talking about now?' Emma asked rudely.

Suze thought it was time Emma stopped underestimating her mother, even if it was a natural trait in your offspring, which was why Suze didn't have any herself. 'Cameron Keene,' she announced, with the air of a conjuror drawing a rabbit out of a hat.

Emma looked at Stuart. 'Who's he?'

'Rock singer.' Stu shrugged. 'Huge in the Sixties and Seventies. Still incredibly popular. I think he's gone on releasing albums, though God knows who buys them.'

'Actually,' Suze replied, needled, 'he had a hit that went platinum and is on every lovers' compilation ever released: "Don't Leave Me in the Morning".'

They nodded in recognition.

'I know the one,' Jesse exclaimed. 'A bit like a male version of "Will You Still Love Me Tomorrow?".'

Suze looked at him in surprise. 'The very one. And do you know who inspired it?'

Emma and Stuart shrugged, beginning to look bored. 'Is this some sort of oldies' pop quiz?'

Suze looked straight at Emma. 'Your mother.'

'Oh, don't be ridiculous,' Emma scoffed.

'He admitted it this very morning on the Mike Willan show. Told two million listeners that the woman he wrote it for abandoned him and went off with a chartered accountant and that her name was Stella.'

'Bloody hell.' Stuart at least was looking impressed. He turned to his mother-in-law. 'And did you actually go out with him?'

'Yes, I did for a while, before he disappeared to America. He wanted me to go with him but I was eighteen and too scared. Then I met your dad, Emma. That was it, end of story.'

'You didn't keep in touch or anything?' Stuart asked.

'Fuckin 'ell, Gran,' Jesse's tone held a new humility, 'you inspired an anthem. Respect!'

'Does that mean,' Izzy's quick wits had made some fast deductions, 'that Gran was *in bed* with this man? When she was only seven years older than me?'

Fortunately for Stella, Ruby saved the day by tossing her beaker noisily onto the floor and making them all jump.

'Right,' Stella got to her feet, 'time to clear the table. Suze has brought cheesecake for pudding.'

'You know, Izzy,' Suze congratulated as she took her plate, 'you are one fast thinker. If they have that as a question in your entrance exam, you will certainly get in!'

'Yes,' Jesse laughed, for once forgetting the tension between his parents. 'I can see it now. If your grandmother, aged eighteen, was in bed with a rock star in 1969, how old does that make her now?'

Stella turned round, laughing. 'Anyone who answers that will not be getting any cheesecake.'

'That's easy peasy,' Izzy piped up, ignoring the threat. 'She'd be sixty-five!'

'Izzy Cope,' Stuart congratulated, 'I am truly proud of you.'

'Before you all get too star-struck by ancient groupies,' Emma intervened abruptly, 'I have an announcement of my own to make.'

They all stared at her except Jesse, who fixed his gaze firmly on the cheesecake, as if it somehow had the power to prevent any lethal developments.

'I have been offered a job and I am pretty sure I'm going to take it.'

'But what about Ruby?' Stuart faltered, as stunned as the rest of them.

Emma gazed beatifically at Stella. 'I rather hoped Mum could look after her.'

Stella sensed the shaky ground in front of her. She adored looking after her granddaughter, and would be happy to do so for part of the week, but had to admit that the joys of grand-parenting were, at least partly, in being able to give the darling grandchild back.

'I'd be delighted to look after Ruby,' she finally managed to reply, 'and of course I'd always drop everything in an emergency, but I don't think I could take it on full-time.'

'That's typical of you!' Emma blurted. 'You think your pet paintings matter more than your grandchild!'

'That's hardly fair, Em,' Stuart intervened. 'I mean you have rather sprung this on us all.'

'And I'm not entitled to a life!' Emma blazed. 'I thought you'd be pleased I was getting off the sofa!'

'Em, I've never implied you were lazy,' Stuart insisted. 'I

realize you have your hands full with the children and that I don't give you enough help.'

'Too right you don't!'

'It's just that we've never talked about this.'

'And when would we talk about it, since you're never home?'

This was something Stella absolutely supported her on but she couldn't help feeling that Emma was going about it the wrong way. Perhaps she'd already tried a more diplomatic route and got nowhere.

'I'll go mad unless I do something that uses my brain!' Emma insisted angrily.

Stella could see that Stuart was on the point of shouting, 'But you were the one who wanted the bloody baby!' so she tried to steer the conversation away. 'How are you getting on with your test papers, Izzy?'

'She's amazing at that non-verbal reasoning stuff,' Jesse chipped in gratefully, seeing the icebergs ahead as clearly as Stella did. 'You know, "Which of the 2D shapes on the right can be folded into the 3D cube on the left?"'

Stella could see how adept Jesse was becoming at heading off conflict between his parents and it made her feel sad. He had difficulties of his own. 'That's terrific, Izzy, well done.'

'Miss Simmons says I'm one of the brightest in the class.'

'Pity your brother can't say the same,' Emma carped sarcastically.

Jesse looked away and said nothing while Stuart threw down his napkin. What on earth was the matter with her? She was usually so supportive of her children. Stella had often thought what a good mother she was. Perhaps too good.

Suze started to collect the pudding plates. 'I thought that

shop-bought cheesecake was delicious, as shop-bought cheesecakes go,' she commented brightly.

Matthew looked at her as if she had gone mad.

'Bomb about to go off there, I'd say,' she whispered to Stella as they loaded the dishwasher together.

'I know,' Stella whispered back. 'I hope I didn't make it worse. But I really don't think I could cope. I'm knackered when I give Ruby back and have to sit down for the rest of the evening. The funny thing is I think you worry more about your grandchildren than you did about your children. They seem so very precious.'

'She couldn't just spring something like that on you. You've got your painting career.'

'And actually,' Stella agreed, 'I never thought I'd say this but I'm doing quite well. I actually made a living wage this year and we can do with the money.'

'And you enjoy it.'

'And I enjoy it,' Stella agreed. 'Apart from the owners.'

They both giggled.

'You don't have to come into the kitchen to talk about me.' Emma was standing behind them.

Stella turned guiltily. 'I wasn't.' She decided she'd had enough of Emma's attitude. 'I was talking about my dog painting and how well it's going. I'm actually pretty busy.'

'Yes, Mum, I get the message. You're much too busy painting pugs to look after your grandchildren.'

'Of course I'll help. I'm just not up for doing it full-time, that's all. What is the job, anyway?' It struck her that Emma hadn't even mentioned CVs, polishing up her work skills or going to job interviews. The world had turned on its axis since she'd last been in an office. Emma was impressively tech-savvy in terms of watching YouTube, and particularly adept at finding things on eBay, but surely that was different from working in an actual office?

'It's for Hal. Do you remember Hal?'

'Hal you used to go out with at college?' Stella remembered a silent nerdy boy with big glasses and a tall daddy-long-legs frame who used to hang around their house all the time in the holidays, rarely speaking.

'He's a tech whizz now. Offices on Silicon Roundabout. He's made millions.'

'What on earth's Silicon Roundabout?' It sounded like a children's TV show presented by someone with a boob job.

'It's in Old Street, the new East End, full of lofts and studios. It's where all the tech offices are.'

'It sounds a long way from Camley.'

'There is this thing called the Overground.'

'I think she means train,' translated Suze.

The vision of Emma as well as Stuart disappearing off to the city every day for long hours, leaving Ruby in someone's care, hers included, daunted Stella. 'Would it be full-time? What is the job anyway?'

'Organizing events. Hal wants to raise his profile. And don't worry, it'd probably only be three days a week. And anyway, he said I could bring Ruby with me if things got tough.'

Alarm bells began to ring in Stella's brain. She knew the modern workplace had changed but what normal techie whizz said you could bring your baby into the office? The words of a song by Jarvis Cocker flashed into her mind – *You can even bring your baby*. But wasn't that song about someone who was still obsessed with his childhood sweetheart, the girl who hadn't really noticed him?

'So how is Hal these days? Settled down with a wife and family?'

'Mum, you are so transparent! As a matter of fact, he's still single. Says he's too busy for love.'

'How did you happen to bump into him after all these years?'

'Is this the Spanish Inquisition? I met him at a college reunion, if you must know.'

'Oh. That's nice. I didn't know you'd been to one.'

'There's a lot you don't know about me, Mum. After all, I'm a big girl now.' She glanced at the clock. 'Time we went, I think, before there are any other explosions.'

'Right. Emma . . .'

'Yes, Mum?' The exasperation was clear in her daughter's voice.

'Of course I'll help out as much as I can if you take the job.'

'OK, thanks.'

Stella waved them all goodbye and turned to Suze. 'Oh dear, Hal used to be completely obsessed with her at college. Worshipped the ground she walked on.'

'A bit like Cameron and you, despite what he pretended. Funny both of you suddenly encountering lost loves.'

'For God's sake, Suze, don't be bloody ridiculous!' Stella snapped, genuinely worried about her daughter's marriage. 'Cameron Keene is probably as drunk as Dean Martin, as grouchy as Van Morrison and as fat as Elvis!'

But later on, as she emptied the dishwasher, she found herself smiling at the memory of those dizzy, happy times when she thought she was in love with Cameron Keene. It all seemed a very long time ago.

Stella woke up the next day with a start, feeling dreadful. Worry about Emma and the whole job thing with Hal had kept her awake. Should she try and discourage her, which Emma would interpret as not only interference, but also selfishness over looking after Ruby, or maybe even have a word with Stuart? She realized that actually she could do absolutely nothing but leave them to sort it out for themselves. The other thing that had woken her up was an extraordinary other-worldly barking, which almost sounded like the Hound of the Baskervilles on a weekend break in suburban Camley, until she remembered it had to be foxes. Foxes were extremely keen on Camley. They appreciated the cordon bleu quality of the rubbish bins belonging to all those posh Waitrose shoppers.

Stella looked out the window in time to witness an incredible fight taking place between two of them right in the middle of her lawn.

One of the combatants was clearly the young contender, all thick russet fur that shone in the early morning mist; the other was the Jack Nicholson of foxdom, an old dog fox with a disreputable look in his eye and a tail with bare patches that had clearly seen plenty of previous encounters. As Stella stood watching at the bedroom window the young one finally admitted defeat and hobbled off while the wily old Basil Brush looked up, his gaze settling directly on Stella. His eyes were the most extraordinary she had ever seen on an animal, pale tawny green, almost yellow, in fact, and yet not the threatening eyes of a Conan Doyle monster, but gentle and world-weary, almost humorous. They must have stood staring for almost five minutes. As noiselessly as she could, Stella reached for her camera and moved in for a close-up. The fox, still looking up at her, waited, almost daring her: 'Go on,' he seemed to be saying, 'see if you can capture me on that contraption of yours!'

'Stella!' Matthew's voice made her jump. 'What on earth are you doing? It's barely six.'

'The foxes woke me.' She wondered if he, too, was worried about Emma. 'I'll make some tea.'

She made the tea and poured hers into her favourite mug. Funny how comforting an object could be when it was a thing of beauty you'd owned for a long time. This one was in bone china. She remembered the arguments with Matthew that tea tasted better in china. He thought she was mad, but she knew he was wrong.

She took the tea back to bed. 'Suze and I are going down to the high street this morning to have a look around.'

'We have to move quickly. The oracle on the corner tells me they're making the decision soon.' The oracle on the corner was the delightful Turkish newsagent who somehow managed to know exactly what was going on in the entire borough without even leaving his seat behind the counter.

'Right . . . Matthew?'

'What?' he replied sleepily.

'Do you worry about Emma and Stuart?'

'What about them?'

Could he seriously not have noticed the tension between them last night and how Jesse had been trying to keep the peace?

'They don't seem to be getting on. And Jesse's so quiet and anxious-looking.'

'Stella, you imagine things. They're perfectly fine. All couples bicker a bit.'

Stella sipped her tea. She wished he was right, but knew instinctively that he wasn't. Were all men obtuse when it came to emotional relationships or was Matthew more obtuse than most?

Stella decided she didn't want to answer that question.

She was meeting Suze at midday, and since it was a sunny Saturday morning Stella decided to take the bus rather than drive. But first she decided to print up the photograph of the fox and see if it really was as good as she'd thought.

She made herself a coffee while the printer chuntered away. Accidentally, she'd forgotten to set the print size to her usual 6 x 4 and set it at full page. As she sipped her coffee the life-size shot of the fox appeared, the russet of its fur, and those extraordinary yellow eyes accentuated by the bright green of the lawn behind it.

Stella considered it, taken aback by the immediacy of the picture. It was as if the fox was standing right there next to her. She slipped the photograph into a hard plastic folder and put it in her enormous shoulder bag to show it to Suze, who would be a more appreciative audience than Matthew, and headed for the bus.

As usual everyone at the bus stop was busily studying their phones. The stop was next to a popular local pub with a large outdoor area which was nearly always inhabited by smokers. But today, even though it was only half past ten in the morning, an eager queue of people were making their way to the pub garden. Stella noted with interest that they were all ages, including quite a lot of hip young mums with their smart Bugaboo strollers. Stella let the bus go past and decided to have a look. She was amazed to find that the entire garden had been converted into some kind of market for the day.

Tables were laid out offering retro clothes in bright satins and velvets – very Suze – and one rather chic 1940s dress in severe black that she was rather tempted by herself. Another couple had bric-a-brac. There was a book stall with lots of alluring orange and blue Penguins, a craft stall and another offering cappuccinos and gluten-free iced fancies. How amazing that it was just round the corner from her home and she'd never even noticed it.

Despite the temptations of the little market she ought to get on as she wanted to slip into the library in the high street – also under threat – to do a little research before meeting Suze. Fortunately, a bus appeared almost instantly. Stella felt the usual small rush of pleasure as she swiped her Freedom Pass. There might be a lot of disadvantages to not being young, but Freedom Passes were a wonderful compensation.

The reference librarian was very helpful and Stella was soon seated amongst the old men who looked as if this was their last refuge and the diligent foreigners of all ages enthusiastically studying English, mostly through reading the *Sun*. The library had a whole selection of material on high streets, thanks to the Mary Portas campaign to save them, which, she remembered, had been greeted with a certain amount of derision from the giant retail parks who claimed the future was with them.

It was fascinating that in the few years since then it was now the retail parks themselves which were in trouble. Shopping habits had changed yet again.

Stella immersed herself in the debate of 'clicks v bricks', the arguments for and against lowering business rates, providing better parking and giving grants to any start-ups which would take on the desolate empty shops. It was noticeable that some schemes actually had been successful in reviving abandoned areas. The consensus seemed to be that a mix of shopping (and not just charity shops, though they had a place), pubs and cafes and some kind of leisure attraction worked best.

Suze was already waiting for her on the corner of the half-timbered high street, a blaze of colour in the rather depressing backdrop of boarded-up shopfronts, tacky takeaways and betting emporia that had taken over from the video store and the extraordinary fashion shop that, for as long as anyone could remember, had sold giant bloomers, bras that could have held up the Empire State Building and crimplene two-pieces to the good ladies of Camley.

'Suze, I've had this great idea and I'm pretty sure it could be done here. A vintage market – just up your street – lots of stalls with books, antiques, food, clothes – they've opened one in the pub garden near my house.' They turned to consider the only pub in the area, the deeply uninviting-looking King's Arms.

'Nothing ventured,' Stella grabbed her friend's arm. 'Let's go in.'

Two middle-aged (OK, a bit older than middle-aged), middle-class women daring to enter the deeply male, deeply working-class precincts of the King's Arms caused the entire clientele to turn round and unite in a stare so chillingly hostile that it reminded Stella of the scene in *American Werewolf in London*. Before either Stella or Suze found their necks being savaged and black wolf-like hair growing on their bodies, they beat a hasty exit. 'OK,' Stella conceded, 'maybe not the King's Arms.'

They stopped to survey the seedy, somewhat discouraging alternatives. Three doors down was a petrol station which did at least seem to attract some trade. Next to it was a square of derelict land behind which a sign, falling off the wall, bore the legend CAR RENTALS: DAILY, WEEKLY, WEDDINGS AND FUNERALS.

'Maybe no one around here gets married or dies,' suggested Suze.

'It might be OK, though.' Stella was mentally measuring up the space. 'You could fit about ten stalls here. Hang up a bit of bunting, a few Indian bedspreads like Camden Lock, some street-food stalls too. I can see this working.'

'Yes, and on the other days you could put seats up and have an open-air cinema,' Suze suggested, her voice heavy with irony.

'Brilliant idea.'

'Actually, I was joking.'

'Come on, Suze, enter into it a bit. Matthew is dead against having a supermarket but I think he's wrong. It would raise the tone and bring people in. And at least there isn't a corner shop for them to put out of business.'

She remembered the photo of the fox she'd brought to show Suze and delved in her bag. As she pulled out the folder, a wild idea occurred to her. 'You know what, pop-ups are all the rage. I could open a pop-up "Get Your Pet Painted" parlour. See Mr Fox here, how good he looks against that green background? There's a man who paints cows like that in huge close-up and gets hundreds of quid for them. I could photograph Bonzo or Brandy and do the same. I'm sure lots of nice young men around here would treasure a portrait of their snarling status dog.'

'OK, OK, I give in,' Suze laughed.

'Why don't we put in something to the council? Nothing ventured, after all. Maybe do a press release, Photoshopping all our ideas, and take it to the local paper before this meeting. I know it's a bit mad and presumptuous but these councils need a bomb under them to do anything.'

'We could put it all on Facebook too, that way it'll have more impact,' Suze suggested.

They spent a happy afternoon downloading images from the Internet of book stalls, food stalls, farmers' markets and bric-a-brac. For the hell of it they even chucked in an outdoor cinema showing a French film. They finished off by interviewing each other about how they would transform the area back into a busy and vibrant high street.

'Optimistic?' Suze grinned. 'I mean, it's all a bit of a long shot. We don't know the first thing about local regeneration.'

'Well, you have to be optimistic. We could have a fresh eye – after all, we actually use these places, unlike the town planners.'

'Ought we to run it by Matthew?' Suze suggested. 'It was his baby after all.'

Normally Stella would have said yes but today she imagined Matthew's carping response, that it was all gluten-free pie in the sky, a load of bloody nonsense.

'Let's just go for it!'

Suze pushed the send button and Stella felt as if she were at Kennedy Space Center about to launch *Apollo 13*. It was an amazing feeling. Of course it wouldn't lead to anything, but at least they were getting involved.

'You did *what*?' It had taken Stella several days to work up the courage to tell her husband that she and Suze had submitted their own regeneration plan. Matthew looked as if he might burst like a tomato roasted in a hot oven.

'Suze and I posted a few ideas of our own on how to revive the high street, that's all.'

'What kind of ideas?' he asked warily.

'A vintage market on a spare bit of land next to the petrol station; food and second-hand book stalls; a pop-up shop where I'd paint pets; even an open-air cinema.'

'How absolutely bloody ridiculous.'

'Yes, I thought that's what you'd say. That's why I didn't tell you.'

'Stella, this was *my* venture, not yours. I just can't believe you've done this.'

'I didn't use your name. I called myself Stella Scott. There's no connection with you, you can simply put in your own thoughts and it'll look even better, as though more people care. Oh, and we included a supermarket. I know you think they're the spawn of the Devil, but they are used by local people. In fact, it's the Metros and the Locals and the Little Waitroses that are putting the retail parks out of business. We're changing the way we shop, haven't you heard? Well, maybe not, since you never do the shopping. We're all French housewives now. Most people don't know what they're having for dinner tonight because they haven't bought it yet.'

'I just don't know what to say. I feel completely betrayed.'

Stella couldn't keep her temper any longer. 'Oh for God's sake, Matthew! You take the fun and excitement out of everything! They probably won't pay the slightest attention anyway. Just put in your submission separately.'

Stella's mobile rang on the kitchen table next to where Matthew was standing. He grabbed it as if he were going to throw it out of the window. 'Yes?' he barked before she could get to it.

He listened to the caller, looking more and more like a bomb that was about to explode all over the kitchen units.

'It's a Stephen Douglas from the *Camley Observer*. Apparently he's just seen your Facebook page about the high street and would like to talk to you about it.'

Stella took the photograph of the fox out of her bag and carried it up to her studio. She had meant to show it to Matthew, because she'd been so proud of it. It was one of the best photographs she'd ever taken. But now she didn't even want to talk to him, she wanted the peace and quiet of some time on her own. Truth to tell, she did feel a little bit guilty, especially now that this journalist had got in touch, as if she were indeed trying to take over Matthew's project. Yet she knew that if they'd done it together, he would have pooh-poohed all her ideas as unsuitable or frivolous. And, really, he ought to be pleased that the paper was interested, if what he really cared about was actually saving the high street. If he hadn't been so high-handed, she might even have apologized and made a real effort to get him on board.

She took down one of the canvases she'd already stretched and prepared for her animal paintings and laid down the background, playing around with different greens and settling on an almost acid tone which immediately grabbed your attention. She was in such a bad temper that she laid the acrylic paint on thickly, so thickly that the strokes of her painting knife were clearly visible. Holding the canvas at arm's length Stella decided she really liked the effect. It was almost sculptural, with the light catching and reflecting on the ridges of paint. Now she would leave it to dry. Fortunately, acrylic was much faster than the oil she would use for the fox's face. And she could always cheat and help it along with her hair dryer just as she did when she'd painted her toenails.

Then she went back into the house to look for Matthew.

He was watching golf on the television in the sitting room. 'Why don't you meet this journalist with us?' Stella relented. 'Then you can put your thoughts across too. Show him your plan. We're meeting tomorrow at twelve.'

'I'm busy at twelve.' Matthew didn't say doing what. 'Besides, it's your ideas he wants to discuss.'

'Look, love, I'm sorry if you feel I've muscled in on your thing.'

'Now why on earth would I think that?' His tone was heavy with sarcasm.

'Right.' If he wouldn't accept any olive branches, he could just stew. 'I'm off to photograph a lurcher. I'll see you later.'

Matthew didn't even bother to look up from the screen as she left.

Once she was in the car and had driven five minutes down the road, she rang Suze. 'Matthew's being absolutely bloody about our scheme, especially as I got a call from some local journo who wants to talk to us.'

'Hey, fast work! Not bad for a pair of amateurs.'

'Can you come and meet him tomorrow at twelve?'

'Try and keep me away. Unless Matthew's going to be there to put a spanner in our little scheme.'

'Oh sod him. He's going for the full twenty-four-hour sulk.'

The lurcher was a beautiful animal named Nijinsky, a bit like a large greyhound but with dark grey shaggy fur and soulful eyes, and clearly in the habit of draping itself sensuously along the wine-coloured velvet sofa. 'He looks so divine,' pronounced his owner, an equally shaggy-haired gent who appeared to be wearing a dressing gown, 'that I can't bear to chuck him off. Aubergine and gunmetal, my favourite colours.' It took Stella a moment to work out that he was talking about the dog. The bungalow itself was a revelation, perfectly ordinary from the outside, yet, inside, it reminded Stella of an auction house – every corner crammed with overstuffed sofas, giant chinoiserie vases, French jardinières and the pièce de résistance, a pair of lamps disguised as life-size Nubian slaves on either side of the hearth, which sported not a roaring log fire but a bizarre 1950s electrical contraption with only one bar burning. 'So, how would you like Nijinsky to be painted?' Stella wouldn't have been surprised if the owner had produced an entire wardrobe of Russian ballet outfits.

49

'Lying on the sofa,' suggested the owner eventually. 'Or it could be upstairs on my bed . . .'

'He's great where he is.' Stella quickly focussed her camera, hoping that Nijinsky wouldn't turn out to be as eccentric as his namesake. In fact, the major challenge seemed to be waking him up, so that, finally, Stella had to resort to her secret weapon, a squeaker toy, which gave him such a fright that he jumped into his owner's arms, but at least this created a photo opportunity that satisfied both of them.

The house was silent when she got back. On the hall table was a note from Matthew to say that he had gone to the pub.

She stowed away her precious camera, and made for the kitchen where the thought of an omelette and a glass of wine were beckoning to her seductively. As she passed through the sitting room she had the sudden sense that there was someone else in the room and almost screamed. Her nerves were already on edge from the row with Matthew and so she slammed on the lights to find her grandson, wearing his usual headphones, curled up on a sofa behind her. He must have let himself in with the emergency key they kept hidden under the window box.

'Jesse! You almost gave me a heart attack! What on earth are you doing sitting here in the dark?'

'Sorry, Gran.' Stella took in how pale and strained he looked and decided not to pursue the reason for his sudden appearance. She had a pretty good idea anyway. If he wanted to, he would bring it up in his own time.

'Have you had any supper?'

He shook his head.

Stella remembered the delicious steak pies she had bought

for tomorrow. Jesse deserved them more than Matthew anyway.

'How does steak and ale pie strike you?'

Jesse smiled wanly. 'Cool. Thanks, Gran.'

'What are you listening to?'

Jesse looked embarrassed. 'You wouldn't know them.'

This was probably true. It was probably some incomprehensible rapper or the heavy metal so often beloved of teenage boys.

Jesse relented. 'They're called The Incredible String Band.'

'Of course I can remember them,' Stella answered, startled at Jesse's choice. 'They played at Woodstock! I was a child of the Sixties, remember.' She racked her brains for a moment. 'Robin Williamson and Mike Heron, right? I can even remember one of their girlfriends who sang with them. Licorice McKechnie. Such a great name. She used to wear long white dresses like Laura Ashley nighties.'

Jesse looked at her with a dawning respect. 'Right. It must have been amazing then.'

Stella smiled. 'Scary, too. Sometimes I felt a bit out of my depth.'

'But the music was incredible.'

'Indeed it was. I can still listen to it and feel eighteen again. So, are The Incredible String Band making a comeback? Everyone else seems to be.' Stella was actually rather surprised if they were, since they had been quite eccentric even for the Sixties. 'What do you like about them?'

'They're the opposite of commercial,' Jesse replied, suddenly animated. 'They're spiritual and they have this amazing purity and . . . well, there's a girl in my class who really likes them too.'

Stella nodded and took the pies out of the freezer.

Revelations about girlfriends were best left unexamined. All the same, she was happy for him. As long as he didn't get his heart broken. She could hear Matthew's dismissive reaction. *Everyone gets their heart broken. That's what growing up means.* Had she ever had hers broken? Had she really broken Cameron's all those years ago? The funny thing was, she hadn't thought he really cared that much. Yet the song seemed to disprove that. Stella forced herself back to the very different reality of the present. 'Green beans or salad?'

'Beans please.'

'Do I need to let your mum and dad know where you are?'

'I told them I was coming.'

'Excellent.' Stella opened the fridge. 'Coke or beer?' Was she corrupting her grandson? Oh to hell with it. He looked as if he needed some TLC and one beer wouldn't hurt anyway, even if it was a weekday.

'Coke, please.'

Stella handed it to him. There had always been something incredibly touching about Jesse. Izzy had all the chutzpah, but also had all the self-centredness of an eleven-year-old; Jesse was different. He wasn't an academic boy, more intuitive and creative. She knew that Stuart longed for Jesse to follow him into the law, but Jesse hated exams and argued passionately that they weren't a true test of a person's talents. Stuart didn't lose his temper but you could feel the well of disappointment, and so could Jesse. The curious thing was, though Stuart was celebrated in his professional life for his ability to relate to people, no matter how unconventional, his son seemed to be the one exception.

The delicious smell of baking pies seeped enticingly from the oven. Stella, on her way to the fridge to retrieve the beans, gave her grandson a wordless hug.

'Why don't you lay the table?'

Jesse collected mats, knives and forks. 'Two or three?'

'Two.'

Jesse grinned. 'Partners in crime?'

'Since when has it been a crime to share a pie with your gorgeous grandson? Have you got some of their music on your phone?'

They sat eating their meal to the strange, haunting sounds she hadn't heard since she had been a student trying to work out what it meant to be Stella Scott and what on earth she should do about her future.

Amazing to think that future was now the past.

How would her life have turned out if she had said yes to Cameron and gone to America with him all those years ago? Stella mentally shook herself. That was a silly fantasy. Her real life was here in Camley.

The melancholy dirge-like tones of The Incredible String Band reinforced those memories of the Sixties, that mad and amazing era when she had been young, when to be an individual and not to conform to outdated values mattered above all else. She saw herself as she was then, shy and uncertain yet passionate and idealistic, full of hope that life would turn out to be a big adventure. She had been telling the truth when she said she'd sometimes been daunted by all that freedom. Yet she'd seen, too, that it was a unique moment, when respect for authority no longer counted and to be young and free was heady and wonderful. And, although they didn't know it, one never to be repeated.

As they cleared up their plates they heard the key turning in the front door.

Matthew was back.

'I'd better be going.' Jesse grabbed his coat and headed for the door, throwing a wave at his grandfather as he left.

'What was Jesse doing here?' Matthew asked as they undressed for bed later. 'Shouldn't he be doing homework or something on a school night?'

'I think things must be rough at home. Maybe he just wanted a bit of familiarity. He's a sensitive kid.'

'Too sensitive. Probably because they called him Jesse. It sounds like a bloody girl's name.'

'No it doesn't. What about Jesse James?'

'He was American. What was that godawful racket you were listening to anyway?'

'The Incredible String Band. You must remember them. They played at Woodstock.'

'Not those nutters with the girls in white dresses and flowers round their heads, who stood there wailing like banshees?'

This was an unkind but not entirely untrue description, Stella had to concede.

'It was the Sixties! Everyone had flowers in their hair, even me.' Stella grinned, making peace gestures with her two fingers. 'Besides, Jesse's learning the guitar and admires their purity.'

'Why doesn't he like normal music? He should be playing "Stairway to Heaven" or "Smoke on the Water" like any other boy his age.' A thought struck him. 'You don't think he's . . .'

'Oh for God's sake, Matthew, listen to yourself for a moment! What if he was?' Stella answered irritably, guessing his thoughts. 'Anyway, he isn't. He was listening to them because a girl in his class is a fan of them too.'

'That's a relief, I suppose.' She could tell he was still angry with her about the high street campaign.

'Look, Matthew, if you feel I've muscled in on your show, just say so. You talk to the journalist instead. I'll make an excuse.'

'I don't care what you bloody do,' was the muttered response. And then he was asleep.

Stella sat up in bed, furious. This was so typical of him. Clearly he minded very much but he wasn't going to give her the satisfaction of a rational conversation.

'Hello, I'm Stephen Douglas from the *Camley Observer*.'

A hip-looking young man dressed in black drainpipe jeans with a surprising red beard was standing outside a boarded-up video store smiling at them. He certainly wasn't Stella's idea of a local journalist. 'Right, fire away. I understand you've come up with an alternative plan for this part of the high street to save it from the wicked developers and the unstoppable spread of convenience supermarkets?'

'Not quite. We've got nothing against Tesco or Sainsbury's . . .'

'Or even Waitrose,' Suze threw in optimistically.

'. . . opening up here. We just want to keep the architecture and get the community here going again. I'm Stella Ains— I mean Stella Scott, by the way.' She held out her hand to show she didn't see the press as the enemy. 'And this is my friend Susannah Welsh. We both live locally and we wanted to show that there are other alternatives to flattening the whole block.' They all glanced around at the discouraging sight of closed shopfronts, the unprepossessing pub, a betting shop and a pay-day loan venture.

Stella outlined their plan – the potential market space next to the petrol station, the street-food stalls and the outdoor cinema, thinking, as she spoke, how ridiculously ambitious it probably sounded.

Suze's phone rang, making them both jump, which greatly amused the young man interviewing them. Probably his mum did the same. Or, more likely, his gran.

Suze turned her back and started an animated conversation with whoever was calling. 'Yes, thanks, Joanie. I'd better warn her now. Grateful for you letting me know.'

'Wow, Stella, you're not going to believe this!' In her excitement Suze forgot about the company they were in. 'That was Joanie Dodds – you know, Joanie, who was at college with us. She says Radio 2's just launched a "Find Cameron's long-lost Stella" appeal. And they're getting hundreds of responses!'

She was so carried away with excitement that she didn't notice Stella's frantic signals for her to shut up.

To Stella's immense relief, if the journalist had picked up on anything, he gave no sign but went calmly on with the interview. 'You mentioned street food.' He nodded. 'Yep, that's all the rage at the moment. And I gather there's something about a pop-up studio taking pet photos? I think that's what grabbed my editor's attention.'

'Yes, well, I'm a pet painter,' Stella explained, 'and I thought people could bring in their dogs and cats and I would photograph them then paint them. Do you want to see some I've done?'

She took out her phone and showed him her recent work.

'Hey, these are great. They say a really good portrait's one you'd buy even if you didn't know the person. Well, I'd buy these even if I didn't know the dog! Could you let me have a couple and we could run them in the paper?'

'Of course, I'd be delighted.' Thank God it looked as if he hadn't picked up on the Radio 2 stuff.

'So, ladies, could I take a photograph of you?' Stephen asked finally. 'Standing here on this patch of ground in front of the bare wall? Both together and then I'll do you individually.'

Reluctantly, Stella posed in front of what she hoped would one day be an open-air cinema while he snapped away.

As he put away his camera Stella found Stephen Douglas's curious gaze fixed on her for an unnaturally long time.

'This Cameron you mentioned earlier. It wouldn't be Cameron Keene, would it? Only our editor heard the interview. Since Cameron's from round here, he's put a reporter on to looking for a mysterious lady called Stella who's married to an accountant. That wouldn't by any remote chance be you?'

'Oh dear,' Suze apologized as he walked off looking extremely pleased with himself. 'I really blew that, didn't I?'

Three

'Yes, Susannah, you definitely did blow that.'

'Relax. He got his story. It was the pop-up pets he was after. Maybe his editor loves Dalmatians. Come on, let's have a coffee to celebrate.' She looked around at the desolate block of abandoned shops and unappetizing takeaways.

'We could go back to yours,' Suze suggested, 'it's only five minutes away.'

Stella grimaced. 'Matthew's probably in.' She wondered if she ought to prepare him for all this long-lost Stella stuff but it would hardly improve his mood. Anyway, maybe Suze was right and it was the pets they wanted.

'Trouble back at 'mill?'

'Suze, he's driving me bloody mad. He's turned into such a narrow-minded old grouch. I keep wondering if it's my fault. He never used to be like that when we were young. Maybe if he hadn't become an accountant and had followed his dream . . .'

'What was his dream?'

'Ironically enough he wanted to play saxophone in a band, but Emma came along so fast.'

'Not quite Matthew's style. Sax players are supposed to be dead sexy. There's something about a horn player women can't resist.'

'He wasn't always like he is now.'

'How long is it you've been married?'

'God, don't ask. Sometimes it feels like a lifetime.'

'I know. People were supposed to die, not stay married forever and ever. Do you communicate properly? That's the key to a good marriage. I read that in a magazine at the hairdressers.'

'Do you mean do I tell him he drives me to distraction with his tunnel vision and his endless obsessions? No, I don't.'

'Maybe you ought to. Being Matthew, he probably doesn't know he's being annoying. How about proper talking? You know, sitting down together over a bottle of wine, telling each other your hopes and dreams, what you want from life. I assumed that was what married people did, or what's the point?'

Stella looked at her friend in a new light. She'd never suspected Suze had such romantic illusions about marriage.

'What *do* you want from life beyond the everyday? You know, the big things?'

'Gosh! I hadn't really thought about it. Health, Emma being happy, and the children.'

'What about *you* though, Stella?'

With a shock, she realized she didn't really know. Was she frightened that if she lifted up the stone of the everyday, what she'd find was disappointment?

Stella was glad she had lots to do to take her mind off her annoyance with her husband. She had the lurcher painting to get on with. She was especially happy with the mournful look in the doggy eyes and the way he'd jumped into his owner's arms. In fact, daringly, Stella decided to do two paintings, one just of the dog and the other of dog and owner. This would take longer and, since she hadn't been commissioned to do it, he might never buy it. Still, it would be an interesting experiment. She looked at all the different possible background colours and chose a dark striking blue which contrasted well with the grey of both dog and owner and the wine sofa.

So absorbed was she in the project that she only just remembered that Emma had asked her to pick up Izzy. She hoped Emma wasn't going to the old boyfriend's office and accepting his Jarvis Cocker-style invitation to take her baby.

She got to the school ten minutes before pick-up time, grateful she no longer had to join the gaggles of school-gate mums, who were always moaning about something – the quality of the teaching, the absence of fresh veg in the school dinners or, worst of all, how many entrance exams they had forced their dazzlingly brilliant child to sit.

Izzy was always easy to look after because she instantly sat down and did any homework without nagging to be allowed to play Minecraft. Stella then gave her tea before they both settled down on the sofa to watch *Shaun the Sheep*. Izzy knew she was really far too old for this and would never watch it with her friends, but with her grandmother she was happy to regress. Quite often she asked for a rug and buried herself cosily beneath it.

Significantly, it was Stuart, not Emma, who came to pick her up, but his black expression didn't encourage any questioning.

At 6.30 p.m., Matthew's face appeared round the door. 'Do you want me to make supper tonight?'

This was an olive branch and she knew better than to ignore

its significance. 'That'd be lovely. There're some lamb chops in the fridge.

'Glass of wine?' This was definitely peace terms since Matthew rarely drank before supper.

'Even better. I think I'll take it out to the studio. I'm going great guns with the lurcher.'

The extra hour proved exceptionally productive and the lurcher was almost completed by the time Matthew called across the back garden that supper was ready.

They avoided all topics of contention over supper – the high street, Jesse, the state of their daughter's marriage – the list seemed longer to Stella than what they did have to talk about.

Afterwards, as they loaded the dishwasher, Stella thought about her conversation with Suze.

'Are you happy, Matthew?' she asked suddenly. 'I mean, are there things you still want to do in life?'

Her intense tone took him aback. 'Where did all this come from? If you mean do I want to disappear to a desert island, no. I like Camley.'

And our marriage? Stella almost added. Do you like that too? But her nerve failed her. What would she do if he told her he hated it?

'How did the newspaper thing go?' That was generous, given the circumstances.

'Quite well, I think.'

'Thursday tomorrow. It might be in the paper.'

Stella hoped that was all that would be in the paper. But if Stephen Douglas had told his editor that he thought she was *that* Stella, surely someone would have called up for a comment by now? Maybe he had been more interested in the pets after all. She wondered if she should mention it to Matthew, but didn't want to spoil the mood. Things had been much better between them now that he was making an effort to be nice. She crossed the room to her husband and kissed him. 'Why don't you go up to bed and wait for me? I'll only be a moment.'

He cocked his eyebrow in surprise, understanding her meaning. 'All right. Don't be long.'

She locked the back door, then remembered suddenly that it was the day for the bins. They would have to wait.

Two minutes later she was upstairs. Matthew was in bed, naked.

And fast asleep.

She was woken the next morning by the phone ringing. Immediately she thought of Emma. Another crisis.

In fact, it was Suze. 'My God, Stella. Have you seen it yet?'

Stella shook herself awake. 'No, I'm still in bed. Matthew said it might be in today.'

'Matthew?' Suze sounded stunned. 'I didn't think he knew anything about it.'

'Suze, what are you talking about?' Suspicion began to dawn on her that all might not be well. 'The *Camley Observer*. Is the story about us in it?'

'I'm not talking about the *Camley Observer*. I'm talking about the *Daily Post*. You're on the front page. "Radio 2 fronts campaign for rock star's long-lost love".'

Stella sat up, her heart racing.

The *Daily Post* was one of the biggest-selling newspapers in the UK.

'There's a huge picture of you then and now. Stephen Douglas must have sold the story to the *Post* rather than telling his own editor about it. No wonder that snivelling little shit wanted individual pictures. Actually, you don't look too bad. They must have been really disappointed.'

'What are you talking about?'

'They obviously wanted you to be a little old lady. Better story. Anyway, good for you.'

Stella scrambled out of bed. Matthew, still naked, snored on. Beside her on the floor her mobile began to bleep.

Stella looked at it as if it were poisonous, then saw that Emma was calling.

'Mum, my God,' she accused, 'what on earth were you doing giving an interview to the *Post* about going out with Cameron Keene?'

'I didn't. I gave the local paper an interview about saving the high street. The weasel of a reporter must have sold it to the *Daily Post.*'

'What does Dad think?'

'He's still asleep.'

'It's got a photo of our house as well. It says you live in a mock-Tudor mansion.'

'Dad'll be livid. It isn't mock-Tudor. It's Arts and Crafts. And it isn't a mansion, it's a semi.'

'Keep me posted. And Mum?'

'Yes?'

'I thought you were making it up about Cameron Keene.'

'It was a very long time ago.'

'You'd better wake Dad up. Stuart says once the press get onto something they'll start absolutely hounding you.'

Stella put the phone down and began to look for her clothes. As she pulled on her tights she glanced out of the bedroom window. There were several unfamiliar cars out in the street which hadn't been there last night. Another bearing the legend SOUTH-EAST TV, with a satellite on its roof, turned the corner and headed towards their house.

Stella sat back down on the bed. They had two choices,

rather like soldiers in a battle – face them or run. Her first instinct was to run. They could slip out the back way and through their neighbours' garden, though next door did have a rather large husky dog which always looked as if it would like to dine on something more substantial than dog food.

Face them, then.

First, she woke up her husband.

'Matthew, there's been a bit of a disaster. That journalist who interviewed me about the high street made the connection between me and Cameron Keene. And he's sold the story to the *Daily Post*.'

Matthew sat up, rubbing the sleep from his eyes, his almost-white hair standing up like Alpine peaks after fresh snow. It rather suited him but this probably wasn't the moment to say so.

'There are about a dozen reporters down there. I wondered about doing a runner, but the Wilkinsons' dog is out there and we'd probably end up on the news being chased by it. So I'm going to get dressed and go and face them. Then let's make a run for it after that. Maybe if I give them something they'll leave us alone.'

Matthew grunted and started to get dressed. 'This is bloody typical. You never think about what you're going to say before you open your mouth.'

Stella ignored this with difficulty and concentrated on finding herself a pretty top. She then spent ten minutes putting on make-up and doing her hair.

She was about to open the front door when she remembered years ago seeing a Page Three girl who'd had an affair with a married footballer take cups of tea out to the waiting press, and how much she'd admired her chutzpah. Stella made ten mugs of tea and added, as an afterthought, a plate of biscuits.

Taking a deep breath she threw open the door. 'Morning, gentlemen and ladies of the press.' She put the tray down on the wall beside them. 'I would just like to say that this a very old story that took place a very long time ago and it had a happy ending. I got married to my husband and Cameron got married to his three wives.'

There was a ripple of laughter at this.

'Is it true "Don't Leave Me in the Morning" was about you, Stella?'

Stella smiled. 'It's a very good line, isn't it? That I left him for a chartered accountant? And, of course, Cameron has got a tour to plug, hasn't he?'

'Did you break his heart, Stella?' The TV reporter thrust a furry microphone under her nose.

'As far as I can tell Cameron's heart is still beating quite adequately. It's his liver I'd worry about.'

Again there was a huge laugh. 'Sorry, everyone, I have to go now. Just leave the mugs in the garden. And no, I didn't bake the biscuits myself.'

She smiled round at them all and disappeared behind her own front door, swiftly slamming it against anyone hoping to follow her.

Matthew was standing behind it with the car keys. 'You know, Stella, you really are full of surprises.'

Stella grabbed her coat, feeling suddenly quite dizzy. 'I'll take that as a compliment, shall I?'

They slipped out of the back door, swiftly locked it, and headed as quickly as they could across their big back garden.

'The fence is quite low behind my studio. Quick.'

Now they were running, managing to jump over it just as

one of the reporters worked out that there was a side entrance. They headed for a clump of pampas grass in their neighbours' garden which Stella had always loathed for being deeply suburban. Just the other side lurked the husky, a delighted snarl on its face and the long-forgotten glint of the hunter in its chilling blue eyes.

'Oh my God,' muttered Matthew.

Stella shoved her hands deep into her pocket, encountering the plastic bag full of doggy treats she kept for particularly prickly pets.

'Here, Shackleton,' she whispered the tasteless name bestowed on the animal, 'good boy,' and threw a trail of treats as far as she could in the opposite direction. Stella and Matthew stumbled across the lawn and into the next garden, where they instantly encountered their other neighbour, ex-army Oliver, strimming the weeds in his herbaceous border.

'Sorry, Olly, we're being pursued by the press.'

'I wondered what they were all doing outside. You haven't knocked anyone off and buried them under your patio?'

'We don't have a patio.'

'Nor do you. That's all right, then. Would you like me to get out the Defender and you can crouch down in the back?'

'That would be brilliant.'

With a swashbuckling smile that indicated that this was the moment Oliver had been waiting for all his life, he disappeared into his garage, beckoning them to follow. 'I'll cover you with the picnic rug. We take it to point-to-points.'

He opened the back door and they climbed in.

A minute later the garage door raised itself automatically and the car drove politely out. Oliver raised his shooting cap at the reporters, maintaining a steady speed just too fast to allow any of them to try and detain him.

After a few minutes he drew in to the kerb. 'Where to, people?'

'Good question. I think perhaps my friend Suze's house.' Stella turned to her husband. 'Matthew, I'm really sorry about all that.'

Unexpectedly, Matthew was smiling. 'Actually, I quite enjoyed it. Not your average Thursday morning. I wonder how long the bastards are going to stay?'

Oliver considered this. 'Do you want to get my son Archie on board? He's a lawyer who specializes in this kind of thing. You could probably do them for trespassing.'

'I think we'll just disappear for a day or two. Can you let us know as soon as the coast's clear?'

'My pleasure. What *have* you been doing, as a matter of interest?'

'Years ago I went out with a rock star and the press have just found out about it.'

'You'd think they'd have something better to do. Economy's going to the dogs. Scot Nats taking over the country.'

Stella smiled. If Oliver chose to give the gentlemen of the press his considered opinion on the policy issues of the day, it might get rid of them sooner than anything she could do herself.

'Thanks, Oliver, you've been a lifesaver.'

'I could get my air rifle out,' he suggested hopefully.

'Just stick to praising UKIP. That should do the trick. And maybe let their tyres down in the night.'

By the time they got to Suze she was already standing outside waiting for them.

'All hail the Dorothy Parker of Camley.'

'What are you talking about now?'

'You. The new queen of the one-liner. Your comment about Cameron Keene's liver. It's gone viral.'

Stella decided she needed to sit down. She really didn't understand the digital world and Matthew still prided himself on writing actual letters rather than sending emails. 'If people really need me, they'll find me,' was his proud pronouncement.

'So what does that mean exactly?' Stella asked, gratefully receiving the large glass of Pinot Grigio Suze poured them both. Matthew piously shook his head. 'I'd forgotten you never imbibe in the daytime.'

'What it means—' Suze was interrupted by Stella's phone, which she had set to ring like an old-fashioned Bakelite one.

It was Jesse. 'Gran, you're not going to believe this. You're trending on Twitter. Wow, Gran, you're famous!'

'Oh dear,' Stella replied anxiously. 'Explain to your old gran how all this works.'

'Probably someone from the press thought it was funny and posted it and the ball started rolling like that.'

'Oh God, poor Cameron. I didn't mean to make him into a laughing stock.'

'As you put it so succinctly yourself,' Suze interrupted, 'he's got a tour to promote. We'd better go and sort out your sleeping arrangements. You won't mind sheets that have only been slept in for three nights, will you? Only laundry isn't exactly my speciality.'

Stella said goodbye to Jesse while Matthew looked around Suze's house, not even trying to disguise his distaste, his sense of adventure clearly evaporating faster than the dregs of red wine in the glasses that gaily dotted the living room. Suze was a confirmed singleton. You could hardly call her a spinster as that would conjure up images of doilies and cats and Suze went in for neither. Her style could only be described as eclectic, which meant that her small house was full of the dark wood furniture she had inherited from her parents (Suze hated throwing anything useful away), plus the IKEA coffee tables and Billy bookcases (ah, Billy bookcases, thought Stella, remembering all the friends' flats they had adorned) which Suze had taken enormous pride in assembling herself. Bunches of once-fresh flowers in enormous vases were in an interesting stage between dead and desiccated. Eccentric *objets* that had caught Suze's eye gave the room a certain individuality. Not everyone could claim ownership of both an intricately painted Chinese screen and what appeared to be a 1940s American petrol pump.

'Don't worry, Matthew,' Suze teased, noting a certain reluctance on his part to sit down, 'remember what Quentin Crisp said about housework. After four years the dirt doesn't get any worse.' Matthew smiled weakly. 'Anyway,' Suze reassured him, 'I spring-cleaned the February before last.'

By late afternoon, and the progression to the second bottle, Suze's boho style was proving too much for Matthew's desire for order and he announced his departure to the Premier Inn round the corner. 'At least the sheets'll be clean,' he muttered.

Guiltily Stella felt a huge relief.

'He isn't as bad as that at home.' She held out her glass for some more wine. 'Well, not quite as bad.'

'You don't have to convince me.' Suze winked. 'I've known him nearly as long as you have.'

'Why is it so hard to be married for forty years? I mean I *approve* of marriage. I think people are made to live in twos, like with Noah and the Ark.'

'Don't you mean Adam and Eve? And look what happened to them. You know what I think the problem is?'

'OK, Ms Relate Counsellor who's never had a relationship for longer than five minutes, shoot.'

'The very thing that attracts people to one another ends up

annoying them. They don't notice so much while the children are around to dilute things, then the children leave, and they give up their jobs and, hey presto, all they've got is each other. And suddenly they can't imagine what they've been doing together all these years.'

'So they split up and they're lonely and miserable,' Stella took over the story, 'not to mention broke, and they fall and break their hip and there's no one to help them and they die on the floor of their hall with the cat meowing because nobody's fed it. And then their husband meets some nubile divorcee who's popped round with a consoling quiche and three months later he's married her and she stops his children ever seeing him again.'

'Bloody hell, you really have been thinking about this, haven't you?'

'Never occurred to me in my life before.'

They both hugged each other and would probably have become quite teary and hysterical had they not been interrupted by another phone call.

'Oh God, what is it this time? I hope some horrible journalist hasn't got hold of this number too.'

But it was only Oliver, their neighbour in Camley.

'Thought you ought to know. An enormous vehicle has arrived and parked right in your driveway.'

'Not even in the road outside? That really is too much!'

'Indeed. I think this is one for my son Archie, now, don't you? Or I could go and wave my air rifle round a bit?'

'No, no, Oliver.' Stella could see the headlines if Oliver managed to wing a reporter with an air pellet. 'Get Archie. And I think I'd really better come back. Are the reporters still there?'

'They seem to have given up the chase. There's just this big bugger now. Probably the television chappies are holed up inside like that thing in Greece.'

'What on earth's he on about?' whispered Suze.

'I think he means the Trojan horse,' Stella whispered back. Then, in a normal voice, she added, 'I must admit, I do think you're right, Olly, this is harassment. I'm coming over right now.'

'Do you want me to come with you?' Suze offered. 'For moral support?'

'No no, I'll be fine. I wonder how I'm doing on Twitter. Maybe I'll overtake Kim Kardashian's bottom.'

'I think you're enjoying this.'

'Makes a change from painting pugs, I'll say that for it. You could call Matthew at his hotel for me. Tell him what's been happening.'

But when Stella arrived home to find that she couldn't park in her own front drive owing to the arrival of a vehicle that looked like a giant toaster, enjoyment was not uppermost in her mind.

She spotted Oliver walking towards her with a younger carbon copy of himself. Stella held out her hand. 'You must be Archie.'

'Yes, hello, Mrs, er . . .'

'Ainsworth,' supplied Oliver.

'All highly irritating for you,' sympathized Archie. 'The curious thing is, there doesn't seem to be anyone inside.'

'You don't think it's a trap?' Stella suggested. 'Some mad Cameron Keene fan out to get revenge on me, and the whole thing'll blow up when I go in?'

They both looked at her a little strangely. 'No, no,' Oliver assured. 'I was in Aden and Cyprus, and they didn't blow up anything as expensive as this. Take a look inside. It's quite a revelation. If it belongs to these news chappies they certainly know how to live. It must be the BBC.'

'If it were the BBC,' his son protested, 'they'd have a satellite on the roof. This thing's like the Café Royal on wheels. And where's the car that towed it here?'

Unable to resist, Stella climbed into the curious vehicle and looked around. From the purple velvet banquettes to the green satin cover on the bed, and the stained glass of the myriad cupboards that lined every inch of spare wall, the tiny space shone like an amethyst caught in sunlight, a veritable hippie nirvana. There was even a champagne bucket by the bed with a beautiful bottle of Perrier-Jouët Belle Epoque, adorned with intricate Art Nouveau decoration.

'Who the hell does this belong to?' Stella finally demanded, stunned.

'Amazing, isn't it?' Archie grinned. 'I have to say, I wouldn't mind going camping in this little number. It'd beat a tent in the Peak District any day.'

They climbed back out and stood on the pavement none the wiser.

'The strange thing is, if it isn't anything to do with journalists or news teams, what on earth is it doing in my driveway with no one inside it?'

Oliver was no longer listening but watching the progress of an unfamiliar figure, who was walking down the street towards them in sunglasses with a lion's mane of hair which he shook as he walked. The stranger, they all noted in silence, sported the unconventional combination of a brown tweed jacket with orange corduroy trousers, a yellow scarf knotted in the European manner, and yellow Nikes, somehow managing at once to evoke both the masculine immediacy of Jon Bon Jovi with the camp grace of Oscar Wilde.

'I wonder,' speculated Oliver, 'if this gentleman might have anything to do with the mystery.'

'Oh my God.' Stella's hand flew automatically to her face. 'It is. It really bloody is. It's Cameron Keene!'

Four

Stella and Cameron stood three feet apart, transfixed, their eyes fastened upon each other, as if both were stunned into temporary silence. And then the years fell away.

'Stella Scott, my God, you've hardly changed!'

'Cameron Keene, ever the romantic, of course I have!'

He took her hands in his as he scanned her face. 'A few lines here,' he touched the crow's feet around her eyes and ran a tentative finger along her lips, 'and here. Time's wingèd chariot's been kind to you, Stella.'

'I didn't make it run as much as you did, Cam.' She shook her head, conscious of mixing her poetic references, hardly able to believe they were both standing here, outside her house.

And then, suddenly, she remembered that they weren't alone.

Cameron turned to Oliver and Archie. 'This is quite a reception committee,' he commented, as if well used to reception committees. 'Would you all like to see around my remarkable vehicle?'

They all followed, dumbstruck, and crowded into the tiny

space while Cameron, as smooth as a caravan salesman, enlightened them about the salient features of his beloved Airstream. 'Hate Winnebagos, the height of vulgarity, driven by overweight Americans. She's twenty-seven feet long, thirty-nine gallons of water on board, plenty for a shower, awning at the side you can pull down if it's sunny, which, of course, in this country it never is, TV, Blu-ray, satellite. The décor was devised by Debora, my first wife, who has a knack for these things.' He treated them to his wolfish smile. 'I designed the fridge.' He pointed to an enormous, gleaming refrigerator which seemed bigger than the adjoining closet, and proceeded to open the door, revealing it to be full of nothing but Perrier-Jouët champagne and a very small piece of cheese. 'Roxy, my current wife, is not a great eater.'

Stella felt as if she had wandered into a strange and curious dream and decided it was time she woke up.

'But do you live here? In a caravan?'

'Stella,' he replied, shocked, 'what sacrilege! An Airstream is not a caravan. It's a top-of-the-range trailer. By the way, I believe I have to congratulate you about the press and Twitter.' Cameron gave her the benefit of his most charming smile. 'I gather you're a sensation on both sides of the Atlantic.'

'Oh, Cameron, I'm so sorry!' Stella said, meaning it. 'This reporter was supposed to be doing a story on our campaign to save the high street and instead he did it on me and you. Then I opened the front door and found all these reporters here. I just said the first thing that came into my head.'

'And very witty it was too. Not to mention extremely astute. My doctor is as concerned as you are about my liver.'

'Oh, Cameron, it was just a joke!'

'No, no. I was wondering how to come across after all these years hiding in America. You have given me a role. The raddled

75

charm of Keith Richards, the wisdom of Leonard Cohen, with perhaps the common touch of Springsteen. And the liver of Dean Martin. Thank you.'

Stella realized her audience was watching them both, riveted.

'Cameron, it's wonderful to see you, but what on earth are you doing in my driveway?'

'The thing is, Stella, I loathe hotels. I tend to be nocturnal by nature and resent the reluctant response I get to four a.m. requests for room service, so I stay in my own accommodation.'

The fact that Cameron might be expecting to stay here in her drive had suddenly occurred to Stella. 'I see, and what are your plans while you're here?'

'Oh, Duncan deals with all that. I just go where I'm sent.'

'He's still with you, then?' Stella felt a flash of shame at the mention of Cameron's friend. Tall, slight and bespectacled, at first he had seemed so much in Cameron's shadow that you could almost walk straight through him, and then, when Stella had refused to go to America with Cameron and he'd disappeared without a word, it had been Duncan, witty, self-deprecating Duncan, who had comforted her. Briefly that comfort had flowered into something more, but Stella had known almost at once that it was a mistake. Duncan's shy caresses were no match for Cameron's. And then Duncan had gone too.

For obvious reasons neither of them had mentioned it to Cameron.

'Oh yes, I don't even breathe unless Duncan tells me to.'

Stella became conscious of how ridiculous it was to have four people standing in the tiny space of Cameron's curious conveyance. 'Cameron, why don't we go and have a drink in my house.' The other two looked deeply disappointed not to be included in the invitation. 'Cameron and I have a lot to catch up on.'

Cameron removed the Perrier-Jouët from the ice bucket and brought it with him. 'Let me look at you again,' he remarked suddenly. To Stella's embarrassment they all turned and studied her. 'I nearly had a heart attack when that DJ said you might be a grey-haired granny. How old are you?'

'Sixty-four, almost sixty-five, and don't quote the Paul McCartney song. Everyone does.'

'You're still beautiful, Stella.'

'I don't look in the mirror if I can help it.'

'Nor me.' Cameron grinned. 'In fact, I've banned mirrors in here. Though I find cleaning my teeth quite a challenge.' He gave a comical little demonstration of looking into a spoon instead of a mirror.

Stella found herself laughing in a way she hadn't for years.

Cameron began to laugh as well. The old attraction between them was clearly still there. Suddenly she wanted him to herself, to catch up on all the lost years since she'd seen him last.

She turned gratefully to her kind neighbour. 'Thank you, Oliver, for keeping an eye on the house. And, Archie, let me know if I owe you anything.'

'I wouldn't have missed it for the world,' Archie insisted. 'Meeting a genuine rock legend!'

Cameron bowed as if this tribute were no less than he expected. Once inside Stella's house, Cameron surveyed the interior with a critical gaze. 'I like your house,' he announced as if surprised. 'A bit bare and chilly, though. Debora definitely wouldn't approve. She's very fond of chintz.'

'Don't use that word to Matthew, my husband. He's obsessed

with Arts and Crafts. I promise my studio at the bottom of the garden is much cosier. So what happened to Deborah?'

'Deb-or-a, no "h". A backing singer.' He began to open the Perrier-Jouët.

'You mean Debora with no "h" was a backing singer?'

'No, a backing singer is what happened to Debora. I fell for one.' He stopped to reminisce. 'Japanese African-American. Her name was Halle, short for Hallelujah.' Stella tried not to giggle. This was all so far from painting pets in Camley. 'Gorgeous girl. Anyway, Debora was prepared to put up with Halle but Halle wasn't prepared to put up with Debora.'

'I like the sound of Debora.'

Cameron ignored this and filled up her glass. 'But then I met Roxanne.' He sighed as if life had somehow unfairly ambushed him.

'Another backing singer?'

'A mistake, though she's a lovely girl. She's too young for me. Her mother called her after that song by Sting.'

'Goodness me, I bought that; she must be young.'

'She was twenty. She's twenty-one now. Stella,' he shook his head tragically, 'you can't imagine what it's like living with someone who thinks Cream is something you put in your coffee.'

'Instead of a band with Eric Clapton, Ginger Baker and . . . ?'

'Jack Bruce, RIP.' Cameron bent his head in reverence at his departed hero. 'And then she wanted to have a baby.'

'And you didn't?'

'I've already got five children.'

Stella felt a fleeting relief that she and Cameron hadn't married. Wives seemed somewhat dispensable.

'I'm too tired, Stella. And I want another hit.' He grabbed her hands and held them in his. 'I need to be re-inspired, that's why I wanted to find you. You were so sweet and hidden – what was that bit of poetry? Like a flower that blushed unseen!' he announced, proud to have located this cultural titbit from the empty fridge of his memory.

'Gray's "Elegy". I love that poem.' Stella tried to remember the lines. '"The plowman homeward plods his weary way . . ."'

'And haven't I known just what he feels like after a heavy night,' Cameron mused.

'The funny thing is, Cameron, you told me that song wasn't about me.'

Cameron shrugged endearingly. 'I'm a man, Stella, what can I say? Men don't like admitting how much women mean to them. Anyway, that poem always made me think of you; I didn't want you to be unseen! I wanted you to be there with me.'

Listening to him, Stella felt a flicker of response. There might be something sweetly comical about Cameron but he still had the old magic.

Behind them the door opened and Matthew appeared with Suze. Stella pulled her hands from Cameron's grasp. 'It wasn't the press in the drive,' she attempted by way of explanation. 'It was Cameron. Cameron, this is my husband Matthew. And of course, you remember Suze? Susannah Welsh?'

'Indeed,' Cameron replied unconvincingly, then turned back to Matthew. 'Ah,' he announced, completely without embarrassment, 'the accountant. You're a very lucky man.'

The two of them stood eyeing each other like a couple of ageing lions. Then, quite suddenly, Cameron caught sight of something behind Matthew's left ear and stepped forward, more or less pushing Matthew out of the way. 'Is that a Keilwerth on that stand over there?' He pointed at a saxophone which Matthew hadn't touched for years.

Matthew's expression immediately transformed from

caveman protecting his property to fellow wandering minstrel. 'Yes. It's a Keilwerth Shadow. Nickel rather than brass.'

'Didn't Raf Ravenscroft play a Keilwerth on "Baker Street"?' Cameron's voice dipped respectfully at yet another recently departed giant of the music scene.

Matthew smiled. 'The greatest sax solo in rock history. I think it was a gold-plated Selmer with Bal action.'

'What language are they speaking?' Suze enquired.

Any mention of what his wife might have been doing staring into Cameron's eyes was entirely forgotten in the brotherhood of the horn. Stella wondered whether to be relieved or insulted.

Eager to defend the honour of the female gender, Suze decided to show off her own musical knowledge. 'What about David Sanborn's sax solo on "Young Americans"? Bowie produced that.'

Both men favoured her with the briefest of glances, while Cameron opened the champagne. 'Couldn't touch Clarence Clemons on "Born to Run".'

'Hasn't he just died too?' Suze enquired.

'Five years ago. Besides, my dear Susannah, nearly everyone who is anyone has just died. Or will do soon.'

This seemed a natural end to the conversation but the deep masculine bond had already been forged.

'Come on,' Stella shook her head, 'let's leave them alone.' The doorbell rang and they all turned and looked towards the door. 'Now who's this going to be?' Stella sighed. 'The paparazzi? Or a horde of over-the-hill groupies?'

In fact, it was their neighbours, the horrible Shackleton in tow, who had come to complain about Cameron's enormous vehicle, which, apparently, was bringing down the tone of the select area and needed to be removed.

'Cameron,' Stella acknowledged, once the ghastly neighbours

had disappeared, 'I hate to give them the satisfaction, but I really don't think you can stay in our front drive.'

'No,' Matthew agreed with more enthusiasm than Stella had seen him muster in months, 'but you could park round the back!' He indicated the wide gravel sweep between the house and the lawn in front of Stella's studio. 'There's even an electrical point for the Flymo you could plug into for your fridge! Stay as long as you like.'

Cameron beamed.

'Are you sure a hotel wouldn't be more comfortable?' Stella asked faintly.

The answer was ominous. 'Ah, the lovely Stella would prefer me to move on. I shall clearly have to find some other location. Pity. I rather like it here. There is one problem, though.'

'Yes?' Stella asked hopefully, her fingers crossed that it would be the tour which would require his immediate presence.

'I can't drive. Or rather, I can drive but I have a temporary problem doing so.'

'You've been banned!' Suze supplied, giggling.

'And Duncan, old woman that he is, unhooked me and took the car.'

'He doesn't trust you!' Suze grinned, enjoying his discomfort as revenge for being ignored for the last half-hour. 'Then you'd better locate Duncan.'

Cameron took himself off so that they couldn't see how unfamiliar he was with his top-of-the-range smartphone.

'Duncan,' he announced grandly, 'will be here first thing in the morning. Time to open some more Perrier, I think.'

'And he doesn't mean the water,' whispered Stella to Suze.

As if sensing resentment from the female quarter, Cameron now transformed himself into a complete charmer.

Much later – two more bottles of champagne later, possibly

three – Suze whispered to Stella, 'What do you think Dull Duncan actually does for Cameron?'

'He seems to be some sort of fixer stroke PA, organizing Cameron's life for him.'

'And stopping him driving his caravan thing out of your driveway.'

'Yes. I suppose it must have been him who drove it *into* the driveway. Strange he didn't even say hello,' Suze remarked.

'We were at your house, remember, hiding from all the horrible hacks,' Stella reminded her. 'Maybe he was in too much of a hurry. Or delighted to offload Cameron onto somebody else.'

'So you were. I think I'm ready for bed,' Suze confessed. 'All those bubbles have gone to my head.'

'We could leave the headbangers to it. You'd better stay too,' insisted Stella.

'I could get a cab.'

'And miss all the fun? Besides, I need you as my minder in case Cameron decides to rediscover my inspiring innocence.'

'He's quite attractive when he lays on the charm.'

'And has three wives to prove it. One of them just twenty-one.'

They gave each other a hug goodnight. Life had certainly got more interesting since Cameron Keene had re-entered it.

A bit too interesting, Stella discovered when she came downstairs to make the morning tea. Their neighbour was at the door again.

'I can't believe your irresponsible behaviour,' accused Mrs Husky from next door. 'Not only have we been hounded by journalists but that vehicle is also still in your drive and someone is prostrate in front of it.'

Stella went outside to discover Cameron lying, face-down, on the patch of green next to his Airstream, apparently unconscious. Stella, still in her dressing gown, attempted to rouse him.

'Come inside for a cup of tea, Cam—' She decided not to use his name in front of the nosy neighbour who didn't seem to have made the connection between the prostrate figure and Cameron Keene, rock legend.

Cameron groaned. 'I can't. I fell down the bloody steps.' He indicated the entrance to the giant toaster. 'I've done my bloody back in.' He handed his phone to Stella. 'Call Duncan. Tell him to get his arse over here now or there won't be any sodding tour!'

'Do you think we should move him?' Suze enquired. 'Or call an ambulance? We don't want anyone walking past and recognizing him and sticking it on Instagram, do we?'

'Maybe cover him up,' Matthew suggested helpfully.

'What, like a dead body?' giggled Stella.

'You bloody well will not,' protested the prospective corpse.

'I know,' Suze suggested brightly, 'we could prop one of those garden umbrellas over his face so you can't tell who it is and cover up the rest of him.'

Which is why, when Duncan arrived half an hour later, Cameron Keene, rock legend, was hidden behind a vast umbrella with the message: I'D RATHER BE F***ING.

Stella forced herself to go and greet him. Probably he'd been as keen to forget their last hideously embarrassing encounter as she had. 'Sorry,' she apologized as he approached. 'It's my husband's fishing umbrella, that's why it's got the asterisks.'

Duncan Miller, looking astonishingly youthful despite his close-cropped grey hair, wore a perfectly cut hedge-fund manager's suit with sunglasses and tennis shoes. His look,

Stella assumed, must be Jermyn-Street-meets-Laurel-Canyon. All he needed was a cashmere jumper slung over the shoulders to make her really loathe him.

'Yes,' he replied. 'I got the joke. Very funny.' He looked around him. 'How is Cameron?'

'I've hurt my bloody back!' announced a voice from behind the umbrella. Matthew moved it out of the way so that Duncan could take a proper look.

'Can you move at all?'

'I haven't tried.'

'Mr Ainsworth, could you help me lift him up?'

Stella watched as Duncan and Matthew gently raised Cameron into a sitting position. He was definitely less Jon Bon Jovi and more Oscar Wilde this morning.

'You took your time to get here! Where the hell were you, anyway?' Cameron carped.

'On the phone to our PR trying to re-establish you as the J. D. Salinger of rock, the man of mystery who hasn't given a concert for ten years.' He glanced at Stella. 'Rather than the bilious sexagenarian glugging Gaviscon that Mrs Ainsworth's helpful comments evoked. After that I was at The Glebe playing a game of tennis.' He pointed to his shoes.

'Well, you should have been here!'

'Why should I have been?' Duncan asked equably. 'If you had agreed to stay with the rest of us, none of this would have happened.'

'You know I hate hotels. And I can't bear to think of The Glebe as a poncy five-star joint that charges a week's wages for a Diet Coke.'

Suze and Stella regarded Cameron. He didn't look as if he often ordered Diet Coke.

'A very long time ago Cameron recorded a demo at The Glebe,' Duncan explained. 'Before he became famous.'

'When it was a lovely broken-down old manor house! Bats in the belfry, damp everywhere,' Cameron reminisced fondly. 'A week's rent was fifty quid.'

'I know,' Stella replied, hurt that they had airbrushed out her presence. 'I was there, remember?'

Suze and Matthew stared. Cameron still seemed lost in his memories.

'So you were.' Duncan suddenly smiled for a moment and his face completely altered. 'Forgive me, I'd forgotten. What we need here is Debora.' He turned to the others by way of explanation. 'Debora always knew how to handle Cameron and his many injuries.'

'Does Cameron get injured a lot?'

'Cameron,' Duncan conceded, still smiling, 'tends to be accident prone. Especially after the third bottle.'

'But aren't he and Debora divorced?' asked Stella, still not up to speed with the etiquette of rock legends' relationships.

'Twenty years ago. But she's still very fond of him. He can be surprisingly lovable.'

Cameron harrumphed from his prone position on the lawn.

'And Cameron was wise enough to be extremely generous in his settlement. Hence Debora is always happy to come to the rescue. She always knew how to manage him.'

'So why did he leave her for Hallelujah?' Suze whispered to Duncan, mystified.

'I suspect Debora knew him too well,' Duncan replied, raising a telling eyebrow.

'Bloody hell,' Suze muttered. 'Women just can't win, can they?'

'And what about the child bride? Roxanne? Is she not good at managing him?'

Duncan shrugged. 'Gone back to her ma and pa.'

'Telling tales of drunkenness and cruelty?' Stella quipped.

Duncan laughed, this time with genuine appreciation. 'Very good. You know your Kinks lyrics.'

'I would never be cruel to a woman,' protested Cameron. 'I love them too much.'

'Actually,' Duncan enlightened them, 'it's her ma she's gone back to. Her pa took off when she was a kid.'

'That figures,' muttered Suze. 'Looking for a father figure. Doesn't he have a PA who could help?'

'He kept sleeping with them. Debora decided it was easier if she took over organizing his life. Besides, Roxy and he are talking divorce. We need to get Cameron on his feet for his opening night.'

'And when is that?'

'Thursday week. The Roundhouse.'

'I wanted the bloody O2,' muttered Cameron resentfully.

'We've been through this. The O2 holds twenty thousand, the Roundhouse just over three. Better to have a full house than empty seats and the music press tweeting that your tour's a flop before it even starts.'

'That makes sense,' Matthew nodded sagely.

'You can curtain off parts of a stadium to make it look smaller but it's always a risk.'

'Duncan doesn't think I could fill the O2,' simmered Cameron.

'Cam, you haven't made a hit record in ten years. And that was in Japan.'

'Yes I have – they just haven't sold as many as my first.' Stella caught Duncan's eye at this Cameronesque rationalization. 'That's why I want to re-release "Don't Leave Me". Unadorned, just as it was then, with just a little bit of jiggery pokery to make it sound cleaner. Everyone who bought it will have to get it again.'

Stella found Duncan looking at her with such sudden concentration that the blood rose to her face. Perhaps he hadn't forgotten after all.

'We'll have to see what we can do.' He looked away equally suddenly. 'Now, if we can lift you into the house, Cam, I can tow the Airstream round the back and make Mrs Ainsworth's neighbours happy.'

'My name's Stella, if you remember!' Stella answered, more sharply than she'd meant. 'For goodness' sake stop calling me Mrs Ainsworth!'

'I do remember your name as a matter of fact, very well indeed.'

With Cameron leaning heavily on Duncan's arm they finally managed to get him inside the house, where they arranged him on the sofa in the sitting room, leaning on a William Morris cushion with the slogan 'Art for All'.

'Art for All,' Cameron repeated to himself. 'That would make a bloody good album title.'

Duncan shook his head. 'Sounds like 10cc.'

The phone began to ring, and Stella answered it.

'Mum, it's Emma. I've got a bit of an emergency. The girl who's looking after Ruby can't come in. Could she possibly come to you?'

'Have you taken this job, then?' Emma had been ominously silent on the subject.

'I'm giving it a go, yes. I'll go mad if I don't do something, Mum. Could I drop her round in a minute?'

'OK, yes, but she'll have to come with me to photograph a French bulldog,' Stella agreed doubtfully.

'I should think she'd love that.'

'I'll try and leave her with Matthew.' Stella suspected that Matthew would mysteriously develop a prior appointment and Cameron Keene was hardly the babysitting type.

Suze had just left when Emma parked outside the front door and rushed in. 'There are spare nappies in the bag and I shoved some jars of baby food in for her lunch. I'll be back about six.' And with that she whisked off, blissfully unaware of the legend ensconced on the sofa.

Stella unpacked the bag with Ruby on her shoulder and put the baby food in the fridge. Shop-bought rather than home-made organic. She couldn't help feeling a little smug that Emma, usually so superior on the food front, was joining the ranks of ordinary harassed mothers.

She jumped, finding Duncan Miller standing behind her, coolly studying her.

'So,' he enquired, in what seemed to Stella an unnecessarily sarcastic tone, 'do you enjoy being queen of suburbia?'

'Love it,' Stella snapped back. 'Full-time grandmother. Underpaid pet painter. Museum curator to my husband's William Morris obsession. What's not to like?' She hadn't meant to sound so sour but his dismissive manner was annoying the hell out of her. What did he know, or care, about what her life had been like?

'Do you ever regret it? Not going to America with Cameron?'

'I cry my eyes out daily. To be honest, I'd never really thought about it till last week.' She jiggled Ruby, who rewarded her with a delicious gurgle. 'You, on the other hand, went with him. Do you ever regret that?'

'Life has certainly been colourful.'

'Yes. I watched *The Osbournes*. I imagine life with Cameron Keene might be similar.'

'With a bigger cast list.'

'More wives certainly. At least Ozzy stuck to Sharon.' Something made her glance at him more closely. 'And you? Is your marital history equally colourful?'

'Oh, I'm very dull. Just the one wife.'

'You didn't bring her?'

'She died last year. It was very sudden. There wasn't anything anyone could do.'

Stella flushed. 'I'm so sorry.' She would have liked to ask more but didn't want to intrude.

'Yes.' Sensing genuine sympathy, Duncan unbent a little. 'Her name was Connie. I met her in New York. She was a painter.' His voice had softened at her memory. 'She was always full of life.'

'Did you have children?'

'As a matter of fact, no. We wanted to but it didn't happen.'

Stella got the impression that this was too private and changed the subject. 'So, what exactly do you do for Cameron?'

Duncan smiled broadly. 'Oh, I make his life easier. Order the cabs. Make sure he gets his Americano.'

'Lucky Cameron.'

'Cameron, as you will have gathered, is charming but a tad impractical.'

'You can say that again.'

'And what about you? Have you been happy all these years?'

Stella was saved from this loaded question by her mobile vibrating in her pocket. The bulldog owner had an urgent appointment and wanted to bring the dog to her at home. 'Could you hold Ruby a moment? I just need to find my diary.'

'How quaint.' He took the baby with surprising confidence. 'You actually write things down in a diary.'

'Yes, and I have a Filofax too. Amazing, isn't it? But at least I don't lose all my contacts when I drop my phone down the loo.'

'Do people really do that?'

Stella had indeed done this herself, though she decided not to admit it on this occasion. His smiling superiority was proving too much for her. 'People do it when they crap. But perhaps you don't crap like other people?' Stella knew this sounded outrageous but there was something about Duncan's manner – mocking and quizzical – that really got to her.

'Obviously not. Talking of crap, this baby needs changing. Would you like me to do it?'

Stella looked at him in astonishment.

'You really don't think much of me, do you?' Duncan asked.

Stella shrugged. 'Maybe it's the sunglasses. Or the tennis shoes. Or maybe it's your constant references to suburbia.'

'Just the one. Appearances can be deceptive. I once thought you were shy and flower-like.'

'So did Cameron.' Stella stared at him, perplexed. 'Plus you don't look like the baby-changing type in that suit.'

'As a matter of fact our tour manager used to bring her babies with her on the bus. I got to be quite a dab hand. And, of course, Cameron had five.'

Stella found her diary and retrieved Ruby, who was happily batting Duncan Miller on the head with her toy rabbit.

'Will Cameron be all right? Doesn't he need to see a doctor or anything?'

'Cameron likes to over-react. Five minutes ago he was talking sax solos with your husband. For an accountant, I hear he's quite a good player.'

'Yes,' Stella quipped sharply, 'I deprived him of his dreams of being a musician as soon as I'd wrecked Cameron's by refusing to go to America.'

'Nice work. And what else have you done with your life?'

'Brought up my daughter Emma. Made a home. And now I paint pets.' It probably didn't sound much to someone in the international music business. 'Speaking of which, I have a canine client arriving soon so Ruby and I will be in my studio, in case there are any more disasters.'

Duncan bowed rather formally. 'Let's hope we won't need to disturb you. Debora will get here as soon as she can so she can take looking after Cameron off your hands. And don't worry, I'll book her a room at The Glebe with me. Your husband says he's happy for Cameron to stay on here.'

'Oh does he?' Stella was halfway across the lawn to her studio when it occurred to her that a bulldog, no matter how French, and a baby were not necessarily a good combination.

She went back to the house to find Cameron and Matthew busy arguing over whether the sax player or the singer were the sexiest members of the band. Really, thought Stella crossly, they were like two old boys in a golf club bar.

When Stella plopped the baby into Matthew's arms, he looked astonished, as if she were some parcel that he hadn't ordered and didn't want.

'It's Ruby. Your grandchild. You need to look after her for an hour.'

'I know she's my grandchild, but as a matter of fact I was in the middle of a conversation.'

'We can all look after her.' Duncan propped Ruby up on a pile of cushions on the sofa next to Cameron, and delved into his pocket. 'At her age keys always seem to do the trick.'

Ruby grabbed his key ring enthusiastically and stuffed it into her mouth.

'I'm not sure her mother would approve,' Matthew commented grudgingly.

'Well, her mother isn't here,' Stella snapped. 'I'll be as quick as I can.'

'Don't worry,' Duncan grinned, 'we'll get her to negotiate a few contracts for us.'

The French bulldog owner was waiting for her outside the studio, a rather beautiful young man, which was perhaps not surprising since the French bulldog, with its pointy little ears and manageable size, was definitely the dog *du jour*.

The distinguishing characteristic of this particular animal, apart from a studded collar with such sharp spikes you could just have thrown it at an assailant with potentially lethal consequences, was the fact that it was wearing socks. Those protective socks made out of blue J-cloth which builders wear on new carpet.

'Millie lives in them at home,' explained her owner. 'I have white rugs and she keeps bringing mud in from the garden. OK if I pick her up at midday?'

He had shot off in his open-top Mini before Stella got the chance to check if he wanted the portrait of the dog with the socks on or off.

Despite her appearance, Millie was a gentle soul and they soon accomplished their task. Stella even had time to make herself a coffee and put her feet up when the phone rang. She looked at it suspiciously. Her attitude to all communication had become wary recently.

Suze's familiar tones reassured her. 'Have you opened your post yet?'

'Oh God, no more surprises! I don't think I'm up to it.'

'Don't worry, it's not another rock god.'

'We haven't got rid of the last one yet. And now his ex-wife's arriving.'

'Ooh, it's like one of those TV reality shows.'

'Yes, but this was my reality first and I was quite happy with it.'

'No, you weren't.'

Stella decided to ignore this jibe. 'So what will I find out?'

'Stella, we've done it! We'll need to do a proper business plan but the council have decided to let us have a go! They've agreed everything – the Local Area of Special Character, zero rates for new businesses, the lot! They're giving us six months to see what we can achieve.'

'But who's "us"? We aren't even a pressure group.'

'We are now. The only thing is, how are we going to fund it? We're going to need *some* money to set it all up.'

A wicked smile spread across Stella's face. 'Cameron! Matthew was right, we'll get him to do a gig. It doesn't have to be huge, if we ask people who'll give. We could even have it here in the garden. If he's going to squat in my back garden using my electricity he can damn well contribute. I'm not having some rock 'n' roll version of *The Lady in the Van* in my drive like Alan Bennett's. His homeless lady stayed fifteen years!'

'Absolutely! One thing, though. Who's going to tell Matthew we've got the go ahead? You or me?'

'I will. It'd be great if he got on board as well. He'd be brilliant at business plans.'

But Matthew, when she approached him to suggest this, was having none of it. 'This is your thing now. Look, Stella, my scheme was to have an art gallery, not this stupid Paint Your Pet scheme.'

'It's me who's doing the painting, but actually, that's a brilliant idea! People could paint their own pets. It might really catch on.'

Matthew had always had the habit of ignoring other people if he didn't agree with them. He employed it now.

'And I suggested an advice shop for people in debt and a community supermarket – not some bloody supermarket chain.'

'Yes, but Matthew, this isn't *The Archers*! Camley's a commuter town. Everyone's too busy to run a community supermarket. The Brownies couldn't even find a Brown Owl because everyone's too busy.'

'But they'll find time to come to your outdoor cinema and your vintage market, will they?'

'We'll need businesses too, but at least the area might start looking inviting again.'

'Look, Stella, I can see we're not going to agree on this. Our ideas are just too different.'

Stella turned away. The problem was that these days their ideas were too different on a whole lot of things.

The next morning, Stella thought she might finally get on with some painting when Cameron, resplendent in a paisley dressing gown and a pair of pointy Moroccan slippers, knocked on the kitchen door and entered with a flourish. His personality was so large that it seemed to fill the whole kitchen. To Stella's surprise he was carrying a tray with coffee and toast on it.

'Stella, my darling, I was about to eat my meagre repast when I thought "breakfast in the garden"! It's a glorious day. Will you come and join me?'

Stella led him to the small table under a weeping willow at the far end of the garden.

'But it's huge!' Cameron pointed out. 'How did you end up with such a big garden?'

'The previous owners bought the extra bit from our neighbours. They wanted to put in a swimming pool and never got round to it. The Huskies next door have never forgiven us. Sometimes I see her staring vengefully out of the window at our lawn. I think she probably sticks pins in a mock-up of my studio.'

As soon as he'd finished his coffee, Cameron demanded a tour. 'I love living in California except for one thing. The weather.'

'I thought that was what most people liked it for.'

'No seasons. And Americans all call their gardens yards. They're for parking or playing basketball in. Just look at this . . .'

They started the tour at the very far end. There was a small pond where newts, waterboatmen and damsel flies scudded happily about in between the pink waterlilies and yellow flags. Cameron breathed in deeply. 'Listen to the birdsong, it's amazing. You'd never know we were only twelve miles from London!'

'I didn't know you were such a romantic, Cameron.'

He took her hand and bowed like an old-fashioned courtier. 'I've always been a romantic. That's why I keep getting married. I live in hope.'

'Tell me about your wives.'

'Debora's a great gal, but so . . . wifely. Halle is just about the sexiest thing you've ever seen and Roxy – Roxy is marvellous. She calls herself an "everyday feminist". I still have no idea why she married me. She's embarrassingly unmercenary. I thought she might divorce me on behalf of all women, but she's extremely kind.' They had arrived at Stella's studio. Not quite sure why, Stella hesitated at the door.

'Come on, show me.'

As they entered, Cameron produced a bottle of champagne from his dressing gown pocket and hunted for glasses. They ended up sipping champagne from paint jars as Cameron studied all the work she'd put on the walls.

'You're really talented, you know, Stella. I think animals have souls and you have caught them.' He turned suddenly. 'In fact, you are a proper woman – the way you manage things – just one husband, family, work, garden, home. You have made a great success of your life.'

Stella, who didn't think she had made a success of life at all, found herself glowing nevertheless in this unlikely approval from one of the world's best-known rock stars.

'Do you ever think about it, Stell? Being young when we were?' He raised her hand to his lips and perhaps because she was feeling so unappreciated by Matthew, she felt for one, brief moment like the innocent young girl who had so inspired him.

'Yes, we were. It was an amazing moment. And thank you for the song, I feel very honoured to have inspired an anthem.'

She was surprised that his reaction was almost bashful in someone so larger than life. 'You were an inspirational girl.' He looked away and added suddenly, 'And not just to me.' He glanced at his watch. 'I think I'd better get back. Wouldn't want your husband finding me with you en déshabillé, would we?'

They started to walk back to the house.

Stella noticed Mrs Husky listening in just the other side of the fence. 'Of course I want to go to bed with you, Cameron,' Stella announced in an extra-loud voice for her neighbour's benefit. 'Would you like me to lay on some groupies too?'

'You're a very naughty girl, Stella Ainsworth,' Cameron announced, chucking his champagne bottle over the fence with impressive precision.

Stella was still laughing when Suze arrived. 'You look happy.'

'Having Cameron around is very diverting.'

'Don't get too diverted. His wife's arriving soon.'

'Number One or Three?'

'One.'

'What do you think she's like? Stick thin with a blaze of blonde hair like Alana Stewart? Or dark and sophisticated like Bianca Jagger?'

'I have no idea. Let's find out what time she's due and you can come and find out.'

The following day they were both waiting eagerly in the kitchen when Duncan arrived with Debora, straight from the airport. Stella had expected a mound of luggage of Joan Collins proportions in the hall, and was stunned to see one small carry-on bag. Maybe the rest was still in the car.

'Tea or G and T, do you think?' she whispered to Suze.

'Oh G and T, definitely. She'll be used to the rock-chick lifestyle.'

'Or in my case,' a warm, friendly voice interrupted them, 'rock hen.'

A motherly looking woman in jeans and a jumper over a simple white blouse, decorated with a single string of pearls, stood smiling at them. She looked as if she had stepped from the pages of *Country Life* rather than *Rolling Stone*.

'Hello, I'm Debora. And firstly I have to apologize for Cameron descending on you like this. I'm afraid he's totally unaware of anyone's needs but his own. I've tried to persuade him to come to The Glebe with me. But no dice. I'm afraid he's rather taken to your husband.'

'And to think I assumed it was me he had come looking for

after all these years. Something about wanting my extra-ordinary glowing innocence to re-inspire him.'

'Of course, that was before he met you again.' They all turned in surprise at Duncan Miller's ironic tone. He stood holding a laminated folder.

'I'm sure he believes it too,' Debora added hastily. 'Cameron's a complete romantic when it comes to women.'

'Aren't we all?' commented Duncan wryly.

'Yes, but at least you were faithful to Connie, Duncan. Cameron uses it to excuse the inexcusable.'

'I've brought you the schedule. It's all there – tour buses, extra musicians, hotels, staging, lighting, parking for the Airstream.'

Stella heaved a sigh of relief at this. At least it sounded like she would get her garden back during the tour.

'I'm hoping Cameron will do the odd grip and grin with the local officials to thank them for the late-night licences.'

'How are ticket sales?' As well as her warmth, Debora had an air of calm authority. Stella decided she really liked her.

'Mostly sold out. Cameron's audience is perfect. They're so old they buy tickets three months in advance and don't throw stuff at the band.'

Debora laughed. 'I'm glad our generation's good for some-thing. Sometimes the kids make us feel like criminals who've stolen their pensions and their future.' Her rich, warm laugh made you think of hen nights and girls' nights in. 'Some of these oldie bands won't even let the audience be shown in their videos. They look too ancient!'

'How outrageous!' Suze tutted, revelling in hearing all this rock 'n' roll-abilia.

'So what are you girls doing for lunch?' Debora asked. 'I'd like to take you out; my treat after all you've done for Cameron, who, no surprise to learn, is perfectly all right. I've arranged for a masseuse to come and give him a work-over later.'

'I hope it's not a Thai one. That'd give Mrs Husky next door something to think about,' Suze giggled.

'As a matter of fact, we're involved in a community revival scheme,' Stella pointed out, 'and we were just going down to have another look. Why don't you come with us?'

'I'd be delighted. I got involved in my local one back in California.'

'I think that might be a bit different from one in Camley.'

As they walked the ten minutes to the high street, Debora laced her arms through theirs. She looked at Stella closely. 'You know, Stella, you look pretty damn good for an old gal of sixty.'

'Sixty-four,' Suze supplied. 'Very nearly sixty-five.'

'Thank you, Susannah.'

'And she hasn't even had surgery. Or Botox!'

'What's your secret?'

'Overindulgence.'

'So tell us about Cameron,' Suze insisted. 'How come he left you for this Hallelujah?' Debora was the kind of person you knew wouldn't mind such personal questioning.

'Have you ever seen Halle Brown?'

They shook their heads.

'Think Naomi Campbell, Rihanna with just a dash of Madam Butterfly, and you've got it. Plus she was his backing singer. Rock singers always fall for their backing singer – if not, they fall for the dancers. They say "She really understands me!" And it's true, these girls really do understand them – this weird life, never mixing with normal people, always on the road. I was fine with it, to be honest. I suppose I knew it was inevitable. I had five kids. Nick was only ten, Sarah, eight, Caroline, five, Karl, three . . . that was my rebellious period—'

'They're not very rock-star names,' interrupted Suze.

'You'd prefer Zowie Bowie or Moon Unit Zappa, would you? Mind you, I did have a Zuleika. That was a moment of madness. We call her Zu. Anyway, it was Halle who didn't want to put up with me.'

'And what about the new wife, the twenty-one-year-old. Isn't she younger than his daughters?'

'A lot younger. It wasn't her fault. It was her mother, Fabia. Now there was the ultimate rock chick. But she's getting old now, and insecure. When your only skills are flattery and blow-jobs life can get a touch worrying. And Fabia won't see fifty again. I think she sees Roxy as her pension.'

'And what does Roxy think?'

'Roxy's a great girl. I think she actually liked Cameron. He's still got it when he makes an effort to be charming and he definitely charmed Roxy. She had a terrible childhood, carted from man to man with Fabia. I think he was a minor aberration. Unfortunately for Fabia, I think Roxy's the one who's over him. Anyway, you'll meet her soon. Once the tour starts Fabia won't be far behind.'

By now they'd reached Camley High Street with its traffic fumes, betting shops and lorries seeking short cuts. It seemed a world away from sun-kissed California, but for some reason Debora instantly took to it. 'I love it! It reminds me of home!'

Stella and Suze stared.

'You know, you could get quite an alternative vibe going here. How about this pub starting to do breakfast or brunch? A lot of bars have started to do that in LA.' She looked at the daunting exterior of the King's Arms. 'Come on, girls, if you don't try . . .'

Suze and Stella could only watch in admiration as Debora, full of American can-do confidence, clapped her hands so that the drinkers round the bar jumped as if they'd been shot. 'Good morning, gentlemen. Can I speak with the landlord?'

Debora then swept him away to return twenty minutes later, the reluctant publican in tow. 'This is Les. He'll give it a go as long as I come and show him how to get started.'

As Debora departed, not giving the poor man a chance to change his mind, the regulars stared at him as if he had just announced he intended to ascend the throne of England.

She was equally enthusiastic about the vintage market and promised to use her contacts to get them a really good movie to kick off their outdoor cinema.

'All we need now,' Stella sighed, 'is some funding. Actually, we thought of asking Cameron to do a gig.'

'Excellent idea. Don't bother asking Cameron. Duncan will organize it all for you.'

'Isn't he just a fixer?' Stella asked, bemused. 'He told me he called the cabs and made sure Cameron got his Americano.'

Debora roared with laughter. 'Naughty Duncan.' She looked thoughtfully at Stella. 'I wonder why he's being so edgy with you? Not Duncan's usual style. Duncan is the business brains. Haven't you wondered how Cam could live so well? It's all down to Duncan and his clever investments. Cameron owns a golf course in California. And a hotel in Cap Ferrat. He's invested in tech companies. Cameron's had a lot of hits but even before the download revolution beggared the business, his sales were declining. Duncan is the one who's made Cameron's fortune – and all of ours, actually.'

'Is he such a good business brain?' Suze was amazed. 'He used to be rather a nonentity. As a matter of fact, we called him Dull Duncan.'

'If you think Warren Buffett's dull, or Bill Gates is dull. OK,

Duncan doesn't flash his position around, but let's say we're all very grateful to him. Long live dullness!'

'So why all this? Why is Cameron suddenly going on tour and coming over here to revive his career?'

'Because Cameron insisted. Cameron wanted to find his lost inspiration.' She smiled wickedly at Stella. 'He wanted to find you.'

'And what do you imagine he thinks now that he has found me? I mean, for God's sake, he remembered me as a pretty young thing. Now I'm sixty-four!'

'That's an interesting question. How's he been so far?'

'Rather sweet, actually.'

'He can be sweet. It's one of his saving graces.'

'Have your children forgiven him for going off with Halle-lujah and now this Roxy?'

'They have now there's talk of a divorce. Anyway, I'm grateful to Roxy for one thing. At least she's shown him how to use his cellphone. He used to ring me in the middle of the night from his hotel room asking me how to do it. Right now,' Debora announced as if she were divvying up tasks for the WI, 'we have to keep Cameron relatively sober and concentrate his energies on rehearsing for his debut. Duncan might have made Cameron rich but he can't stop the vultures descending if he can't carry off these concerts.'

'Surely they wouldn't, would they?'

'They'd enjoy nothing more. I can just see it now. Forget a comeback, this is a throwback to times best forgotten. That's why we all have to look after him.'

Suze rubbed her hands together. 'Then it looks like we're in for an interesting summer.'

'There is one benefit to touring,' Debora pointed out. 'At

least Cameron will move his Airstream out of your back yard for a bit.'

'You mean he'd consider coming back?' Stella asked faintly. She had rather hoped life would go back to normal.

'Almost certainly. But go on, admit it, I bet he's made things a lot more colourful.'

Five

As it turned out, Cameron's arrival in their midst was only a temporary distraction from Stella's everyday problems. When she returned from her newest pet commission a couple of days later, it was to find two of her grandchildren ensconced on her sofa watching *The Simpsons*.

'Hello. Was I supposed to be picking Izzy up?'

'Hiya, Gran.' Izzy gave her a small smile but with none of her usual look-at-me bravado.

'Mum and Dad were both out,' Jesse explained. 'Rube's at the babysitter's and Izz needed a hand with homework. Eleven plus maths. I'm sixteen and I still can't fathom all those pie charts and rotating cubes so I couldn't really help.'

'Me neither,' Stella sympathized. 'Have you asked Pappy?'

'He's too busy on some incredibly important Internet search. It seemed to involve power tools.' Power tools now vied with William Morris among Matthew's current obsessions.

'Right,' Stella announced in a tone of steely decisiveness. 'We'll see what we can do about that.'

'He said he'd help later,' Jesse added, clearly not wanting a confrontation.

Stella strode towards Matthew's den.

'Gran,' Jesse got up and followed her, quietly closing the door, 'maybe best left. She got into a terrible state about it. I've never seen Izzy lose it like that. She's usually brilliant at these test papers. She likes competing with herself. But not today for some reason.'

'Something at school?'

Jesse shrugged.

'Oh dear, something at home?'

'Mum and Dad don't seem to be talking to each other at the moment. As soon as one comes in the other goes out. It's pretty tense.'

'OK, I'll just sit down and have a cuddle. Are you OK?'

He shrugged, sweeping his usual curtain of hair across his face so that she couldn't see his eyes.

'Always come and see us if you want to.'

'Yeah.' He seemed to deliberately straighten his shoulders. 'It's great having you round the corner. A lot of kids in my class don't have grandparents. They lost contact when their parents got divorced. That wouldn't happen with us, would it?'

Stella held out her arms and he came into them in a brief and bumpy embrace. 'Never. And your parents aren't going to get divorced.'

She made a cup of tea and brought it back with a plate of chocolate biscuits and sat down between them. Thank God for *The Simpsons*. Funny that such a dysfunctional family could seem so normal and comforting.

Izzy had always reminded her of a more extrovert version of Lisa Simpson. They watched three episodes before the doorbell went. Stella jumped up, expecting her daughter or son-in-law, but it was Debora with Duncan Miller in tow.

'I've just been discussing the "Concert for Camley" you'd

like Cameron to do. Duncan says no problem at all if it can wait till after the tour's finished.'

'Fantastic! You're sure Cameron'll be up for it? I mean, he may not want to admit he comes from around here. It's not exactly the Bronx or the Badlands of New Jersey.'

'Cameron'll be fine,' Duncan reassured her.

'By which he means Cameron'll do what he's told,' Debora translated, helping herself to a chocolate biscuit. 'I love the way you Brits have tea whenever there's any kind of crisis. What's been the trouble today, people?'

'Oh, nothing at all. Izzy was struggling a bit with her ghastly test paper and I'm about as much use as a fish on a bicycle, so we're having tea and telly instead.'

'My granddad said he'd help,' Jesse smiled winningly, 'only he's a bit taken up with power-tool attachments.'

'I hear you're a pretty good guitarist,' Duncan commented.

Jesse blushed.

'You must come to one of our concerts. Not your kind of music, but we could show you backstage.'

Jesse lit up like a light bulb.

'We'll have to sort something out. Can I have a look?' Duncan picked up one of Izzy's papers. 'I used to quite enjoy these, though I expect they're all different now. Right. Why don't we pool our brainpower?'

'Better than *Countdown*, anyway.' Jesse grinned, knowing *Countdown* was one of Matthew's favourite programmes. Duncan started reading aloud: 'Look at the bus timetable on the right.' They all stared at it helpfully. 'Jemima lives on Hart Street. She wants to arrive at Maple Lane before ten-fifteen. What time should she catch the bus from Hart Street?'

'Nine-ten?' Izzy asked tentatively.

'Absolutely!' congratulated Duncan. 'Next. A bar chart! I

used to love making bar charts!' He showed Izzy the illustration. 'Twenty-five per cent of children like ham. How many like tuna?'

Izzy studied it. 'Fifty per cent?'

'Wah-hay! Who said you couldn't do it?'

Izzy giggled, looking considerably happier.

'Here's another one. Shania has three pieces of wool . . .'

'Shania?' demanded Debora. 'As in Shania Twain?' She grabbed Stella's hand and they both started to sing the chorus of one of her greatest hits: '. . . *Let's go, girls!*' so loudly that Matthew appeared at the door. 'What the hell's going on?'

'We're all helping Izzy with her test paper.'

'For God's sake, Stella,' he fumed. 'The whole point of these tests is that they're done to time and she doesn't get any help, else what's the bloody point?'

He grabbed the paper and demanded, 'OK, if you're all so clever: what is twenty-one point seven times nine point four? Is it a) two hundred and eighty-seven point sixty-eight; b) four hundred and thirty-two point forty-two; c) one hundred and seventeen point twenty-four; d) two hundred and three point ninety-eight; e) four hundred and twelve point ninety-six?'

'D – two hundred and three point ninety-eight,' Duncan replied, winking at Izzy, who was beginning to look distressed again.

Maybe Duncan's involvement was making him feel guilty at his own lack of grandparental input but Matthew grumpily reached for the answer sheet. 'It says here you can use estimation to work it out. How bloody ridiculous! Whatever happened to mathematical accuracy? Imagine if NASA tried estimation to get rockets to the moon!' He turned to Duncan. 'Shouldn't you be doing something useful like setting up security or booking tour buses?'

'The promoters book security,' Duncan answered calmly, refusing to take offence. 'And our tour manager books the buses.'

'Then what the hell *do* you do?'

Duncan eyed him evenly, refusing to take the bait. 'As I told you,' he replied, 'I get the Americanos.'

'Well, why don't you go and get some now? I want some peace alone with my grandchildren.'

Debora laced her arm through Duncan's. 'Come on, Duncan dear, we've overstayed our welcome.'

'As a matter of fact,' Stella blazed, 'you're welcome any time you want!'

She went to the door with them. 'I'm so sorry. That was outrageous.'

'Don't worry,' Debora soothed, 'we're used to outrageous, aren't we, Dunc? Outrageous is when Cam has an audience of five thousand people waiting and doesn't turn up.'

'He's never done that?'

'It has been known.'

'By the way,' Duncan added, 'I really like your grandson. The way he looks out for his little sister. Not many sixteen-year-olds would do that.'

'Yes,' Stella nodded, 'Jesse's a good guy.' She just wished he didn't need to.

When she went back into the sitting room Matthew ignored her and began ostentatiously to change channels on the television.

'I'll take Izzy and Jesse home,' Stella announced. 'I may be some time.'

When they got the car out, Izzy jumped in the back without staking her usual claim to the front seat.

'What was the matter with him today?' Jesse shook his head

in amazement. 'He used to be quite fun. When did Granddad turn into an old grouch?'

Stella busied herself with reversing out of the drive. It was the question she'd been avoiding asking herself.

When they'd met a year after Cameron's abrupt departure, Matthew had been the only person apart from Suze who could cheer her up. He was no Cameron Keene, but in his own way he loved music and there had been something touching in his desire to take care of her.

It had struck Stella that Matthew's mix of wild enthusiasms and down-to-earth-practicality was just like her beloved dad who'd died a few years earlier.

Stella had been going to ask Matthew one more time if he wanted to get involved in the Save the High Street campaign, but she was so angry with him that she decided to just get on with it without him. It would be a delight to get away. Besides, it was a gorgeous sunny day, the kind of day when people had to get out into their gardens, or sit outside in pavement cafes. The kind of day people felt would bring good things. With all the criticisms Matthew would raise about her ideas, he would somehow manage to make the sun go in. It was quite a skill.

She decided to start with the pop-up studio instead of at home. If she turned it into a reasonable working space, she could spend a lot of time there and since she had expertise in this area she'd at least know what was needed. Of the row of shops, the site of the now-defunct video store looked the most likely. It was big enough to have a photographic area to the left, and a studio space to the right of the store. There was even a tiny kitchen and an even tinier loo at the back.

Before anything else it would need a new coat of paint and some furniture, most of which she could bring from her studio at home. She wondered if she could persuade Jesse to give her a hand. Since the council had only given them a short window to prove themselves she'd better get on with it. She texted Jesse to see if he could round up some friends in aid of a good cause, if they were provided with pizzas and Coke.

What colour should she go for? She surveyed her recent paintings which were stored on her iPad. She really liked the new brightly coloured backgrounds she'd started using and decided that the acid-green one was the most effective. Home-base in Camley had a whole selection of acid-greens and she chose one which was the colour of a new leaf. To her delight she found a bean bag in their sale section which would do perfectly for the pets to pose on. She added filler, cheap brushes and yellow gloss paint for the front door and window frames. It might not be tasteful but it would certainly be eye-catching. Now she'd have to think up a clever name.

The total came to more than she'd expected and it made her stop and think. It was one thing to pay for tarting up a single shop, but there was a whole row to be renovated. Stella flagged momentarily, realizing that they were going to have to get hold of money now, and, more than money, people too. As an artist who worked alone, Stella had a horror of committees, with their incessant arguments and bickering that seemed to take up far more time and energy than the task in hand.

It was Debora who came up with the solution in the end. California was way ahead of Camley in these things, it seemed. 'You should use Facebook! Remember all those horror stories about party invitations going on the Internet and five hundred people turning up? That's what you want here. But first you need to draw up a list of exactly what needs to be done. Good-will doesn't last long.'

'But what about the funds?'

'Oh, Cameron'll donate something. It'll be good for his image. In fact, why don't you get Duncan on the case? He could get Cam to come down here – for the press, obviously – and announce the date of his Campaign for Camley concert and hand over a cheque.'

'But we haven't even sorted out a venue for the concert yet.'

'Didn't you say something about your garden? It's plenty big. You don't need a million people. Just ask the ones with money. You could make it a mini rock festival!'

'We could sort that out, Stell,' Suze endorsed.

'As well as the renovations?'

'Weren't you just a bit bored with life before all this?'

Stella thought about it. There was something in what Suze said. Without realizing it, she had adopted a certain mindset that said 'I'm sixty-four, I've raised a family, have a career of sorts, made a home, have terrific grandchildren. It's enough.' She remembered a visit to the Chelsea Flower Show of all things, which seemed populated by happy octogenarians, walking hand in hand amongst the roses and lilies, and hoped one day to be just like them. But Matthew didn't seem to be interested in spending time together. And he certainly didn't want to hold her hand.

'Right. What are we hanging about for? Let's get on with it!' Suze and Debora both clapped.

Following Debora's advice, Stella started by looking for Duncan. Debora had suggested he'd probably be at their hotel, since he'd set up his informal office there. She'd heard a great deal about how luxuriously The Glebe had been transformed from the run-down manor house where they'd recorded 'Don't Leave Me' so long ago.

The Glebe had been owned for centuries by the Woodfield

family. Its last owner, Celia Woodfield, an enthusiastic but dead-broke socialite, had enjoyed irritating her aristocratic neighbours by renting it out to various rock bands for such a reasonable rent that they ignored the manor's shortcomings – antediluvian plumbing, rising damp and the occasional infestation of mice or bats. But that was all a distant memory. The Glebe had been sold to a luxury hotel chain long ago.

Stella realized that she actually felt quite nervous as she gave her name at reception and asked to speak to Duncan Miller.

While she was waiting she wandered out into the glorious garden. The borders blazed with colour – roses in every shade from palest pink to vermilion tumbled over the rope trellises, filling the air with their heavy perfume. Bees hummed and the occasional thrush or blackbird trilled its tune, as delighted as she was with the burst of glorious weather. The ancient house with its gabled roof and mellowed honey-coloured stone seemed to doze in the midday sun.

Could it really be nearly fifty years ago since she'd last been here, a shy eighteen-year-old, with so little confidence that she never believed anyone who told her she was beautiful? Stella could see now that she'd had the right looks for the extraordinary moment of the Swinging Sixties. The aristocratic models of the Fifties had been thrown out of the window by ordinary suburban girls like Twiggy and the barefoot Sandie Shaw and Stella had fitted the mould. Slim and waiflike, with her long blonde hair and huge eyes, which she'd lined with kohl so as to make them even bigger, she'd embraced miniskirts as well as the floating silky garments of the hippie trail.

Yet she'd been frightened as well as excited by all this tearing up of rules. Drug-taking, so much a part of the scene, had made her nervous, as did the outrageous behaviour which it fuelled. She'd had none of the apparent confidence of a Marianne Faithfull or a Linda Eastman, the determined natural beauty everyone hated for marrying Paul. Maybe she'd just been a conventional girl caught up in a heady yet terrifying whirl of rebellion against everything that had gone before. And yet the Sixties had had its own conventions. Like saying yes to sex.

She remembered with sudden clarity that she had been really nervous when she'd first slept with Cameron and how amazed he'd been that she was a virgin and not only that, that she didn't have the slightest idea what to do in bed. Maybe it had been her inexperience that had made Cameron so obsessed with her? That male delight in teaching and writing their own script on a blank page. And she'd turned out to be a fast learner.

Looking up at the manor house, seeing it as it had been then, damp and dilapidated, yet somehow a symbol of the old order changing, she vividly remembered the day she'd come here to watch Cameron.

Duncan's question came back to her. 'Do you wish you'd gone with him? Have you been happy with your life?'

She'd been so sure that she'd had no regrets when he'd asked her that. Had it really been only a few short days ago? But Cameron's return had stirred things up far more than she had realized. Suddenly Stella wasn't so sure. Now it seemed that habit was what sustained her marriage rather than choice or satisfaction.

She was lost in reverie when a voice behind her interrupted her thoughts. 'It's all changed a bit, hasn't it?'

She swung round to find Duncan emerging from the bar holding two long-stemmed glasses.

He handed one to her. 'To thank you for all this hospitality you've been giving Cameron.'

Stella smiled, relieved he couldn't read her mind. 'I have to admit my hospitality wasn't entirely voluntary.'

'He seems to be very happy there.'

'Yes, he does, doesn't he?'

Duncan glanced up at the manor. 'It was quite a moment, wasn't it?'

Stella laughed and raised her glass. 'It was quite a decade. I wish we'd known at the time that we were living through a revolution. I was really just a shy girl from the suburbs. I felt out of my depth most of the time.'

It was funny how much more attractive he'd grown with the years. There was no sign now of that awkward youth she'd shared the embarrassing night with.

'And I was a boring boy from South London.' He paused, studying her. 'I did know your name for me, by the way. Dull Duncan.'

Stella felt herself changing colour. How ridiculous at her age. 'There's nothing like the young for being cruel.'

'You and Susannah especially. They say the Afghans used to give prisoners to the women to torture.' He seemed to lose all his expensively acquired sophistication and sounded like a bitter boy. 'I can see why. Of course, you were the beautiful Stella Scott.'

She hoped to God he wasn't going to bring up their disastrous encounter.

'I'm sorry if I was cruel. I didn't mean to be. And it was all a very long time ago.'

Duncan seemed to shake himself as if he hadn't meant to be this personal. 'Indeed it was.' He made an effort to retrieve his usual suave persona. 'You must all come to the Roundhouse and see the tour kick off. I'll sort out some tickets for you.'

'That's very generous of you. We'd love that.'

'Good PR as well. You can demonstrate to the press that the woman who was Cameron's inspiration doesn't really think of him as a boozy old bore.'

Stella felt suddenly nettled, as if what had seemed a kind gesture was simply a tactic in Cameron Keene's career revival. 'Is that all you think about? Cameron's PR and how things look?'

'Why?' he challenged. 'What would you like me to be thinking about?'

Stella drained her glass and put it down. Was he implying that she wanted him to be thinking about her?

'Friendship perhaps? Shared times?'

'Of course.' He raised his glass, watching her as though she'd said something secretly funny. 'Why not? To auld lang syne.'

Stella had no more time to ponder on the state of her marriage, whether she should have run off with Cameron or what on earth Duncan had been getting at. What with the business plan and making lists of all the tasks involved in saving the high street, assembling names and phone numbers for all the negotiations that still needed to be done, buying paint and decorating supplies, wondering where to get tables for the vintage market and a thousand other things, she was run off her feet. Finding herself at a loose end, since Duncan had already completed the tour plan, Debora had announced she loved a cause and had got stuck in too.

Even Matthew, after taking the third phone message from a pet owner who was hopping mad with Stella for not delivering their dog painting on time, realized how much she'd taken on and decided to get involved after all.

'Wow,' whispered Suze, 'the sheriff's come to town. Now everything'll be hunky dory.'

Stella, picking up the irony in her friend's tone, grinned back. 'Come on, it's better than him grumping around. He can deal with the council.'

'I thought he saw them as the enemy.'

'He can do a bit of collaboration. If the Vichy government could do it, so can Matthew.'

'Not a very happy analogy. Look what they got up to.'

'I'll persuade him he's really the Resistance, just pretending to collaborate. At least we don't have to deal with any private landlords. The council bought the whole row so they could redevelop.'

It was just as well Stella had planned ahead. The response to their call for help was overwhelming. From grannies (hey, Stella reminded herself, you're a granny) to teenagers, including Jesse and an extremely pretty girl who rejoiced in the name of Isadora. No wonder she liked The Incredible String Band. Jesse had a smile on his face she hadn't seen for months and Stella had to stop herself embracing the girl who had put it there.

'Please call me Dora,' she insisted. 'I loathe Isadora. My parents were going through a Bohemian phase.'

'What would you prefer? Prepping or painting?'

'Painting please,' they chorused.

'You'd better do the pet studio, then; that's already been prepped. Are you wearing old clothes?' She eyed Dora's faded print dress. It looked just the sort of thing she hoped they'd soon be selling. 'Are you sure you wouldn't rather get involved with the vintage market?'

'I love retro stuff.' Dora's brown eyes kindled with enthusiasm.

'Could you make a list of local vintage and charity shops who might take a stall and then go and visit them? Explain what a good cause it is and that the stalls will all be free? The council's agreed to give the land so all we have to do is hire the tables.'

'Why don't you use wallpaper-pasting tables?' Dora asked. 'They're really cheap in B&Q.' She thought for a moment. 'Actually, my dad's a head teacher. I wonder if his school would lend theirs to us. They've got loads they use for the Christmas bazaar.'

'I don't suppose he has a van too?' Stella sked hopefully.

'Afraid not.'

'I know a man who does,' interrupted Debora, who had just arrived to help. 'And it's sitting in your back garden.'

'Not the Airstream? It's his pride and joy.'

'Time it earned its living. Most of the time it's a glorified bar.'

'But who would tow it?'

'I would.'

'OK,' Dora smiled her lovely, optimistic smile, 'I'll give Dad a ring. As long as I can persuade him it isn't distracting me from revision! Fortunately, Mum's away. She's the tough one. Anything else?'

'We need lots of people to take stalls – car booters, home bakers, crafty people.'

'Right, we'll get on to it.'

Stella looked around her at the ant-like industry that filled every corner of the parade of shops. Even the sleazy denizens of the betting shop came out to take a look and the landlord of the King's Arms surpassed himself by appearing with free pints and packets of out-of-date pork scratchings. 'If you can really get this place going again, it'll be bloody good for me,' he announced, rolling up his sleeves to reveal tattoos that owed more to prison DIY than the tattooist's art.

'What about those breakfasts, Les?'

Stella was amazed that Debora had become such good friends with the unappealing publican. But then Debora was probably on first-name terms with the entire world, from the Almighty downwards. No doubt she started every day looking up and shouting, 'Morning, Jehovah!' And, because she was so amazing, he probably shouted back, 'Morning, Debora!'

'You bring the people and I'll do the breakfasts.'

'You betcha! I can't wait to spread the word about your great British bangers!'

Dora trotted up, beaming, to say that her dad had talked to the school caretaker and they could pick up ten trestle tables any time they liked as long as they were back in good time for the bazaar.

'No time like the present,' announced the amazing Debora. 'See you kids later.' She disappeared into the traffic fumes of the Camley Road with Jesse and Dora in her wake.

An hour and a half later, the entire locality ground to a halt to make way for Debora towing a large aluminium vehicle round the roundabout. It signalled left and drew up in the slip road in front of them, ignoring the double yellow line with stately grandeur. The door opened and like the aliens in *E.T.*, its occupants descended, each carrying a pasting table. The last, to Stella's utter amazement, was Cameron Keene.

It felt like the curious lull before the tsunami. The tide seemed to go out and stand still for a split second, then came rushing back as a tidal wave.

The youngest volunteers went on working, but gradually the whispering began as more and more people worked out who it was, until the sound became so loud that everyone simply stopped dead.

One of the regulars of the King's Arms finally broke the awed silence that followed. 'Fuck me, it's Cameron Keene!'

And gradually they all began to clap.

Cameron grinned and took a bow. 'Right,' he demanded, still grinning, 'where do you want these bleedin' tables, then?'

Stella was the first to recover. 'In the pet studio would be best. At least we can lock that up.'

Half of the crowd stood staring at Cameron, as if he had just descended from the right hand of God the Father, while the rest stared at his extraordinary vehicle.

They stacked the pasting tables in the far corner.

Cameron glanced round at the half-painted studio. 'Great colour. Acid-puke. It reminds me of the gents' toilet floor in half the dance halls I played before we had a hit. Here,' he grabbed a brush from one of the bemused volunteers, 'I used to be a dab hand at this. My dad was a housepainter.'

Stella had a sudden inspiration. 'Jesse! Tweet a photo of Cameron with a brush. Put "'Paint it Green' – rock legend Cameron Keene helps bring his local high street back to life".'

'Gran, "Paint it Black" was the Rolling Stones.'

'I know that! It's just a cultural reference.'

Cameron smiled engagingly while the acid-puke paint dripped onto the floor, narrowly missing his expensive yellow Nikes.

Behind Jesse a burly fan appeared carrying a pint from the landlord and requesting that Cameron autograph his Led Zeppelin tee shirt.

'Sorry, Cam,' the huge man apologized shyly. 'I'd have worn plain white if I'd known I was going to bump into you.'

'No problem.' Cameron signed his name right across Jimmy Page's face. 'I like the Zep myself, but if you want to see a real band, come and see us at the Roundhouse.'

'Good for Cameron,' Stella whispered to Debora. 'He's putting on quite a show with the public.'

'It's not a show. He's enjoying himself. I can tell when he's putting it on,' Debora replied. 'The trouble with being famous now is that they're all terrified of being caught out on someone's phone. Passed out. Or pissed. Or in the act. It's not like the old days any more, when the only risk to a rock star was kiss 'n' tell. It's lonely as hell. They don't trust anyone and social media has made it ten times worse. I can tell you, Stella, being famous is horrible now.'

As if on cue, one of the teenagers rushed up with his phone on the end of a selfie stick, shoved his arm round Cameron, and snapped away.

Everything went quiet for a moment and Stella thought Cameron might snap the contraption in two. Instead, he turned gleefully to Debora. 'Here, Deb, have you seen these things? Bloody clever, aren't they?'

The teenager, who had also sensed incipient trouble, immediately released his phone and handed the selfie stick to Cameron. 'You have it.'

'Come on, Cam, let's get back to the Airstream before you get a genuine British parking ticket. Thanks, everyone.'

Cameron, the man who could have everything, gleefully brandished his cheap plastic selfie stick, reminding Stella of a child at Christmas who prefers the wrapping to the present.

Just as they were leaving, a very old man pushed his way through the crowd, then stopped, looking confused and waving a photograph of a dog. He clearly had no idea who Cameron was.

'Lost your dog, mate?' asked Cameron sympathetically. 'I lost my Persian cat last year. Just wandered off, never to be seen again.'

The old man didn't look as if he found this very reassuring.

'Do you want us to stick your photo on the door?' Cameron enquired, reaching for the photograph.

The old man held it to his chest protectively as if Cameron were trying to steal a precious possession. 'I was told there was a pet painter opening up here.'

'Yes,' Stella stepped forward, 'that'd be me. We're hoping to start trading next week.' The photo he was clutching was crumpled and indistinct and Stella suspected it would be hard to get a good likeness from it. 'Why don't you bring the dog in and I'll take another photograph. Then I can work from that.'

The man looked at Stella as if she were mad. 'Because he's bloody dead, that's why. He died three years ago. The best friend a man could have.'

They all contemplated the blurred photo of an overweight black Labrador. It had the kindest eyes Stella had ever seen on an animal. She almost felt like crying herself.

'Tell you what,' Cameron had put a comforting arm round the old boy, 'what's your name, by the way?'

'Desmond,' he replied, looking momentarily confused.

'OK, Desmond, why don't you come with us? We'll go back to my place and have a toast to absent dogs.'

'Desmond's the bloody dog,' he protested testily. 'I'm Bernard.'

'Bernard, then. I'm Cameron.'

They both headed back towards the Airstream.

'That was kind.'

'Yes,' Debora sighed. 'I'd better get on and drive them. Cameron likes people who've got no idea who he is. At least they won't keep trying to take his photo to post on Instagram.'

'No,' Stella grinned, 'this time it'll be Cameron. With his new selfie stick!'

When she got home she and Suze were dropping with

exhaustion and were stunned to find Matthew greeting them with a happy smile and the offer of a cup of tea.

'How did it go?' he enquired, handing out chocolate biscuits.

For once, Stella realized with relief, Matthew seemed reasonably content with the world. He was spending hours on the phone negotiating with his enemies at the council. Stella almost felt sorry for them. Clearly they'd had no idea he was involved when they'd given the go-ahead to the campaign and were probably bitterly regretting agreeing to it all. Matthew's battle style was to barrage them with so many calls and emails that eventually they just lay down and surrendered.

'Not bad. We've almost finished the pet studio and Jesse's girlfriend came up trumps with ten trestle tables for the vintage market.' She grinned at Suze conspiratorially. 'You'll never guess who delivered them.'

'Carrier pigeon?'

'Cameron Keene! In person!'

'I'm surprised Cameron could recognize a pasting table, let alone deliver one.'

'That's where you're wrong. His father was a housepainter. Cameron used to be allowed to go with him and clean his brushes.'

They didn't have long to contemplate this affecting scene because the door opened and an excited Cameron, with a smiling Debora in tow, burst into the kitchen.

'Stella!' He shook his head in delighted amazement. 'You'll never bloody guess. Bernie knew my father! He only owned the company Dad worked for! He says Dad worked for him for thirty years!'

Stella almost giggled that Cameron Keene, such a rebel at nineteen, should treasure the news that his dad had been a steady worker. Just in time she caught the significant look in

Debora's eye that told her this revelation was an important one.

'He was such a good dad.' Cameron sat down and poured a cup of tea. 'OK, he liked a drink or two, but even when he'd done a ten-hour day he'd try and be there for bath time. ' Cameron paused, as if staring back over the years. 'If he'd been working outside, his hands would be so chapped that he'd literally wince when he put them in the bathwater.' He looked down at his own hands. 'What would he have thought about what I do with mine?'

So intent were they on Cameron that no one had noticed Duncan quietly opening the kitchen door.

'He'd have been proud as hell if he'd seen this.' Duncan threw down a copy of the evening paper on the kitchen table. The photograph Jesse had taken on his phone was splashed across the front page under the headline 'ROCK FOR REGEN-ERATION – legend Cameron Keene returns to help save his roots.' Underneath was a list of his tour dates.

'Thanks, mate.' Cameron got to his feet and put his arms round Duncan.

'Can you save roots?' Suze enquired, deciding that there had been more than enough emotion. 'I have this mental picture of Cameron with an armful of swedes and turnips.'

Stella looked at her quellingly. 'Didn't you live just off the Brighton Road?'

Cameron nodded. 'Acacia Avenue. Talk about classic suburbia. I didn't even know it was called after some yellow flower till I was twenty-one.'

'We should go back there one day. Take a look.'

'Maybe. I always swore I'd avoid it like the plague.'

'Cameron,' Duncan gestured towards the Airstream, 'some things we need to iron out.'

After they'd left, Debora sat down in Cameron's place. 'That was rather a rosy picture, I'm afraid. The truth is his dad was a drunk, but Cameron's sort of canonized him anyway. He died when Cameron was twelve, so I think he needs to believe this stuff. And his dad did seem to love him.'

'That's really sad. I didn't know any of that. He still had a mum, though?'

'Yes, she died a couple of years ago but his dad was the one. So,' she deliberately lightened the mood, 'I hope you're all coming to the Roundhouse? Duncan invited Jesse and Dora, and guess what, Cameron's just asked Bernie, his new father figure. It's going to be quite a party!'

Stella thought guiltily about Emma and how she must include her daughter and son-in-law as well. She'd forgotten Emma and her problems in all the excitement of the campaign. She realized with a sinking heart that she probably ought to call her and ask her how things were going. 'If it's not too outrageous to ask, could Izzy come too, or is she too young?'

'I'm sure venues like that are used to it,' Debora reassured. 'Rock legends tend to go in for flocks of offspring. I heard one boasting that he had children between the ages of forty-four and six months!'

'Any news of Roxy and the famous Fabia? Still no word?'

'Don't worry. Fabia specializes in making entrances. Usually at the most inconvenient moment.'

Six

Stella sat in her nice warm kitchen, the cosiest room in the house and the one, apart from her studio, she truly considered to be hers, admiring the bunch of roses from her garden on the kitchen table and savouring her first cup of coffee in her favourite dark green cup. She tried not to think about how much she had to do today.

The owner of the three pugs was quite rightly fretting about when her painting would be delivered, Stella hadn't even finished the louche lurcher, and the first vintage market was happening frighteningly soon. They had put the outdoor cinema on hold for the moment, and there was still the bric-a-brac and food stalls to get underway. Far more important, dwarfing all these other concerns, was the question of what she was going to wear to the concert.

She and Suze had already had several sessions going through their respective wardrobes.

'How about that slinky black dress from Zara with your black leather jacket with the studs on?' Suze had suggested.

'I haven't worn that jacket in thirty years.'

'Why do you hang on to it, then?'

'Sentimental value. Because of the good times I had in it. Besides, Emma might want it.'

'Emma!' Suze had snorted. 'Emma is the acme of subtle understatement. Only the Farrow and Ball palette for Emma, all the way from cream to daring taupe. If she wore a colour she'd probably faint. And as for studded black leather . . .'

'That's because she wouldn't want to look like an ageing rock chick and neither do I!'

They sat happily flicking through magazines for inspiration.

'Oh look, Stella! She's wearing your hat!'

And indeed there was a lovely young girl in a huge floppy felt hat the spit of the Biba one Stella had loved so much at eighteen.

'Can it really be forty-seven years ago?' Suze demanded. 'Do you remember when we couldn't even imagine *being* forty?'

'But that was when forty was old. Now even sixty isn't old – or so we tell ourselves!'

In the end they'd hit on a simple electric-blue silk which Suze had insisted she wear with a green taffeta jacket.

'Green with blue?' Stella had protested. 'Do they really go?'

'Stella Ainsworth, you are sounding like your mother! "Blue and green should never be seen . . ."'

'". . . without a colour in between!"'

'No wonder everyone looked so dull in the Fifties with rules like that!'

She stood behind Stella as they peered together into the long mirror. Actually, Stella had to agree, somehow the clashing colours worked with the shade of her hair. 'Anyway, you're a muse! If you're not breaking the rules, God help the rest of us! I suppose you could always go in a tasteful two-piece.'

'Heaven forbid I actually look my age!' Stella shook her head.

For herself Suze chose a Ghost dress in black chiffon with giant flowers appliqued on it, teamed with rather ambitious high heels.

Muse or not, Stella decided, she would leave the ridiculously high heels to her friend. She might want to cut a dash but she insisted on doing it in comfort.

Matthew mostly kept his overt disapproval of their Save the High Street schemes to himself, apart from announcing that flogging tat and showing romcoms, even French ones like *Amélie*, would hardly be a drop in the ocean against dilapidation and crass development. What the council really wanted in the area, he insisted, as if he were the only person who'd been privileged with this information, was cheap office space.

Stella decided that between bludgeoning him to death with the briefcase he had started carrying everywhere and ignoring him, the latter was probably the better option.

But only just.

'I will not let his negative energy bring me down,' Stella repeated her new mantra to herself. This and sitting on the floor doing her mindfulness exercises was keeping her chakra, or maybe her karma, or even her dharma, God alone knew which, open to calm and peace.

Only today it wasn't working. She was halfway through taking deep breaths, hand on abdomen, and letting her mind empty of all distracting thoughts, when the doorbell rang. She thought of ignoring it but her inner being wasn't sufficiently evolved to let her.

It turned out to be Cameron, which was a surprise as, for the last few days, he had kept himself to himself, only allowing Matthew into the inner sanctum of the Airstream to reminisce about sax solos and chord sequences. And now Bernie, the replacement father figure, had been granted admittance as well. Stella wondered if Bernie knew how honoured he was.

Perhaps he'd come for a cup of sugar (did anyone really ever ask for a cup of sugar?) or a pint of milk? The thought of Cameron actually going to a shop and purchasing such things did rather stretch the imagination. Usually he called up Duncan or even his PR to run his errands, no matter how high-powered a meeting they were in.

'Morning, Stella.' In the time since his sudden arrival she'd begun to get to know his moods and had to admit that he looked more than usually rough today. He had several days' stubble blurring his chin and the front of his hair stood up in tufts like a parrot that had been plucking out its feathers.

'Are you OK, Cameron?'

'Never better. Do you happen to have any tonic water? Not that crap diet stuff. Proper Indian tonic water. In a glass bottle preferably.'

'I'll go and have a look.' Given that it was only nine in the morning, Stella hoped it was for indigestion or a minor stomach upset. They did say flat Coke was good for calming the digestion. 'Why don't you sit down?'

She disappeared off to the larder, wondering whether to call Debora or pretend they were out of tonic water.

In the end she found half a bottle which was probably flat anyway. She'd ring Debora as soon as he'd left.

'I must admit, Stella, you've made this room very pleasant.'

'Thank you.' She handed the bottle over to him.

'I don't suppose you've got any lemons?'

This was definitely a bad sign. 'Afraid not,' she lied, hoping he didn't spot the lemons on the worktop.

Cameron's glance alighted on a bowl of tangerines. 'Would

you mind if I pinched a few of these?' He helped himself to a handful. He was just about to leave when the kitchen door opened and Emma appeared. Despite her usual soigné appearance, her eyes were red and she was holding Ruby.

'Oh,' she blurted, as if she might disappear as quickly as she'd come. 'I didn't know you had company.'

'Emma, this is Cameron Keene.' Emma almost dropped the baby. 'I expect you've heard of him. My daughter Emma, and my delicious granddaughter Ruby.'

Ruby waved her hands gleefully and Cameron suddenly bent down and kissed her bare feet. 'I love them when they're this age. Before they can answer back.'

'Do you have children of your own?' asked Emma, taken aback.

'Only four.' He shook his head as if, in the annals of rock musicians, this was akin to the Chinese one-baby rule.

'Five,' Stella corrected automatically. She was beginning to sound like his wife.

'Gosh.'

He clambered back to his feet. 'I hope you're coming to the launch of my tour at the Roundhouse.'

'When is it?'

'Next Thursday. Your mother's coming. Bring the family. You can all come in the Artists' Bar. You get a really good view. And free drink.' He looked at Ruby. 'Maybe not the baby.'

'And you're doing a concert for Camley too? In our garden!'

'Bit of a fundraiser. For your mother's scheme. Bring the old 'hood back to life – though, God knows, it was dull enough in my day.'

'Mine too,' agreed Emma. 'Do you remember Sundays? How everything was closed.'

'You don't know what boredom even means!' Stella was

about to insist, and stopped herself. What was the feminine equivalent of an old codger?

'Good. See you there.' Cameron headed off with his tonic water and his tangerines.

'God, Mum,' Emma complained as soon as Cameron had left, 'your life's more exciting than mine!'

'If you mean having a rock star in residence, I can assure you it's a mixed blessing.'

'Not just that – this campaign, a concert in your garden, your pet painting! You can see why I had to get out of the house or I'd go mad.'

'Yes,' Stella could see that Emma was upset and didn't need her mother to disapprove of her choices, 'though I'm at a very different stage of life to you. You could get involved in the campaign too, you know,' she offered eagerly. 'We'd love to have you. You'd be brilliant at it.'

'Then I'd still be dependent on Stuart. I need some independence and some money of my own.'

'And how's it going?'

'It's brilliant!' Emma's face lit up. 'I'm really enjoying it. Hal's being terrific, letting me be really flexible.'

Stella wondered how to ask the next question without starting another argument. 'And how are the children getting on?'

'Absolutely fine,' Emma insisted in a tone that didn't brook further discussion. 'Ruby loves her childminder. Jesse's infatuated with this Isadora. And Izzy' – she hesitated for a fraction of a second – 'Izzy's fine too.'

'And Stuart?'

Her daughter's happy face darkened. 'Oh well, Stuart's always working anyway.'

'And how's the thera—' She had been going to ask about

the couples counselling but realized that, quite possibly, she wasn't supposed to know about it.

'The therapy?' Emma demanded angrily. 'How the hell did you know about that?'

'I just deduced from what one of the children said.'

'We're giving it up, as a matter of fact.'

'Oh dear, is that a good idea?' It sounded to Stella as though this was the moment they really needed it.

'Just keep out, Mum!' Emma flashed back furiously. 'We'll sort this out ourselves.'

Stella picked up her coffee cup and began washing it up. It was so hard being a parent, let alone a grandparent! You so desperately wanted your children and grandchildren to be happy and not perpetuate the mistakes you'd made. And yet your advice was never welcome. But were there times when it was your duty to speak out?

Not sure if she was being cowardly, Stella decided that this wasn't one of them. 'It'd be lovely if you all came to the concert. Maybe we can even tempt Stuart away from his asylum seekers for once.'

'I'll see if I can get a babysitter for Ruby,' Emma replied in a flat voice. She found her bag and had begun to lift Ruby onto her shoulder, when she suddenly remembered why she'd come.

'By the way,' she asked, almost awkwardly, given their argument. 'Could you possibly have Ruby for the day on Tuesday? The childminder's got to take her own kids to the dentist.'

'I'd be delighted. She can come with me to the new studio. You'd like to see all Grandma's paintings of doggies, wouldn't you, Ruby?'

Ruby wriggled her toes enthusiastically. Tentatively, Stella and her daughter smiled.

When Emma had gone, Stella sighed, changed her mantra

to 'I will not let *anyone*'s negative energy bring me down', and then decided that was a bit unfair. Emma was normally a good mother. But what were you supposed to do when your children brought you their problems but wouldn't let you suggest even the smallest solution? It struck her that actually Emma hadn't brought the problem, Stella had picked it up from Jesse and Izzy. And anyway, people never listened to advice, no matter how good it was. Had she even done so herself? And what about all that stuff about being allowed to make your own mistakes? The trouble was when it was your own flesh and blood making the mistake, and maybe wrecking her marriage, and hurting her own children into the bargain, it took the patience of Job to just stand by and do nothing. Besides, she'd always thought Job's patience highly overrated.

Debora was fortunately still at the hotel, helping Duncan and the tour manager with all the last-minute arrangements, double checking the extra musicians, the buses and hotels, lighting, staging and security at every venue on the tour from Glasgow to Brighton. Stella could imagine Debora's supremely unflappable nature was very welcome indeed.

'Debora, it's Stella. Sorry to interrupt, but I'm a bit worried about Cameron. He's just come round and borrowed tonic water and tangerines.'

'Did you say tangerines?' Debora enquired. 'Shit, that is bad.'

'Why are tangerines bad?' Stella felt she had fallen into a topsy-turvy world where normally good things were suddenly harmful. 'He's not allergic, is he?' She had memories of ghastly children's parties where some wretched child would announce after scoffing a peanut butter sandwich that they were nut intolerant and they would go into anaphylactic shock any moment and have to be rushed to A & E.

'He only uses tangerine peel in emergencies.'

'I'm not sure I follow.'

'It means he's drinking gin and tonic. At nine-thirty a.m.'

'Ah.'

'I'll come right round. At least I know where I am with drink. The heroin was a bastard.'

Suddenly life in suburbia didn't seem that boring after all.

Less than half an hour later, Debora was on the doorstep. To Stella's astonishment she removed a portable drip from the car which she had managed to blag from a private hospital that specialized in boob jobs and liposuction. Maybe Cameron would be the only known case of having fat piped back into him.

'Debora,' Stella demanded, 'what the hell is that?'

'Deathbed relief. It's what med students use when they've been out on the town and have to be back on the ward with no sleep and more alcohol in their bloodstream than Oliver Reed.'

'What on earth's in it?'

'Intravenous rehydration. When you drink one pint of beer you pee out two pints of liquid. That's why you get that headache from hell. This puts back all the salts and stuff. Potassium, calcium, anti-nausea and all that shit. Let's hide it in the kitchen and see if he needs it.'

Once the rehydration unit was safely hidden, they knocked on the door of the Airstream.

After a moment or two Cameron opened it. His new friend Bernie sat at the small table, a half-bottle of Bombay Sapphire in front of him. The tonic was finished but two of the three tangerines remained.

'Good morning, ladies, come to check up on the old winos, have we?' There was a dangerous glint in Cameron's eye, but his speech was clear and he didn't seem to be at all the worse for wear. 'Sorry to disappoint you.' He gestured to the table where a black-and-white photo was propped up against the empty tonic bottle rather like a little altar. 'Bernie brought round that photograph of my dad and we were just having a little toast to him.'

'Isn't that nice?' Debora, though not one hundred per cent convinced of his innocence, smiled at them both in her all-embracing motherly way. 'I'm sure he'd appreciate being saluted in gin before it's even time for a coffee break.'

'Oh, my dad could put it away, believe me. He carried two bottles in his work bag, one of vodka and the other of white spirit.'

'I never knew that!' protested Bernie. 'He hid it bloody well.'

Debora and Stella glanced at each other, sharing the thought that it must have been tough for Cameron even if he did love his dad, if he'd been that far gone. 'Let's hope he didn't ever mix them up,' Debora said brightly. 'Now, I hate to break up the party, but you're needed over at The Glebe.'

'I'll drop you there, if you like,' Stella offered. 'I need to go out anyway. We can give Bernie a lift on the way.'

While Cameron and Bernie readied themselves, Stella and Debora headed back to the house.

'Apologies for the false alarm,' Stella whispered.

'Better to be safe than sorry. I'd only worry if they'd got to the third tangerine.'

'How did you ever cope with all the dramas?' Stella asked in genuine admiration. 'Heroin, Hallelujah. Roxanne.'

Debora smiled slowly. 'I'm an exceptionally calm woman. Plenty of wives cope with husbands that drink and stray. Cameron just does it on a rather epic scale. And I quite like the old bastard. Of course he runs off with the backing singer.

Who else does he get to meet? And when Fabia found she'd got too old to pull rock stars and pimped her beautiful young daughter at him, how was Cameron going to resist? He can't even resist cookies or dessert. But the thing is, he's always paid up and he's never been grumpy about it.'

They dropped Bernie off first then drove on to The Glebe. It was another glorious morning.

As they parked next to the old manor-house-turned-luxury-hotel, Cameron smiled his sexy seen-it-all smile. 'They were good times, weren't they, Stell?'

'Amazing,' she agreed, smiling back. 'And do you know, till you came back, I'd almost forgotten quite how wonderful.'

He reached over and took her hand. 'I never really got over you, you know. That's why I had to come back after I went to America that first time, to make sure you hadn't changed your mind.'

'Really?' Much as she might like to, Stella couldn't resist being honest. 'I thought it was to record "Don't Leave Me".'

Cameron ignored this pinprick to his romantic balloon. 'Do you know you're the only girl in my whole life who's chucked me over? Do you still feel anything for me, Stell?' Stella was grateful he didn't wait for an answer but ploughed straight on. 'Do you know,' he laughed to himself at the ludicrousness of the suggestion, 'there was a point where I wondered if something had been going on with you and Dunc.'

Cameron smiled indulgently at the crazy idea that anyone could prefer Duncan to himself.

'What was his wife like?' Stella couldn't resist asking.

'A bit highbrow for me. I never really get art.'

'But you were an art student when I first met you!' Stella reminded him.

'I saw Andy Warhol making all that money with the soup

cans,' Cameron laughed. 'Thought I might have a go. Connie was the cultured type. And I think it was downright weird the way she wanted to fix him up with this other woman painter when she knew she was dying.'

This was the first Stella had heard of Duncan being fixed up with anyone by his dying wife. It seemed an almost saintly act. 'Maybe she loved him and didn't want him to be lonely.'

'She could have chosen someone a bit more normal, then. You know he's meeting up with her later in the tour?'

Stella made a mental note to find out more from Debora. After all the emotion that had been swirling about she was grateful she had the launch of the vintage market next weekend to keep her busy.

'How's it all been going?' she asked Suze, who had proved herself remarkably efficient and practical.

'Not too bad. All of the tables have been taken. Quite a good mix of clothes, books and bric-a-brac, even if it is stuff they can't even shift at car-boot sales. We could do with a couple more food stalls and I'm going to try and get the pub to make an effort and produce hot dogs. The place could look quite inviting if they put out some bunting and chased the smokers out of the garden.'

'Rather you than me,' Stella replied sceptically.

'Come on, where's your fighting spirit? We can't rely on Debora to charm him now she's got so busy. Let's go down there now. It'll only take an hour.'

It turned out to be considerably longer since on the way Suze remembered she needed to pick up some stuff for her stall that she'd put into storage.

'I didn't know you had stuff in storage.'

'I couldn't bear to throw away that hideously ugly furniture my mum and dad owned.'

'Why, if it's hideously ugly?'

'It's all I've got left of them. Stupid, I know.'

Stella had been going to add 'And expensive', but she saw that Suze, rarely given to sentimentality, was close to tears. 'I think you should hang on to your parents' hideously ugly furniture as long as possible. One of these days we'll all go off IKEA and it'll be just what we want.'

They turned into the entrance of the Camley StoreSafe, a giant yellow warehouse just off the main road, and parked the car.

'Morning, ladies,' the receptionist greeted them with a big smile.

'She's very cheerful.'

'You'll see why when you get inside. You need to be cheerful to survive,' Suze replied.

As they pushed open the hospital-style swing doors, Stella saw what she meant. They were greeted by echoing empty corridors in total darkness that lit up eerily when the movement detector registered their presence. Otherwise there was blackness and complete silence.

'God, it's creepy here,' Stella shivered.

'I know,' Suze looked over her shoulder, 'it always makes me think of that serial killer who stored the body in a storage unit and kept visiting it.'

'Charming! I think I might wait in reception.'

'And abandon me to my fate?' Suze began to open the padlock to her storage unit.

'There's a woman over there getting her stuff as well. You should be OK unless it's a female serial killer. Do you want me to take anything?'

'As a punishment you can carry this.'

Suze handed Stella the bust of a Roman emperor. 'Somebody might want it,' she explained hopefully.

Stella staggered off with Tiberius or Claudius or Vespasian in both arms. She was almost at the lift when she encountered such a strange sight that she stopped to stare. In perhaps the tiniest storage unit in the place a young woman about Emma's age sat behind a desk that took up three quarters of the space with a laptop and mobile phone in front of her.

'Gosh,' Stella couldn't help exclaiming, 'is this your office?'

'I know,' replied the young woman, 'totally weird, isn't it? And cold too! But there's Wi-Fi and a phone signal and I can rent it by the month or the week. There's no other office space I can afford in Camley and I can't work from home because I need to be near my clients!'

'Don't you get nervous with the lights going on and off?'

'It used to freak me out at first, like working in a thunderstorm, but I've got used to it now.'

'Isn't it a bit lonely?' Stella thought of her daughter sitting alone in this Scandi Noir environment and shuddered.

'Horrible. I dream of having other people to talk to so we could share ideas and even costs, but it ain't gonna happen. Not in Camley, anyway. So it's just me and the receptionist. Nice statue.'

Matthew's declaration that what the council really wanted was cheap office space came back to her. Now she could see why. She waved goodbye to the young woman and carted her emperor thoughtfully back to the reception area.

Five minutes later, Suze joined her.

'Do you think there's enough here for a whole table?' she asked Stella.

'Is it for sale?' asked the smiling receptionist, indicating the bust. 'I mean, it might brighten this place up a bit. It's so empty and faceless. A Roman emperor might be company for me.'

Suze thought about it. 'A tenner?'

'Done! Now you won't have to cart it around with you.'

They helped her place the bust on a cheap MDF shelf next to the water cooler.

'Now I've got a friend!'

'That was the strangest place I've ever been,' remarked Stella as they unloaded Suze's stuff into the pet studio for storage with the tables.

Stella caught sight of her fox painting and decided to put it up there and then. She found her hammer and picture-hanging gear and positioned it in pride of place right opposite the entrance.

'Just so that anyone with a pet fox can see what a dab hand you are at wildlife painting?' teased Suze.

The fox's amber eyes stared out from the green background, world-weary and mournful, as if he had seen all human life and nothing more could shock or surprise him.

'I think it's amazing.' They both turned, startled, to find Duncan had just come into the studio.

'Don't sound so astonished.' Stella felt irritation rising that he clearly hadn't expected her to be any good.

'You know who it reminds me of in some strange way?'

'Fantastic Mr Fox?' suggested Suze.

'Cameron.' Duncan grinned, ignoring Stella's tone. 'There's something about his charm and guile and total untrustworthiness that definitely reminds me of him.'

'I'm not sure he'd appreciate that,' Stella commented, still bristling at the patronizing tones she'd detected in his voice. 'Aren't you busy at The Glebe, or do you want your pet painted?'

'I don't have a pet. Too much travelling.'

'What would you have if you did? Let me guess.' She looked at him thoughtfully. 'A terrier wouldn't be suave enough for you.'

'I am not suave!' he snapped. 'I just dress like this for business.'

'Something fashionable. A Hungarian Vizsla, perhaps? They're sufficiently haughty and distinctive.'

'Actually,' Duncan refused to be drawn, 'if I had a dog, I would go for a poodle.'

'A poodle?' Stella repeated, stunned.

'A big one. They're the most intelligent dogs there are. Anyway, forget poodles, I came here to say thanks for keeping an eye on Cameron. He's probably dreading the concert. It's been so long since his last live gig and the music press will be out in force. He wants to stay as near as possible to the venue so we'll move the Airstream to their car park on Wednesday.'

'Not long now.'

'Absolutely.'

Stella realized that, forget Cameron, she was feeling quite nervous herself.

Duncan produced a wallet from his jacket pocket. 'Here are all your tickets, plus passes to the Artists' Bar area. Have fun.'

'Is everything all sorted? For the concert, I mean.'

Duncan shrugged. 'Everything except Cameron.'

As the concert finally approached, Debora was deputed to be on Cameron-watch, so she had camped with him in the Airstream, playing backgammon, listening to Pink Floyd at top volume and watching endless reruns of *Cheers* and *Happy Days*. At last she emerged the night before the concert, her hair slightly out of place and with no lipstick, which, in anyone else, would be the equivalent of a complete mental breakdown.

'Phew,' she took a deep breath. 'That was hard work. Cameron's like a little kid. He has to be entertained all the time or he gets bored. I've given him a Valium and a large brandy. He'll sleep like a baby.'

Stella gave her a hug, realizing how fond she'd grown of Debora in the short time they'd known each other. 'He's lucky he's got you.'

'Goodnight, hon. I'll be back for him in the morning. By the way, I've taken the precaution of locking him in.'

'Is that wise? What if he starts a fire or something?'

'You'll hear the alarm. It's very loud, believe me.'

Stella finally retired after her usual tour of the house, pulling curtains and checking locks before tumbling into bed.

As usual Matthew was fast asleep.

She fell into a light sleep, only to be troubled by a strange dream. It seemed to feature one of her favourite novels by Mary Renault about the legendary Minotaur in Ancient Crete. Suddenly the Minotaur, half-man, half-bull, let out a bellow that was such a terrifying mix of anger and hopeless abandonment that Stella woke up with a jolt. The sound wasn't coming from classical Crete, it was coming from her back garden.

She whipped on her dressing gown and ran downstairs to look for the key Debora had left to the Airstream before the whole of Camley was woken up, with Mrs Husky first in line.

Fortunately, there was a torch by the back door that she kept handy in case she needed to cross the lawn to her studio.

She unlocked the door of the Airstream and Cameron burst

out as if gasping for air. 'Stella!' he clutched her to his considerable chest, 'I thought I was going to die in there!'

'It's OK, Cam,' she stroked his hair, adopting the tone she used for Izzy or Ruby; firm but kind. 'Calm down now. You just hyperventilated a bit. Just sit on the step and I'll get something.'

Back in the house she found a paper bag in the recycling. When Jesse was little he sometimes used to have minor panic attacks and the GP had shown them how to get him to breathe into a paper bag.

She rushed back out and tried to hold the bag over Cameron's nose and mouth.

'For fuck's sake,' Cameron protested, 'I'm not going to throw up.'

'It's to calm you down. Just hold it yourself and breathe into it. Just normal breaths. Then take it off and start again in a minute.'

After three attempts he did seem a bit less agitated. 'Now take deep breaths from your diaphragm.'

Once the emergency was over, Stella took in the fact that Cameron was stark naked. Thank God it was quite a dark night. 'Cameron,' she shoved him back into the Airstream, 'put some clothes on.'

'I will if you come in with me. Otherwise I'm staying right here.' He gave her a cunning look that made her see immediately why Duncan had likened him to the fox. 'Give your neighbour a thrill. She doesn't look as if she's seen a cock in a while.'

'I'll come in if you promise to cover up.'

Once they were inside he did at least reassure her by putting on a tee shirt proclaiming MAKE LOVE NOT WAR.

'Stella, Stella,' he insisted passionately, 'you were always the only one who could inspire me. Why didn't you come with me to the States? I could have written such amazing songs for you.' He shook his head as though it were all her fault that though he had made plenty of records, only the one about her had become an anthem. 'You will stay with me tonight, won't you, Stell?' he appealed in a voice that was suddenly fearful. 'I'm scared, Stella. What if those vultures of music hacks tear me apart?'

Stella felt herself overwhelmed with sudden tenderness for the man she'd shared such amazing moments with. Both from humble backgrounds, they had felt the tectonic plates of society moving, and had learned to whoop joyously, throwing themselves into music, into freedom and into new experiences. Was it possible to feel it again so much later?

She sat down next to him. 'Everyone loves you, Cam. You're practically a British institution, like Tom Jones or Rod Stewart. No one is going to tear you apart. Now come on, just lie down and I'll massage your neck.'

Cameron Keene, world megastar, lay obediently down and she began to knead his rigid muscles. In a matter of moments he was asleep.

Too emotionally exhausted even to crawl back into the house she lay down and slept by his side.

It was the neighbours' horrible dog that woke her, barking at the postman. Good God, he didn't come till nearly ten!

She jumped up, scrabbled around for her shoes, and flung open the door to the Airstream.

A bewildered Matthew was standing outside their house, obviously looking for her. By his side was Emma, holding their granddaughter plus her baby bag.

'It must be another emergency.'

But neither of them was giving her their full attention.

Behind her, rubbing his eyes and yawning, stood Cameron Keene still wearing only a tee shirt.

'Peace and love,' he pronounced, holding up two fingers in the time-honoured hippie salutation. 'Well, this is a bit awkward.'

Seven

'What the fuck is going on?' Matthew exploded.

'Yes, Mum,' Emma seconded, almost as horrified as her father, 'what *is* going on?'

The only way to play this, Stella decided, was to treat the situation as the joke it almost was. She glanced at Cameron's member. Fortunately, it was curled up and harmless, like a dog in disgrace.

'Don't be ridiculous, the pair of you.'

'Ridiculous, when you've clearly spent the night with the world-famous rock singer who wrote a song about you?' Matthew demanded pugnaciously. 'Pathetic more like!'

'What's pathetic about it?' demanded Cameron. 'A lovely woman spending the night with a man who's always loved her?' He turned to Stella, with a tender look. 'I have, you know, Stella. I still love you now.'

'And you have three marriages to prove it,' Stella replied crisply, in a passable imitation of her old headmistress. 'Stop all this self-indulgence right now and pull yourself together!'

They all looked at her in shocked awe. This wasn't a Stella

they had yet encountered. 'Cameron had a panic attack and I stayed to calm him down. Nothing happened.'

'You gave me a massage.' Cameron smiled mischievously, looking like a lecherous pixie. Was he trying to sabotage her marriage deliberately?

'Come with me, Stella, after the tour finishes. It's not too late!'

Before she had the chance to answer they heard the sound of clapping and swung round in unison.

Duncan Miller stood in the kitchen doorway with Debora. 'I had no idea I was interrupting a drawing-room comedy,' he congratulated. 'No, make that a psychological thriller.' Stella looked at him gratefully. He did seem to have the knack of calming troubled waters. 'I'm afraid I have to remove the romantic lead rather sharpish.' He looked Cameron up and down, dwelling for a second on his absence of underwear. 'Or possibly the pantomime villain. Just for the record, I believe Stella.'

'So do I,' laughed Debora. 'Cameron always panics before a concert. Thanks, Stella, for calming him down.'

'Just as well you two aren't really planning a surprise elope-ment.' Duncan smiled round blandly. 'We've just heard from Fabia. She and Roxy will definitely be coming to the concert.'

'Christ, that's all I need,' muttered Cameron, closing his eyes.

'Nonsense, Cam,' Duncan shepherded Cameron into the Airstream. 'A gorgeous young wife to wipe your fevered brow? Any man would envy you.'

Cameron looked as if he might sack Duncan on the spot, but he finally allowed himself to be led inside.

'Right,' Stella held out her arms for her granddaughter,

'that's enough drama for one day. What time are you picking Ruby up?'

Matthew, always a terrier when it came to hanging on to an argument, still looked deeply unconvinced. 'Even if he did have a panic attack, someone else could have stayed with him. You're married to me,' he hissed, and disappeared inside, banging the door. From past experience he'd now give her the silent treatment and they would remain stuck in mutual antipathy for days. She'd once tried to persuade him to go for couples therapy, as Emma had done, but he'd blankly refused. 'I'm not listening to all that ridiculous pyscho-twaddle!' had been his firm and final response.

Ten minutes later, Cameron emerged looking almost smart in his tweed jacket and corduroys, with the familiar yellow Nikes, smiling unrepentantly.

'Are you all still coming to the show? After all the drama?' asked Debora.

'You bloody bet we are. I wouldn't miss it for the world.' She winked at Debora. 'Especially now the famous Fabia's back. I'm dying to meet her.'

She was just putting Ruby into her high chair when she noticed that Duncan had come into the kitchen and was leaning on the Aga. 'Who needs stand-up comedy?' he asked, still laughing. 'That was one of the funniest things I've seen in a long time. I hope you didn't mind my butting in. I thought maybe you could do with a distraction.'

'Funny!' Stella's tension metamorphosed into outrage. 'That was my marriage Cameron nearly destroyed!'

Duncan stopped smiling and looked at her intently. 'If your husband was so ready to believe you'd be unfaithful, maybe it isn't worth saving anyway.'

'And of course you were never unfaithful in your perfect

marriage!' Stella flashed angrily. 'All those groupies and backing singers and dancers and gorgeous little girl fans. You never even thought about it!'

'Of course I thought about it,' he replied, almost as angry as she was. 'But I didn't do it. It always seemed rather unfair on my wife.'

Stella remembered that his wife had died suddenly only last year and felt herself flush with shame. 'I'm sorry. That was unforgivable of me.'

'Don't worry,' he was suddenly smiling again. 'I expect you were jealous of my long and happy marriage.'

Really, the man was too much! Implying that her own marriage didn't live up to his! Stella plucked Ruby out of her high chair and stalked upstairs to get dressed without even rewarding him with so much as a goodbye.

'Is Matthew coming tonight or does he still want to call Cameron out to defend your honour?'

Suze and Stella were in Stella's and Matthew's bedroom getting dressed for the concert. Stella sipped the champagne she had just poured for them both.

'To be honest, Suze, I don't really care. Come on,' she held up her glass, 'let's have fun getting ready. I'll put some music on to get us in the mood. James Taylor or Joni Mitchell?'

'Little ol' lovin' man JT. Do you remember when we used to get changed to it at college?'

'It was usually more fun than the date.'

They started giggling like silly teenagers. Suze did up Stella's zip and then Stella did up Suze's. They took it in turns to apply their make-up and when they were finally ready they appraised each other in the mirror.

'Not too bad for a couple of old broads!' Stella laughed, and they gave each other a giggly hug just at the moment Matthew walked into the room.

'I don't know why you two don't just move in with each other,' was his grumbling mutter, and Stella refrained from replying, 'Neither do I, it'd probably be much more fun.'

He hurried into the en suite bathroom and without even closing the door began to have a pee.

'Why is it,' Stella whispered, 'that what seems bold and outrageous because your parents would never have done it, like peeing in front of each other, just ends up irritating you in the end?'

'Look at it this way,' Suze reassured her, 'you're lucky to have someone to pee in front of you in the first place.'

'Come on,' Stella squeezed her friend's arm, knowing Suze was perfectly happy living on her own, 'let's get our coats. Taxi'll be here in a min.'

'Oooh, a taxi! We are pushing the boat out!'

'Muses don't arrive on the bus, even if they do have a Freedom Pass. Besides, we're picking up the others on the way. Matthew,' she shouted, 'are you coming with us? Because if you are, we're leaving in five minutes!'

She was greeted with silence. 'That's another of his delightful tricks. Pretending he hasn't heard me.' When she got into the bedroom the bathroom door was locked. 'I'm leaving your ticket on the bed,' she shouted through the door. 'Up to you whether you make it or not but everyone else is coming and we'd all like it if you did.' Absolute silence. Overcome with irritation, Stella banged on the door. 'If you're not coming just to spite me, that's really stupid because it's going to be a fun occasion and no one will miss out but you!'

'You did your best.' Suze shrugged. 'The taxi's here.'

Stella gave him one more try. 'Matthew! We're going now. See you later, I hope.'

'No you don't,' Suze dug her in the ribs as they sat in the back of the people carrier.

'Not if he's being like this, I don't.'

'Now we're alone you can tell me the truth. Did you and the rock god get it on?'

'Suze, how can you ask?'

'Well, why not? He's quite attractive as raddled rock gods go.'

'For a start, I'm married and so is he.'

Suze raised an ironic eyebrow. 'Aren't you curious? I mean, he is Cameron Keene.'

Stella shook her head.

'OK, were you worried about him seeing your ageing tits?'

'No!'

'You want him to still be in love with you and ask you to run away with him!'

'Actually,' Stella couldn't help admitting proudly, 'that's what he did. Of course he didn't mean it for a moment. Or if he did, he's a complete fantasist.'

'Well, I think it's sweet and flattering that he still fancies an old lady like you!'

'I don't think he's actually faced up to my age at all. If I'm sixty-four, that means he's sixty-five!'

'How romantic! A relationship based on mutual denial and regular Botox.'

'I don't use Botox,' Stella protested.

'No, but Cameron does. No one could have a forehead that smooth when they've lived the life he has. He ought to have more lines than an OS map!'

'Can you stop here, please?' Stella asked the driver when they reached Emma's house. 'I'll just give them a call.'

Five minutes later they all spilled out happily onto the driveway. Jesse had dressed up in a smart new shirt. Dora, the Incredible String Band fan, had avoided copying their singer Licorice at Woodstock in her white bridal wear with flowers in her hair, and had stuck to a pretty blouse with a neat Peter Pan collar. Izzy wore a grown-up dress with a denim jacket, and Emma looked quite beautiful in blue jeans tucked into cowboy boots with a floaty pale silk top. Even Stuart was there. Ruby waved them goodbye from the arms of her babysitter.

Stella felt her heart overflow with pride.

As they got into the cab, Emma sat down next to her, holding her handbag against her chest as if it were incredibly precious.

'Come on, Mum,' Izzy teased. 'You're going to have to put it down some time!'

Stella and Suze both stared at the bag. It was pale-blue softest leather, brand new, the ultimate object of desire. Right in the centre was the tell-tale triangular brass panel with the word PRADA on it.

Neither Stella nor Suze said a word, but they were thinking identical thoughts. They had no idea how much the bag cost but they were certain about two things. First, neither of them would ever dream of buying such a ridiculously costly item and second, whoever did buy it for her must be very rich indeed.

'So, how did you first meet the great man?' Stuart interrupted her thoughts. Stella turned and smiled at him. He had come straight from work and had a slightly rumpled look, but it suited him. His hair, longer than usual, almost covered his collar. With his interesting, angular face and black-framed spectacles he looked even more like Elvis Costello. Stella tried to picture Hal, but surely he wasn't anything like as attractive as Stuart? Except perhaps for his success. And perhaps because he noticed and flattered Emma at a moment when she was feeling trapped, even if it had been her own decision to have a baby, and needed to feel wanted and valued.

Had Stuart noticed the Prada bag or had Emma managed to dazzle him with some tale of bargains on eBay? Perhaps it might be better if he did notice.

'We were at art college together,' Stella replied. 'I was eighteen and he was a year older. We met at a concert and started going out. He was just dreaming about music then, playing records of his heroes all day and night, practising chords and riffs on this little girl who hardly knew the Beatles from the Stones.'

'She doesn't really mean that,' Suze broke in. 'She was actually in love with Jim Morrison. She used to keep The Doors album under her pillow.'

'Suze!'

'Did you really, Gran?' Jesse laughed.

'I did, actually. I know I'll sound like an old bore, but it's hard for your generation to imagine the Sixties.'

'I can,' Dora broke in passionately. 'I so wish I'd been born then!'

'You'd have made a wonderful flower child,' Stella agreed.

'And how did the song come about?' Jesse took Dora's hand and squeezed it lovingly. 'Did you really leave him in bed and break his heart?'

'Cameron's an artist,' Stella replied quickly. 'He's allowed to make things up.'

'The funny thing is,' Emma threw in, 'I always thought that song was about a one-night stand. You know, that agonizing feeling when one of you is in love and the other one just gets out of bed and goes.'

Her words were imbued with such intensity that they all looked at her.

Emma flushed uncomfortably. 'I mean, what does anyone else think?'

'I just thought it was a wonderful love song,' Dora rescued her with the optimism of youth. 'And how amazing to have it written about you!'

By now they had left the suburbs of Camley far behind and were driving through the leafy beauty of Regent's Park, not far from the venue. Stella began to feel quite nervous. She hoped Cameron had recovered. At least with Debora on hand things should be all right.

They turned down a back road and found themselves in the sudden craziness of Camden Lock. Even at this time it was more like a souk than an English market, enticing tourists with its displays of Indian bedspreads emblazoned with the elephant-headed god Ganesh, joss sticks, cheap jewellery, tee shirts of Bob Marley and David Bowie cheek by jowl with street food from every corner of the globe. Outside the pavements were thick with every fashion era from goth to punk to New Romantic.

'God,' said Suze, 'it's like walking into fashion history.'

'Yes,' breathed Dora ecstatically, 'isn't it wonderful?'

Another five minutes and they had arrived.

'Bloody hell,' Emma pointed, 'look at the queue.'

The queue was indeed impressive.

'And they're not all old people,' she added, surprised.

'No,' Suze commented, 'some of them are still alive.'

Emma ignored her. 'They must be in their twenties.' She pointed to a hip young couple.

'Maybe Cameron is becoming an ironic icon,' Stuart suggested. 'Like heavy metal, so unfashionable it's fashionable.'

The taxi came to a halt. 'To think,' breathed Suze, 'we don't even have to queue up!'

They walked down the steps into the one-time railway shed with the amazing rotunda shape that gave it its name. A security guard immediately approached. 'We have tickets,' Stella announced proudly. 'To the Artists' Bar.'

'Go to the desk on the left-hand side,' he replied with new respect. 'They have the guest list there. They'll give you your wristband.'

'Oooh, a wristband!' Izzy jumped up and down. 'I can add it to my collection. I already have One Direction, Olly Murs and Make Poverty History.'

'Are they a band?' Suze asked Stella.

'No – as far as I know, it's a worldwide campaign to eradicate hunger.' They started giggling again. The receptionist ticked off their names from her list and helped them put on the wristbands.

'I feel like I'm seventeen again,' Suze whispered. 'Do you remember that dive in Camley where they stamped your wrist in infrared so you could come back in again when you'd been out for a fag?'

'Or gone outside to snog?'

'Gran!' Izzy opened her eyes wide in shock. 'You never snogged!'

'Hard to imagine, isn't it?' Suze seconded. 'I mean, she's such a frightful old bag now.'

'No she's not,' Izzy defended. 'She's quite pretty for an old lady. Even Mum says so.'

'Now that *is* a compliment.' Stella glanced at Emma, who

was putting on her wristband with the help of her husband. She was still clutching the bag as if it were the Crown Jewels.

'I'll get someone to take you up,' said the receptionist.

'How's it all going?' Stella couldn't help herself asking.

'Pretty good. Full house. Nice well-behaved people who'll buy wine instead of beer and not throw it at the stage like the Madness fans.'

'Stella,' Suze hissed, 'stop behaving like Cameron's mum!'

Stella ignored her. 'Do they really?'

'Well, mainly,' the girl grinned, 'they throw it over each other. When they're pogoing.'

'Pogoing!' Suze repeated mistily. 'I remember pogoing . . .'

'Before you got so arthritic!' teased Stella.

'Sounds very silly,' Izzy commented. 'I prefer trampolining any day.'

They followed their guide through the byways of the amazing building, past posters of past acts.

'Look,' Suze hissed. 'The Stones, 1971 . . . Bowie, Elton John, Blondie. Cameron's in good company!'

There was a greeter waiting for them in the bar. 'Welcome. I'm Vivienne. A glass of champagne? Courtesy of Mr Keene.'

'Wow, we really are getting the rock-star treatment!' Stuart grinned.

'By the way,' Vivienne gestured at a coat rack behind her, 'would you like to leave your things here? They'll be perfectly safe.'

'Isn't this amazing!' Stella couldn't help laughing. A couple of weeks ago she'd been a grandmother from the suburbs, now she was drinking champagne in the Artists' Bar at the Round-house! 'It's so kind of Cam to send us the champagne.'

'Actually,' the girl confided, 'I think it was really Mr Miller.' She indicated the auditorium below. 'You get a great view from here, but the crowd can't see you. The artists like the privacy for their friends and family.'

At the front of the bar was a row of small tables with high bar stools. Stella perched on one and looked down at the crowd gathering below. They were mostly like her, people who'd followed Cameron from their teens, but as Emma had pointed out, there were twenty-year-olds too. 'Quite an age range,' she commented to the greeter.

'"Don't Leave Me" tends to be 'our song' for an amazing number of people,' the girl replied.

'But it's so sad!'

'We've all been there, though, haven't we? That's why it's such an anthem.'

Behind them, the door to the Artists' Bar opened and two figures stood silhouetted by the light behind them.

The first was an extraordinary figure in a fur coat, with bright red lips and sunglasses. She reminded Stella faintly of Cruella de Vil and imagined every Dalmatian in North London cowering unconsciously in its bed. Behind her was a stunningly beautiful young girl with masses of dark hair, in a 1940s-style print dress and a fur bolero.

'It's Foxy Roxy!' breathed Izzy, rooted to the spot in awe. 'I follow her all the time on YouTube!'

The two newcomers surveyed Stella and her party in startled surprise. 'I'm Fabia de Rosza and this is my daughter Roxanne,' announced Cruella, raking them all with a gimlet eye. 'Who the fuck are all of you?'

Stella found everyone suddenly looking to her for the answer.

Stella stepped forward. 'I'm Stella Ainsworth, an old friend of Cameron's, and this is my daughter Emma and her husband

Stuart, my old friend, Susannah, and my granddaughter, Izzy. Oh and my grandson Jesse and his friend Dora.'

'Right. Got you.' Fabia looked very pleased with herself at this dazzling feat of memory. 'You're the grey-haired granny Mike Willan was going on about.'

'Except she's not grey-haired, is she, Mum?' her daughter enquired sweetly.

'How many times do I have to ask you, Roxanne, will you stop calling me Mum?' Fabia replied wearily.

'What should I call you?'

'How about Cruella?' Stella almost suggested.

'I've told you. Fabia. It is my name after all.'

'All right. As I said, she's not grey-haired, is she, Fabia? And I think she's beautiful. Hello, Stella, delighted to meet you.'

'Are you really Foxy Roxy?' breathed Izzy shyly, as if greeting a goddess just down from Mount Olympus.

'Yes,' Roxanne laughed uproariously. 'Hilarious, isn't it? But yes, I am.'

'She gets a million likes,' explained Izzy proudly. 'Would you mind if we took a selfie?' She couldn't wait to share it with Freya and Bianca.

'Likes?' Fabia pooh-poohed. 'Facebook Friends? What does it all mean? She doesn't know any of these so-called Friends. Roxanne just records her life and lets all these strangers watch it.'

'You don't understand any of it, Mum . . . Fabia. You still read *Hello!* magazine.'

'Glass of champagne anyone?' Stuart offered. Stella smiled at him gratefully. She could see he was used to dealing with tricky customers. It was a pity his politics banned him from expanding his client list from refugees and asylum seekers to deposed dictators and superannuated groupies.

'Can I take your coat?' he asked Fabia when she accepted the champagne. 'It looks very expensive.'

To anyone else this might have been crass but Stuart had judged Fabia perfectly. 'It was,' she replied proudly. 'It is Arctic fox and they are an endangered species.'

Suze spluttered into her champagne. 'Highly endangered with her around.'

Fabia allowed her coat to be removed, strode to the front and placed herself at the most prominent table while Roxanne shrugged in embarrassment and retreated to chat with Izzy.

At last she removed her sunglasses and Stella saw that the once-beautiful face was surprisingly lined and the red from her lipstick had trickled into the runnels above her top lip. It gave her the air of a vaguely melting waxwork. Stella was surprised she hadn't gone in for plastic surgery. She hardly looked the type to have scruples about it. Maybe she couldn't find anyone to pay for it.

Intrigued, Stella studied her more closely. The ankle boots she wore, clearly designer, were scuffed and down at heel. Maybe Fabia, so glossy at first glance, was finding it hard to keep up appearances. Debora was clearly right about Roxy being her insurance policy and her pension.

Yet how could such a sweet girl have fallen for a grizzled, if charming, over-sixty-year-old like Cameron? Clearly it must be connected with Roxy's insecure upbringing. Stella had a sudden flash of what she would have had to endure with someone like Fabia as a parent, dragged about from man to man and hotel to hotel, never putting down roots or having a proper home. She could see how, at least for a while, Cameron, with his fame and money, not to mention his occasional twinkly charm, could offer an attractive alternative. Equally clearly, the illusion hadn't lasted long.

The door of the Artists' Bar opened and Duncan Miller appeared. Before Stella had the chance to thank him for the champagne he began to speak in a quiet but urgent voice.

'Stella, could you spare me a moment? Vivienne, could you come too?'

Stella put down her drink and followed him out of the bar, leaving Fabia looking outraged not to be included.

'Sorry to interrupt your fun,' he expanded once they were in the corridor. 'Debora says can you go and get the Deathbed Reviver? It's in the Airstream. It's parked just behind here. Vivienne will show you. Here are the keys.' He tossed them over to her.

'But why? What's the problem? The show starts in half an hour.'

Once they were in the corridor where no one else could hear, he told her. 'Thank God for support bands. It's Cameron. Debora and I just found him lying in a pile of cheap beer cans. He's out cold.'

Eight

Stella and Vivienne raced to the car park and opened up the Airstream. The Deathbed Reviver was just inside the door. Debora seemed so well prepared that Stella wondered if this had happened before.

They shoved the throw from the sofa over it and ran back to the venue. 'If we bump into anyone, we'll just have to say it's for my friend Suze who's just out from hospital. She won't mind.'

Vivienne led her back through winding corridors and up via a lift for band equipment to the dressing-room area.

Cameron's backing band stood around looking deeply pissed off while Debora, Duncan and a doctor gathered round Cameron.

'He's already puked about twenty-five times, so that has to be good,' Debora greeted them with her usual amazing calm. 'Bring it over and we'll hook it up.'

'Wha' the fuck?' demanded Cameron, trying unsuccessfully to get to his feet.

'It's OK, Cam,' soothed Debora. 'It's just a drip of Dioralyte, like when you get the shits. It helps you recover quicker.'

'Where's that triple espresso?' the doctor demanded. 'It's easier with smack addicts; at least you can give them a shot to revive them. Bloody alcohol. It's a menace.'

'Can't you just cancel the show?' Stella asked Duncan. 'Say he's got a bad throat and get them to come back another day?'

Duncan shook his head. 'Apart from the complexity there are too many "bad throats" in this business. The twitterati and music press would have a field day, which is what Cam was nervous about in the first place. We've got to sober him up.'

They stood silently as the saline and electrolytes flooded into Cameron's bloodstream. The doctor produced a vial of anti-nausea medicine and vitamin B12 and injected them into Cameron's arm, finishing up with a large dose of painkillers.

'With luck that should revive an elephant,' he said as he rolled back his sleeves.

Cameron caught sight of Stella sitting next to his couch and reached out his hand. 'Stella, you came. You know this concert is for you.'

'I don't care if it's for Joan of Arc,' Duncan commented brusquely. 'Just get the fuck up, Cameron, or I'm resigning.'

Cameron sat up slowly.

'Have some more coffee.' Debora handed him another cup.

'Hey, Debs,' he replied. 'What would I do without you?'

He looked around in wonder at how and why all these people were gathered round him. 'I'm sorry, everyone, I just wasn't sure I could do it.' He smiled magnanimously. 'Now I think I can. I know I can.'

The band exchanged weary smiles.

'How long till we're on?'

'Fifteen minutes. Watch him, all of you. Don't even let him go to the bog on his own.'

'Duncan . . .' There was a world of reproach in his voice. 'Would I?'

'Yes. Remember your dad and the white spirit. Have you got any more booze hidden anywhere? Test those water bottles, Deb.'

'Nothing.'

Cameron smiled beatifically.

'What's that?' Duncan indicated a small bottle marked 'Dunlop 654 Guitar Polish'.

'Since when have you ever polished your guitar? Hand it over.'

Reluctantly, Cameron passed him the bottle. Duncan sniffed it. 'It smells like bloody absinthe!'

'Nothing wrong with the green fairy. Natural product. Only the finest wormwood.'

'The only natural product you're getting is water.'

There was a warning knock on the door. 'Ten minutes.'

'Is everyone sure of the running order?'

They nodded. 'One thing,' Steve, the drummer, hesitated. 'Cam says we shouldn't play "Don't Leave Me" and save it for the encore. Won't that seem like a wedding without a fucking bridegroom?'

Duncan thought about it. 'No, it'll be OK. Go out on a high. Thank God he did a sound check earlier.'

They headed off towards the stage.

Debora momentarily seemed to sag. 'I'd forgotten what it was like. Someone's going to have to keep him on the straight and narrow and I suspect it won't be Roxy. Has she arrived?'

'Yes.' Stella grinned at Debora. 'And Fabia too. Wearing half the world's Arctic foxes.'

The Artists' Bar was even more crowded by the time they got back there. Fabia, still in prime position at the front, was surrounded by an admiring audience of two – Matthew and Bernie. Matthew, she noted, was eagerly refilling Fabia's glass with more champagne.

'How did you get here so quickly?' Stella asked her husband.

'I got a text from Cameron asking me to pick Bernie up in a cab. Apparently it's important he's here, for some reason,' Matthew explained stiffly, eager to make it obvious he hadn't come for her sake.

'That was nice of him.'

'Have some champagne,' Stuart rescued her. 'Problem solved?'

Debora smiled round at the box. 'If it isn't, you'll soon know about it.'

A roar silenced any further questioning. The roadie was on stage checking the band's equipment. The audience began to pound their feet and clap slowly in anticipation of the big moment.

The bass guitarist walked on, smiling broadly, followed by the keyboard player, sax and two backing singers. Next came the drummer and finally the man himself.

'Ladies and gentlemen,' announced a disembodied voice, 'I give you the voice that breaks hearts and shatters glasses . . . Cameron Keene!'

To a storm of applause, Cameron, in black shirt and black 501s, and his trademark cowboy boots, sauntered on stage with a huge smile on his face and all the confidence that took six shots of liquor to achieve.

'Are you happy to be here?' he shouted to the audience. Ignoring the murmurs of assent he shouted again, this time louder, 'Are you happy to be here?'

This time the response was a roar.

He grabbed the microphone and began to walk up and

down at the front of the stage. 'Before we start, there's one person I'd like to dedicate this concert to, someone who helped to make me the person I am . . .'

In the bar all eyes turned to Stella, especially Fabia's. Even Duncan, who had slipped in to join them, fixed his gaze on her face.

Cameron paused, looked down at the audience then up for maximum effect. 'My father, Billy Keene!'

There was a gasp from Suze. Debora just shook her head.

'Yes,' Duncan broke the silence. 'Here's to Billy Keene, the man who couldn't tell paint stripper from vodka. He's certainly made Cam the man he is today. I'd like to add another toast. To Stella, who welcomed us all back into her life. I hope you're not regretting it after today.'

Stella raised her glass at the assembled gathering, her dignity restored, and began to laugh, struck by the ridiculousness of expecting to have a concert dedicated to her at sixty-four, as if she were some medieval lady hoping to give a knight her colours, when both the knight and the lady in question were almost in their dotage.

'Nonsense,' and as she said it, she realized she actually believed it, 'Matthew and I haven't had such fun in years.'

They settled on their stools and began to watch the show. All the seats in the balcony were full, the aisles even had one or two wheelchairs – another comment on the reality of age – and the standing-only space below the stage was packed as well.

'Every seat sold,' Duncan explained. 'Cam will be on at me about why we didn't book a bigger venue. This is perfect, iconic, efficient and the music press can see it's overflowing. The ideal kick-off to the tour.'

Stella studied Cameron. It was as though he was born to

be on stage. He came alive under the spotlight, all vestiges of the unreliable, semi-alcoholic sexagenarian disappearing in a puff of dry ice as soon as he walked on. This audience, leaning forward eagerly, reliving their youth as they sang along, would have been stunned to know that half an hour ago he had been lying in a drunken stupor.

How joyous and amazing the power of music was. Just listening to the songs they had first heard all those years ago transported the audience back to their youth as no other experience could. Maybe, like Stella, they were all thinking about the passage of life, the choices they'd made, the decisions taken or not taken. Or just remembering what an amazing moment they'd experienced when being young was suddenly exciting, heady, dangerous and wonderful. When you could put flowers in your hair, wear ludicrous loon pants, dress up in silks and velvets, and terrify the older generation with your careless insouciance and lack of respect for anything they stood for.

She looked around at her family. Jesse and Dora stared at the stage, entranced by Cameron's rambling yet wonderfully witty introductions.

'Almost as long as the songs are,' Duncan commented.

Fabia, seated cosily next to Matthew, was scanning the audience for anyone worthy of note and shrugging dismissively that they were ordinary fans. Even Izzy, despite the proximity of her new idol Roxy, was watching with fascination.

'Gran,' she asked to raucous laughter from Suze, 'is that really the old man who's been staying in your driveway?'

'He is not an old man!' Fabia corrected crossly while Roxy, Stella noted, just laughed and nodded her head.

And it was an amazing transformation. For ninety solid minutes Cameron rocked his audience at ear-splitting maximum decibels. 'It's amazing he hasn't gone deaf,' Suze commented, covering her ears.

On the vast space beneath the bar they bopped and jiggled and tapped their feet, roaring applause at the end of each number, savouring every moment as the atmospheric blue spotlights raked the audience, pausing occasionally to pinpoint a pair who danced away, unconscious of their surroundings, abandoned to the music as if they really were young again.

As the concert neared its end Stella became aware of a restlessness in the auditorium. Couples looked at each other anxiously, a few people shrugged and looked at their watches. One or two even started to leave like at a football game when your team's losing.

All at once the show was over and Cameron thanked everyone for coming and abruptly left the stage without playing the one number they all really wanted to hear.

The sense of disappointment hung in the air like fog hiding the sunshine. Cheated of the reason a lot of them had come, they began to stomp on the floor and catcall, not entirely favourably.

'Oh dear, he's losing them.' Stella bit her lip anxiously.

'Don't worry,' Duncan reassured, 'Cam's a sly old beast. It's all showmanship.'

And then he was back on stage and straight into 'Don't Leave Me in the Morning', while all around the venue people jumped from their seats and looked deep into each other's eyes, suddenly nineteen again, roaring their approval.

Listening to the song live, at maximum volume, was an extraordinary sensation. The raw longing and fear of rejection, the cruel one-sidedness of love, the desperate need to believe, united the entire room in exquisitely painful memory.

Stella found herself glancing at Jesse, who was just entering into this tunnel of unavoidable suffering himself, and found Duncan's eyes on her. He must, she supposed, be wondering what she was feeling now, listening to the song she'd inspired so long ago.

The slightly shocking truth was that she felt nothing at all. It was all so many years ago and she had no real complaints with her life. She could hardly persuade herself that she and Matthew were soulmates, but wasn't that an illusion, a romantic cliché that had nothing to do with real life?

Cameron and his band played one more track and the show was over, ending on an uproarious high.

Stella watched the auditorium empty. Cameron had done it. He had given the audience what it wanted. A brief moment to forget rheumatism, divorce, loneliness, whether or not your children were happy, and how long you might still have on this earth, and recapture the joy and pain of being young when everything was still ahead of you.

'What happens next?' she asked Duncan.

'Another ten minutes and we can go down. The venue lays on food and drink so that the rock god that is Cameron Keene or Elton John or Mick Jagger can eat here and wait till the public and press have safely dispersed outside. Are you all right?' he added in a low voice as she looked for her handbag. 'I suspect he meant to dedicate it to you and got sidetracked. Cameron is supremely unaware of other people's feelings. I suspect he finds it a very useful quality.'

'Why would I expect him to? It would have felt really strange.'

'Where *is* Cameron?' Fabia interrupted with a sweep of fox fur that knocked over three champagne glasses. To Stella's amusement, Fabia didn't even turn. Some minion could sweep it up. 'I am sure he is longing to see his wife.' She dismissed

Matthew, who had been helping her on with her coat, and grabbed Roxy, who looked distinctly underwhelmed. 'Come on, Roxanne, let's go and find your husband.'

'By the way,' Duncan thanked Stella quietly, 'thank you for not telling anyone what happened earlier.'

'Does it happen often?'

'Only on first nights. Cameron needs to be loved. He's fine once he knows he's still got it. It can be quite wearing.'

'Why do you stay with him?' she asked curiously. 'Not for the money, surely? Debora tells me you've made Cameron a rich man.' Suddenly she realized how rude and intrusive this must sound. 'Sorry, don't answer that.'

Duncan smiled. 'For the fun, I suppose. My other interests are rather dull.'

'Not golf?'

'Redistribution of wealth. I make money and spread it about.'

'And Cameron benefits?'

'Him and some rather more deserving causes.'

'Speaking of deserving causes, do you think Cameron really will do a concert for Camley?'

They had started to follow Vivienne out of the bar and downstairs. 'Absolutely. Can I come round tomorrow and check your garden? Then Cameron and his vehicle will be out of your hair at last.'

Stella smiled. 'Do you know, I'll probably miss him.'

'And I won't have any more excuses for dropping round.'

'Do you need an excuse?' she asked, surprised. 'You're always welcome.'

Duncan stopped suddenly in the corridor with all the guests and staff swirling around them. 'Am I really?'

'Yes, of course. Any time at all. Just give me a call.'

'I'll look forward to it.'

The stage was now completely clear of all the band's equipment and a delicious buffet from the local Greek restaurant had been laid out – octopus salad, spicy meatballs, hummus, taramasalata, black olives with their skin wrinkled like an old Greek lady's, cheese pastries, slow-cooked aubergine and warmed pitta bread.

'Thank God the wine's not Greek too,' Suze said, pouring them both a glass.

'You're out of touch, Suze,' Stella laughed. 'It was only terrible when we were students and could only afford that awful stuff that tasted like Dettol.' They clinked their glasses.

Now that the show was over the excitement and the relief were palpable. Everyone talked a little too loud and drank too fast. Dora was in a little group with Roxy and the adoring Izzy, Emma and Stuart seemed to have made it up over the meze. Bernie had struck up enthusiastic conversation with Cameron's bass player and Fabia had discarded the Arctic fox to reveal a black bodycon dress of eye-popping obviousness.

'She must have been eased into that with K-Y jelly,' commented Suze enviously. Then added: 'Her skin's a bit leathery round the cleavage, though. Big mistake to show that off. First sign of ageing.'

'Amazing, isn't it?' Debora agreed. 'And equally amazing that Roxy's so different. She's a really sweet kid. Fabia's flat broke, you know,' she added in a low voice. 'Just been thrown out of her flat in Primrose Hill. I actually feel quite sorry for her. Always the mistress, never the bride. Even the guy who gave her the fox has dumped her. It turned out to be a kiss-off gift. Hold on to your husbands, girls.'

'I would if I had one,' Suze nodded.

'If Fabia wanted to be provided for in her old age, she should have found her own old rich guy. Speaking of old rich guys,' Debora looked around the party, 'where *is* Cameron?'

Just as she spoke the stage door flew open and Cameron burst into the room. 'Greetings, everyone! Hope you all enjoyed the show. Right, who's coming out with me for a Ruby?'

'What's he talking about?' Fabia demanded, angry that he didn't seem to have even noticed her or his missing wifelet.

'I rather think,' Matthew translated, 'Cameron wants us to go out with him to an Indian restaurant. Ruby is short for Ruby Murray. It's rhyming slang. Ruby Murray. Curry.'

'But Cameron,' Fabia protested, 'everyone has eaten.'

'I'll come,' Bernie offered loyally.

'Me too,' seconded Matthew.

'But why does he want to go to an Indian restaurant?' Fabia was still confused at this curious English custom. 'There is plenty of food here.'

'Because they still serve alcohol till three in the morning,' Suze explained.

'But so does The Glebe,' protested Fabia, shuddering.

'Yes, but I bet they don't serve it with extra hot vindaloo!'

Now that the excitement and tension of the concert were over Stella could concentrate on the high street. She based herself full-time at the pop-up studio and decided it was time to gather Matthew, Suze and Debora together for a serious meeting.

Matthew seemed unusually cheerful, especially for someone who'd been out carousing in curry houses till dawn's early light. He had recounted how Cameron had persuaded the other guests plus waiters to form a backing group while he belted out a few of his best-known songs to a delighted audience.

It had all been such a resounding success that the owner treated them to several free rounds of Kingfisher lager and offered Cameron a free curry any time he was passing. He would even, he told Cameron delightedly, send him a take-away down to Brighton for his final gig.

'I just thought I'd mention,' Matthew announced casually, 'that Fabia says she'd like to get involved in saving the high street.'

'*Fabia?*' they all chorused, as stunned as if he'd announced that the Pope had sent a message from the Vatican that he wanted to join them all in Camley for a spot of suburban regeneration.

'Yes, Fabia,' Matthew replied huffily. 'I don't see why it's such a surprise. Apparently she started her own campaign in Buenos Aires to save the real tango from being turned into some awful commercial travesty.'

'Single-handedly, I assume?' Debora commented, trying not to smile.

'Or single-footedly?' suggested Suze. They all giggled.

'Look, we need all the help we can get,' Matthew pointed out with irritation. 'We've only got six months to show the council we're turning the area round.'

'Matthew's right,' Stella conceded. 'All hands to the pump are obviously welcome.' She looked at the others. 'Even hands with long red nails.' They giggled again.

'Actually,' conceded Debora, 'Fabia's got more contacts than Jade Jagger. She could bring the whole of Primrose Hill to Camley. She could even make it fashionable!'

'Yes,' Suze protested in a rare moment of practicality, 'but we don't need Primrose Hill here at the moment. What we need is things for them to see when they get here. The vintage market, the open-air cinema, and anything else to occupy the empty shops. Those all need to be properly organized. The stalls are all taken. Debora, you're good at this sort of thing, could you look at the other vacant sites and see if you have any ideas?'

'Hang on,' Stella insisted, handing round some coffee, 'surely Debora's got other things to do; we can't just co-opt her for Camley. Aren't you going on tour with Cameron? What if he needs another Deathbed Reviver?'

'He only does it once. Besides, it's much more fun here.'

'More fun in Camley than being on tour with a rock legend?' Stella asked incredulously.

'Duncan will have to look after him. Anyway, what about Roxy? She's the current wife. Time she paid her wifely dues and held the basin for a while.'

'Fabia is having a bit of trouble with Roxy,' Matthew confided.

'You seem to know an awful lot about Fabia,' Suze pointed out.

'She came along to the curry house.'

They all sat awestruck, trying to imagine Fabia in her Arctic fox ordering a chicken biryani.

'She just needed someone with a sympathetic ear,' Matthew insisted pompously.

'And you just happened to offer one?' Suze raised an eyebrow at Stella. Matthew was famously autistic in his lack of empathy for anything non-William Morris based.

'And exactly what is the trouble Fabia is having?' Debora asked mock-sympathetically.

'Roxy wants a divorce. She's claiming Fabia pushed her into it as if it were an arranged marriage in Bangladesh.'

'Oh dear. And what does Cameron say?'

'He seems quite relieved, which is making Fabia absolutely furious with both of them.'

'I'm sure it is,' chuckled Debora. 'So the gravy train's coming off the rails. Good for Roxy. I didn't think she was a chip off the old block.'

'You've all got Fabia wrong,' Matthew insisted earnestly. 'She got stuck into the chicken curry and even drank a pint. By the end of the evening she was in the kitchen asking for the recipe. Cooking is her hobby, apparently.'

'Obviously she has hidden shallows,' quipped Suze.

'I think you're all being quite unpleasant,' Matthew threw in huffily. 'This is the woman who's offered to help us.'

'Yes, you're quite right,' agreed Suze piously. 'We should be grateful for any help we can get. I just hope she doesn't bring the fox coat. A lot of the stallholders are vegan. I think she might get massacred.'

'I know,' Stella suggested, 'why don't we ask Roxy to tell all her followers about the vintage market. Maybe we could get her to open it. Could you ask her, Debora?'

'I'm not sure it's the place of Wife Number One to make requests of Wife Number Three, but I'm sure she'll do it. Just ask her. I'll go and chat to my friend the publican. See how he's getting on with his hot dogs and bunting. Maybe we could get Fabia to offer tango lessons at the King's Arms. The right kind of non-commercial tango, obviously.'

Debora was joking but Stella jumped on the idea. 'Absolutely! Matthew, can you ask your new friend if she'd consider it? It would have to be tomorrow or Sunday, so not much warning.'

'Really, Stella,' Matthew replied crossly. 'Fabia's offering her services as a campaigner, not some rose-in-the-teeth tango dancer.'

'Have you *met* Fabia?' Debora teased him. 'Given the choice between boring backroom phone-bashing and being in the spotlight, instructing handsome young men in how to hold her, which do you think she's likely to go for?'

'I'm not so sure about the handsome,' Suze admitted. 'Or the young. Have you seen the clientele in the King's Arms? Most of them haven't got their own teeth.'

'Yes, but we're getting a new clientele in,' Stella reminded her. 'That's the whole point of the exercise. And afterwards they can eat the landlord's hot dogs, then everyone'll be happy.'

'She'll never do it,' Matthew predicted. 'She's a charming and sophisticated woman of the world, not some suburban dancing teacher.'

Stella looked at Matthew in amazement. Clearly he'd been dazzled by Fabia's exotic charms.

As it turned out, Matthew was wrong. Fabia declared herself happy to offer an introduction to the tango if it would help their campaign.

'I will buy myself some new dancing shoes from the Internet,' she announced. 'You must have the correct shoes when you tango.'

'And you can bet your last cent they won't be low-heeled and unflattering,' Debora said, and grinned.

At last Stella found that she had a moment to sit at her desk in the back of the pop-up studio and complete the last few brush strokes of the pugs, whose owner had been getting impatient. She was examining her handiwork and feeling really rather pleased. Somehow she had managed to capture a different expression in each of their sad-looking bulgy eyes.

'Very engaging,' congratulated a voice behind her. She turned to find Duncan Miller standing by the door. 'Matthew said I'd find you here.' He looked around the studio, his eyes fixing on the oil painting of the fox he'd liked so much. For no reason she could discern he began to laugh.

'It's not that bad, is it?' Stella demanded defensively.

'Not bad at all.' The laughter seemed to completely convulse him till she thought he might actually choke. 'Here, have a glass of water.' She removed her paintbrushes from the jam jar she kept them in, rinsed it out and handed it to him.

'I'm not that close to death,' he protested. 'Besides, those brushes are probably badger and I'll end up with badger TB and have to be culled.'

'You certainly do have a colourful imagination for a businessman.'

'Actually, I was admiring your fox again. The seen-it-all expression is so exactly like Cameron's when he wants to bamboozle you into thinking he's right and you're wrong. May I?' He lifted the canvas down from the wall and studied it. 'Look at those eyes! They're even the same colour as Cam's. Are you sure he didn't pose for this?'

Stella laughed. 'Of course not. It was a wily old dog fox I caught in my garden. He'd just seen off the young contender before mounting a vixen right under my window.'

'Perfect. It really *is* Cameron. How much will you take for it?'

'Well, I don't really know . . .'

'Come on, Stella, you've got a campaign to run. We might even use it for the new album cover.'

'Two hundred?' Stella suggested tentatively.

'Three!' suggested Duncan.

'OK,' Stella laughed. 'Three.'

'No, four,' he countered, still grinning.

'I don't think you've got the hang of this,' Stella protested. 'I thought the buyer was after the cheapest price.'

'OK, five! You're a hard woman to bargain with. Sold to the man in the hedge-fund manager's suit for five hundred pounds! Now when are you free to show me around your garden?'

'Would this afternoon about four be OK? Only I've promised utterly and completely to deliver these paintings and we've got so much to do for the market this weekend. I don't suppose you want to commission something?'

'I don't have any pets. Too much travel. Maybe one day. Though I do like that chap up there.' He pointed to a particularly engaging fluffy-haired bull with a belligerent stare that belied its cuddly toy appearance. 'Reminds me of myself. Soft on the outside but rampantly male within.'

'Are you?' Stella heard herself ask.

'Oh, absolutely,' he replied modestly, tucking the fox under his arm, 'ask any woman of my acquaintance. They run from the room as soon as I enter for fear of being mercilessly ravished.'

'I'll bear it in mind.'

'See you at four. You can give me tea in the garden.'

He shut the door and disappeared, whistling, up Camley High Street.

Stella Ainsworth, her conscience upbraided her as soon as he had left, *you were flirting! With Duncan Miller!*

Fortunately, she didn't have time for mea culpas. Before she delivered the pugs, Stella wanted to try and get the French bulldog completed as well. The louche lurcher had been dispatched yesterday and the owner loved it.

Stella found herself in the awkward positon of opening up a pet-painting studio and hoping for no new customers for a day or two, she had so much on her plate. Better than being bored, she kept reminding herself, which made her think of her mindfulness mantra and how she'd been neglecting it.

Sod mindfulness, she caught herself thinking, and in a somewhat inappropriate addendum, I'm just too busy for it at the moment!

The almost-finished French bulldog in his carpet-protecting socks was standing proudly on her easel when yet another interruption arrived in the form of her granddaughter Izzy, with a smiling Roxy in her wake.

'Gran! Gran! Roxy says she'd be happy to open your vintage market!'

'Hi, Stella. And of course I'll tweet about it too so you get some publicity for it. It's a really deserving cause. I hate seeing boarded-up shops, it looks so sad and abandoned. Plus, I love shops!' Roxy caught sight of the portrait Stella had painted of the French bulldog in socks. 'Oh, isn't it the cutest thing you've ever seen!' Roxy began snapping away on her phone. 'Look at this, Izzy, a dog in socks! I've never seen that before. Why is it wearing socks?'

'I know,' Stella replied, lowering her tone conspiratorially. 'The owner has white carpets!'

'That is the funniest thing I've ever seen! I'm just going to share that.' She pressed a button on her phone.

'Roxy,' Stella panicked, 'I'm not sure that's a good idea. The owner might not be happy.'

'Too late! The cute bulldog's already out there. If the owner's your generation, he probably won't see it anyway, if you don't mind me putting it like that.'

'Excuse me!' Stella glimpsed someone coming into the front of the shop, who couldn't see them because the easel was half hidden by the stack of tables for the vintage market. Not another bloody interruption! Reminding herself it might be a perfectly reasonable customer wanting their pet painted, she emerged to find an anxious-looking young man whom she instantly recognized, from his years of hanging about their house as an almost-silent teenager, as Hal.

'Mrs Ainsworth!' He looked startled, as if he hadn't expected her. Stella surveyed him not entirely kindly. He didn't look like a mogul. Far from it. His hair, which had been long and luxuriant when he was going out with Emma, was now short and faintly receding. He wore serious specs and a tee shirt over jeans and Nikes. Thank God he didn't have one of those bushy hipster beards, though he looked like the kind of man who quite easily might. 'I was looking for Emma.'

'Her daughter Isabel is here,' Stella pointed out firmly.

Izzy was looking at him with considerable interest, as if he might hold the answer to some question she'd been wondering about, which he probably did.

'Why would Emma be here?' Stella asked discouragingly.

'I thought she was going to ask you to look after the baby. We've got a bit of a crisis at work.'

'Have you indeed? Well, as a matter of fact, it isn't very convenient.' Stella knew she shouldn't say what she was about to, and that Emma would kill her, but she couldn't have him barging in here like this in front of Izzy. 'As a matter of fact, Hal, I'm not sure it's a good idea for Emma to be rushing back to work like this.'

'Isn't that rather up to Emma?' Hal replied, a glint of the steel which he must possess to be so successful in his expression. He seemed to notice Roxy suddenly. 'My God, aren't you Foxy Roxy? I'm Hal Meadows. My company is called Green Meadows.' He seemed to expect her to recognize it, so it must be big. 'We've been talking to your agent about getting you involved in some of our ideas.'

'Small world, eh? This is my new friend Izzy.'

This seemed to bring starry-eyed Hal back down to earth.

He held out his hand very seriously. 'Hello, Izzy. I've heard lots about you.'

'Have you?' Izzy enquired, knowing the answer perfectly well. 'Who from?'

'Your mum. I'm her boss.' He seemed to feel he was stepping over some kind of line. 'I'd better shoot. Can you ask Emma to call me urgently?'

'About the crisis at work?' Stella repeated frostily.

'Yes,' Hal seemed to have lost some of his belligerence, 'about the crisis at work.'

He hadn't been gone five minutes when Emma appeared, looking harassed and carrying Ruby in her car seat.

'You've just missed your boss,' Stella informed her. 'Apparently, there's a crisis at work. I see you've still got your bag.'

'Mum, for God's sake, don't start . . .'

'I'm out of my depth here.' Roxy could tell there was something going on in the subtext. 'Why don't I take Izzy off with me? Leave you both to it. I've got my car outside.'

'Because she's got to do her maths test papers, that's why!' snapped Emma.

'Fine. We'll download some. I love those papers. We could race each other and see who does one first.'

'That'd be great!' Izzy's eyes were shining at the unlikely prospect of doing eleven plus maths papers with her divinity.

'It's not just the speed you do them . . .' Emma lectured.

'You have to do them on your own. I had got that.'

Emma watched their departure sulkily. 'Izzy talks about nothing but Foxy bloody Roxy. Roxy this. Roxy that.'

'Stop being small-minded, Emma. It doesn't suit you. Besides, you should be glad someone's taking Izzy's mind off her home life.' She looked her daughter firmly in the eye. 'Emma, this has to stop. Hal can't barge in here in front of Izzy

179

like this. I'm pretty sure she knows something's going on. I'm happy to have Ruby when you need me to.' She lifted Ruby from her car seat and nuzzled the soft, warm baby against her neck. 'But I am not providing an alibi for you to wreck your marriage.'

'I'm thirty-eight, Mum. It's up to me whether I'm involved with Hal.'

Stella ignored her daughter's angry tone. 'But not with my assistance.' It was really tough, but she had to help Emma see what was at stake. 'I'm sorry, darling, you know I love you, but I can't do it. I'm afraid you'd better take Ruby home.'

Lifting Ruby off Stella's shoulder and angrily grabbing her car seat with the other hand, Emma stalked out.

Stella was almost in tears when her mobile began to ring. She hated having to give her daughter an ultimatum like this.

'Hello?'

'Hi, Gran, it's Izzy. Gran, check your phone. The French bulldog's a star! Thousands of people have already shared it!'

'Oh great,' Stella murmured crossly. 'That's all I need.' Now the owner would go absolutely berserk.

She'd behaved badly with Duncan Miller, antagonized her only child and offended a paying customer.

All told, what a wonderful day it had been.

Nine

When Duncan arrived in her garden he was surprised to find that Stella, still angry with herself over their last conversation, treated him with a brusqueness that bordered on hostility.

'Right. What do you need to know?' She raced straight on without waiting for him to answer. 'The garden is an acre. We have had fundraising parties here before a couple of times, though nothing with musicians that needed to plug anything in, just string quartets, that sort of thing.'

'Classy as opposed to noisy, you mean?'

'We usually put up one of those marquees like a sail that stay open at one end. They're cheaper and you can fit more people in.'

'Do you think we need a marquee? More expense for you out of your fundraising?'

'You've been in California too long. Even in summer it may pour with rain.'

'That didn't stop them at Woodstock.' His grin was surprisingly appealing in an essentially serious man, but Stella was not going to respond to it.

'Yes, well, Camley's hardly Woodstock.'

'What time do you want the great man to come on?'

'About two would be perfect. Oh God, we haven't even thought about how to organize it yet.'

'Treat it like any concert. Decide how many you can accommodate and only sell that many tickets. You can throw in raffles and auctions, if you want to make more money.' He looked around the garden assessing where lights and speakers would go. 'Is there electricity in your studio?'

'Yes. I often paint there all day.'

'Can I see?'

She led him towards the studio, feeling suddenly flustered because they kept a large bed in there for occasional guests who didn't fit into the house. How ridiculous of her. She pushed the door open. There was a scrabbling sound inside. 'Oh my God. I hope it's not that fox at it again.' She couldn't bring herself to look.

When she opened her eyes Duncan was smiling. 'Not unless he likes to do it in a double bed.'

The back door of the studio was open and Jesse and Dora were halfway across the lawn. Jesse was trying to say sorry in sign language.

'Oh my God, he's only sixteen!'

'You were only two years older when we first met,' he said, his eyes on her face.

Stella couldn't admit that she'd hardly noticed him then, so overshadowed had he been by his glamorous friend Cameron. Things had changed when she'd got to know him better, and begun to appreciate the quiet wit behind his social ineptness, but that wasn't a quality eighteen-year-olds tended to fall for. 'There's all the difference in the world between sixteen and eighteen,' she insisted, her sudden embarrassment making her tone harder than she'd intended.

'She looked confident enough to be in charge, by the look of it. I'd say he was in safe hands.'

'That is such a sexist thing to say,' Stella burst out angrily. 'The woman as temptress!'

'I didn't mean that women were temptresses at all,' Duncan replied calmly. It made Stella furious that he seemed to think the whole thing was simply funny. 'I just meant that this girl seems very cool and sophisticated. I would certainly have welcomed that at sixteen. Sex is terrifying at his age. Boys are supposed to know what to do, yet they haven't the slightest idea. Girls are these remote terrifying beings, far more together than boys are. A girl has a mental age at least two years ahead of a boy and yet he has to understand the mysteries of giving her pleasure!'

Stella stared, taken aback by the sudden passion in his voice. Was he talking about her? Their encounter came back to her in all its excruciating detail.

'Stella . . .' he began and she knew he was going to mention that occasion so long ago. Suddenly she felt eighteen again, and just as embarrassed and shy.

Deliberately she steered the conversation to safer waters. 'So it's all right for us to announce the concert and start selling tickets?'

'Certainly.' He seemed amused that she needed to change the subject so abruptly. 'What are you calling it?'

'We thought Rock for Regeneration. Actually it was the headline in the *Evening Standard*.'

'Perfect. We will need to come and do a sound check on the day. We don't want to make Cameron look like a prat. Though he does seem quite capable of doing it by himself.'

'Thanks a lot then, Duncan. We really are grateful.'

'Think nothing of it.' Duncan had clearly taken a cue from her sudden brisk manner. 'Cameron and I couldn't get out of Camley quick enough. Time we came back and paid our dues.'

She saw him back through the garden. 'Good luck with the tour.'

'Thanks, and thanks again for your help. I hope we don't need to call you again.'

It was only when he'd gone that she realized she hadn't even offered him the cup of tea she'd promised.

When Stella switched on her phone, she found six messages from the owner of Millie, the French bulldog. Oh God, she was going to give the man his money back. When you got your dog painted, particularly if it was wearing socks to protect your white carpets, you didn't expect to find it going viral on YouTube or whatever it was. The final message was from Jesse. It read: *So sorry, Gran, didn't mean that to happen. Will call later.*

She decided it might be more politic to actually visit the dog's owner rather than ring. She stopped and picked up a placatory bottle of fizz on the way. He lived in a rather faceless modern block on the outskirts of Croydon.

Stella rang the bell twice and was about to go away, feeling relieved, which was stupid as the whole point of coming had been to apologize in person. *Stella Ainsworth, you wimp*, she was just telling herself when the door opened.

'Stella!' the beautiful young man who owned Millie almost shrieked. 'You got my messages, then?'

Stella held out the sparkling wine. 'Yes, that's why I came. To apologize.'

'But Millie's a star! All my friends are getting socks for their dogs and I even got a tweet from a Swedish manufacturer who wants to feature her in their ad campaign!'

'You're not annoyed, then?'

'No, I'm absolutely thrilled. Let's open the champagne now!' They went into his flat which was almost entirely white apart from the eye-popping painting of Millie in pride of place in the centre of the wall. 'Who needs a feature wall? I'm featuring Millie!'

And Millie did indeed look very pleased with herself, lying on the taupe leather sofa with her head on a cushion.

'Isn't she priceless?' demanded the delighted owner. 'You'd think she knew she was a star! She's not really allowed on the sofa but I thought I'd make an exception. Millie, darling, you're princess for a day!'

The message from Jesse was harder to resolve. What did the modern grandmother do in these circumstances? Almost being caught in the act by your own gran would probably put the brakes on and sixteen, after all, was hardly a child. The only real worry was that she hadn't seen any sign of a condom, but then maybe it hadn't gone that far. Dora seemed such a confident girl that she probably carried her own. In Stella's youth, that magical decade post-Pill and pre-Aids, they'd thought condoms horrid slippery things. Now she knew they were de rigueur. How difficult modern sexual etiquette had become.

She wouldn't mention it to Emma, she decided. Her life seemed to have enough complications already.

Without the Airstream in the back garden, or any emergency administration of fluids, life could seem rather flat and Stella was grateful for the launch of the vintage market tomorrow.

When she got home, Matthew was excitedly waving an

official-looking letter at her. 'It's from the council! They're so pleased with what we're doing that they're offering a grant if we can regenerate some cheap office space in the area as well.'

'Where on earth are we going to find office space?' Stella read the letter through, remembering the girl who had set up her desk in a self-storage pod because it was the only place she could find. 'Maybe the council should just approach Big Yellow Storage.' She noticed that Matthew was putting on his coat. 'Where are you off to?'

'Down to the King's Arms. Fabia wants to check it out for these tango lessons she's supposed to give.'

'Right.' There were a million things she ought to be doing but she couldn't miss Fabia's arrival at their unappealing hostelry. 'I'll come along with you. We need to make sure they've ordered enough hot dogs anyway.'

Matthew didn't point out that she could just as easily achieve this by phone.

Through the gloom of the public bar, which seemed tobacco-stained even though smoking had been banned for almost ten years, they discerned that the landlord had not exactly achieved a Grand Design or even a quick makeover. The pub looked much the same.

Debora, wearing her usual calm smile and an enormous flowery tent dress, emerged from the gloom looking remarkably cheerful. 'Don't despair,' she whispered, 'it's much better outside. He's promised to put up the bunting and install half an oil drum filled with charcoal. He says the other half of the drum is played by his friend's steel band and they'll be coming too. So as long as we make sure the customers only go in the garden and not the pub it should be OK.'

Debora, to their amazement, had managed to get hold of a

glass of white wine. 'It isn't too bad, actually. I should grab the bottle. It may be the only one they have.'

'Thank you so much for all your hard work.'

'Actually, I'm really enjoying it. You'd be surprised how dull life can be when Cameron's behaving himself. There's very little for me to do.'

'Have you seen Fabia?' Matthew peered through the gloom.

'Gone to put her shoes on in the Ladies. I imagine it's not an experience she's used to. It'll be freezing cold, have a ten-watt bulb and no toilet roll. Ah, here she comes! I told you those shoes wouldn't be flatties!'

Fabia, in a slinky black dress in some expensively clingy material, a flower in her hair, tottered towards them in red shoes with extremely high heels and an ankle strap.

'OK.' She snapped her fingers and, to general amazement, the music came on. 'I will start with Matthew.'

'Lucky man,' breathed Debora.

But before the show began they were treated to a potted history of the dance, whether they liked it or not. 'Tango from Argentina must not be confused with the Flamenco or, God forbid,' she stared at Stella and Debora as if they were exactly the kind of cultural lightweights who would make this mistake, 'that stupid Apache dance where the man flings the woman all over the room. Tango is subtle. Tango is erotic.'

She took Matthew's hand and placed it firmly on the middle of her back. She put hers in the same position on his, then placed her hand in his. 'What makes tango the dance of seduction is that the man has the woman completely in his power. It is his hand on her back that impels her, gives her no choice but to follow him.'

Matthew, Stella recognized, was looking frankly alarmed. The KA regulars, clutching their unerotic pints, stared stolidly at their fellow man in this, his hour of potential humiliation. Fortunately for all concerned, Fabia had adopted the man's role for the purposes of demonstration.

Slowly they progressed across the pub floor. Tango seemed to be a kind of quickstep, but with your feet sliding sexily as you moved, and your movements slower than in conventional ballroom dancing. 'Not sure they'd win on *Strictly*,' Stella whispered.

'Thank God that's over,' Matthew confided as the music finally stopped. 'What I need is a pint of Sheepshagger PDQ.'

'I thought you were doing very well at being subtly erotic,' Debora congratulated.

'Thank you, Debora. I do my best.' Matthew raised his Sheepshagger.

They all sat down in a corner of the pub, feeling like the lady mayoress who'd arrived to open a bazaar.

'Thanks so much, Fabia.' Stella decided some PR was in order. 'We'll knock up a banner and hang it up outside the pub. The idea is that the cost of the lessons will go towards the Regeneration fund; that way we can charge much more than usual.'

A thought struck Fabia. 'What if nobody wants a lesson?'

'Matthew will, won't you, Matthew? Especially as you've shown him some steps. And Bernie. And I'm sure we can persuade my son-in-law Stuart onto the floor. Plus with your lovely Roxy tweeting about it I'm sure hundreds of people will show up for the market and be dying to learn the tango!'

This, Stella realized, was a faux pas. Fabia did not like to be upstaged by her daughter. 'All this technology,' Fabia announced grandly. 'It is not real life! They look at their screens all the time and do not see the grandeur of nature!' She swept her arms operatically to embrace her surroundings.

Les arrived at that moment with a plate of hot dogs for them to sample.

'Mustard, ketchup or mayo?' he offered them proudly.

Fabia took a bite and spat it out theatrically. 'But what is in this disgusting travesty of a meat product?'

'She's from Argentina,' Stella whispered to Les in mitigation of this harsh pronouncement. 'They take their meat very seriously.'

'I dunno,' Les began to look hunted. 'It's a frankfurter.'

'You cannot give this abomination to people who pay to come to your local market!' Fabia announced grandly.

'What do you propose to give them instead?' Debora enquired, trying not to grin.

'*Parillada*!' Fabia announced with a flourish.

'Eh?' Les shook his head dubiously. 'What's that when it's at home?'

'A proper Argentine barbecue. Beef, pork, ribs, blood sausage. And I will make pancakes filled with dulce de leche for the sweet tooth!'

'What's dulce de whatever it was?' Les asked, looking like the survivor of a train crash.

'I think it's a bit like condensed milk,' Stella explained. She'd seen some ice cream made of it in Waitrose. 'You'll do all this, plus the tango lessons?'

'This is nothing.' Fabia nodded modestly. 'In Argentina the gauchos leave their women behind on the *estancia*, but not de Rosza women! We go with them into the pampas and milk the cows and cook the food whether they like it or not!'

'Not in those shoes, you wouldn't,' Debora murmured under her breath, beginning to feel sorry for the de Rosza men.

'We are used to hardship!' Fabia announced, clearly relishing the role of saviour of their sad little venture. 'I will talk to the

Argentine meat board. I did some dancing for them. I am sure they will remember me.'

'So am I,' confided Stella to Debora.

'By tomorrow? It's very kind of you, Fabia. Maybe for next week.'

'Tomorrow is long enough,' Fabia announced, heading for the Ladies to change out of her tango shoes. 'The meat market opens very early.'

'I must admit,' Stella conceded with dawning admiration, 'Fabia's quite something, isn't she?'

'I know,' agreed Suze. 'All that energy. She'd have been an exhausting groupie. Probably made them try every position in the *Kama Sutra*. I wonder why she's bothering with us?'

'Same reason as Debora, maybe. Volunteering makes you feel good. Surveys prove it.'

'Wait for this, though. She told Debora she wants to take on one of the empty shops! She's always wanted to open a retro emporium, apparently, and always been too busy travelling the world!'

'Why would someone like Fabia want to open a shop in Camley?'

'Because it's free! According to Debora she's flat broke.'

'But wouldn't she have to buy stock and all that?'

'She's intending to sell her own clothes. She's got quite a collection.'

'I can well imagine. Not that there's much of a market for Arctic fox in the outer boroughs.'

'She says she's going to make this little corner the new Primrose Hill!'

'By the way, girls, where do you want me to put this?' Debora brandished a huge sign proclaiming VINTAGE

MARKET THIS WAY. 'I hate to be sexist but we need a man and a ladder to put this up, preferably one that's handy with a screwdriver.'

'I wonder what my nephew Jesse's up to? Apart from misbehaving with girls and not revising for his AS's? I'll see if we can get him down here for a bit. He got an A star in woodwork. His parents weren't impressed, poor lad. He got a C in everything else.'

Jesse was only too happy to escape revision for an hour or two and was soon merrily hanging the vintage market banner according to Debora's demanding directions. He whispered an apology to Stella about the other day and begged her not to tell his mother.

'How's the tour going?' he enquired as he climbed up the ladder.

'Oh, fine. Cardiff loves him,' Debora replied, handing him the sign. 'They've declared him an honorary Welshman and given him the key to the city. I just hope the key doesn't open too many pubs.'

But while Jesse was happy to escape, his mother took a different view. Emma arrived an hour later, clearly on the warpath.

'Mum!' she berated. 'How could you be so irresponsible? You know how important these exams are!'

'I'm sure he'll study better after a break,' Stella replied, trying not to feel guilty. Maybe she had been a bit cavalier. 'Now you're here, why don't you lend a hand? You're incredibly creative at this sort of thing. We're trying to make everything look irresistible for tomorrow.'

It soon became clear that Emma had a subtext to her visit. As soon as Debora and Jesse had left to hang another banner, she started up. 'I don't know what's got into Jesse – well, no, I *do* know what's got into Jesse. It's that girl Dora.'

'What's the matter with her?' Stella could imagine how mad Emma would be if she knew about the studio incident.

'The family's nothing like ours. The father's a headmaster and the mother works in the City and they're completely obsessed with her getting into Oxford. Everything she does is for her CV – including Mandarin and Grade Eight cello. They seem to think Jesse – Jesse! – is a bad influence. Something about long hair and weird tastes in music. And anyway,' Emma grumbled on seamlessly, 'what kind of a name is Isadora?'

'I imagine it's after Isadora Duncan,' Suze supplied helpfully. 'You know, the woman who danced with all the scarves?'

'Do you remember the Ken Russell film?' Stella reminisced. 'The one with Vanessa Redgrave when she gets strangled by her scarf getting stuck in the wheel of her lover's car?'

'I know who Isadora Duncan is, thank you,' snapped Emma. 'I studied English literature, which is more than either of you did.'

'But I thought she was a dancer, not a writer?' Suze enquired innocently.

'Maybe she wrote as well,' Stella replied.

'Oh for God's sake, it's just a very affected name, that's all.'

'I expect she thinks so too, that's why she calls herself Dora.'

'Anyway, she's far too sophisticated for Jesse. I'm sure she's stringing him along. I bet you she'll drop him just before his exams start. That's exactly what happened to my friend Liz's son. When I told him he'd have to stop seeing her unless he did some work, he just said, "Mum, you don't understand, I *love* Dora". It's so completely ridiculous.'

Stella was tempted to point out that it was neither as

ridiculous nor as potentially harmful as falling in love with your old boyfriend when you were married with three children, but knew it wouldn't help anyone.

Debora had joined them and was listening quietly.

As soon as Emma had gone, she made a suggestion. 'Maybe Duncan could get Jesse interested in playing in bands. About the only thing teenage boys like more than girls is bands.'

They stood and surveyed their sign. 'Good for Jesse. He's got it straight.'

'Right.' Stella put an arm round each of her friends. 'Tomorrow it finally happens. Let's hope after all our hard work a few people turn up!'

Ten

Six o'clock in the morning, Stella discovered, was very, very cold. They had organized a team of volunteers to put out the stalls ready for the onslaught. Fortunately, she had remembered to pick up croissants and the electric kettle was on in the studio ready for the coffees and teas. She had even remembered real milk.

By six-thirty, the stallholders were starting to arrive. Some of them were old hands who travelled from car-boot sale to antique market. They soon chose the best pitches near the entrance and enthusiastically threw old lengths of chenille over the pasting tables to give their stock a more dramatic background. Instantly they covered the space with interesting objects – old pharmacists' bottles, pretty china, painted vases, art deco ladies, saucy playing cards, old-fashioned champagne glasses and in the case of one stall, a car horn that would have delighted Toad of Toad Hall.

Besides the bric-a-brac there were clothes stalls featuring rows of wonderful silks and velvets. There were embroidered handbags, hats made of feathers, silk chemises and gorgeous vintage sandals. Stella felt herself drawn like a magnet to a fox tippet just like the one she'd worn herself forty years ago but then remembered the old fox in her garden and decided against it. It might be some distant ancestor.

She was delighted when Matthew appeared and sent him off to dispense the teas and coffees to the grateful stallholders, one of whom had actually erected a tiny changing room, complete with floor-length mirror. At nine she heard from a startled Les at the King's Arms. Half a cow had arrived and twice its weight in sausages and blood pudding!

'What time's the official opening?' Suze enquired, taking in the long queue already snaking round the block. 'I see the jumble-sale vultures are already gathering at the gates of Rome.' She indicated three ladies who were rolling up their sleeves preparing for action. 'They can empty a church bazaar faster than you can say piranha fish.'

'Well, I suppose that's the idea, though I think some of this stuff will be too expensive for them. Opening is ten o'clock. Still an hour before Roxy's due.'

Izzy might have tried to explain it to them, but like Richard Dawkins and God, they had underestimated the impact of a real divinity.

It started with posses of pubescent girls, some dropped off by their parents, others arriving by bus. Hundreds of them, so that the queue began to resemble less a charity jumble sale and more a One Direction concert. Next, the older ones appeared, by tube or train, mostly female with the odd snake-hipped male, each one clutching a phone or iPad at the ready to capture the moment of the goddess's arrival.

A sudden frisson in the queue told them the moment was at hand. Fabia, never one to miss an entrance, had purloined a gorgeous drop-top sports car, with an equally gorgeous driver. She opened the door and placed one high-heeled sandal on the pavement then paused for effect only to find herself almost knocked to the ground by the tidal wave of teenagers who wanted to see not her but Roxy.

'Well, really,' she protested, catching sight of Stella, who had stepped forward diplomatically, 'I call that downright rude!'

'Come on, Fabia.' Debora held out a hand to steady her. 'The grown-ups will be much more impressed by you.'

As if on cue, Matthew appeared out of the crowd. 'Wow, Fabia, you look amazing!'

She fished about in the huge bag that accompanied her everywhere and proudly produced an apron which she proceeded to put on. 'Before the dancing, let us see what is happening to my *parillada!*'

He led her off reverently towards the relative peace of the bunting-festooned pub garden, which the smokers had grudgingly vacated for the day.

'Since when did Matthew become Mr Tactful?' Suze shouted from behind her stall.

'It's not tact. He means it.' Stella watched her husband retreat in Fabia's wake. 'I fear Matthew's been tangoed.' She looked round to see a huge crowd of pre-teens engulfing Roxy. 'We'd better rescue Roxy from her fan base or she'll never get out alive.'

Debora and Stella politely pushed their way through the shrieking crowd and grabbed her.

'I must admit,' she smiled as they led her towards the red ribbon, 'you two make very good bouncers.'

They even had a small step ladder for Roxy to climb as she declared the event open. 'Hello, everyone. Thank you all so much for coming. I suspect that you, like me, love shopping.'

A cheer went out from the crowd. 'And, like me, you think it's really sad what's been happening to our town centres. So today I hope you are going to spend lots of money to help bring Camley High Street back to life!'

There was no more time for thinking as the stampede had started. It was shopping bags at dawn as about a hundred seasoned jumble salers took on four times their number, who might have had the handicap of youth, but were prepared to shell out more cash, much to the disgust of their elders.

'You can't be asking five pounds for *that*,' a Dot Cotton lookalike insisted to Suze, eyeing up a stretchy leopard-skin top. 'It isn't even real polyester!'

Meanwhile, a gorgeous young girl, dressed entirely in black, handed over the fiver, removed her blouse to reveal perfect black-bra-encased breasts, and slipped on the leopard-skin top right there and then to the sound of delighted applause from her friends.

'Well, I never,' commented Dot Cotton, outraged. 'The bloody cheek of it. She'll get what she deserves if she goes round taking her clothes off like that.' But her adversary had already moved on to another stall where, with impressive decisiveness, she chose a pair of retro sunglasses and a battered pork-pie hat, both of which she immediately put on to create a vision of such instant stylishness that no further argument was possible.

By lunchtime, almost every stall had sold out and people were still arriving. 'Bloody hell,' Suze whispered to Stella, 'what are we going to offer them? If we're not careful, there'll be a riot!'

Stella climbed up the step ladder Roxy had used earlier. 'Ladies and, err . . . ladies.' This was a good start because it got a laugh. 'Our event has been such a runaway success that we have almost sold out, but – and I think I can promise this – it's been *so* successful that we will make it a weekly event from now on. But, for the moment, our local pub, the King's Arms, invites you to sample a real Argentinian barbecue and to listen to a steel band in its glorious garden!' Right on cue the band struck up with Bob Marley's 'Three Little Birds'. 'And later on there will be tango lessons for all those *Strictly* addicts among you!'

Even the sun obliged by coming out, possibly ordered by Fabia, along with the half-cow and the ton of sausages.

Les, the landlord, was all smiles as Fabia instructed him and his minions in the art of *parillada*.

'How's it been going, Mum?' Emma and Izzy had appeared, Izzy looking very down in the mouth. 'She has her entrance-exam coaching on Saturday mornings,' Emma explained.

Roxy, wonderful Roxy, made up for it by beckoning Izzy over to join her and showing her all the silly things she'd bought at the market. Together they looked at the brooch, bag and elegant art deco watch Roxy had found among the stalls.

A thought occurred to Roxy. 'Why don't you have it?' She pressed the watch into Izzy's hand. 'Make sure you get to your exams on time!'

Izzy looked as if she could hardly believe her luck, especially when Roxy took a photo of them together, with Izzy wearing the watch, and Instagrammed it.

'Freya and Bianca are going to be so jealous!' Izzy announced, thrilled. This was clearly a result.

'I bet the watch doesn't even bloody work, and she'll end up missing her entrance exam,' grumbled Emma.

Before Stella had time to wonder if she should let this pass, Debora jumped in. 'Lighten up, Emma, did you never have a pash at school?'

Emma thought about it. 'Susan Warren,' she replied, her voice suddenly dreamy. 'She was captain of the netball team and had legs that went on forever.'

'There you are. Izzy's much less in love than you were.'

Emma laughed and hid her head in her hands at her own mean-spiritedness.

Watching them, Stella marvelled at Debora's amazingly sure touch. How had Cameron ever dumped Debora for Hallelujah and, even more extraordinary, ended up marrying Roxy? Her only possible rationale was that rock gods might behave differently to lesser mortals.

In the pub garden, the steel band stopped and the insistent, pulsating strains of the tango took over. 'Come on, Em,' Debora linked arms with her, 'let's go and see someone make a fool of themselves.'

The area in the centre of the floor was clear and Fabia, now without the apron, stood centre stage with Matthew, his hand in the small of her back.

'Oh my God, it's Dad. I hope she's going to be gentle with him!'

To their complete amazement, as the music began again it was Matthew who seemed to be in control. Fabia, her eyes wide with surprise, found herself propelled across the dance floor, his arms tightly around her, his feet sliding in a silent glissando. As the audience stood, hypnotized, Matthew and Fabia twirled and kicked, locked together as if joined by Superglue, in a display that was as intense as it was surprising, climaxing in a final move where Fabia was made to lean so far back that if Matthew hadn't held her fast she would surely have fallen over.

Everyone in the garden roared their applause.

'Wow. Whatever's happened to Dad?' asked Emma, seeking out her mother in the crowd.

Wasn't it obvious? Stella thought, a distant warning bell going off in her head. Fabia had happened to Matthew.

When the applause finally died down, Matthew uncoupled from Fabia and came to join them, looking faintly embarrassed. 'I sat up watching how to tango on YouTube,' he confessed as a line of KA regulars queued to take his place. 'It shows you how to do it, step by step.'

'You were amazing, Pappy.' Izzy ran into his arms.

Matthew seemed to light up in the warmth of all this female admiration. 'Was I? Maybe there's life in the old dog yet!'

Before the crowds began to disperse, Stella sent Roxy and Izzy round with labelled buckets to collect for the campaign. Roxy laughed uproariously. 'Of course we'll do it, but this is a bit old school, you know, Stella. I'm sure we can do better than this! We'll do you a Facebook page; you'll get far more money that way.'

As the crowds finally began to disperse, Stella realized how exhausted she felt but there was no doubt the day had been a success. 'Do you know, even without the Roxy factor, I think we could make a go of this. The pub's delighted too. If Fabia's serious about opening a retro clothes shop, all we need now is to get takers for those two empty shops in the parade and this place will start taking on a life of its own. What do you think, Matthew? This was your idea in the first place.'

She suspected he would still feel it was all too frivolous and quite probably unsustainable.

But nothing was going to dent Matthew's new-found enthusiasm. 'If we could keep it up and fill those empty shops, I think we could convince the council to drop their plan to redevelop, but we have to keep reminding them how well we're doing.'

'Why don't we put Izzy in charge of all this social media

malarkey,' Stella suggested. 'She's the only one of us young enough to really understand it.'

'Izzy is doing her eleven plus,' Emma reminded them.

'Think how good it would look on her university entrance,' coaxed Suze temptingly. 'I bet no one else will claim they've run a PR campaign to save a high street at eleven.'

Emma was giving this serious consideration when she saw her husband Stuart striding through the crowds towards them, holding Ruby in one arm and her pale-blue Prada bag in the other.

'Oh dear,' breathed Suze to Stella, 'something tells me he hasn't just bought that in the vintage market.'

'Emma, what the hell has been going on?' he demanded, angrier than any of them had ever seen him. 'I found this bag . . .'

'Stuart, I've had that bag for ages.' Emma tried to keep cool in the face of his onslaught.

'And what about this phone? Have you had that for ages?' He produced a cheap pay-as-you-go mobile. 'Since you started working for Hal, for instance?'

Emma seemed to be desperately trying to think of some defence. But Stuart wasn't a lawyer for nothing. 'Are you going to try and deny it? Or would you like me to read out some of the messages?'

Eleven

Stella caught sight of Izzy running towards them clutching her collecting bucket, her eyes alight with happiness at spending a whole day with her idol, and tried to head her off but it was too late. 'Hi, Mum, hello, Dad, I didn't know you were coming.'

With an instinct borne of experience, Izzy knew things were wrong between her parents even before she heard them speak. There was something about the way they were standing, her dad towering over her mum in a way he never did, his face rigid with anger, tightly holding on to Ruby yet not even looking at her.

'You're going to call him now on your private hotline,' Stuart demanded, holding out a phone to her mother, 'and tell him that you resign. Now.'

Emma hesitated, furious at being told what to do so publicly. 'Why the hell should I?'

'Because if you don't,' Stuart insisted, refusing to budge an inch, 'you can pack your stuff and move in with him right now.'

Izzy clung on to Stella's arm, terrified and powerless.

Stella removed the collecting bucket and found herself

wondering what Debora would do in this situation. Her years with Cameron and his dramas hadn't even wrinkled her calm. Distraction rather than confrontation, she suspected.

Before he even registered what she was doing, Stella reached over and took the baby from Stuart's arms. 'We're all just going to see if there's any food left and leave you two to sort things out.' Stella smiled at them with Debora's smile. 'Maybe you should go home and talk this through in private. Jesse and Izzy can come back with me.'

Bereft of their audience they seemed to come to their senses a little. 'You're right, Stu,' she heard Emma say in a chastened voice, 'I'll give up the job. It was probably a mistake anyway.' She looked at the offending Prada handbag, in all its expensive pale-blue beauty. 'I'll give the bag to charity.'

It would probably have been all right, Stella decided later, if Hal hadn't chosen that moment to stake his claim in person.

Stella's heart began to race as she spotted his tall frame pushing its way through the departing crowds just as Emma made her declaration.

Emma and Stuart looked on horrified as he grabbed the bag. 'We chose that together,' he shouted at Emma. 'It was a symbol of what we feel for each other.'

Stella thought Stuart was going to punch him when Roxy suddenly appeared from the crowd and grabbed the bag out of Hal's hands. 'Pretty damn stupid, then. If Prada bags are a symbol of anything, it's of silly women with too much money and no self-worth.' Before he could protest she grabbed him firmly by the hand. 'We need more volunteers for the tango and you've got just the right body for it.' She gave him her most devastating smile. 'Besides, if you stay here and cause more trouble, I might have to clock you one.'

'Is it going to be all right between Mum and Dad?' whispered Izzy anxiously.

Stella hugged her. 'Let's go home and leave them to talk things over. They probably need a bit of time together.'

Roxy, meanwhile, was working her magic. 'You're a very attractive man,' Stella heard her murmur as she carried Hal off to the pub garden, 'you don't need to go getting involved with married women.'

In fact, Roxy was doing such a sterling job in distracting Hal that Stella decided not to point out the fact that she happened to be married too.

Just as they were about to leave, Roxy reappeared and started to help them pack up.

'Thank you for distracting Hal,' Stella said quietly. 'I thought it might turn quite nasty.'

'Don't worry,' Roxy smiled ruefully, 'I've got plenty of experience in defusing dramas. A mother like mine tends to attract them. Believe me, I've defused from Monaco to Marrakech.'

It was amazing, given her ghastly childhood, that Roxy had turned into the delight she was. So many children like that ended up having to be the parent instead of the child.

As if in endorsement of this, Roxy stopped packing up Suze's bric-a-brac. 'By the way, I'd like to thank you for letting Mum take over – the food, the tango lessons and all that. She can be a bit full-on.'

'Actually, we were really grateful. She must have made us a mint with her Argentinian barbecue – and she got the meat free!'

'The thing is, she hasn't had much of a shot at ordinary life. It's her own fault, obviously, but the glam image, it's only skin deep. She's having a tough time at the moment. Following bands isn't the greatest career choice. Definitely not to be recommended.'

Stella smiled encouragingly, wondering if this was an element in Roxy's decision to split with Cameron.

'She had high hopes of the guy who gave her the coat, until she realized it was a goodbye gift.'

'Poor foxes,' Suze said, and almost added, 'sacrificed to be a romantic kiss-off', but caught Stella's eye. Roxy was trusting them with this revelation.

'I think she'd be happier if her life were more normal. Look at your life here. It's a real place with friendly people. You know she's being chucked out of her flat in London? Maybe, if she does get this shop she's talking about, she should move in upstairs.'

Stella and Suze exchanged a very speaking look.

When Emma came round the next morning to fetch Ruby and Izzy, it was obvious from her clear skin and shining eyes that Stuart and she had had a reunion. Perhaps the involvement with Hal had been what Stuart needed to remind him that his wife and family couldn't always remain behind asylum seekers and refugees on the list for his attention.

'Is everything OK, Mum?' Izzy asked anxiously.

'Absolutely fine, darling. I just need to get myself something else to do or I'll go mad.'

'I know it's not the same,' Stella suggested, expecting to have her head bitten off, 'but why not come and join us in the campaign? There's still lots to do. Three shops that need tenants – well, two, if Fabia's serious – and the cinema show to organize. And what the council really wants is cheap office space for start-ups. Your experience with –' Stella stopped, deciding it wouldn't be wise to mention Hal – 'in tech would be really useful.' Emma hadn't said no yet so Stella ploughed ahead. 'Even if you just did a day or two a week. You could bring Ruby with you or leave her with me in the pet studio.'

'I'll think about it,' Emma conceded.

Stella remembered that she had an appointment with a rather dashing Dalmatian. 'I've got to get off to see a dog owner, I'm afraid.'

'I really will think about your offer,' Emma said as she hugged her. 'I don't suppose I'd be paid? Oh well. I didn't think so.'

'You'd have to look on it as work experience.'

'Work experience! At my age? Where's Jesse, by the way? Still in bed?'

'Jesse?' Stella asked.

'Yes, Jesse. My son. Tall and dark with floppy hair. Your grandson. He told us he was going to stay with you.'

'But he didn't!' Stella immediately started to worry. 'I texted him to come but got no reply. I assumed he'd just gone home.'

A dreadful thought occurred to Stella. 'Oh my God, what if something's happened to him?'

But Emma seemed more angry than concerned. 'I don't think we need worry about that. I've got a pretty good idea where we'll find him. I bet you Miss Grade Eight Cello sneaked him under the headmaster's nose. That'd be just like her.'

Feeling reassured, Stella was relieved to have half an hour to herself, even if it was with canine company, after all the emotional buffetings she'd been through. The trouble with grown-up children was that they could behave exactly as they liked but to you they were still your responsibility. If they decided to wreck their lives, you couldn't help feeling it was your fault.

If Hal hadn't walked in yesterday and made a scene that

forced Emma to choose, Stella suspected she would have gone on having an affair with him. Stella, who told herself she believed in marriage, found it hard to understand. On the other hand, now Emma was beaming like the cat that had got the cream. Maybe, if she'd behaved more like Emma, Matthew would have stopped seeing her as part of the furniture; more interesting than a bookcase, but a lot less beautiful than a William Morris fireplace. *Hang on,* Stella put her chin up rebelliously, *you are beautiful* and *useful.* Well, Matthew wasn't going to tell her, so she'd have to tell herself.

The funny thing was, now that it had departed, she was missing the caravanserai of Cameron, Duncan and even Bernie much more than she'd expected. Camley was suddenly dull in a way it had never been before they'd swanned into her life and turned it upside down.

But her boredom didn't last long. Around lunchtime Fabia arrived, dressed in black jeans and a black shirt with a huge floppy black hat like the one she'd owned herself from Biba aeons ago. She was clutching a vast black bin bag which she deposited on the floor before fetching another dozen from the back of her car.

'Fabia! How nice to see you. What's all this stuff for?'

'My retro emporium! I've decided to make Camley fashionable. I know, I know, you will say it isn't possible. Why should anyone come out to this ... this *suburb!* But I have made a little bet with myself, to see if I can do it, because if I, Fabia de Rosza, cannot do it, nobody can!'

Clearly Roxy had been right about her mother putting down roots. Stella just wasn't sure about wanting her to put them down in Camley. 'OK. I've got the keys. Let's go and take a look at the empty premises and see what you think.'

Fabia thought they were all hideous and entirely

impossible, but the final one, which adjoined the garden of the King's Arms, was slightly less entirely impossible than the other two. This unit had two sides made of glass. At the moment it was boarded up and dingy as Dickens, but Fabia could see a vague glimmer of potential. Stella tried not to let herself get discouraged. If Fabia could see the potential, she certainly ought to as well, but it seemed to Stella that there was so much to be done, stripping, painting and, from looking at the state of the leads hanging from the ceiling, probably rewiring too. How on earth were they going to find anyone to do it without being paid?

'Bernie!' Stella suddenly exclaimed, making Fabia wobble on the ladder they had borrowed from the bookie's next door. 'Bernie used to have a painting firm that employed Cameron's dad. Maybe he'd still have some contacts!'

Since Bernie enjoyed a pint or two of IPA every day, they were able to pop into the King's Arms and enquire.

The reaction to Fabia's arrival would have put Jamie Oliver in his place. Les, the landlord, rushed across and almost kissed her feet. 'We had the best day here on Saturday since Charles and Di's wedding!'

Stella smiled to herself at the idea of the King's Arms regulars doing a commentary on Princess Diana's fairy-tale wedding dress as they toasted the happy couple in bitter and stout.

'Have you seen Bernie, by any chance?' Stella enquired.

The landlord looked up at the clock. 'He'll be here in ten minutes. You could set your watch by him. Now, what can I get you ladies?'

Stella opted for a G and T since that was pretty safe anywhere. Fabia was made of sterner stuff. 'I would like a sea breeze please, landlord.'

'The name's Les, Fabia. It's short for Leslie. And what's a sea breeze when it's at home?'

'Vodka, with grapefruit and cranberry juice.'

Les reached down below the dusty bar, ringed with the imprints of years of wet glasses. 'We have grapefruit.' With a beaming smile he produced a small bottle of Britvic. The ten or so assorted regulars gave him a round of applause at his foresight in stocking so exotic an ingredient. He held the bottle up to the light. The sediment at the bottom was an inch thick. 'Hunky dory, if you shake it a little. Cranberry's a bit beyond our touch.'

'I'll settle for a screwdriver, then,' Fabia conceded. Les looked so puzzled that she enlightened him. 'Vodka and orange juice. You do have orange juice, I take it.'

Les poured it out. 'Well, blow me, I never knew that was a screwdriver. Hey, lads, we can do cocktails!'

Behind him a clock, consisting of nothing but photos of Elvis, chimed midday by playing 'Hound Dog'.

'Isn't that clever!' Stella laughed.

'Not when you've heard it every bloody hour for ten hours,' mumbled the prune-like octogenarian who served as pot man, collecting the empty glasses, and downing any abandoned dregs as his perk.

Any further discussion of horrible fates for Elvis were cut short by the arrival of Bernie, as predicted, on the dot of midday.

'Bernie!' Stella welcomed him as an old friend.

Bernie pretended not to show even a blink of surprise to find two ladies sitting at the bar, one of them sipping a screwdriver, in the entirely masculine ambience of the KA.

'Morning, girls.' His welcoming smile made his small eyes disappear into the furrows of his face like a friendly Shar Pei.

'Rare to see someone of the fair sex in here on a Monday and, I must add, a great improvement.'

Stella glanced round. Bernie was right. Of the twenty or so tables scattered through the vast echoing Victorian tavern, not one was populated by another female. There were probably more women on Mount Athos.

'Actually, we came in especially to look for you.'

'Why is that?'

'Fabia is hoping to take over the shop next door and turn it into a retro emporium.'

'What, Mount, the draper's shop on the end there?'

'I don't really know if it was a draper's.' To be honest, Stella wasn't even sure what a draper's was. But Bernie had disappeared back into his childhood. 'We used to buy all our clothes there when I was a kid. They had this old cash-delivery tube they put the money in and it went upstairs to old Mrs Mount who'd send back down a receipt in the tube. I always wanted to put a gobstopper in and see what the old girl made of that.'

'What is a gobstopper?' enquired Fabia to a raucous response from the drinkers.

'It's a large boiled sweet you suck,' Stella enlightened her. 'They lasted for hours. People at school used to take them out for lessons and wrap them in a hankie and put them back in again afterwards.'

Fabia shuddered. 'How uncivilized.'

'Fancy a pickled egg or a pork scratching?' Les offered, eager to impress his exotic guest. 'They're local delicacies.'

'Leslie.' Fabia turned to him haughtily.

'Les.'

'Les. I may have a foreign accent but I have lived in this godforsaken country for years. Long enough to know that I never, ever, want to eat a pickled egg.'

'Fair enough.'

'So what do you want to do with Mount's?' Bernie took a long swallow of his beer and gave them his full attention.

'We want to completely renovate it. Wiring. Carpentry. Any plumbing that's needed.' Stella smiled at him winningly.

'And you want to pay as little as possible?'

'Exactly.' At least they'd have the money from the fox painting and that was a start. 'It's all part of our campaign to regenerate the high street. Make it more like it was when you were a boy.'

Bernie laughed. 'They still had trams and horse-drawn carriages in those days.'

'We won't be bringing those back, but we do want to stop this block being demolished and turned into a huge superstore.'

'Is Cameron involved?'

'He's doing a fundraising concert in our garden. Rock for Regeneration. You'll have to come along.'

'I've been thinking about Cameron.' Bernie turned his head away as if lost in contemplation. 'He loved his dad but Billy Keene was a bad lot. I feel responsible, in a way, as Billy was my worker and I turned a blind eye, but I knew what was going on. I'll do what I can to help you.'

Bernie glanced around the bar. 'Stan over there's a spark, Norman's a plumber. I still have contacts in the decorating trade. We'll sort something out for you, won't we, lads?'

An inaudible grumble arose from the assembled drinkers.

'Just leave it to me.'

'Bernie'll see you right,' asserted Les. 'And next time you come in here we'll be doing cocktails. You see if we don't!' A hideous thought struck him. 'You will be coming back next Saturday with your parill-wotsit, won't you?'

'*Parillada*. That would depend on whether I can get the free meat again.'

'I can get the meat for you. In the market.'

'*I* will choose my own meat,' Fabia announced grandly, as if any meat Les purchased would turn out to be horse.

'And the ballroom dancing too?'

Fabia treated him to a deathly stare. 'Argentine tango is *not* ballroom dancing. It is an act of passion, more erotic even than making love.'

'Blimey,' the pot man murmured, 'and in broad daylight too!'

'Goodbye, Stella,' Fabia announced. 'Can you let me know when the workmen can start?'

Stella watched her departure in slightly stunned amazement.

The force of nature that was Fabia was clearly coming to join them in Camley. If Fabia was getting stuck in because she was looking for a more normal life, Stella had had the opposite motive. She had been looking for a change from a routine that had become all too predictable. She hardly even needed to keep a diary because she knew exactly when everything would be happening in their peaceful and ordered life.

But not today. Stella's heart lifted at the sight of something she certainly hadn't been expecting.

The giant toaster was back in her driveway.

She rushed inside the house to find Cameron installed in a large wing chair in the sitting room with his leg up on a stool watching Sky Sports on television. Matthew was with him and they had opened a bottle of Matthew's best red wine. Behind them the French windows were open to the garden. There was no sign of Duncan. To Stella's relief her guest seemed to be perfectly sober.

'Cameron!' Stella exclaimed anxiously. 'What on earth's the matter?'

'Oh, good, you're back' announced Matthew, stating the obvious in a highly irritating manner. 'I was just wondering what we could have to eat.'

'But what's happened to the tour? Why are you back here so soon?'

'We've got two days' break and I needed a bit of peace and quiet away from all the fans. They worked out I was living in the Airstream and wouldn't leave me alone.'

Stella had visions of Cameron besieged by crowds of screaming sixty-year-olds.

'I can see that would be uncomfortable.'

'Uncomfortable! I couldn't even get out of the door to buy a pint of milk!'

As she doubted Cameron had bought a pint of milk in forty years, Stella decided there had to be another more convincing reason for his sudden departure.

'Also I discovered I've got a rather awkward medical condition.'

All sorts of possibilities raced through Stella's mind, from prostate problems to sky-high blood pressure.

'Cameron! What is it?'

Cameron grinned broadly, raised the large glass of red wine and indicated his foot resting on the embroidered Arts and Crafts footstool Matthew had paid far too much for in a chi-chi antique shop. 'Gout!'

He and Matthew rocked with laughter. 'Obviously, I've got to be pretty careful it doesn't get out. OK for overweight country squires in the seventeenth century, but not so hot for ageing rock stars relaunching their careers. Not to mention that it was bloody painful! I can see why Oliver Cromwell massacred the Irish when he was having an attack of gout. In fact, he was being quite lenient, really.'

'So what's the treatment for it?' Stella had visions of rolls of bandages and men being wheeled in basket chairs.

'Just these nice little pills. As long as I remember to take them I should be fit as Yehudi Menuhin's fiddle. The only thing is I have to walk with crutches till they work, which isn't very rock 'n' roll, but it's better than a wheelchair. You can just see the headline in the press: Don't Wheel Me in the Morning, or some such crap. I am telling everyone I've cracked a bone in my foot. Preferably a metatarsal like David Beckham. I'm hoping his glamour can help me carry it off. Matthew, you couldn't pour me a glass of that excellent Malbec, could you?'

Matthew, Stella noted, filled his own glass at the same time. Clearly he wasn't keeping to his rules in Cameron's company.

'There's one little problem. I want to nip down to The Glebe tomorrow and sort out this recording we want to make but I don't dare call a cab or it'll be all over Surrey that I can't walk.'

'So you wondered if I would give you a lift?'

'Stella, lovely Stella, always so generous and obliging.'

'Why can't Duncan do it? He usually sorts this kind of thing out.'

Cameron looked positively puckish. 'Because Duncan's lady friend is back.'

Maybe it was exhaustion at overdoing things lately, but Stella felt the sudden need to sit down.

'She's been taking her ghastly art around Japan. Pity it didn't stay there, if you ask me.'

'Of course, she's an artist.'

'If you can call it art. She knew Duncan's wife Connie a bit.'

'Yes, I think you told us about her. What's her name?' Stella asked casually.

'It's hilarious. Poncy as you like. Scarlett? Lola? No, I'd remember that. Amber. Amber O'Somebody. An Irish name. Amber O'Reilly?'

'Not Amber O'Riordan?'

'The very one entirely!' congratulated Cameron in a cod Irish accent. 'You never know, maybe it's love, begorrah. It's time he got over Connie and found someone else. He's always been a one-woman man, our Duncan. What's that Byrds song about a time to love and a time to hate? Maybe Dunc's found it's a time to love again. Pity it had to be her, though. They got together in California. I was rather hoping he'd forget about her when she was in Japan, but no dice.'

'What's she like, then, this Amber O'Reilly?' Matthew enquired.

'O'Riordan,' corrected Stella. 'She's quite famous. She paints enormous 3D wombs and breasts, rather like medical scans.'

Matthew refilled their glasses again.

'Typical of Duncan!' Cameron continued. 'Trust him to fall for some crazy painter. He's always had this hang-up about High Art. He even dated an opera singer once. The lads and I thought she'd smother him in bed.'

Personally, Stella thought Amber O'Riordan's work, from what she'd seen of it in magazines, was showy and pretentious, the opposite of High Art. But there was no doubt it was collected and that gullible people paid large sums for it.

Listen to you, Stella told herself sternly, *anyone'd think you were either narrow-minded or jealous. Possibly even both.*

She left them to it and retreated to the peace of the kitchen, where she found herself staring at a fly buzzing pointlessly in its attempt to get out of the closed window. Outside, the weather blazed, but Stella felt oddly disconnected. When Duncan had admired her painting of the fox and even talked of using it, she'd been elated, had even believed it held a touch of genuine talent. Now, hearing that he had fallen for a celebrated artist, even one she didn't personally rate, she felt she was just a painter of pets. She could well imagine what Amber O'Riordan would think of her modest output.

Stella poured herself a glass of white wine and held it up to the light, seeing in it the greenish glow of summertime. How stupid she'd been, believing she was still young, that if you kept the spark alive in your heart, that moment of gilded youth could last forever. She ought to content herself with the amazing fact that Cameron had once written a song about her. She would have her tiny moment of immortality, which was more than most people had. She held the glass up again, cheered by the thought. 'Here's to you, Stella Ainsworth, remember you're a muse and pull yourself together.'

Like a million women before her, she calmed her soul by fulfilling small familiar tasks: the laying of the table, beating eggs for an omelette, the assembly of a salad, the preparation of a smooth but tart vinaigrette. Then she announced lunch.

She could see that if she didn't accept Cameron's request to take him to The Glebe, he would behave like a sulky teenager all evening. So it was with an air of veiled irritation, trying not to think of the million tasks on her list which no one else considered important, that Stella brought the car round the next day and she and Matthew helped Cameron in.

The manageress at The Glebe greeted them eagerly, mainly because Duncan had phoned ahead to warn her of the likelihood that she would be visited by a god. Stella smiled to herself, imagining Duncan saying something like 'Don't worry, he probably won't be disguised as a swan like Zeus,' and the girl's puzzled incomprehension.

'Mr Keene! This is an honour.' The young woman had the high good sense not to add the usual response from someone her age: 'My mother loved you.' She added that she had been going to take him on a tour of the hotel but, given his injury, maybe they should put that off till another time. 'I have been doing a little research,' she announced proudly. 'The place where you made the original recording was in the ground-floor lounge.'

'Perhaps you could show me that?' Cameron favoured her with one of his wolfish smiles.

She led the way along various corridors to a large sunny room, decorated with trellis wallpaper adorned with sweet peas, echoed by an enormous arrangement of flowers in a vast vase in the middle of the room. French windows led into the garden. Tables and chairs, mostly occupied by chatting women, were scattered throughout. It was almost unrecognizable from the freezing half-empty room adorned with fading brocade and Indian bedspreads and reeking of patchouli that she remembered so well.

'What's that godawful pong?' demanded Cameron.

'That'd be the sweet peas.'

'It's not air freshener, is it?' Cameron swept on regardless. 'I hate bloody air freshener. Duncan's forever spraying it in the bog whenever I've had a crap. I have to say to him, "Dunc, old boy, before, it smelt like I had a crap. Now, it smells like I had a crap in a flowerbed".'

'What a lovely room,' congratulated Stella, trying not to laugh. 'Such a great view of the garden.'

'This is where we normally celebrate special occasions,' the manageress enthused.

'Of course, all the furniture will have to come out.' Cameron shrugged. 'Probably the carpet and curtains too.'

'Excuse me?'

'You can't have them muffling the sound. The place was almost empty when we did it before.'

'I'm afraid we can't possibly consider that,' was the appalled reaction. 'We're really booked up for weddings. We've invested a lot of money to make this a premiere wedding venue.'

'You'll just have to cancel them, then, won't you?'

The manageress looked at Cameron as if he were an escaped lunatic. 'I'm afraid that's entirely out of the question.'

'For Christ's sake, woman,' bellowed Cameron, making all the flowery-hatted occupants jump, 'don't you realize you'll be making musical history? Where's Duncan, anyway? He should be sorting this kind of thing out.' He got out his iPhone and sacrificed any small street cred owed to rock stars by having to ask Matthew how to work it. None of them could blame him when Duncan did not pick up.

It was obvious to Stella that without Duncan, Cameron was like a Rolls-Royce without an engine.

'Does this godforsaken place have a bar? Or is it too full of wedding planners and pushy mothers having afternoon bloody tea?' He stomped out of the room on his crutches.

'You'd better go with him,' Stella murmured to Matthew. 'I'm afraid I'm due at Emma's.'

The fact was, Stella was still worried about Jesse. She assumed he must have come home or she would have heard, but the disappearance with no word wasn't like him.

Although Emma and Stuart's house was on an executive estate handy for the station with twenty identical others, Emma had managed to make theirs individual. It was a three-bedroom house, and one of the points of contention, when Ruby had come along, had been that for six months she had to sleep with Stuart and Emma. Izzy, although she had liked the idea of a baby sister a lot more than her father, was outraged at the idea of suddenly having to share her bedroom just when she wanted to be private. The only solution had been a loft conversion, which cost them a lot more than they could afford, but at least it meant an extra bed and bathroom. Jesse had been allowed to change rooms to general relief as he preferred listening to such weird music. Ruby inherited his old bedroom.

The months of builders had only added to the household stress but finally things had seemed to calm down at last.

But when Stella rang the doorbell, it was answered by a tearful Izzy, who flung herself at Stella. 'Gran! I'm so glad you're here. It's Mum and Jesse! She's just got back from seeing his teacher. They're in the kitchen shouting at each other.'

Stella's relief was short-lived since she, probably along with the rest of the street, could hear that any fragile family peace they had achieved was in the act of being shattered.

'Your teacher says you haven't been in school for two days,' accused Emma furiously. 'Your bed hasn't even been slept in last night. I know it's down to that little slag Dora.'

'How dare you call her a slag!' Jesse looked angrier than Stella had ever seen him. 'If anyone's a slag round here, it isn't Dora.' Things must have got very bad for lovely Jesse to speak to his mother like that.

'Right, I'm not taking this from you . . .'

'You don't need to,' Jesse insisted quietly. 'I'm going. Right now.'

'Gran!' Izzy begged. 'Stop them!'

'Emma,' Stella tried not to let the annoyance she was feeling seep into her voice. 'I know you love Jesse and he loves you.'

'Not as much as he loves the little slag, obviously.'

Stella walked across to her daughter. 'Don't, Emma. He really likes this girl. If he goes, you'll only regret it.'

219

Emma seemed to come to her senses. 'You're right. I over-reacted.' She started to walk towards the stairs just as Jesse almost tumbled down them, holding his backpack and his guitar. 'Jesse, I'm sorry . . .'

'I'm going, Mum. I stayed because I thought maybe you and Dad were going to be all right, but do you know what? I feel sorry for him. It would have been better for us all if you'd left.'

He hugged Izzy. 'Don't worry, Izz, I'll be fine. And remember, you've always got Gran. Give Rube a kiss from me.' And he was out of the door.

At these words Stella almost wanted to cry herself. How had Emma got so caught up with Hal and this stupid job that she couldn't see what was happening to her own family?

Emma sat down heavily at the kitchen table and began to cry.

Twelve

Stella made Emma a cup of tea and kept her peace, hoping that she would have drawn her own lessons without further parental interference.

Emma looked as if she might collapse. She reached out to her daughter. 'I'm sorry, darling. I shouldn't have said that to Jesse and especially not in front of you. Maybe if Mum could make you a sandwich, I'll help you with your homework.'

'We're only doing test papers and I did some with Roxy.'

She could see that Emma was about to protest and thankfully thought better of it.

'What about supper?' Stella asked.

'Oh shit, supper.' Emma clutched her head.

It was odd, Stella decided, because she used to be so fussy about stocking all things organic. 'I'll see what I can rustle up.'

Stella found some rather sad-looking vegetables in the bottom of the fridge and some Parmesan cheese that had taken on the consistency of cement and threw it all together with a packet of frozen peas and some pasta.

'This is really nice, Gran,' Izzy commented, when Stella served her some.

Stella saved some of the sauce, put it aside till it was wanted for Stuart's and Emma's supper.

'Dad's going to be livid. About Jesse, I mean.' Izzy sounded depressed rather than nervous.

'Do you want me to stay?'

She shook her head. 'He'll just wait till you've gone and then be livid.'

Emma appeared with Ruby enveloped in a giant fluffy bath towel. Oblivious to the volcano erupting around her she kicked her bare legs and put out a hand to try and grab some pasta.

'Wait a minute, Greedy-guts.' Emma smiled and dried her lovingly, stuffing one gorgeous plump arm into her pyjamas, then the other. 'Thanks a million for supper, Mum, it smells delicious. You've saved my life. Oh God, Mum, what am I going to do about Jesse?'

'Where do you think he's gone?'

'To see Dora. He's totally obsessed with her. Just when he ought to be revising. And she's cool as a cucumber, getting him to test her all the time for *her* exams. She's so much more grown-up than him.'

'I'm surprised at her parents allowing him to stay so close to their exams. I got the impression they were pretty strict.'

'They've got quite a big house. Maybe they think it's better for Dora's calm approach to exams not to have a fight about it. I'm sure they'd be in separate rooms. Izzy, would you get me Ruby's socks?'

Izzy got up and looked at her mother levelly. 'I know what you're going to tell Gran when I'm out of the room. You think they're having sex. Which socks do you want?'

'The blue ones,' Emma replied in a chastened voice. 'God, Mum, how do kids know *everything*?'

'Mainly because adults talk to their friends in front of them.'

222

Stella wondered if she ought to mention the incident in her studio, then remembered Jesse's plea not to tell his mother and decided to respect it.

They both heard Stuart's key turning in the door. 'I must go.'

'Mum, stay.' The urgency in her daughter's voice made Stella sit down again.

'Hello, Stella,' Stuart greeted her. 'I didn't know you were coming. Mmm . . . something smells good.'

'Mum made it. Stuart . . .'

Stuart, halfway through taking his coat off, looked at her warily. 'What?'

'Jesse's taken off.'

'Where to?'

'Where do you think? Gone off to that little slag.'

Stella shot her a look. Hadn't she learned her lesson after all?

'Right. Well, I'm going to have some supper and a beer, as it's been a long day, and after that I'll go round and see if he's there.'

Stella hugged Izzy, kissed her son-in-law on the cheek, and nuzzled Ruby. 'Good luck.' She smiled hopefully. 'He's not a bad lad.'

'I know,' Stuart seconded, casting a stormy look towards his wife. 'Thanks for helping out, Stella.'

'Let me know when you find him, won't you? A text will do.'

Stuart nodded. He was looking exceptionally tired.

After all the emotional upheaval, Stella realized how tired she felt herself. There was nothing that wore you out like worrying about your children, and it didn't matter if they were three or thirty-three. She'd probably still be worried when they were sixty-three. The one thing she longed for was a bath, preferably with a glass of wine, and an early night.

Stella was surprised to see Suze's car in the drive, next to the Airstream, and wondered why she'd dropped in. As soon as she opened the front door, she was hit by the sound of clinking glasses and laughter. Obviously there were far more people in the house than just Suze. Stella wondered if she could make a quick getaway and hide in the studio at the bottom of the garden, but Cameron had already spotted her. He was enthroned like Henry VIII, his gouty leg on a stool, surrounded by his courtiers. Or, in this case, a rather drunk Matthew, who sat next to Fabia. Debora and Suze were in armchairs near the fire.

But the real shock was who was sitting on the sofa.

Duncan had leaned forward to laugh at something the woman next to him had just said. She was tall and Junoesque, about thirty-five, with dark curly hair and bright red lips and a clinging red wrap dress, displaying a cleavage the size of the Grand Canyon. At her feet dozed an enormous drooling boxer dog.

Debora was the first to her feet. 'Stella, darling girl, Matthew invited us all back to celebrate Cameron finally persuading The Glebe to let him do his famous recording. Well, actually, it was Duncan who persuaded them, but still.'

'How kind of Matthew.' Stella tried not to sound sour. 'The only thing is I haven't got any food to offer you.'

'I will cook,' Fabia announced grandly. 'Debora has brought some scallops and I will prepare them with lentils and bacon. If you will let me use your kitchen?'

'Stella,' Duncan had got to his feet, 'may I introduce you to Amber O'Riordan?' His tone, she noted, was almost apologetic.

Amber nudged the dog with her foot and stood up. 'Wisht,

Donleavy, out of the way now!' She was taller than Stella had thought, almost six feet, certainly as tall as Duncan, though she was wearing ridiculously high heels.

'Hello, Amber, obviously I'm familiar with your work.'

'Duncan says you paint as well.'

'Oh, well, animals mostly.'

Amber laughed with a hint of patronage. 'Maybe you could paint Donleavy here!' She looked coyly at Duncan. 'Men always say I care more about the dog. Always making a fuss of him and petting him instead of them.'

Stella decided she didn't want to contemplate this affecting image. 'Has Matthew given everyone a drink? I hope you'll excuse me while I get one myself.' She beckoned Debora into the kitchen and shut the door.

'My God,' Stella whispered, 'how long has he been seeing the Irish Valkyrie?'

'They've been going out for a while but we didn't know if it was serious. He hadn't really got over Connie, if you ask me. Then she went off to Japan. She must have just got back. Someone should tell her that wrap dresses are *so* ten years ago.'

'She must look like the Statue of Liberty to the Japanese!'

'Do we detect a sour note from lovely Stella?' Debora teased.

The door opened. It was Suze come to join in the gossip. 'She really should put those tits away before someone gets hurt diving into them!'

Matthew appeared on her heels, swaying gently as if in a strong breeze. 'Girls, girls, do I detect a little jealousy from the post-menopausal towards the abundantly fertile? Men are always drawn to women with overt sexuality. It's all down to the primal need to reproduce.'

'Fuck off, Matthew,' Suze greeted him. 'That's just another excuse for men to drop their drawers.'

'I must admit, I'm surprised at Duncan,' Debora commented, helping Stella look for ingredients for Fabia. 'I thought he had more discrimination than to fall for someone so obvious. Connie was so subtle and sophisticated.'

'And dead,' reminded Matthew to a response of such universal outrage that he grabbed a bottle from the fridge and scuttled off.

'I thought he had his eye on someone else altogether,' Suze announced, not looking at Stella. 'She's just a posh casserole lady.'

'What is a casserole lady?' Debora asked, intrigued by this unfamiliar British jargon.

'You must have them in America. They appear after death or divorce, whenever a man's on the market. *Oh, you poor thing, it must be so lonely, have this casserole I've lovingly prepared.* Three weeks later, they're in his bed and in three months, they've bagged him. I've seen it time and time again.'

Debora shook her head. 'And fancy calling a boxer a silly name like Donleavy.'

The kitchen door opened and Amber appeared on the hunt for ice. 'Is this a private coven?' she asked breezily, unaware that she was the topic of conversation. 'Or can anyone join in?'

Stella filled up the ice bucket and sent her back to summon Fabia.

Stella had to admit, Fabia was indeed a wonderful cook. The barbecue at the King's Arms had been no fluke. Fabia really knew her stuff. The scallops with bacon and lentils were divine.

Throughout the evening Stella kept checking her phone for news of Jesse, but there was none.

Fortunately for her ragged nerves, the party began to disband fairly early.

'Right,' Duncan drained his glass and became businesslike,

'from tomorrow we're on the road again. I'll be round at nine a.m. sharp to collect you, Cam. Do you think you can walk on stage without crutches? If not, we can always invent some funny story about you tripping over a roadie.'

'Hang on, mate,' Cameron protested, his pride piqued. 'I'm as fit as you are. I could somersault onto the stage if you wanted me to.'

Duncan grinned and looked at Cameron's foot sceptically. 'Just ambling would be good enough for me. And Matthew –' He turned to say goodbye to Matthew and found him gently snoring in a wing chair. 'Good, at least he won't be leading you astray. You've both had quite enough. Just remember what happened at the Roundhouse, will you?'

Cameron regarded him balefully. 'I don't see why you should harp on about one little slip.'

'Jaysus,' Amber demanded, trying to rouse her somnolent boxer, 'so what happened at the Roundhouse?'

'We had to bring Cameron back from the dead. He tried to drown himself in several gallons of cheap beer. Debora and Stella were amazing.'

'Angels of mercy, were you?' Amber managed to make it sound vaguely insulting. 'I like a good session myself. Why do you think I called the dog Donleavy?'

'No, do tell,' Suze replied innocently. 'Could it be after J. P. Donleavy, author of that classic tale of Dublin drunkenness and dissipation, *The Ginger Man*?'

'Indeed it is,' Amber replied, a note of sourness behind her determined gaiety. 'Well spotted, ladies.'

'So, Amber, have you had any shows on lately?' Stella could see that Suze had taken one of her rare dislikes to Amber O'Riordan.

'Oh I've dispensed with all that sort of nonsense. Only a

mug would stand by and let galleries take fifty per cent just for providing some crap white wine for a private view and a bit of wall space. I only show on the Internet.'

'Do you dispense with reviews as well?'

'Who needs reviews? They're only from old white men, anyway. When I want publicity I create it myself.'

'And how do you do that?' Suze asked sweetly.

'I sat naked on a plinth in St Stephen's Green for two days,' Amber boasted, sticking out her considerable frontage. The men all watched her, fascinated.

'I hope you didn't frighten the pigeons. And did you get lots of publicity?'

'I did till this stupid guard kept putting his coat over me. Some nonsense about reminding him of his daughter.'

'How very inconvenient. I hope you told him where to get off.'

'Too right! I don't think he'll be forgetting me in a hurry. Come on now, Donleavy. Time to get back to the hotel.'

Stella wondered for a brief moment if Amber and Duncan would be sharing a room. How bloody ridiculous. Of course they would. Perhaps it would be Duncan who would need waking in the morning for once. Amber O'Riordan looked like the type who would keep him up for quite a lot of the night.

Really she should be happy for Duncan. He wasn't the kind of man who went into relationships lightly. Telling herself she'd thought quite enough about the subject, she made herself a cup of tea and decided to ignore the clearing up.

Cameron, to everyone's surprise, was up bright and early. If the amount of alcohol he'd put away last night hadn't affected him, God knows how much he must have drunk the time he'd been out cold. Matthew, on the other hand, was neither bright nor even conscious. He had burrowed beneath the duvet as if it were a tent pitched in a polar landscape so that no part of him was visible.

'Matthew,' Stella attempted, pulling the top of the duvet back and shaking him gently. 'Wake up!'

Matthew only groaned.

His clothes littered the floor like one of those clichéd Hollywood movies where the couple have torn their clothes off to have wild sex. He had actually collapsed insensible and had proceeded to snore loudly for most of the night.

Since Matthew was clearly not going to move she dressed quickly and went downstairs to see Cameron off herself. A small knot of people, including the ghastly Mr and Mrs Husky from next door, had gathered to see the last of the Airstream.

The only problem was that Duncan had still not arrived to drive it. Damn that Amber woman. Duncan was always so quietly efficient. Stella realized her reaction to Amber was morphing from determined tolerance to active dislike.

She was just about to call Duncan when a car hove into view and disgorged Duncan and Amber, who was wearing an equally revealing ensemble, and ridiculous high heels of the kind that Naomi Campbell had fallen off. Stella watched hopefully for a similar performance.

'Sorry we're late,' Amber smiled in a manner she no doubt supposed was roguish, 'we overslept.'

She caught sight of the husky sitting obediently on the pavement and tottered over to stroke it.

In a rare burst of good taste, Shackleton growled. 'He can probably smell my dog on me,' she tittered, making even this simple statement sound faintly suggestive.

'I don't suppose Cameron's up?' Duncan enquired.

'Been up for hours. I've fed him toast and coffee with lots

of orange juice. Actually, he's in an excellent mood. He's watching *The Simpsons* in the sitting room.'

'It must be The Glebe agreeing to the recording. It's turned Cam into a spring lamb.'

'I wouldn't go that far.' Stella grinned. 'More of a happy ram.'

'I'll settle for that. How's the gout? He has been taking his pills, hasn't he? I'm hoping he might be able to walk on stage tomorrow without the crutches. So far the gout story hasn't got out.'

But Stella was unable to answer this. She had spotted Emma's hatchback speeding down the road towards them. Emma, still wearing her pyjamas, tumbled out. 'Mum,' she blurted, her face blotched with crying, 'it's Jesse. He isn't with Dora after all!'

Stella put her arm round her daughter and shepherded her inside, away from the fascinated gazes of Amber O'Riordan, Mr and Mrs Husky and Shackleton.

'The thing is,' Emma sobbed as soon as they were inside, 'we've no idea where he's gone. And it's all my stupid fault for having a go at him!'

She slumped down on the sofa next to Cameron, who seemed so engrossed by the dilemmas of Homer and Mr Burns that he didn't even notice.

Duncan and Amber followed them in. With his usual presence of mind Duncan suggested that Amber go and make some tea.

'I'm not your bloody skivvy,' she protested, her bosoms heaving inappropriately.

'I didn't think you were,' Duncan replied calmly. 'Stella and Emma need a moment together, that's all.'

'Why don't *you* make the tea, then?'

Duncan very sensibly ignored her and she stomped off.

'Where's Dad?' Emma demanded.

'Still in bed. He and Cameron had a bit of a night.'

'Oh great. Just when I need him he's got a hangover.'

'So what happened?' Stella took her hand to try and calm her down.

'Stuart went round there last night but no one was in. We didn't really think anything of it. Then he had to go in for an early meeting at Belmarsh prison, so I said I'd ring. I managed to get hold of Dora on her mobile. The thing is, Mum, he hasn't been there at all!' Emma began to cry again. 'And Stuart doesn't even know yet. I couldn't get hold of him. Oh, God, Mum, what if something's happened to him? He's only sixteen. And he's so trusting. He always thinks the best of people. I know I blamed Dora, but it was my fault too. I can see that now. And I shouldn't have gone on about his exams.'

'Have you tried his friends?' Duncan asked. 'When I ran away after a row with my parents, I went to my best friend's.'

'Did you?' Emma asked, as if he'd thrown her a lifeline.

'He wouldn't be the first teenager to run away after a row.' Stella glanced at him gratefully.

'But didn't they make you ring your mum and dad?'

'They didn't know. Neil just smuggled me in.'

'How long were you away?'

'A couple of days. When I got back, my dad went berserk, but I could see that they had been really worried, so we all sat down and talked about it.'

'Tea, anyone?' Amber plonked the tea down with a disgruntled air. It had slopped all over the tray.

Somehow her arrival made everyone instantly clam up. 'OK, OK.' She shrugged, in a rare moment of sensitivity. 'I'll go back and take Donleavy for a walk. He's probably crapped on the hotel carpet by now anyway. How do you get a cab around here?'

They were saved by the arrival of Suze. Before she could even take off her coat or ask what was going on, Stella had given her a meaningful look and delegated the task of driving Amber back to The Glebe to her.

'The thing is,' Emma admitted, taking in the significance of this statement for perhaps the first time, 'he doesn't really have a best friend. Jesse's always been a bit of a lone wolf. He doesn't really go in for friends. Not till this Dora.'

'She's not exactly a friend, is she?' Stella said gently. 'He must have had someone, Em.'

'Well, there was one girl, what was her name? Kirsty? But she's moved to Brighton. I remember he was quite upset.'

'Do you remember her surname?' asked Duncan. 'I'm sure we could track her down. I suppose the question is, do you tell the police?'

'*The police?*' Emma repeated, beginning to shake. 'Yes, we really ought to, I suppose.'

'Maybe you'd better get hold of your husband. It sounds as if he's used to dealing with the authorities if he's a human rights lawyer.'

'Oh, God,' Emma wailed. 'I'm such a crap mum! He's going to be furious with me.'

'Come on, Em,' Stella put her arm round her daughter, 'don't worry about Stuart. It's Jesse we've got to think about. I'll come with you so you can look for this girl's details. You're too shaky to go alone.'

'I know,' Emma brightened for the first time, 'I've got the school lists . . . but they'll be no use if she's only just moved.'

'There you are,' Duncan reassured her. 'Crap mums don't keep school lists. Look, once we've done the last show in

Glasgow we'll be ending the tour in Brighton. If you haven't found him by then, we'll put out a Facebook appeal for him to come to the show.' He saw her anguished expression and realized this was a mistake. 'Don't worry, you'll have him back long before then.'

Emma burst into tears again causing Cameron to suddenly take in the drama unfolding around him.

'What the fuck's going on? I never touched the girl!'

Duncan dropped his head into his hands. 'Never mind, Cam. You just concentrate on Homer.'

'Do you want me to stay for a bit?' Stella asked when she drove Emma home.

'Would you, Mum? I need someone to be home for Izzy and pick up Ruby from the childminder later on. She gave Stella a sudden hug. 'And just having you there would be such a comfort.'

Stella stroked her daughter's face, feeling unbearably touched. She wasn't allowing herself to imagine all the appalling things lurking at the back of her mind that could happen to Jesse because that would be no help to anyone, least of all herself.

They had only been back at Emma's a few moments when an unfamiliar car drew up outside. Stella's heart soared when she saw it was Dora, accompanied by both her parents.

But the expressions on their faces soon put her right; the father's angry, the mother's sour as an under-ripe lemon.

'Mrs Cope? My wife and I would like a word.'

Once they were inside they refused all offers of refreshment and even declined to sit down. 'Mrs Cope, did you know that your son and our daughter have been having sex?' Stella dreaded what was coming next. 'It must have been down to your son because Dora would never do such a thing without pressure. She's far too focussed on her exam results.'

'Well, he isn't here. Besides,' Emma was morphing into a Tiger Mother before Dora's and her parents' startled eyes, 'you can stop talking as if this was still the nineteenth century. Your daughter isn't some little backstairs skivvy forced into it by the young master, she's a highly competent young woman and it's far more likely that if they're having sex she's been taking the lead.'

Dora's father started to protest, but Emma was tolerating no interruptions.

'As a matter of fact,' Emma turned the conversation skilfully, 'I was about to come and ask you, Dora, if you had any idea where he might have gone. Did you know Kirsty who moved to Brighton, for instance?'

'It wasn't really Brighton,' Dora pointed out coolly, 'it was outside. Somewhere near the Marina, not the cool bit up by Hove where the famous people live.'

'And what was her other name?'

'Kirsty Weatherall. Maybe the school could help.'

'Has he contacted you at all?'

Dora shook her head.

'So he isn't here?' demanded Dora's father.

'No, he's not.'

'Can you make it clear to him that Dora wouldn't welcome hearing from him?'

'Till after the exams,' chipped in Dora.

Her father ignored her.

'I expect you need to get back to your revision, Dora,' Emma said briskly, leading them towards the door. At the last moment she clutched Dora's arm. 'You will let me know, won't you, if you do hear from him?'

Dora's parents hustled her out before she could reply.

'I'll pick up Izzy from school,' Stella offered when they'd gone, 'and make her tea. Do you want me to get something for Stuart and you too?'

'Oh, Mum, you're an angel.'

'You're my precious daughter,' Stella replied simply. 'And I really love my grandchildren. Though what I really wonder is what the hell's happened to their grandfather when you need him.'

As soon as she was outside she rang him to find out.

Matthew, still sleeping it off in bed, woke with a start, unable to believe it was almost 3 p.m. 'Stella, where are you?' he demanded in an almost belligerent tone which made her want to kill him.

'If you must know, I have been at Emma's. Jesse is not with Dora. Indeed, Dora and her parents have just been round to break the happy news that Dora and Jesse have been sleeping together and it's taking her mind off revising for ten A stars!'

'They sound ghastly.'

'Yes. Emma told them to get lost.'

'Good for her.'

'Yes, but what about Jesse? We may need her help. She may be all we've got. I wonder if this was part of the reason he ran away. It could have all been too much for him. Anyway, I've offered to make supper and help out. I'll stay there if they want me. Suze can man the pet studio until further notice. She can organize the vintage market from there. How's Fabia doing, by the way? Is she really up for all this stuff she's taken on?'

'I think she's enjoying it,' Matthew answered, sounding extraordinarily pleased with himself. 'As a matter of fact, she's asked me to be her permanent partner.'

It was only after she'd rung off that it struck Stella that that was a very odd phrase indeed.

Stella thought about his words. Should she be wary of Fabia? Fabia had seemed too exotic a bird to roost in suburban Camley. Yet it seemed that she was a sadder figure than anyone had suspected. There was vulnerability underneath that painted exterior. And that could be far more dangerous than out-rageous self-confidence.

But today she was too angry with Matthew to care. He should be here supporting his daughter, not staying up all night boozing with Cameron. Had he always been this annoying, and in the everydayness of life, she hadn't seen it? Or had she made too many allowances for an easy time? Whatever the reason, she didn't feel like doing it any more.

Stella waited for her granddaughter outside the school gates as the exodus of school children began, the little ones first, skipping gleefully, then the older ones, inevitably on the phones they'd been deprived of all day, shepherded across the road by the lollipop lady, which was just as well since they might have been on Mars for all the attention they were paying to the traffic.

Stella spotted Izzy looking nervously around and the smile of relief that it was her gran, rather than an unpredictable Emma, who had come to meet her wrung Stella's heart.

Stella had taken her mind off the waiting and the moaning mummies by running through all they should be doing in the hunt for her grandson. By now, with luck, Stuart would be home and any fireworks hopefully exploded by the time she and Izzy arrived. Deliberately, she suggested they stop for an ice cream.

'Ooh, Gran, you are naughty. Mum never lets me.'

'What are grandmothers for, if not to let you do what your mother doesn't? Especially if you promise not to tell her!'

Izzy chose butterscotch and vanilla in a crunchy sugar cone. Stella opted for her favourite, lemon sorbet.

'Do you want a flake in that, love?' enquired the cafe owner.

Stella decided, unorthodox though it might be, that the combination sounded delicious. She was right.

'We're just going to pick up Ruby from the childminder,' she explained to Izzy, 'and then I'm going to make your tea. Shepherd's pie with real shepherds.' They both giggled. This had been their joke since Izzy was tiny.

'Can we have baked beans with it?'

'You certainly can.'

Ruby was thrilled to see her gran and her big sister and chuckled away to herself as they fitted her into her Bugaboo pushchair, carefully doing up the straps. 'Can I ride on the back?'

Stella hesitated, worried that Izzy might break it, but she was a tiny little thing for her age. 'Why not?' So Izzy climbed aboard.

By the time they reached home it was 5.45 p.m. and Stuart's car was in the drive.

'Dad's home early.' Izzy looked at Stella anxiously. 'They think I don't know about Jesse still being away, but I do.'

'Did he say anything to you?'

'He asked if he could borrow some of my Christmas money. I asked everyone for cash this year because I want a new phone and Mum won't buy me one.'

'Did he say where he was going?'

'No, but he took his little surfboard thing.'

Stella wondered if Emma had had a proper look around his room. If not, this should be the next thing on the list.

'I hope Mum and Dad aren't shouting at each other.'

This wish was unfortunately not to be granted.

'I can't see why you didn't ring the police straight away,' Stuart was saying angrily. 'We've lost another whole day. All you have to do is dial one zero one, and they'll put you straight through if the child's under eighteen.'

'You're the expert on the law, Stuart,' Emma defended herself, 'how could I know that?'

'You could have gone online. We don't live in the middle ages. What have you been doing all day, anyway?'

'Sitting on the sofa eating chocolates!' Emma flashed back. 'What do you think? I've been ringing anyone I think is friendly with him and their parents too. Everyone seems to think this Kirsty is our best option.'

'But I don't suppose you've managed to track *her* down?'

'Stop it! Stop it, both of you!' Izzy shouted and put her hands over her ears.

Overcome with guilt, Stuart opened his arms. 'Sorry, Izz, I'm really sorry. C'm here.'

Izzy buried herself in his embrace, still weeping.

'I'll call them in a minute,' Stuart announced. 'Sorry, everyone. That wasn't helpful.'

'Sit and watch TV for a bit, Izzy. Ruby can stay in her walker while I start the supper.'

Emma shot her a grateful look.

Five minutes later, Stuart was off the phone. 'They're sending someone round later. That's the kind of treatment you get if you're a nice middle-class family. If it were one of my clients, they'd suggest the kid was in a gang or on drugs.'

'Leave it out, Stuart!' snapped Emma. 'Spare us the right-on lecture.' She paused a moment, struck. 'You don't think he is on drugs, do you?'

*

Stella was impressed by how quickly the police arrived. They had just finished supper when the doorbell rang and a young man and woman introduced themselves as the 'initial investigating officers'.

Emma invited them into the cosy-if-somewhat-chaotic living room. Ruby was still in her high chair at the kitchen table while Izzy was helping with the clearing up. To Stella they looked like the most normal of families. She wondered how quickly police assessed any situation.

'Actually, I'm a lawyer so I know the ropes,' Stuart stated with a slight but discernible air of hostility. Stella assumed he was simply telling them they were dealing with a professional here, on the assumption that this would make them treat it more seriously. She hoped it worked.

'Right.' The male officer looked at him. 'So when did your son actually disappear?'

'Yesterday.'

'Less than twenty-four hours ago?' His tone implied a certain over-reaction on their part.

'Yes, but as you know, if the child is under eighteen, that is the correct procedure.'

'Indeed. And his name?'

'Jesse. Jesse Cope.'

'Age?'

'Sixteen.'

The woman officer was looking around the room, taking in family photographs, books, the size of the television. In some ways, just being a woman and working out her instinctive take on the family.

'Did anything happen to explain his departure? Pressures at school? Fall-out with friends? Any quarrels with you?'

Emma hesitated. 'Well, yes. We did have words, as it happened.'

'*You* had words,' Stuart commented.

The policewoman ignored him. 'And what was that about?'

'A girl. I felt he was neglecting his studies and getting too intense about a girl.'

'And have you talked to the girl he was . . .' she paused and Stella sensed she thought Emma one of those pushy mums who only cared about exam results – 'getting too intense about?'

'Yes. That was the first thing we thought of. That he might have gone there, but he hasn't.'

'Has she heard from him?'

'She says not.'

'And he hasn't contacted anyone? No phone calls, texts, Facebook messages? None of his friends or anything?'

'Not as far as I know. He's quite a solitary boy.'

'And you have no idea where he's gone yourselves?'

'We did wonder if he might have gone to find an old friend, a girl, who moved to Brighton.'

'Right.' The male officer made a face. 'Brighton.'

'Why do you say it like that?' Stuart asked testily.

'A lot of runaways go to Brighton. They think it's cool, apparently.'

'My son is not a runaway!' flashed Emma.

Neither officer reacted. 'For tonight we need a photograph and some DNA.'

'DNA?' Emma repeated, horrified. 'My son's not a criminal!'

'Calm down, Em, it's routine practice,' Stuart insisted. 'His toothbrush will do.'

'And we'd like to search his bedroom, if that's all right with you. By the way, has he ever run away before?'

This was too much for Emma. 'No he hasn't! We're a happy family!'

As if on cue, Ruby began to wail.

'I'll take her up for her bath, shall I?' Stella suggested. 'Izzy could help me.'

Emma nodded gratefully. The officers had gone upstairs to Jesse's room where they stayed for half an hour.

'What on earth are they doing?' Emma demanded, getting more and more wound up.

Eventually they came down.

'Did you find anything useful?' Stuart enquired before Emma could speak.

'We'll put Jesse's details out on our website. Good idea if you follow your own leads too, though. It can be a long process. Two hundred and seventy-five young people go missing every day. I assume you've tried his phone?'

'Only about a thousand times.'

'Then perhaps just send a text telling him you love him, no pressure.'

Stella thought of Jesse out there somewhere, probably alone and scared, and decided that tomorrow, interfering or not, she would get involved in finding him as well.

The officers took their leave.

'I'd better go too,' Stella announced, feeling that they might cope better with this alone.

'Thank you, Stella.' Stuart got her coat. 'You've been a great help.'

'Well, whatever I can do, don't hesitate to ask.'

'Thanks, Mum,' Emma called out.

In the car she realized how worried she was about Emma. It was bad enough when your child was in trouble, but a hundred times worse when you felt that they were in some way responsible. Emma needed to find a way of mending her relationship with her son.

But before that they had to find him.

All she wanted now was to get home and have Matthew make her a nice cup of tea and talk it through with him. Talking things through wasn't exactly Matthew's great strength, but with something of this magnitude, she was sure he would do his best.

But when she got home she found the whole house was dark and empty.

On the hall table was a note from Matthew explaining that he had gone to help Fabia with something, and he was sure Stella would understand.

Well, she didn't bloody understand.

The red light winked on the answerphone and she rushed to it in case it was from Emma about Jesse.

In fact, it was Duncan. If Jesse wasn't back by tomorrow, he suggested, they should put his photo on their website, as he'd suggested, and ask him to contact them so that they could arrange for him to come to a concert in Brighton. It was a long shot but at least they'd feel they were doing something.

Although Stella longed to go to bed, she made herself stay up till midnight, and she heard Matthew's key turn in the door.

'Matthew!' she greeted him. 'How the hell could you go out when Jesse has disappeared and everyone is desperately looking for him? We even had the police round!'

'Oh, for God's sake, Stella, Fabia's being really helpful. I thought you wanted this campaign of yours to succeed! Jesse'll come back, just you wait. As soon as he runs out of money he'll be on his phone in five minutes.'

'I can't believe you don't care when even Duncan has been

on the phone suggesting we put something on Cameron's website to help find him.'

'Perfect bloody Duncan! You'd think he was Jesse's granddad, the way he goes on! As a matter of fact, I'm knackered and now I'm going to bed!'

It occurred to Stella that instead of a caring grandfather Matthew was behaving more like a love-struck teenager and the shocking and startling fact struck her that sometimes she really didn't like her husband.

Thirteen

'So what's happening about Jesse now?' Suze asked when Stella arrived at the studio the next day. It seemed months since she'd painted any pets, but actually it wasn't more than a week or so.

Stella almost crumbled. 'Stuart's blaming Emma and Emma's blaming Dora and Dora's parents are blaming Stuart and Emma. The police came round and seemed about as interested as if they'd lost a cat rather than my beautiful grandson and told us that a hundred thousand children run away each year. Duncan came up with a really kind suggestion that they should put an appeal on their website, but I can't honestly imagine Jesse ever going online to check out Cameron Keene, even if he hadn't run away. They think he may be in Brighton. A friend from his school has just moved there.'

'Has he got his phone with him?'

'Yes. Everyone's been leaving supportive messages but no response so far. I think the best idea is to find this girl Kirsty, but, annoyingly, she's only just moved there and no one seems to have her new address except the school and they won't give it to us because of data bloody protection or some such thing.'

'Has anyone tried Directory Enquiries? You'd be surprised how effective it is, even in these days of social media. And why don't you go on one of those mummy websites and enlist the giant support group that is the Internet?'

'Anything's worth a try, I suppose,' Stella replied doubtfully. She opened her iPad and logged on to 4Mums, then searched for 'missing teenagers'. To her surprise there was quite a lot on the subject, including an advice page put together with a young people's charity on what to do if your teen ran away, but they had done most of the things already. There was one bit of advice they weren't following: don't go into meltdown because most teenagers return safely.

Stella decided to follow the thread and see what other families had found useful, but soon discovered that she didn't understand what on earth anyone was on about. It was as if they were speaking entirely in acronyms.

'I don't get it. What's all this gobbledegook they're talking?'

Suze laughed. 'You have to learn to speak Internet, that's all.'

'OK, what is AIBU when it's at home?'

'It stands for Am I Being Unreasonable?'

'And YANBU? It sounds like a Nigerian dialect.'

'You Are Not Being Unreasonable.'

'Here's a good one: AYSOS.'

'Are You Stupid Or Something?'

'Gosh, that's rather rude. And what are all these DD, DS and DH's?'

'They mean Darling Daughter, Darling Son and Darling Husband.'

'And what's PITA?'

'PITA is Pain In The Ass.'

'OK, it may not be Shakespeare, but I'm beginning to get

the hang of this. My DH is a PITA: My Darling Husband is a Pain In The Ass. You can say that again! Do you know my DH went tango dancing with Fabia when everyone else was worrying themselves silly about Jesse?'

'Well, he is Matthew. What have these Internet mums got to say now you understand the lingo?'

Stella applied herself to the heartbreaking stories of runaway children, lack of police interest, and the sense of utter helplessness felt by most parents in the face of their lost teenagers. The plight of one very pretty fourteen-year-old girl was being discussed at length. Missing for three weeks with no word to her parents, she had only been found when celebrities supported a Twitter campaign to track her down.

'Do you think Duncan's offer of an appeal on their website is a good idea? I just couldn't see Jesse seeing it. Cameron's not exactly his kind of music.'

'No, but other people might see it and start talking about it.'

'Suze! I've just had an incredible idea!' Stella pushed her iPad away. 'Cameron Keene might not exactly be a buzzword among the twitterati, but *Mrs* Cameron Keene certainly is!'

'You mean Roxy?'

'Absolutely! I feel a bit bad because she's already done so much for us, but still. I'll give her a ring.'

Stella felt so much better that she was able to spend the next half-hour assessing where they were on the vintage market, how much they'd made from Fabia's barbecue and the profit from the tango lessons. 'I'd hoped Emma would get on board and help find this office space the council's so keen on, but this is hardly the moment.'

'And what's happened to Debora? Has she gone on tour with Cameron?' asked Suze.

'Duncan says she's standing by.'

'At The Glebe? Nice place to stand by.'

'She's doing a cookery course. Their chef teaches cordon bleu to the rich and famous. Using only the very best ingredients.'

'Even I could cook if I were handed a fillet steak and foie gras.'

'Suze, I'm not sure about that.'

'Neither am I! On the subject of cordon bleu, Fabia's a bit of a revelation, isn't she? Who'd have thought she could swap those foxes for a pinny? Speaking of food, let's nip into the King's Arms and grab some.'

As they approached the pub Stella and Suze congratulated themselves on one small achievement: thanks to them the pub was a great deal more inviting than it used to be. Before, it had appealed only to the desperate, the alcoholic and the raucous overspill from the betting shop who drank only pints of the cheapest lager with utter dedication until they started a fight or passed out. Today the clientele was relatively normal, even including men in suits and – more amazing still – women! Les the landlord greeted them with a delighted smile. The barbecue had proved so popular that he had added burgers and pizza, he announced, as if he were Marco Pierre White revealing a new five-star menu. 'And when somebody asked for a mojito,' he added with simple pride, 'Mick the barman knew what it was! Plus we've got a new barmaid, Nicky. A college girl. If we're getting a better class of drinker, we need a better class of bar staff; stands to reason.'

He nodded in the direction of a lively blonde. 'Nicky, come and meet these nice ladies who're trying to bring some life back to the old manor.'

'Stella,' Stella smiled, 'and this is Suze.'

'Which of you ladies has got the hot husband? The one that was dancing with the lady from Buenos Aires?'

'That'd be me,' Stella replied, startled at this new view of Matthew.

'He's really something, isn't he?'

If Stella and Suze had been sitting on bar stools, they would have fallen off.

'We were watching them the other night. Made me quite hot and bothered, it was so sexy. The lady said people just come in off the street and dance like that on the way home from work. With complete strangers. If people round here knew about that it'd put dogging out of business in no time.'

'Well, there's a thought.' Suze tried not to giggle. 'Matthew and Fabia clearing the car parks of doggers. Did you know Matthew had turned into a Latin American lounge lizard?'

'I knew he was dancing with Fabia a lot, that was what made me hopping mad when we were so worried about Jesse, but not that he was quite so talented. I'm as amazed as you are.'

'To think dull old Matthew has hidden depths.'

'Yes,' Stella mused, 'I wonder if there are any others she's going to uncover.'

'Oh come on, Matthew's not in Fabia's league. He couldn't even keep her in Arctic fox!'

'No, but Roxy says the man who gave her the fox has dumped her. Fabia knows her charms are fading and there's something reassuring about Matthew.'

'Gabriel Oak to Fabia's Bathsheba?'

They both laughed, but Stella couldn't help thinking it wasn't a bad analogy. And then she remembered she'd never liked Gabriel Oak.

As they came out into the bright sunshine, Stella almost tripped over a young man with his ancient Labrador sitting on the ground outside the exit, begging. He had made a large sign out of cardboard with one word written on it: SMILE.

There was something so vulnerable and touching about him that Stella could hardly bear it. Before Jesse disappeared she'd seen the homeless as part of the backdrop, now she noticed every fragile young girl or boy, realizing that they were somebody's missing child.

She pulled a fiver out of her purse and gave it to him.

'Thanks, missus.' He looked up at her, surprised.

'Suze, I've made up my mind,' Stella suddenly decided. 'If Stuart and Emma can't find this Kirsty, I'm going to.'

'You don't think they'd class that as interference?'

'Sod interference! Duncan and Cameron are in Brighton next week. I'll pretend I'm just going to watch the show. I can't just sit here doing nothing.'

'Speaking of shows, what's happening with this fundraiser in your garden?'

Stella looked stricken. 'With all this stuff about Jesse I hadn't really given it any thought.'

'Why don't you delegate it to Matthew? Give him something else to think about apart from the Argentinian tango queen. Unless you want him to help with Jesse?'

'He's worse than Stuart. Stuart's just busy, Matthew actually thinks Jesse is hopeless. Apparently, it's all his parents' fault for giving him a girl's name. Do you know, he once asked me if I thought Jesse was gay?'

'Well, Emma may call Dora a little slag but at least she's put everyone right there.'

They were about to get back into the car when they both stopped and stared at each other. The brown paper lining the window of Fabia's Retro Emporium had come down, revealing an amazing interior.

In the window was a display unit made up of about twenty irregularly sized wooden boxes, all painted a different colour; orange, jade, bright blue, yellow and red. Inside each box was a different item – an art deco cake stand, a pair of leopard-skin stilettoes, a silver teapot, a vase, a jewellery box and 1940s hat on a bronze wig stand. Through the gaps in the boxes customers could glimpse the rows of alluring clothes: Twenties beaded jackets, floor-length satin gowns, kimonos and tea dresses, silk nighties and feathered boleros. Along another wall exotic curtains were displayed in velvet and chenille, lace and tempting Indian fabrics.

'Bloody hell!' Suze said, amazed. 'You have to hand it to her. This on top of all the other stuff she's doing. It's like walking back into Carnaby Street or Kensington Market! Where do you think she got all this stuff?'

'From her own wardrobe, according to Debora. If she's really flat broke, that'd be one way of making money.'

They peered in to see if anyone was inside but the shop was obviously empty.

'All that trouble to make it look inviting and then it isn't even open!' Suze complained. 'That's one way to piss off your customers. I loathe shops that say, "Back in five minutes" and still aren't back in half an hour.'

'I'm not sure it's officially trading yet.'

'One good thing.' Suze looked at her friend sneakily. 'At least once it opens she'll be too busy to tango with Matthew.'

'I wouldn't be too sure. I bet this was what he was helping her with. He's quite handy with a hammer.'

When Stella got home Matthew was out again, so she couldn't find out or approach him about organizing the concert. She went upstairs to change. The usual wet towels decorated the floor of the bathroom. Stella bent to pick them up and decided, no, why the hell should she?

She had just put on a skirt and clean top when she heard the front door open. Matthew came in and stopped to see what post was on the hall table. He was humming 'Hernando's Hideaway', and what struck Stella was how happy he sounded.

Stella stood at the top of the stairs listening. There was, she had to admit, something indefinably different about Matthew. He seemed younger somehow, jauntier, less grouchy.

Suddenly Stella found she wanted to cry. As cranky and conservative Matthew grew younger before her eyes, she was feeling older. What was the matter with her, for heaven's sake? If Matthew and the police thought Jesse would walk back in, why didn't she?

Not suspecting she was watching, Matthew did a funny little side step as if he were on the dance floor, and smiled to himself.

Stella held tightly onto the banister. Her anxiety wasn't just about Jesse. It was about her and Matthew as well. The truth was unavoidable. Matthew was falling for Fabia. And Stella had a question to face that was much harder than she had ever imagined: did she want to fight for him or stand back and let him go? Stella was shocked to find that she wasn't sure.

The sound of a text beeping on her phone made her jump. A message from Duncan telling her to look at their website.

It was a welcome distraction from facing Matthew and his new-found happiness. She searched Cameron Keene's website for the details of his tour. At the end there was a mysterious message. *Jesse: get in touch or come and see the show – The Hangman's Beautiful Daughter awaits you.*

What on earth could it mean? To Stella it even sounded

faintly sinister and cultish. She was about to contact Emma and see if she understood it any better when the doorbell rang.

She heard Matthew answer it then shout up to her, 'Stella, someone to see you!'

To her amazement it was Dora. 'I hope you don't mind me coming round like this. I didn't dare go to Jesse's parents. I felt I'd caused enough trouble already.'

'Have you heard from Jesse?' Stella asked hopefully.

'No, sorry. But I have found the address for Kirsty Weatherall. Someone in our class had it.'

Stella could have kissed her. 'Thanks, Dora, I really appreciate it.'

The girl hesitated. 'I really like Jesse, you know. You will let me know when you find him?'

'Of course. Thank you, Dora. It's a real help.'

Stella opened the front door to let her out. Dora hung back as if there were something more she wanted to say.

'He's really fond of you too,' Stella added gently.

'I have heard from him!' she blurted suddenly. 'He *is* in Brighton. Only he told me not to tell anyone!'

'Do you know where he's staying?'

'He didn't say anything else. I don't know if he wants to be found. He's pretty angry with his mum.'

'Thanks so much, Dora. We just want to make sure he's all right.'

Dora nodded and turned towards the door.

This time it was Stella's turn to hesitate. 'By the way,' she said, getting out her iPad, 'do you have any idea what this means? A friend put it on Cameron Keene's tour website.'

Dora smiled, displaying perfect teeth. She read the cryptic words out loud. '"The Hangman's Beautiful Daughter awaits you." *The Hangman's Beautiful Daughter* is an album by The

Incredible String Band. Clever of your friend to think of it. He obviously understands Jesse a lot better than his mum and dad.'

She saw the girl out, feeling as if a huge stone had been lifted from her chest. Her beloved grandson was only forty miles away in Brighton.

'What was that all about?' Matthew asked.

Stella debated whether to tell him that Dora had heard from Jesse and decided to wait. 'She's found an address for Jesse's friend who moved to Brighton.'

'Does she know why he ran away?'

'She said he was very angry with Emma.'

'I'm not surprised. If I thought my mother was having an affair with a tech millionaire I'd be angry too.'

The thought of Matthew's mother, aged ninety and in a care home, having a liaison with anyone was so funny they both laughed.

'We may laugh but Ma told me they have a big problem with Alzheimer's,' Matthew announced, suddenly serious. 'Apparently, people keep forgetting they're married and start falling for someone else. It's really sad.'

'I can imagine it would be.' This was the moment when she could say, 'So are you having an affair with Fabia?'

Instead she asked if he could take on organizing the Rock for Regeneration concert.

The old Matthew would have said, 'Bloody typical of you, Stella, you never do what you've promised.' The new Matthew smiled and said, 'Yes, why not, it sounds rather a laugh.'

Then she rang Emma. To her huge disappointment there was no reply.

She knew how worried they must be so she left a message that Dora had heard from Jesse, that he was indeed in Brighton and that Dora had also found the address for Kirsty. All in all,

Stella thought, Dora was far from a slag. In fact, they all ought to be grateful to her.

Although she might appreciate the improvement in his mood, there were other aspects of Matthew's transformation from grouch to gigolo that were beginning to infuriate Stella.

'He's taken to shaving every morning!' she told Debora as they lunched next day at The Glebe to try out the products of Debora's cookery course. 'And leaving all the hair in the sink for me. And he's suddenly obsessed with looking old. "I look like a bloody judge!" he announced yesterday. Debora, this pâté is amazing!'

'Thank you.' Debora smiled delightedly. 'I totally understand how you feel about all this crap. Men are so transparent. Of course, with Cameron, I worried more if he was sober, because if he was sober it meant he was *really* misbehaving. When he was drunk he couldn't get it up anyway, so that was OK, though some of these girls did their best, I can tell you. They probably got repetitive strain injury just trying. The pâté *is* good, isn't it?'

Stella giggled; the trials and tribulations of being married to a rock god rather put her own into perspective. She tried to resist it but found herself asking what Debora thought about Amber O'Riordan.

A cloud appeared on Debora's calm face. 'I'm not sure. I mean, I'm happy for him in one way. He's a good guy, he loved Connie and he was actually faithful to her. They weren't like anyone else. They were like lovers! Always catching each other's eye and smiling. Connie liked Amber. She said her honesty reminded her of Tracey Emin, but Amber hasn't got a tenth of Tracey Emin's charm. She's about as subtle as a

Russian Internet bride. I know it's kind of ridiculous, but I mind on behalf of all women!'

'Do you think he wants to have children?'

'When he already has Cameron, you mean? Christ, I hope not. I loathe those men who boast about being fathers at his age. They're all over the music business, men with no hair and great fat paunches, with wives that look younger than their children.'

Stella found, for some reason, that she didn't want to think about Duncan and Amber having a baby. 'And yet you had to cope with Hallelujah and Roxy. It sounded really tough to me.'

'Yes, but Cameron gets what he deserves. Duncan's different. Anyway,' Debora grinned, 'I don't think Roxy counts. It was all Fabia's doing. Roxy knew it was a mistake from the start.'

'Why aren't they divorced, then?'

'The situation must suit them, I guess, weird though it sounds.'

It was time, Stella realized reluctantly, that she gave her own marriage some serious thought.

She looked around the restaurant. Informality was not the order of the day at The Glebe. Each table boasted a crisp white tablecloth, pink linen napkins, a bunch of fresh roses which were changed every day, polished silver and a plethora of shining glasses. Even the set lunch was fifty pounds, so God alone knew what à la carte would come to.

A new guest arrived in the room. She was a woman about Stella's age. She was blonde and attractive in a motherly sort of way, her clothes comfortable rather than smart.

'Table for one, madame?' Was it Stella's imagination or was there a slightly dismissive edge to the maître d's tone?

The woman was led not to a discreet table in the corner

which she might actually have preferred, but to one where she was highly visible to anyone coming in or out of the restaurant.

With a display worthy of a music-hall conjuror, the waiter removed the place setting opposite her which, conversely, had the effect of drawing attention to her single state.

The new arrival scanned the menu and placed her order.

'Will you have wine, madame?'

Her head went up. 'Yes, I will, thank you. I'll have half a bottle of white.'

'The house white?' the waiter enquired, face deadpan.

'No, I'll see the wine list.' After she'd ordered, the woman looked around. Phones, those saviours of the uncomfortable social situation, were banned and she hadn't thought to bring a book.

Stella hoped to catch her eye and give her a smile of solidarity, but then felt embarrassed at the intrusion and looked away, as you did with someone in a wheelchair, not out of rudeness but because you didn't know how to respond.

The woman noted her reaction and raised her chin. She stared at Stella combatively. 'Because I am a woman alone you are treating me with pity. How dare you?' her look said. And Stella almost died of embarrassment because it was true. That was exactly what she had done. And worse, it was because Stella was thinking, what if soon I am that woman alone?

'Stella. Stella! Are you all right? This is the pièce de résistance. Pig's cheek stuffed with apple. I always thought this rather reminded me of Cameron. What do you think?'

Grateful for wonderful Debora, she turned to the amazing dish on her plate meaning to give a normal, pleasant smile to the woman on the way out, but when she next looked up the unknown guest had gone.

*

When she got home the house was still empty. Still no word from Emma. Stella decided to go down to her studio in the garden and finish the oil painting of a rather sweet schnauzer which was way overdue. It was a glorious afternoon with the sun filtering in through the open door. She looked round at the row of photographs she'd taken of all the work she'd done in the last year. They were lively and likeable, and showed a certain talent, she knew. What made the difference between someone like her and a painter the art world valued and lionized?

She flipped open her iPad and searched for Amber O'Riordan.

The images that came up were startling. The first was of a woman's torso painted in bright blue as if it were in 3D. At first glance the blue woman seemed to be wearing a pink bikini, but on closer inspection it became clear that the pink top was *inside* her body, formed by the flower-like arrangement of her milk glands and the bikini bottom, her uterus and ovaries. The shocking effect was somewhere between medical illustration and pop-art porn. The painting even had a catchy title: *Airbrush this, Mr Hefner*.

The next painting was simply a vast uterus with the two ovaries attached, forming the shape of a giant sheep's skull. Again the clever slogan: *One ovary or two?*

But the one that Stella found really disturbing was the six-foot-large depiction of uterine cancer. Again the ovaries and uterus were in 3D, and all around were what appeared to be beautiful red flowers but were actually the invading cancer cells. This time the question was: *Am I going to get better, doctor?*

Studying it, Stella felt slightly sick. Amber O'Riordan had certainly done what the art world wanted: created work that was highly original and bore her individual signature. For an artist, as Damien Hirst attested, that was the way to get rich and famous.

But there was also something harsh and exploitative in the paintings, as if Amber had discovered this admittedly clever technique, but had no real feeling for the subjects. These weren't real women, but animated illustrations. Clearly Amber had not had close friends or loved ones who had actually asked those questions, dreading to hear the answer, knowing that their futures depended on it.

They made Stella think not of the powerful questioning of the real artist but more of the sensationalism of those Allen Jones tables made out of women's submissively kneeling bodies.

Was she just experiencing the jealousy of the older woman for the young? She turned to her wall of pets. 'OK, guys,' she grinned, 'we're not going to earn a million but maybe we're not doing such a bad job after all! At least we make your owners feel a little bit happier.'

She had a feeling that Amber O'Riordan would not appreciate the argument.

She sat for a moment, Jesse intruding into her thoughts, and tried her daughter again. This time she got through.

'Mum, this is fantastic! I was just about to ring you. I can't tell you how relieved I am. At least we know he's safe and we've got something to go on. Though she could have told us when we saw her, little bitch.'

'I think we should be grateful to her that she's told us at all. Jesse didn't want her to so it was obviously hard for her to do it.'

For once Emma seemed thoughtful. 'I'll tell Stuart as soon as he's back and we'll decide what to do.'

Stella was in no doubt about what she intended to do herself.

She sent a message to Duncan thanking him for the Hangman's Daughter message and saying that now she understood it, she thought it was a great idea.

The answer came back surprisingly quickly. 'Come to Brighton and we'll all pitch in. Tour almost over now and no major mishaps. PS. Maybe I shouldn't have said that. Duncan.'

She heard Matthew's car come to a crunching stop on the gravel outside and realized that rather than rushing out to say hello, she preferred the solitude of her studio. The realization hit her with a shock. How much of their life did they really share any more? She couldn't say that he didn't have the power to ever surprise her because he *had* surprised her in the last few weeks, but it had been Fabia, not she, who had brought the transformation about. Trying to recapture a sense of normality, Stella made herself get up and cross the garden, think about supper and pick up the pieces of everyday life.

Matthew was in the kitchen mixing himself a G and T. 'Do you want one as well?' he asked her. 'I'm feeling rather pleased with myself.'

'What've you been up to?'

'Sorting out the concert. The tickets are all printed. Marquee booked for the band. The Glebe have agreed to do some food. The wine's organized. Cloister Wines are offering free fizz if they can be official sponsors.'

'For a concert in our garden? That's amazing!' Stella was genuinely impressed.

'Fabia gave me a hand. She's brilliant at this sort of thing.'

'I would have thought she'd be too busy with the shop she got for zero rent thanks to our campaign.' Stella couldn't keep a slight edge of peevishness from her voice. This sudden emergence of Fabia the charity benefactor as well as everything else was too much to bear.

'She's been incredibly generous with her time.'

This was true but Stella was beginning to feel that if she fell under a bus Fabia would move in before they'd even called an ambulance.

'We're going to start looking for auction prizes tomorrow. That's how you really make money at these things. Fabia's been to loads of them.'

'My, you have been busy.'

'Stella,' it was Matthew's turn to be peevish, 'I'm only doing what you asked me to do.'

'I know,' Stella conceded, realizing she was being a bitch. 'I'm really impressed. It's just with this business over Jesse I can't think straight.'

Matthew shook his head. It was obvious it hadn't even occurred to him to worry about his grandson. Was this just being a man, Stella wondered, or being Matthew?

'I've decided that if he isn't back I'm going to Brighton to look for him,' Stella announced.

'Stella, I realize you're worried but it really isn't anything to do with you.'

'Of course it's to do with me! He's my grandson!' Stella replied angrily, convinced this was another of Matthew's emotionally autistic responses.

'Imagine if my mother had suddenly interfered over Emma. How would you have taken that?'

This was a sore point, as Matthew well knew. When she was younger, his mother Marjorie had infuriated Stella with her continual criticisms of their parenting techniques. 'That child . . .' was a common preface to the usual carping comment about Emma's unusual table manners, punctuality and general appearance.

'But Emma didn't run away!' Stella protested.

'And if she had? And Ma had steamed down to Brighton to look for her?'

This was such a ludicrous prospect that Stella almost laughed. Marjorie rarely put herself out for anyone and now she was too old anyway. And yet how would Stella have felt if she had done so?

'You're the first to point out that Emma and Stuart's marriage is a bit shaky,' Matthew persisted. 'If you just blunder in it will look as though you think they don't care. Can't you see it could make things worse between them?'

Although she didn't want to, Stella could see his point of view. 'But Emma should be going herself!'

'Then why isn't she?'

'I don't know. She loves Jesse. Maybe it's something to do with Hal. He could be telling her it'll all be okay.'

'What does Stuart think? He's a sensible chap.'

'He thinks they should see what the police do.'

'Maybe you haven't got the monopoly on caring. Had you thought of that?'

Stella shut her eyes, suddenly close to tears, which was ridiculous since she never cried. It was the inaction she couldn't bear, while Jesse could be out there, lost, cold and in danger. Why did she feel as though she was the only one who could see it?

'The only way you can possibly go is if Emma agrees. Besides, what about the concert? Are you just going to leave all that to Fabia and me?'

Stella could see the obvious pitfalls in that, but what should she do? Stay here and keep an eye on Matthew, or try and find Jesse?

'You seem to have it well in hand. You might ask Suze to help as well.'

'So she can keep an eye on me?'

'Does she need to?'

Matthew turned round, his face unusually serious. 'Come on, Stella, you know what's going on. I haven't tried to hide it. I look forward to getting up in the morning. I've started to play the sax again. Fabia said I should. I know we probably look odd – she's so glamorous and I'm . . . well, I'm me, but we have a surprising amount in common. I feel energetic. Excited. And I tell you what . . .'

Stella steeled herself. He was going to ask for a divorce.

'. . . we're going to open a chain of dancing clubs – not just tango but salsa, rumba, merengue!'

If it hadn't been so desperately sad, Stella might have smiled. It was so like Matthew to take passion and make it practical.

Fourteen

As Stella drove through Camley town centre she remembered that she needed more oil paints to finish her latest portrait, and there was a parking space outside the art shop she liked to patronize. They were incredibly helpful and it was having a hard job surviving the Internet. She found a parking place near the shop and nipped into it with neatness and precision. Matthew liked to say that she was a terrible driver, but, left to her own devices, she was remarkably efficient.

The usually bustling town centre was quiet since all the mums had gone off to the school gates and it was too early for the after-work scurrying for buses and trains.

Stella hummed as she walked past the Caffè Nero next to the art shop, then stopped, as if she had been Lot's wife turned into a pillar of salt. Seated in two leather chairs, right in the window at the front, was Emma. She was in tears and, next to her, Hal was holding her hand tenderly and mopping her face with his Caffè Nero napkin. Stella didn't think twice about what she did next. She walked straight in.

'Emma, could you come outside a moment,' she said, trying to keep her temper.

Hal stood up protectively. 'I'm not sure this is your business, Mrs Ainsworth.'

On another occasion Stella might have been impressed by his desire to protect her daughter, however misconceived, but not today. 'If you don't mind, Hal, this is nothing to do with you. It's up to Emma if she chooses to throw her marriage away. What I care about at this moment is my missing grandson and why no one has gone to look for him.'

By now all the other customers were staring at them, some from behind the coffee menu, others openly.

Stella walked out of the cafe and waited for her daughter. 'Emma . . . darling . . . I know you're upset, but crying on Hal's shoulder isn't going to help find Jesse, so why don't we go to Brighton and look for this girl Kirsty?'

Emma burst into tears. 'Stuart still thinks it's all my fault!' she announced in the tones of an operatic heroine. 'He says Jesse's going to miss his exams and screw up his future and it's all because of me!'

Much as she liked her son-in-law and had misgivings about Emma's behaviour she felt Stuart wasn't handling the situation very well. Accusing Emma like this was simply driving her towards Hal. Besides, missing exams was hardly the point.

'I'm sure he doesn't mean it,' she soothed diplomatically. 'He's probably feeling angry and hurt and he's lashing out at you when he should be thinking about how to find Jesse. This is your son who's run away, the baby you cradled in your arms! I can remember how much you longed for him. How you said he'd changed your life completely.' She looked at her daughter evenly. 'You said it was like falling in love.'

Emma reached out a hand to her mother.

'Well, that's how I feel about Jesse too,' Stella said quietly. 'And Izzy and Ruby. I love them for themselves, but I also love them because they're *your* children. It's as though the love has been doubled. So why don't we go and look for him together?'

'All right,' Emma answered, still wavering. 'As long as Stuart will look after Izzy and Rube. I'll come.'

'Good. I'll find somewhere for us to stay.'

Stella walked away from the cafe feeling shocked at herself. She had discovered that as well as loving her daughter, she could quite seriously disapprove of her.

The staff in the art shop were as helpful as they always were. Stella stocked up on both acrylic and oil paints, some white spirit, a new rubber and three pre-stretched canvases for the portraits she would need to complete in the coming weeks.

When she got back to the car the window of Caffè Nero was empty.

The bright sunlight bounced off all the hard surfaces in the street, so strong that shoppers dashed from shade to shade. One old lady was using her black umbrella as a sunshade. In front of her a toddler in a buggy was holding an ice cream that melted in the heat and slid to the ground. His tragic expression would usually have made her smile.

But not today. Today she couldn't help wondering whose marriage was going to survive, her own or her daughter's? And then, another painful question, had she been right to interfere? If it hadn't been for Jesse, she probably would have walked past and left Emma to sort out her own life.

She drove home, trying to stop these thoughts whirring uselessly in her head and found herself stuck in traffic at road-works on the outskirts of Camley. By the side of the road, on some wasteland running down to the canal, stood a stack of about ten containers, faded and peeling, the kind you usually saw loaded into ships. The way they were piled on top of each other, balanced like a child's bricks, so resembled the structure

Fabia had erected in her shop window that they caught her attention. Next to them was a sign that they were offered for purchase or rental. She wondered how much of a market there would be in second-hand sea containers?

Just as the lights changed the thought came back to her of that young girl who had set up her office in a storage unit because it was the only cheap place she could find. It hadn't been that long ago but somehow it seemed like years. And then she had a flash of excitement. Was there any way they could possibly be converted into cheap offices?

She stopped, got out her phone and began to search for 'Containers as offices'. To her amazement there were clearly a number of container communities in and around London. One – calling itself The Box – was made of units just like these, all painted in different bright colours and sited on a canal in East London not unlike this one. It was full of young techie tenants who praised the sense of community it gave them – and especially the short-term leases which enabled them to start their own businesses.

Camley, of course, didn't have the hip edge of East London, but the suburbs also cried out for cheap office space. The vast prices of London property meant that young people were living further and further from the centre and the cost of travel was so prohibitive they were desperate for local workplaces.

Stella pulled back into the traffic and sped off, grateful to have something else to think about, and full of a sense of challenge. She would have to find out the practicalities and discover how much was needed to convert containers. But she wasn't an artist for nothing and was confident she could create a convincing mock-up to put to the council. She might even head over to The Box before she went to Brighton and have a look. Doing something constructive would take her mind off the fact that so much of the rest of her life seemed to be falling apart.

When she got home, full of plans, it was to find the house bursting with activity. Matthew had taken her at her word and got Suze involved, which was a relief as it meant she would not only know what Matthew and Fabia were up to, but also what was being planned for the concert in her own garden. Typical of Matthew; having said his piece, he would ignore the subject of their marriage from now on.

'Oh, and we had another thought,' Fabia added. Was that a malicious gleam in her eye as she said this? 'We might ask Duncan's new friend Amber to give us one of her paintings for the auction. What do you reckon about that?'

'Good luck to you.' Why should Fabia think she would mind about that? 'Though I'm not sure Camley's ready for Amber O'Riordan. People around here prefer art that goes with their wallpaper.'

Even Bernie had been drafted in to organize the teams of tent erecters, chair providers and clearer-uppers while Roxy had been as good as her word. There she was, her long legs draped over a chair, tweeting away at this very instant.

A loud argument broke out between Matthew, who supported practical plastic, and Fabia, who insisted on glass champagne flutes for the free fizz. 'I will resign now this minute,' Fabia announced dramatically, 'unless we give out proper glasses. To do anything else would be an insult!'

'I'm with Fabia on this one,' Suze seconded. 'Divine decadence, darling. Champagne has to be provided in a glass.'

All that was left for Stella was to make them all tea and consider sneaking off to her garden studio to think about the down-to-earth topic of converting containers. But first she turned to Roxy. 'Could I ask you one really huge favour?'

Roxy looked up, intrigued.

'Help us find our grandson? I've been reading up about this lovely young girl who disappeared in South London. She was only found thanks to celebrities tweeting about her. I wonder if maybe you could do the same with Jesse?'

'Sure,' Roxy replied, all sympathy. 'I'm so sorry he's gone off. I really like Jesse. He's so kind to his little sister.' Again Stella detected that wistful tone of the only child dragged from place to place. 'Can you get me a photo? Plus a paragraph about him – what was . . .' her pretty face flushed at her tactless slip-up – '*is* he like. Maybe I'll make it funny. Sort of "Do you remember fighting with your parents and saying you'd walk out? Jesse actually did it." It'll get retweeted more if it's entertaining. And maybe he won't be so cross with you when you find him.'

Stella tried to smile at Roxy's light-hearted certainty. But she had picked up that tell-tale slip. She couldn't let herself think like that, but her relief was intense that she was actually *doing* something to find him, even if he and his parents would resent her for it.

She found a photo for Roxy then left them to it and went to her studio to look up B & Bs in Brighton, which turned out to be remarkably expensive. Brighton's image as the dirty weekend capital of England seemed to have morphed into something altogether classier and pricier. The average room per night seemed a lot more than she'd hoped to pay. She'd have to paint a lot of pets to pay for a week in Brighton.

Eventually, she found a last-minute hotel room in a Regency square near the seafront for a remarkably reasonable price. It offered only a double bed, which Emma would moan about sharing but would have to put up with, tea-making facilities and a shared rather than an en suite bathroom. It had been longer than she could remember since she'd had to walk down a corridor to share a bathroom, but for that price she would be prepared to share a toothbrush too. The large message on the hotel's website made her laugh: THE HOTEL DOES NOT ACCEPT STAG OR HEN PARTIES. She could well imagine the problems which sharing a bathroom with a stag or hen would throw up.

She was just about to book when she stopped for a moment. Was she certifiably insane to throw Matthew and Fabia together, after what he'd told her, and then disappear for a week? She could already hardly recognize the beaming, clean-shaven, well-dressed person masquerading as her husband since Fabia had come on the scene.

But, as Duncan had suggested, if she couldn't trust her husband after all these years, what was their marriage worth anyway?

She pressed the button to book the room. There, it was done.

An irritating advert jumped up in the margin. Ten Things to Do in Brighton. After a visit to the pier, a stroll round the Lanes, admiring the madness of the Brighton Pavilion, and a swim in the English Channel, the next suggestion was to drop in to 'the most talked-about art show of the decade'. Beside the ad popped up another of Amber's horrible brightly coloured wombs. This one featured both the uterus and ovaries illustrated in fluorescent Mediterranean blue. Underneath was the seriously stupid statement: *Blue is the colour of Heaven.*

Stella blitzed it with her mouse. 'Not if you're in it, Amber!'

She heard Matthew shouting to her and emerged gratefully from Amber's blue womb.

Matthew was standing at the garden door, his arm round their granddaughter.

'Izzy, darling, what a lovely surprise,' Stella greeted her, feeling full of misgiving. Izzy must have walked here on her own. It was only about twenty minutes but she wouldn't have done it unless something was seriously up.

She took in Izzy's tearstained face and held her firmly by the hand. 'Come on, let's go inside.' Thankfully Fabia and Roxy had retreated to the expensive luxury of The Glebe, presumably funded by Cameron.

Only Suze remained and she was tactful enough to remember a sudden engagement.

Stella took Izzy to the sofa and pulled her down next to her into its comforting softness. 'OK, what's been happening?'

'It's Mum and Dad. They're shouting at each other all the time, and, Gran, I so miss Jesse. When they shouted before he used to just wink at me and we'd go off and watch *EastEnders*. It always made it seem all right because the people on the telly were shouting even more than Mum and Dad.' She started to cry again. 'When's he coming back, Gran?'

'As a matter of fact,' Stella held her close, 'your Mum and I are going to Brighton to look for him. We think he may have gone to find his friend Kirsty.'

'The policeman came round yesterday and Dad shouted at him too, because they don't seem to have done anything. And he said to Dad that maybe they should be asking themselves why Jesse left, and that made Dad tell Mum it was all her fault because of that stupid handbag.'

'Everyone's very overwrought at the moment. It'll help once we really start looking for him. You do know the police think Jesse's probably fine? He's not a child. And between you and me, I think Jesse's pretty sensible. He's not the kind of boy who'd take drugs or go wild.'

'Could we say a prayer for him, Gran, like we do in Assembly for the children who've got Aids in Africa?'

Stella nodded, a little startled. She wasn't a great one for prayer. 'Why don't you make it up and we'll both say it together?'

'Dear Higher Being – we say that because there're kids at my school who believe in lots of different gods – could you make sure my brother Jesse is safe and sound and that he comes home soon and tell him that I really, really miss him and I won't complain about him borrowing my scooter any more even though he looks stupid on it? Amen.'

'Amen,' endorsed Stella, giving her another hug.

'You will find him, won't you, Gran, and bring him home again?'

Stella hesitated, torn by the desperate desire to reassure, but equally scared of making empty promises. 'I promise you this: I'll do my damnedest!'

'Thanks, Gran,' Izzy offered a small smile, 'you actually sounded quite fierce. Like someone in *Game of Thrones*.'

'I assure you,' Stella hugged her granddaughter, '*Game of Thrones* hasn't got anything on me. Now, since it's a school night, I think we'd better ring your mum and dad and get them to come and take you home.'

'It's OK,' Izzy shook her head, 'I've got my scooter with me. They think I'm out with Freya and Bianca. They'll only make a huge fuss if you say I've come here.'

Stella waved her goodbye. 'Take care now, remember to stop at all the roads!' She turned away, unbearably saddened that at eleven Izzy had already learned how to negotiate the complicated world of adult relationships.

'Are you sure you're all right, going to Brighton on your own?' Matthew asked her as she packed a small case. 'Do you think you'll manage? Do you need me to come with you?'

He made it sound as if she were travelling to the Hindu

Kush rather than forty miles away. Poor Matthew, even when he meant well it came out as patronizing.

'I won't be on my own. I'll have Emma.' Stella realized that no, she definitely didn't want him to come. He would only get diverted by something completely different – some Morris-y antique he found in the Lanes, for example – and be of no use whatsoever. Stella repressed the thought that this wasn't really it, that she actually wanted to be alone, and what this might mean. She suspected it wasn't entirely to do with Jesse.

'No, we need someone to keep the home fires burning. Be a refuge in case things get even worse between Emma and Stuart and Izzy needs us. She's going to their neighbour and Ruby will have her childminder but she could still turn up here. Who knows, Jesse might even turn up here. Besides, your hands seem to be full.'

He looked up at her quickly, suspecting sarcasm. He knew she was no fool, even if he occasionally treated her like one. 'Well, there is a lot to do for the concert,' he conceded. 'How many shows have they got in Brighton?'

'Two, I think. The last one's on Friday.'

'And you're planning to stay down for it?'

'No idea. The main thing is to find Jesse and try and get him to come home.'

He took her hand briefly. 'You're a good grandmother.'

She squeezed his back. 'Maybe a better grandmother than mother. I'm not sure I did such a good job on Emma.'

'Em's all right. She just needs to learn a few lessons. Maybe all this will help her.'

Stella thought of Emma and Hal clinging on to each other in the coffee shop. 'I bloody well hope so.'

*

272

The next morning Stella set out for Brighton, making a giant detour to look at containers. She had printed out all the information she could find and hoped it would be worth it. Emma was coming later.

The Box was hard to miss. It stood out like a set of child's bricks piled on the edge of the Regent's Canal, a stone's throw from the hip Broadway Market. Forty units were ranged in two tiers with a wooden deck in front overlooking the canal. The back of each unit was a vast panel of glass and the front painted in bright pinks, oranges, yellows and greens more reminiscent of beach huts than office space. A nice young thing called Eleanor, who only seemed to be a year or two older than Jesse, showed her around.

'The whole point of The Box,' Eleanor enthused, 'is cheapness and community. Renting a desk is three hundred pounds a month and you can rent one for as short a time as you want, so you can start your own business here with no vast overheads.'

'Are most people starting up on their own?' Stella asked, amazed at their nerve. She would never have dared start a business at their age. She got out her phone. 'Would you mind if I recorded our conversation so I can include it in the package I give our local council?'

Eleanor giggled. 'Lady Gaga, eat your heart out, here comes Eleanor Douglas! Yeah, go for it!'

'So how is it different working here from the average office, apart from being cheap?'

'The people! If you think about it, you spend longer at work than at home, so you ought to enjoy it. We do yoga at lunchtime and have talks from various bods about business development and exciting shit like that. Ooh, should I not say that?' She put her hand in front of her mouth, remembering she was being interviewed.

'I think council officials can cope with the odd swear word. They probably find themselves sworn at quite a lot, poor things.'

'OK, there's a cafe – actually, it's a business, but we all use it too.' She pointed to one of the units which had tables and chairs dotted all around on the deck in front of it and pots of geraniums in the same shade of bright fuchsia as the paintwork. It looked very enticing.

Stella thought about the girl in the storage unit and how much she'd enjoy being here instead of that horrid scary place she was using.

'We even have a communal Nutribullet!' enthused Eleanor.

'That sounds ominous. What on earth's a Nutribullet?'

'It makes the best smoothies on the planet. My favourite's kale and spinach.'

'Right.' Stella nodded doubtfully.

'But the best thing of all is these units were cheap to build. And quick! They were all made off-site and swung into place on a giant crane. It only took a few days.'

Stella's phone rang, breaking into the conversation. To her surprise, it was Duncan. 'Sorry, Duncan, I have to be quick. I'm in a wonderful office made out of shipping containers called The Box. Why are you laughing?'

Duncan was suddenly in fits on the other end of the phone. 'Only in England! Do you know what a box means in the US?'

'No idea.'

'Only a woman's vagina!'

'Duncan!' Stella corrected, almost getting the giggles as well. 'I think maybe you've been seeing too much of Amber.'

Duncan pulled himself together. 'Anyway, I just phoned to tell you. The Tour has landed. Without drunken brawls, seductions of minors or cars driven into swimming pools. So far. Any news of Jesse?'

'He contacted his girlfriend. He is in Brighton. Roxy's doing an appeal and I'm on my way down to look for him.'

'Where are you staying? We're at The Old Galleon. Right on the front. It's not five-star, but we've got the whole hotel. Lessens Cameron's chances of giving offence. Come and find us whenever you want.'

'I will.'

'Stella? Don't worry too much. We'll all look for him. You're not on your own.'

Why she should believe that an ageing rock star and his exceptionally rich manager were likely to spend their time combing the streets of Brighton to find a lost boy, she had no idea. But she felt comforted all the same.

She said goodbye to Eleanor.

The journey to Brighton took less than an hour, yet as soon as Stella got off the train she felt as if she were hundreds of miles away. The station was filled with light and the blue-painted steel arches above the concourse had a jaunty seaside air, even though it was a ten minute walk from the beach. She bought herself a Millie's cookie and laughed as the seagulls attempted to share it with her, swooping down mischievously from their vantage point in the sky. She decided to walk to her hotel, breathing in the salt air mixed with traffic fumes as she went.

At last she could really look for Jesse. Emma was due to arrive in Brighton in the evening and Stella had promised to pick her up from the station in a taxi so that they could go straight to Kirsty's house and start their enquiries.

For now she had the rest of the day to check in and have a look around for herself.

The hotel was perfectly nice, clean and in a good position and had none of the over-familiar, nylon-sheet-and-cruets atmosphere of an old-fashioned seaside B & B. Fortunately, she reminded herself, Brighton had always had an attitude that was anything but provincial. No wonder it was called London-by-the-Sea.

When she opened the door of her room, she didn't know whether to laugh or cry. It would have been small even for a cabin, with just enough room between the bed and the wall to fit in the smallest of beside tables. The rest of the room was taken up by an enormous dark wood wardrobe of the kind that no one had wanted since the IKEA revolution and which you could probably pick up in one of Brighton's countless antique shops for a fiver. Inside were five or six bent coat hangers which no doubt had come with the dry cleaning of previous occupants. Still, the duvet cover and valance were at least in plain white cotton, so that was a start.

God knows what Emma would say but this was what you got for the money she could afford – well, actually, which she couldn't afford, but which she was prepared to shell out in an emergency like this.

Obviously, there was no sea view but, Stella found, if you opened the window, you could climb out onto the crenellated flat roof of a big bay window – health and safety must have missed barring it – and there, in the distance, was the English Channel.

She unpacked her toothbrush and hung up the few clothes she'd brought before deciding to make a start. A map would help. She asked for one at the desk and was handed a version featuring all the interesting landmarks from the Brighton Dome, where Cameron would be performing, to the Prince Regent Swimming Complex (poor Prince Regent, with his vast bulk, he probably couldn't get into the water at all), to such useful venues as the Brighton Buddhist Centre, and the Laser-Zone. Stella sat down on the bed overwhelmed by the memory of Jesse, aged twelve, having his birthday party at one of these places and being disqualified for running too fast. No appeals that he was the birthday boy could overrule the decision. Jesse had almost cried and Stella had wanted to kill the stupid jobsworth who had ruined his day. Dear, sweet, thin-skinned Jesse! If only they could find him and bring him home!

Armed with the map, Stella set out into the bright afternoon towards Brighton's famous seafront. Even though it was a weekday and not even the official holiday period there were crowds everywhere and a permanently festive feeling in the air. People smiled and walked slowly, enjoying the sunshine. Brighton had always been a special place, unconventional and exuberant, as colourful and eccentric as a pantomime dame, but with a sprinkling of sophistication.

There were so many foreign students clogging the pavements, chattering in German, French, Spanish and Swedish that Stella decided every school in Europe must surely be empty. There were nearly as many of them as the famous starlings she had heard about that gathered in their thousands to roost on the West Pier at dusk.

She wandered past the gracious but slightly peeling hotels lining the promenade down onto the lower path which bordered the beach. Here there were rows of fishing boats, a carousel with small children squealing happily as they rode the brightly painted horses, and rows of deckchairs occupied by lots of happy sun worshippers. And everywhere the atmospheric cry of seagulls.

She stopped to look at the sandwich board advertising a 'clairvoyant to the stars' with black-and-white pictures of faded luminaries from Frankie Vaughan to Joan Collins. If she hadn't been such a sceptic she might have paid for a consultation to see if the gypsy could throw any light on where to look for Jesse.

Her heart thudded. Crouched on some kind of drain cover, right in the middle of the beach, his hoodie pulled up so he resembled a marooned pixie, was a young man she convinced herself was Jesse. At first she had thought he was a statue or one of those buskers who pretended to be Yoda, then she saw his fingers flying over the keys of a mobile phone.

Stella stumbled across the shingle towards him. Just before she got there, he turned, fear in his eyes at being descended on by this ageing madwoman.

It wasn't Jesse.

'I'm sorry,' Stella flopped down beside him, 'I thought you might be my grandson.'

The young man looked her up and down. In fact, he was older than Jesse, probably about eighteen, and his face had a hard look that Jesse's entirely lacked. His pale skin looked grey, and his eyes made her think of a fish that had been laid out too long on the slab.

'Run away, has he?'

'Yes.'

'How old?'

'Sixteen.'

He shrugged. 'Trouble at home?'

Stella nodded; it was true after all.

'Stepfather? I had a sodding stepfather. He wanted my mum and the brat but I didn't figure in the happy ending. He'd hit me and she just sat there doing fuck all to stop him. She probably wanted me out too.'

Stella felt the familiar anger and frustration creep up on her. No, Jesse didn't have a stepfather, especially a violent one.

He had two perfectly good parents who ought to have been able to sort this out.

'Has he got a dog?'

Stella looked startled. 'Not as far as I know.'

'Easier to find him if he has. There's only one hostel that takes dogs. Eight quid a night and all the dog food you can eat.' He grinned at his own joke and Stella wanted to hug this young man with his wry sense of humour whose life had already gone so wrong. 'You could try the Hostelpoint or the YMCA.' He pointed back towards the pier. 'But they're pricey – think they've gone into the hotel business, all en suite bathrooms. Brighton's not too bad. They don't like the homeless frightening the tourists. They have a rough-sleepers team who find you places to stay. You need a referral, though. They could give you a list of shelters.'

'Thanks, I'll try that.' She got out her purse and handed him a fiver. The look he gave her back was full of world-weary cynicism. 'Maybe I should set up as a homeless information centre.' And then, as an afterthought, he added, 'Has he brought a tent? There are sometimes a few tents up by the Max Miller Walk. Till they get moved along.'

Stella stood up. If Kirsty didn't have any firm information, they were going to have to be a lot more organized in their search. She turned back towards the seafront, noticing with surprise that they were directly opposite The Old Galleon where Cameron and Duncan were staying. For now, though, she wanted to fetch Emma from the station and go straight to Kirsty's.

She was right about Emma's response to the hotel room. Her daughter took one look at the bed and said, 'Mum, we can't sleep in that!'

'Well, we're going to have to.' Her encounter with the young man with the violent stepfather had not made her more sympathetic to Emma's protests. 'It's all I can afford. Now let's get straight off and find this Kirsty.'

The address Dora had given them was in Prince Regent's Close. It seemed, like Shakespeare in Stratford, that everything in Brighton from fish-and-chip shops to massage parlours were named after poor old Prinny.

It was a small end-of-terrace house, painted pale lilac, with an ancient camper van parked in the drive. Kirsty's parents had, it seemed, left London for the laid-back atmosphere of Brighton and its lower house prices. They were helpful but baffled when Emma and Stella knocked on their door. Neither of the parents could really remember Jesse and Kirsty announced, as if this settled the matter, that she hadn't even heard from him on Facebook.

In that time-honoured British fashion they were offered tea and biscuits, as if this might help, and they all sat in the small sitting room discussing her grandson.

Finally, Emma remembered to get out the photo she'd given the police to show Kirsty's parents in case they happened to see him.

'Oh my God,' Kirsty's mother suddenly enthused, 'this is the boy Foxy Roxy's been tweeting about!' They looked genuinely interested for the first time.

'Isn't he into that weird music?' Kirsty offered. 'The Incredible String Band?'

'Yes,' Stella replied, feeling she had to defend her grandson. 'He says he likes their purity, how they haven't been tainted by the usual commercialism.'

'He hasn't joined Hare Krishna, has he?' Kirsty's mother asked, offering them more Bourbon biscuits. 'They're quite big in Brighton. I'm always seeing them chanting in Churchill Square.'

'I don't think so.' Stella suddenly realized with a sinking heart how many possibilities there were to explain Jesse's continued absence. 'No, I'm sure he wouldn't.'

'I'm sorry we couldn't be more helpful. Leave us your number so we can get in touch if we do hear anything,' Kirsty's father said kindly as they got up to leave.

Stella looked around the room for her handbag, her attention diverted by the family photos. One in particular caught her eye, clearly taken in a beach hut. Kirsty and her younger brother sat smiling next to the parents and probably grandparents. A young man in his twenties, an uncle perhaps, sat barefoot in front of them. They were all tanned and happy. It was the kind of moment every family treasured. Of course, anyone could look happy in photographs. It didn't mean they actually *were* happy. All the same, Stella felt a stab of jealousy at what looked like a lovely family outing.

She saw Kirsty studying the same photograph, then look swiftly away. Was that a look of guilt in her eyes? Stella told herself she had to be imagining it.

They stood up and said goodbye.

'So where does that leave us?' Emma asked in the taxi on the way back.

'I met a young man today who suggested we look at hostels. And also an area where some young people camp out. Did he take a tent, by any chance?'

'I don't know. He does have a tent for festivals. I'll get Stuart to see if it's still there.'

They wandered down to the seafront and shared a pizza and half a bottle of wine. Stella realized how gloomy she was starting to feel, how much she'd banked on Kirsty having some clues to Jesse's whereabouts. Now it seemed to be a dead end. Still, she had to keep her spirits up for Emma's sake.

She got out her notebook. 'Let's make a list of all the places we can check on tomorrow.'

Suddenly Emma burst into tears. 'How can we be sure he's really in Brighton? That girl Kirsty was our only clue and she says she hasn't even heard from him.'

Stella put her arms round her daughter. 'He told Dora he was here, and I'm not sure I believe Kirsty.'

'But why would she lie?'

'I suppose she might, if Jesse had asked her not to tell us anything.'

'Oh, Mum, this is all so awful. Stuart and I have really screwed up. When you have a baby it all seems so simple,' Emma said tearfully. 'If you love them and feed them and change them, everything will be all right. But it isn't. Not even when they're babies! They cry and you don't know why. And then they grow up and sometimes you even resent them. You have to be so unselfish.' She looked appealingly at Stella. 'I know I've been selfish, Mum. But I'm not going to be any more.'

Stella touched her daughter's tearstained face with a gentle finger. Emma seemed to be realizing at last that actions had painful consequences.

'We'll just have to trust to Jesse's good sense. I have a lot of faith in him.'

Emma sighed. 'I hope to God you're right.'

But the next morning was deeply discouraging. The small crowd of young people in tents had never seen the boy in the picture and neither had anyone at the homeless shelters, nor the small groups hanging around outside.

They were just walking along the seafront back to their

hotel when they saw Duncan emerge from The Old Galleon. One look at their faces told him the news wasn't good. 'No response to our offer to have him on stage, I'm afraid. Probably a silly idea.'

'Kind, though.' Stella smiled.

'Why don't I get the crew involved?'

Stella smiled again. The idea of everyone from Cameron Keene down to Laurie, the doped-out looking roadie, on the hunt for Jesse was so improbable as to be amusing.

Emma's phone buzzed and she went off to answer it.

She returned looking even more frazzled. 'It's Ruby. She's ill and Stuart's really worried. I'm going to have to go back for a bit. Will you be all right on your own? You will keep looking, won't you, Mum?'

'Of course I will. We haven't nearly exhausted the possibilities yet.' She waved as Emma headed back to the hotel to get her stuff.

'You look done in.' Duncan studied Stella for a moment. 'Why don't you come and have a drink?'

It was too tempting an offer to refuse. Matthew wouldn't have noticed if she had bubonic plague – except to worry if it was infectious.

'I've just got to stop by the Dome to make sure all's in order and we'll find somewhere quiet where we can chat.'

Stella followed him, relieved that they weren't going to The Old Galleon. She didn't feel up to Amber or Cameron.

Despite her worries, Stella couldn't help finding a backstage tour of the Dome fascinating. They went in through the side entrance, via the vast doors where the trucks had been parked since early morning. It made Stella laugh to see that even the garage doors in Brighton had Regency crenellations. They passed the small reception desk and were issued with backstage passes. The production team was already there and were busy setting out sound and lighting. Caterers were arriving with big plastic cases of pre-prepared food which they placed on a lip at the front of the stage which, Stella was amazed to see, could be raised up and down. After the show there would be a party in the Band Room, Duncan explained, where the bigwigs of Brighton would come alongside the punters who'd paid up to £150 for special tickets that meant they could meet Cameron afterwards.

'Everyone does it now,' explained Duncan. 'Another way of bringing in the revenue.' Once he'd satisfied himself that the roadies were in control, checking each instrument carefully, he led Stella back out into the sunshine.

'What time does Cameron get here to rehearse?'

'About five. We have to watch him like a hawk. No stimulants stronger than PG tips. And that's pushing it.'

They found a cafe next to the mad but wonderful Pavilion with its green onion domes and lacy Eastern stone carving, mixing Indian, Chinese and Persian styles and somehow ending up with a curiously beautiful whole.

The clusters of slender minarets looked for all the world as if they were about to summon the good people of Brighton to prayer. Except that the only religion in Brighton tended to be hedonism.

Duncan brought two large glasses of wine back to their table. Stella took hers gratefully.

All around them people laughed and chatted and soaked in the welcome sunshine. There was an air of holiday in Brighton all year round. That was why people flocked here. And somehow it had avoided the dilapidation and seediness that had befallen so many seaside towns. Brighton still blazed with enough colour, style and downright eccentricity to have warmed the heart of its patron, the dandyish and decadent Prince Regent.

Stella was equally grateful when Duncan skipped the small talk and went straight to the subject close to her heart.

'Right. Let's think about this logically. How much cash did Jesse have?'

'It couldn't be much or he wouldn't have borrowed Izzy's Christmas money.'

'So if Jesse is here, he has to earn money. What could he do?'

'Work in a cafe, I suppose,' Stella replied. 'He's too young for a pub. Maybe be a washer-upper, something illegal immigrants might do who don't want to be visible.'

'Right. Well, we could try the smaller fast-food joints.'

Stella found she was immensely comforted by the 'we'.

'I wondered about something to do with records,' she suggested, sipping her wine. 'He's always talking about the revival of vinyl.'

Duncan laughed. 'Good thought.' He started to check his phone for record shops. He looked up at her, shaking his head. 'Don't you love Brighton? There are no fewer than six second-hand record shops here and five of them sell vinyl! Who said the recording industry's dead? I haven't got much time today, but why not tomorrow? We've got a couple of days between shows, thank God. We'll go and look together. Come to the hotel at eleven?'

Stella finished her drink and looked for her handbag. There was something distinctly reassuring about Duncan. Cameron might be the star but you got the clear impression that it was Duncan who had created the firmament.

Fifteen

Bed was deliciously comfortable, Stella thought guiltily, now that she had it all to herself and didn't have to share it with either her daughter or her husband.

She had been woken by the raucous cry of seagulls; so many of them, in fact, that they sounded as if they were auditioning for Hitchcock's spooky film *The Birds*. She had made a cup of tea and to her delight had found a tiny jug of fresh milk in the fridge, plus two shortbread biscuits, which was amazing considering how cheap the hotel was. She might even become one of those enthusiastic people who left reviews on TripAdvisor.

She had finished the first cup and was wondering whether to indulge in another when the phone rang. It was Emma informing her that Ruby had chicken pox. Stella listened guiltily. What kind of grandmother was she to be lying here delighting in tea and biscuits when she should have rung her daughter to find out how Ruby was?

'The thing is, Mum, I think I'm going to have to stay with her. She can't go to the childminder with chicken pox.'

'I quite understand. As a matter of fact, Duncan's coming with me to look.'

'I would have thought he'd be too busy with their shows.'

'He's become very fond of Jesse. It seems he was an ISB fan too.'

'What on earth is ISB? It sounds like some kind of bowel complaint.'

'That's IBS. It stands for The Incredible String Band,' Stella explained. 'Jesse loves them. Their fans stick together because there weren't that many of them.'

'I'm not surprised, if that's the ghastly music he's always listening to. Like cats with catarrh. Are you all right, Mum? You sound a bit odd.'

Stella realized why she sounded odd. If she hadn't been worrying about Jesse, she would be greatly relishing her independence.

'I'm fine. I'll let you know as soon as we find anything out. What's happening your end? Still no word from his friends? What about the police? Still nothing?'

'I don't think they honestly care. They think he'll just come home.'

'Maybe he will.' Stella said goodbye, but her indulgent pleasure had evaporated at the news of the lack of police enthusiasm. It seemed as though more fuss was made over a cat up a tree than her beloved grandson.

She didn't have much time before her peace was shattered again. This time by Suze.

Stella glanced at her watch. 'You're up early.' Suze was a notoriously late sleeper.

'I'm on tango watch.'

'Sorry?'

'The tangos are getting steamier.'

287

Stella laughed.

'Stella, I don't think you're taking this seriously. Fabia's cooking for him every night. Proper cordon bleu stuff.'

Stella realized that for some reason she hadn't told Suze about Matthew's admission. Maybe she didn't feel ready to face up to it yet.

'And he's got absolutely fanatical about dance, always droning on about the cultural significance of the mambo in Cuba or some such thing. You know Matthew. I never thought I'd say this but I wish he'd go back to William Morris and the council. And this thing about starting up dance studios with Fabia. They're like bloody Fanny and Johnnie Cradock! All I know is I just don't think you should stay away.'

'Well, I've got to be back for Saturday. I can hardly miss the concert in my own garden, can I?'

'It's a long time till Saturday. Stella, listen, this is serious. Matthew's a new man. Charming, considerate, can't do enough for everyone.'

Stella almost laughed out loud. 'And you think I should be worried about that?'

'In Matthew, yes, I do.'

'But if I can't trust my husband alone for a few days, what does that say about our marriage?' She realized Duncan had said the same thing.

'That's all very well, but most people's marriages don't have to cope with an Argentinian firecracker being thrown into them.'

Stella had to concede that this was true.

And then, the final nail in the coffin: 'Stella, she actually seems to like him.'

To Suze's baffled exasperation, Stella changed the subject.

'Anyway, what else is happening? How are the preparations coming along?'

'Fantastic, actually. Food and drink under control. Fizz already arrived. Auction prizes rolling in. The dreaded Amber has donated a giant uterus with ovaries attached. It reminds me of a dead sheep's skull and Matthew says it's a steal from a Black Sabbath album cover but that it'll probably go for quite a lot. Oh, and one of your pet owners is hopping mad. The owner of the French bulldog you painted in his socks. The dog's become such a celebrity he's getting no peace.'

'Oh dear.' She got dressed musing on the peculiar nature of modern fame. Amber and her enormous wombs and bulldogs in socks going viral. She wondered if Roxy's tweeting about Jesse had led anywhere. But surely she'd have heard about it if it had?

When she arrived at the hotel Duncan was nowhere to be found. Instead it was Cameron who pounced on her, looking dissolute and unshaven. He pulled her into the small room off the lounge where he had been playing bar billiards with Laurie, the roadie.

'You know Laurie, don't you?' Cameron asked.

'Hello, Laurie. Such a great name for a roadie.'

They both looked at her blankly.

'Well, you know. Laurie. Sounds like Lorry.'

They exchanged a significant look.

'Where's Duncan?' Stella threw in hastily. 'I'm supposed to be meeting him. How did it go last night?'

'Pretty good. Full house. Got them on their feet rockin' away at the end. Told them to throw away their Zimmer frames.'

'He got them up on stage,' Laurie endorsed. 'It was fuckin' amazing.'

'Right. Like in *Hair*,' suggested Stella.

They looked blank again.

'You know, *Hair* the musical. "Let the Sunshine in". The audience all went on stage at the end.'

'Before my time, darling.' Cameron grinned.

'So where did you say Duncan is?'

'Upstairs being lectured by Amber. She doesn't like it here, apparently. Too noisy, by which she means too near me. She wanted to stay at The Grand. Duncan says The Grand's full of salesmen who fuse the electrics by all blow-drying their hair at the same time and suffocate you in the lift with their after-shave. Apparently the décor here offends her artist's eye. Answer me one question, Stella.'

'I'll do my best.'

'What the fuck does he see in her? Apart from the tits, obviously.'

'She's very much her own woman, a successful artist, apparently Connie liked her, and she does have an elemental kind of sex appeal.' Stella wondered what she was doing selling Amber to Cameron. Maybe it was because Duncan seemed to like her and Duncan was being very kind.

Amber chose that moment to sweep majestically through the lobby and out of the revolving door onto the promenade.

'Well, I don't get it. It's like that thing in *Jurassic Park*,' Cameron announced, much struck by the philosophical truth of his own perception.

'What thing?' asked Laurie.

'The mosquito trapped in amber. That's Dunc. He's trapped in Amber.'

They both laughed uproariously.

'I'd better go and look for him. What room's he in?'

'Ten. At the front. It's bigger than my room, I can tell you.

And I quite like the décor.' Cameron and Laurie went back to their bar billiards.

The lift was busy so Stella took the stairs, remembering that she'd meant to ask Cameron about the gout. He seemed fine and maybe he wouldn't want to be reminded of so embarrassing an affliction in a rock star.

To her surprise the door of the room was wide open. She knocked and when she got no reply, peered in.

It was a pretty room with a big bay window looking out on the promenade framed by huge swagged curtains in sea blue. Even the wallpaper was sea blue, dotted with white seagulls.

But it was the bed that caught her attention. It was vast and, fitting into the nautical mood, shaped like a boat. No matter how unhappy Amber might be with their surroundings, the tumbled sheets spoke of recent use.

Despite herself Stella found her eyes drawn back to it. An unexpected emotion flooded through her. Surprise? Jealousy? Shocked that she should be feeling such a thing, Stella turned away to find Duncan standing in the doorway. For a fraction of a second their eyes met. 'Sorry, I was just looking for Amber, she went off in a bit of a huff.'

'So I heard.'

'Yes,' he grinned, surprisingly boyishly, 'no secrets around here. She does have a soft side, you know. You meet a lot of bullshitters in this business and Amber's got this amazing honesty, a sort of take-it-or-leave-it attitude. I've always been a bit scared of what people think of me. Maybe because I was so shy when I was growing up, but Amber doesn't even notice. And she cares a lot about art.'

Stella felt a pang of guilt that she probably hadn't helped with his confidence by labelling him 'Dull Duncan' all those years ago. She didn't quite know what to make of this unburdening but she could see that Duncan wanted her to understand why he was drawn to Amber. And the curious thing was, she was resisting it. It was easier just to dislike Amber. Yet, for Duncan's sake, she ought to try.

'I can see she's very original and refreshing.'

Duncan laughed. 'But you can't stand her.'

'She's very different to me. Let's leave it at that. Shall we go?'

They headed out onto the seafront, avoiding the rollerbladers, who seemed to be mostly incredibly fit retirees, and turned north, away from the sea, wending their way through the tiny streets known as the Lanes packed with antique shops and expensive jewellers.

They cut through the Pavilion Gardens, full of picnickers even at this hour, with the Pavilion on their right, and passed the Dome, where Cameron had performed last night.

'How are tickets going?' Stella asked.

'Sold out weeks ago.' Duncan grinned. 'The great thing about being a Sixties rocker is that your audience is as old as you are. They book ahead, pay whatever you ask, and don't start fights or puke over the upholstery. They're a dream. You are coming, aren't you? I'll get you a backstage pass.'

Stella almost laughed out loud. How she would have longed to be able to say, 'I'm with the band,' forty years ago. Now, for the first time in her life, she could say it at over sixty. Life was certainly full of surprises.

They took a right turn and all at once it seemed to Stella that they had walked into their own past. The date might profess it to be the twenty-first century, but in Brighton it was still a hippie paradise. A vintage clothes shop boasting the title To Be Worn Again was full of the silks and velvets, embroidered shawls and peasant blouses Stella had worn at eighteen as a rebellion against all that was dull and suburban in her background.

They wandered into a souk-like shop full of beaded silver necklaces, Tuareg camel bags and colourful Eastern rugs. 'Oh my God,' Stella breathed in and closed her eyes, transported by the spicy aroma of joss sticks. 'Patchouli! Now that does take me back!'

She remembered with a flash of embarrassment that she'd been so enamoured of all things exotic that she'd attended lectures in a Berber wedding dress.

'I seem to remember,' Duncan teased, his blue eyes crinkling at the memory, 'you had an Afghan coat which was so smelly it ended up as a rug on the floor!'

Stella nodded, amazed he could remember.

He picked up a chillum pipe, used for smoking the illegal substances so familiar in those liberated times. 'Did you indulge?'

'Once or twice. Too scared most of the time. You?'

'Me neither.'

'But you're in the music business! What about sex and drugs and rock 'n' roll? I thought it was obligatory!' Stella stared down at the chillum. Suddenly the question seemed too intimate.

'I'm the boring businessman, remember.' He smiled winningly so that little creases appeared in his Californian tan.

It seemed ridiculous now that they had ever thought of him as Dull Duncan.

'Did you ever go to the Starlight Rooms? *The* club you had to go into Brighton?'

'Of course I did.' Stella could still remember running for the late-night trains back to Camley after watching her favourite groups there.

'And the infra-red stamp on your wrist? How it seemed the height of cool? And you didn't want to wash it off for days!'

'I saw the Yardbirds there,' Stella boasted. 'With Eric Clapton!'

'So did I!' They began to sing 'For Your Love', the group's biggest hit, oblivious to the strange looks they attracted from passers-by.

They wandered back into the street past shops devoted entirely to dream catchers, beautiful turquoise Navajo jewellery, a shop selling wonderfully named vegetarian shoes and another, inappropriately next to JoJo Maman Bébé, devoted entirely to witchcraft. 'Handy for *Rosemary's Baby*,' quipped Duncan.

A sharp-suited man on a smartphone leaned outside a pub, looking as if he were an alien from the twenty-first century who had mistakenly landed in an earlier era.

At the far end of the street a raggle-taggle band of shaven-headed young people dressed in orange turned the corner singing:

Hare Krishna, Hare Krishna,
Krishna, Krishna, Hare Hare,
Hare Rama Hare Rama,
Rama Rama Hare Hare.

Stella grabbed Duncan's arm and began to laugh helplessly. 'Pinch me. I think we really have landed back in the Sixties.'

He smiled, then looked at her intently for a moment. 'Would you really mind?' She had no chance to answer. They caught sight of a young busker, who reminded her so much of Jesse that her heart turned over.

'Come on, less of this wading in the past,' she said trying to be stern. 'Where's the first record shop?'

'Just down here.' He indicated a small shopfront a minutes' walk away.

Stella threw a pound in the young man's hat and he gave her a melting smile of gratitude.

She felt a hand touch hers and realized that it was Duncan and that he understood. 'Don't worry. We'll find him.'

They went silently inside the shop, manned by two bearded assistants. It was quiet at this time of day. The stock was a mix of CDs, vinyl records, books about rock music and posters.

Stella glanced at the iconic album sleeves displayed on the walls.

'They look a lot better than CD covers, don't they?'

Duncan shrugged. 'And even CD covers are almost history.'

Stella approached one of the two beards and got out the photograph of Jesse. 'We're looking for this young man. He's my grandson. He's very into old records. Have you by any chance seen him?'

They both studied it. 'Nice-looking kid, but sorry, no. Have you tried Vintage Vinyl up the road?'

Vintage Vinyl turned out to be only a few hundred yards away. On the way Stella stopped for a moment, looking around. She pointed excitedly. 'That used to be one of the first Body Shops! You could bring your own bottles and they'd fill them up for you!'

Stella thought about the wonderful Anita Roddick, who'd founded the Body Shop. She hadn't got stuck in the Sixties but had gone on striding forwards to try and change the world.

Vintage Vinyl turned out to be surprisingly big for a second-hand record shop. Albums were at the front and then there were rows and rows of old forty-fives that seemed to go back forever.

As if pulled by a magnet, they started looking through the singles.

'Al Stewart. "The Year of the Cat".' Stella sighed.

'Girls' music. We boys preferred Roy Wood. Look, *Tubular Bells!*' Duncan bowed his head in awe. 'We're uncovering history here!' He suddenly grinned delightedly. '"For Your Love"!' I'm buying that for you. To bring back old times.'

He took it to the front of the shop.

Stella watched him, smiling. She didn't like to mention that she didn't have a record player. What did it matter anyway? She'd stick it on her wall. She pushed away the question creeping into her mind about where that wall would be.

The next shop on their list was called Feeling Groovy.

'Like hairdressers,' Stella commented.

'Sorry?'

'Hairdressers always have these funny names. Mane Attraction. Lunatic Fringe. Curl Up and Dye. And a fabulous one I saw the other day – Ryan Hair!'

Feeling Groovy was upstairs, above a tattoo parlour. Stella got out her photograph again. The assistant, who had large holes in his ears, kept open by stainless-steel rings that made Stella think of stationery reinforcements, shook his head. He'd never seen Jesse, he said.

Duncan had wandered to the back of the shop.

What had grabbed his attention was a small display dedicated to The Incredible String Band. Not unusual in Brighton, but quite a coincidence all the same. He was about to call Stella over, then stopped and decided to do a little research of his own before getting her hopes up. He knew she was pretending to be strong but he sensed the fragility beneath. Family happiness had been such a strong part of Stella's idea of what she'd achieved in life and lately, with her daughter's affair and her grandson's disappearance, all that seemed to be falling apart. He'd like to help give it back to her.

It was funny. So many people had asked him if he'd missed having children and he'd always said no, out of courtesy to Connie. But when he'd met and liked Stella's family and glimpsed what it was like to be a grandparent, for the first time he had felt a sense of loss.

All the more reason to help her find Jesse.

He'd get Laurie or one of the other members of the crew to take it in turns to keep an eye on this place for a day or so. They were free now till the final show. Hanging around in a record shop would be Laurie's idea of fun anyway.

She left her mobile number with the reinforced-eared assistant, just in case, and they headed down the stairs. Stella was all for continuing the search but Duncan, eager to brief Laurie, wanted to get back to the hotel.

The Old Galleon seemed oddly quiet. Normally there would be sounds of chatting, glasses clinking, music and the tap of snooker cues. But not tonight.

They turned the corner into the dim interior of the horse-shoe-shaped bar. It was empty except for Amber. She was sitting alone, wearing a red dress that matched her lipstick. Even her drink was red. Just above her was a spotlight. The whole effect reminded Stella of that painting by Hopper, *Nighthawks*. Except that this was, in Stella's view, undoubtedly a pose. Right down to the teardrops that sparkled on her cheek. But would Duncan see through it?

'Amber . . .' Duncan approached her with genuine concern in his voice. 'Are you OK?'

'Not really.' She held up a piece of A4 paper. It was a photograph of a large bead of honey-coloured liquid inside which a dead insect was clearly visible. Underneath it, in large letters, were the words TRAPPED IN AMBER.

'Oh, for God's sake,' Duncan muttered irritably. 'We all know who did this. Stella, why don't you order yourself a drink?' He strode angrily out of the bar towards the lift.

Reluctantly, she pulled up a bar stool and asked the waiter for a glass of wine.

Amber turned to her. 'You may not have put it up, but I know you'd like to.'

Stella stared at her in astonishment. 'Why on earth would I want to do that?'

Amber sipped her red drink. 'Because you're jealous. Because you can't accept it's someone else's turn. Because you're old and you're still pretending to be young and it's really pathetic.'

For one glorious moment Stella almost threw her wine in Amber's face. But that was probably what Amber wanted. Instead she climbed down from her bar stool.

'The sun's come out on the terrace bar. I think I'll share my wine with the seagulls. The company's more congenial.'

With the sweetest of smiles she turned her back on Amber and walked to the front of the hotel.

Duncan, discovering Cameron's room was empty, returned to Amber in the bar. 'What happened to Stella?'

'She went to sit outside. I expect she finds the pace a bit exhausting. At her age.'

'Stella's the same age as me,' Duncan reminded her, his sympathy diminishing, just as Cameron and Laurie came in through the revolving doors with Stella in tow.

'Hello, playmates,' Cameron greeted them.

'Did you stick up that sign on our door?' Duncan demanded.

'I might have.' Cameron smiled insultingly at Amber. 'How did you know it was me?'

'Maybe because you're the only one who's watched *Jurassic Park* eighty-three times. Why, for God's sake?'

'There are those amongst us who feel you are becoming a trifle uxorious.'

'What the hell is he talking about?' demanded Amber.

'I think he means Duncan is thinking more about your comfort than his,' enlightened Stella.

'Is this about the size of your room?' Duncan demanded.

'It is a lot smaller than the bridal suite you are occupying,' agreed Cameron. 'But it's not just that. We rarely seem to be sharing your company these days.' Stella almost jumped to Duncan's defence by pointing out that he was actually spending his time looking for her grandson but decided it would only fan the flames.

'I think you owe Amber an apology.'

'Your Royal Wombness, I abase myself,' Cameron announced with a bow, not looking sorry at all.

'Apology accepted.' Amber was smart enough to know when to back down.

Stella decided it was time to leave them to it. 'Now if you'll all excuse me, I have some quite important things to be doing.' She headed through the bar towards the Ladies. Once inside, she took several deep breaths. She looked in the mirror, adjusted her lipstick and ran a comb through her hair. Behind her in the mirror she caught sight of Amber entering.

'I just wanted to say that there's one thing you should remember. Duncan's wife introduced us because she thought I would cheer him up, which I intend to do. So don't get any ideas about him. He just feels sorry for you.'

Stella turned round to face her, realizing that Amber was clever enough never to show this animosity in front of Duncan.

'Then it's a pity for Connie's sake that she didn't know what a silly bitch you are, isn't it?'

As she walked briskly back towards her hotel, Stella wondered again what it was that Connie had seen in Amber. By all accounts Connie had been a lovely woman and she had obviously loved Duncan. It took a huge act of unselfishness to imagine your beloved husband's future without you and not be bitter. Even more so to imagine him with another woman.

But in a less dramatic way, wasn't that what was happening with her and Matthew? But Stella wasn't at all sure she was as unselfish as Connie.

The two remaining record shops were on her way back to the hotel and she decided to check them out briefly. With both of them she drew a blank.

Just before her hotel she came across a cafe right on the beach and flopped down, watching the sun sparkling on the sea, with the pier beyond, its rollercoasters and amusement arcades, its toffee apples and candy floss, beckoning invitingly to holidaymakers.

She checked her phone and found four messages from Emma. Clearly she was desperate for news. Stella wished she had some. Before she could reply her phone rang.

It was Debora.

'Hi, how are all the arrangements going for the big day?' Stella asked her.

'Not bad. Mortal combat threatens between Suze and Fabia.'

'Oh dear.'

'In your interests Suze is insisting that Matthew and she keep one foot on the ground at all times to prevent any hanky panky. Why is sex called hanky panky in this country, by the way?'

Stella felt a flash of purest anger at her husband. All this time she had been tolerating his interest in Fabia and while she was here trying to find their grandson he was openly parading it.

'It was all getting a bit too much for me,' Debora continued calmly, 'which is why I am walking towards you at this very moment.'

To Stella's delight she saw her friend approaching along the seafront only a few yards away.

She jumped up and embraced her.

'This is so great. It's getting hairy here too. Cameron can't stand Amber.'

'Can anyone stand Amber?'

'No, but not everyone puts up a photograph from *Jurassic Park* with "trapped in Amber" written on it.'

'He didn't! He always was a stirrer. That's why I've been summoned. To keep a bit of an eye on him. I didn't realize I'd have to be a referee too. And now tonight we have to go to her damn show.'

'Not me.'

'Yes, you. It's time we wives stood together against the invasion of the younger model. I liked Duncan's wife. She couldn't have really known what Amber was like or she wouldn't have introduced her husband to him. I feel the need to right the wrong on her behalf. We need to open his eyes. If we could only think how. What do you think it is he sees in her? He's usually such a sensible man.'

'He said something about admiring her honesty. And that she doesn't care what other people think.'

'That's what makes her so ghastly. And stop being so reasonable about her.'

'All right, I think she's utterly dreadful and I couldn't bear it if he settled down with her.'

'Then let's *do* something about it.' Debora smiled her most motherly smile. 'Let's get the bitch before she gets him.'

'Well, actually,' Stella's eyes twinkled, 'I do have a little plan. The only thing is, I will need Cameron's cooperation.'

The preview of Amber's exhibition was from six-thirty to eight-thirty in a small but stylish gallery in the Lanes. The walls were also adorned with other hideous works of art that Stella couldn't imagine anyone wanting to possess. There was a crucifixion featuring Jesus with a scarecrow's face; a version of Ganesh the elephant god wearing false eyelashes; giant replicas of various Ecstasy-like tablets with smiley faces on them; a vast neon sign bearing the single word YES, and then there was Amber's work: a series of enormous uteruses in different colours, with the occasional ovary or bladder for light relief.

'God they're ghastly,' murmured Stella. 'Someone should remind the customers about only owning things that are useful or beautiful.'

'Ah,' Debora replied with a smile, 'but the art world would collapse if people followed that. And these are reassuringly expensive. The big ones are twenty grand.'

But Stella was only half listening. She had just caught sight of someone the other side of the crowded room and it had set her mind whirring.

Yes, it might be possible. She would have to see.

A scarily elegant woman in an asymmetrical dress arrived to refill their glasses, handing them a list of the works on sale and a note about Amber being one of today's foremost young artists.

A red dot suddenly appeared on one of the biggest and most expensive paintings, signifying a sale. 'Jeez,' Debora muttered, 'I hope they're not hanging that in the dining room. It'd certainly put you off your muesli.'

'Congratulations, Hal,' Stella edged her way through the crowds, 'you've obviously got a taste for the eye-catching.'

'Hello, Mrs Ainsworth,' Hal replied nervously, obviously thrown to see her here, given the circumstances of their last meeting. 'I'm starting my own collection. I thought it made quite a statement about modern life.'

'Yes, Stella,' Debora winked at her, 'it's a *Womb with a View*.'

'I hope we'll see you at the Cameron Keene concert we're hosting on Saturday. One of Amber's works is up for auction at that too. Could be a terrific bargain for your collection.'

'Of course,' he mumbled, looking stunned to be invited.

'That was Hal,' Stella explained, as they walked back together. 'The rich idiot who's involved with my daughter Emma.'

'I got that. So why are you inviting him to the concert?'

'He's part of my plan,' was the mysterious reply.

'So how's the search for your grandson going?'

Stella stared out at the darkening sea. 'Oh, God, Debora,' her voice suddenly cracked at the edges. 'We've got nowhere. Maybe I shouldn't have come.'

'Hey,' Debora stopped in the middle of the prom and hugged her, 'you've been doing your best. More than anyone else.'

They had reached their destination.

'Come in and have a glass of champagne,' Debora tempted. 'Cheer us both up.'

One good thing about The Old Galleon, apart from its great

position on the seafront and the fact that it was near the Dome where Cameron was performing, was that there were various inviting nooks and corners where you could be private.

Stella selected an inviting alcove with two armchairs upholstered in black-and-white devoré velvet dating from its headier days of art deco grandeur.

'You stay, I'll go and order,' she told Debora.

She arrived at the reception desk at the same time as a statuesque young woman wearing a pink tulle tutu over a black body with leggings and Doc Martens plus a pink sash proclaiming LOU'S HEN PARTY. The whole thing was topped off with a fetching fake tiara.

The newcomer was as well upholstered as the devoré chairs, with generous breasts that spilled out of the front of her dress, luxuriously unruly long red hair and an infectious smile. She also reminded Stella of someone.

The receptionist's smile froze over like a glacier as the girl approached and Stella remembered the sign at her own much less posh hotel.

Hen and stag parties were not welcome here either.

She listened, fascinated, as the newcomer addressed the frosty woman behind the desk. 'Hi, I'm looking for Bernadette O'Riordan. I gather she's staying at the hotel.'

With a haughty air, as if the girl might have dog shit on her shoe, the receptionist consulted her screen. 'We have an Amber O'Riordan.'

The girl in pink smiled engagingly. 'Aye, that'll be her. Is she in?'

So Amber was really Bernadette. It didn't quite have the same ring to it.

'I'm sorry, madam. Can I take a message?'

'Only to ask her if she's really going to miss her own sister's hen party?'

'Do you want me to write that down?' the girl on the desk enquired.

'No, no.' She shook her head and the fake diamonds in her tiara winked sadly in the light of the lobby. 'Just tell her that her sister Dolours called and can she get me on my mobile. Here's the number, just in case she's forgotten it.' This last was in a tone heavy with irony.

She wrote the number down and passed it over.

'Excuse me,' Stella interrupted, 'my friend and I know your sister and we were about to have a glass of champagne round the corner. Why don't you come and join us? To mark such a special occasion?'

'I don't mind if I do.' Dolours grinned, to the evident dis-approval of the receptionist. 'Hoity-toity old cow,' she added just loudly enough for the woman to catch her words.

Debora had appeared behind them. 'I think you'd better make that a bottle,' she announced. 'And three glasses please.'

Their new friend followed them into their alcove and they pulled up another chair.

'So you're Amber's sister?'

'Indeed I am. You know her, you said? Her real name's Bernadette, after Saint Bernadette of Lourdes, the one that does all the miracles. She must have done one on Bernie, turning her into an Amber!'

'And you're getting married?'

'To Brendan. He's a plumber. Not quite up Bernie's street.'

'And your name's Dolours?'

'Desperate name, isn't it? My mam is religious, as you can probably tell! People call me Lou.'

'It's a pity about Amber missing your hen night.' The champagne arrived and Stella began pouring it.

'We're not exactly in touch. In fact, we haven't spoken for months. Bernie was always a bit up herself. She's frightened we'll all get hammered and end up in the papers and embarrass her.'

'Is she that well known?'

'She thinks she is. She was always a bit of a killjoy. It comes from being the eldest of nine. My mam used to go on about how having nine children was a piece of piss, but that's because Bernie did all the work; it was really her who brought us all up. She had no life. My mam drank, you see.'

Debora and Stella exchanged glances at the revelation. This was a whole side of Amber they'd never suspected. Maybe there was more to her than they had seen so far.

'What about your dad?'

'Our da ran off when we were wee. So you can see why Bernie had it hard. Why she couldn't wait to get away and turn into Amber. She always says one thing's for sure. She's never going to have any children of her own. She says the Pope can have the children if he cares about them so much.'

'He may be liberal,' Debora grinned, 'but I don't think he'd go that far.'

'Bernie made sure she couldn't, though; she had the operation and everything. It caused a big scandal in Ireland. Well, you can imagine, she's only a young woman. But maybe it explains why she doesn't like bad publicity. It doesn't mean she should turn down my hen party, though. That's downright mean of her.' Dolours drained her champagne. 'I'd better be getting along. It wouldn't do for me to have a hangover for me own hen night, would it now?'

After Dolours had left, Stella looked thoughtful.

'Well, that was unexpected,' Debora confessed. 'I may not like the woman but I shouldn't have been so quick to judge her.'

'Maybe it explains the wombs,' Stella suggested, and they both burst out laughing.

While Dolours had been drinking champagne with Debora and Stella, Duncan had been waiting in the small bar the other side of the hotel for Laurie, who had spent the day sleuthing in record shops.

'Any news?' Duncan asked, ordering them both a pint of Camden ale.

'I went back to that Feeling Groovy place and hung about a bit.' Laurie sipped his beer. 'This dog came in, obviously at home there, and the kid behind the counter called it – "Licky! Licky!" Now that might have been referring to an unsavoury habit of the dog licking its balls, but it turns out Licky is short for Licorice.' Laurie was looking exceptionally pleased with himself. 'You know that daft bird who sang with The Incredible String Band? Do you remember what she was called?'

Duncan grinned. 'Licorice. Licorice McKechnie.'

'Too right. And that was what the dog's called too, so I deduced this had to be where your kid is.' He grinned at Duncan like a mischievous leprechaun. 'The one in the photo. He works there three days a week. As a matter of fact, he's there tomorrow.'

'Thanks, Laurie – you're wasted as a roadie, you should be a private eye. I can't tell you how pleased Stella will be.'

'Good, she's a nice lady, not like that—'

'Thanks, Laurie,' Duncan interrupted quickly. 'Another pint?'

'Don't mind if I do.'

Duncan downed his and went up to his room. Amber was still out celebrating her show, he noted with relief. He couldn't cope with any more emotion tonight. He needed to think.

He really felt for Jesse. His own parents hadn't given a toss about him. No matter how well he did at school, they never came to his parents' evenings. He used to watch the kids with the mums and dads who pinned down the teachers with endless questions about their children's progress and envy them. He even envied the kids who complained that their parents were never satisfied and that they gave them a hard time no matter how well they did. At least they cared. So Duncan had stopped working, stopped getting straight A's. And his parents hadn't even noticed, even when his teachers did. One teacher, who'd taught him English, had even cared enough to visit them at home. The last thing he'd expected, in a school full of pushy parents, was to hit a brick wall of indifference, but that was what he had got even when he'd tried to explain that their son had a real feeling for poetry and wrote the best essays about Shakespearean tragedy in the class.

After that, Duncan had given up. He'd started messing about on guitars with Cameron while his grades slipped week by week. He'd made a last-minute effort just before A levels when he'd realized he wouldn't even get into college and all his mates were going. In the end he'd just scraped in. Of course, his parents thought college was a waste of time and money and hadn't supported him with a penny.

So he thought he knew a little bit about what Jesse must be going through with parents who didn't seem to care about him that much or surely they would have tried harder to find him?

*

It was after eleven by the time Stella left The Old Galleon. She stood for a moment on the seafront breathing in the clear night air. The stars were out and the sliver of a moon trailed a fine line of light across the water. She sat down on a bench, mesmerized by the loveliness.

After a few minutes she made herself remember what she was doing here and got out her phone. There was a message from Roxy passing on a tweet she'd received from her appeal. It was from one of Roxy's followers in Brighton. It showed a young boy in a hoodie with a dog on a piece of string walking past a row of beach huts.

Stella sat up, electrified. You couldn't see the boy's face but there was something about his stance, slightly stooped and bending forward as if he were in a strong wind, that instantly made her think of Jesse. The dog was some kind of lurcher cross, a little like the one she'd painted.

The backdrop of the beach huts sparked something in Stella's memory. And then she remembered it. The family photo at Kirsty's house. The one she had envied and she had then told herself that photos could lie. It had been taken in a beach hut. Stella closed her eyes and tried to picture it. It had been pale blue with lime-green doors. She remembered now how distinctive it had been, because her grandparents had owned one in windblown Suffolk, which had been plain white, peeling and dilapidated, though much loved; a prefab compared to the palace that appeared in Kirsty's family photo.

She wanted to go and look now but knew it would be madness. She wouldn't be able to tell what colour any beach hut was at this time of night and she would look highly suspicious poking about on the beach at midnight. No matter how excited she felt it would have to wait till tomorrow.

On the other side of the road she saw a taxi stop and

Cameron emerge rather unsteadily. Rather to her surprise he was alone, with neither Duncan nor any of the other band members in tow. She wondered how he'd managed to shake them off, given that he was supposed to be being minded carefully. Only two more nights till the final show here at the Dome, then back to Camley for the concert in her garden.

Stella realized with a shock that she'd hardly thought about Camley, the concert, or Matthew. Somehow things had seemed more vivid here. And yet, in the blink of an eye, real life would return. Stella recognized that this was a truth she'd been avoiding, but it was one she was going to have to face. She couldn't let things drift like this. She knew that her life in Camley was a lot less than perfect, but till now she'd been prepared to accept the compromises. Why? To stay married? To keep a comfortable roof over her head? The hope of a secure and settled old age? She'd always believed in staying together if you could, and sharing all your memories, and it had always seemed important to be near Emma and her grandchildren, but even that had been problematic lately. What if Emma actually left Stuart for Hal?

She crossed the road to find that Cameron, the rock legend, didn't seem to have enough money on him to pay for his cab. This made Stella giggle as she delved into her wallet and retrieved a tenner.

'Sorry about this, Stella.' Cameron grinned his famously lopsided grin and took hold of her hand. 'Come on, one for the road.' The bar and lobby were as dead as a graveyard at midnight. 'We'll have it upstairs. You can see how much smaller my room is than Duncan's.' He signalled to the night porter. 'A bottle of Bolly. Room twelve. Thanks.'

'Cameron,' Stella started to protest.

'Shut up, Stella.' Cameron softened the words with a crinkly smile. 'I'll drink it on my own, if you won't join me, and don't give me that crap about watching the drink before the last show. I get enough of that from Dunc.'

With understandable misgiving Stella followed him to the lift. But although he might attempt a kiss he was hardly going to throw her on the bed and ravish her. Not at her age. He probably just wanted to talk about himself as usual. What was that great line Debora had used about Fabia? 'She's always there when she needs you.' That was even truer of Cameron.

The room was indeed smaller that Duncan's, but it was still a delightful room with a big bay window looking out at the moonlit sea, a huge bed, and bunches of flowers on every surface – 'from grateful fans,' Cameron smirked – and piles of CDs. 'I'm not up to all this downloading crap.' Cameron shrugged. 'Debora got them for me. Obviously I'm too famous to walk into a record shop myself.' His grin undercut the boast. The mention of record shops made her think of Jesse and a cloud crossed her features.

'You all right, Stell?' Cameron asked in a rare moment of sensitivity.

For a split second she considered telling him about Jesse and the beach hut but Cameron wasn't really interested and would soon stop listening.

The champagne arrived and Cameron began opening it. He filled the glasses and brought one over to her. She would regret this in the morning but reality would soon be back and drinking in hotel rooms with rock stars a distant memory.

They clinked glasses.

Suddenly he put his down and looked at her fixedly. 'There's something I want to say.' He took her glass and put it next to his. 'You've always been special to me, Stella. I know I'm a romantic. It gets me into trouble. I like the world to be the way

311

I see it. Maybe it's because of when we met, but to me you'll always be the innocent girl with the blonde hair and the big eyes, who was there with me when it all started to happen. I can remember it like it was yesterday.'

Stella smiled at him. 'We really *were* stardust and golden. I don't suppose anyone after us would really understand.'

Cameron raised his glass to hers.

'Here's to never forgetting!'

They clinked their glasses again and Cameron raised her hand to his lips. 'To Stella Scott. My inspiration.'

The door opened behind them and Duncan stood on the threshold. 'I saw the waiter with the champagne and didn't want to interrupt a tender moment.'

To Stella's surprise his voice was heavy with irony. 'Oh for goodness' sake, Duncan,' she replied, suddenly irritated at the implication. 'Cameron and I are just old friends. What else would we be at our age?'

'Stella,' Cameron looked at her as if she'd plunged a knife into him, 'is that all I am to you? A friend?'

Duncan began to laugh and Stella joined him, struck by the ludicrousness of the idea of her, at almost sixty-five, being Cameron's new lover.

But Cameron didn't see the joke. 'I'd like you both to leave,' he announced grandly as if he were Louis XIV dismissing his courtiers, 'and give me some time to prepare for my show.'

Sixteen

Well, that was clever, Stella told herself, as she walked briskly back to her hotel. She had obviously managed to wound Cameron's *amour propre* just when she was expecting him to give his services free for their concert in three days' time. What if he took umbrage and pulled out? They'd already sold all the tickets, provided food for two hundred guests and assembled a dozen auction prizes on the back of Cameron Keene performing in their back garden.

'Hello, Stella, how's it going?' shouted a woman's voice. Stella turned to find Amber's sister Dolours and her hen party approaching from the direction of the lower promenade beyond the Sea Life aquarium. They were an impressive sight.

'Are you OK? Only you looked a bit mournful walking along,' Dolours said.

'We were just remembering the giant stingrays we saw this afternoon,' commented one of her friends.

'And isn't one of them the spit of Brendan?' added another.

Dolours linked arms with Stella. 'You can't be thinking of

going home yet! The night's young. We're off to Dirty Martini, some new place near here where I'm guessing they sell . . . ?'

'Dirty Martinis!' chorused her friends.

Laughing, Stella let herself be led towards a narrow staircase to a basement dive. 'Watch out for these stairs now, girls,' sang out Dolours. 'They're desperate for getting your heel stuck and ending up arse over tits, and we wouldn't want that, would we? Not with my sister being such a big noise in the town.'

Dirty Martini turned out to be a bare room with loud music, strobe lighting and zero atmosphere. Everyone was so young, Stella began to feel like the unwelcome parent who'd come home early at her teenager's party. But the Martinis were surprisingly good and she really liked Dolours.

'So when's the wedding?'

'Not for another two weeks. We wanted time to sober up before the next round.'

She explained how Brendan had wanted to get married in Las Vegas or even the Isle of Man, anywhere to escape the entire O'Riordan clan descending on them, vying with each other in their thirst.

'But, sure, what would be the fun in that? I said we could go to Las Vegas for the honeymoon, if he wanted, but, surprise, surprise, he's booked all-inclusive in Majorca, the mean old sod!'

'Where do you live in London?' Stella enquired and was delighted to find the answer was Streatham, only a few miles up the road from Camley. 'You really must come to our concert on Saturday afternoon. Cameron Keene is playing.'

'Now isn't he the one Amber's boyfriend is the manager of?'

'He is indeed. The very one. Though unfortunately I have

just wounded Cameron's masculine pride, so I'm hoping he won't change his mind and cancel.'

'What did he do to deserve that, at all?' demanded Dolours. Then she nudged Stella in the ribs. 'As if we didn't know. They're all the same, men. No better than the beasts in the field.'

Stella decided against trying to explain that it was Cameron's heart rather than his sexual prowess that had been at issue in this case.

'Just drop us a text if it's all on and I'll be delighted to come. Give me a chance to get away from Brendan's mother and the serviette-folding session she's got planned for the wedding.'

Stella took her leave as another enormous jug of Martini arrived, sent by a young man the other side of the room. The group gave him and his friends a big thumbs-up. She hoped Dolours was going to behave herself or there might not *be* a wedding.

The following morning she got up earlier than usual and put on jeans and sneakers to go to the beach to look for Jesse. She was surprised to find Debora sitting on a wall outside her hotel with a hot chocolate and a bag of croissants.

'What are you doing up so early?'

'I was going to go for a run and I got waylaid by these croissants. Why don't you have one? They're delicious. Duncan told me about you and Cameron last night. Don't give it a second thought. You won't dent Cameron's ego. He's impermeable. Things just run off him. So cheer up and have another croissant. They're remarkably good, even though I bought them in the gas station.'

'Debora, you are entirely wonderful. Thank you for the croissant and the chocolate. I'm going to have to desert you to go and look for my grandson. One of Roxy's followers says they might have seen him in Hove. Near the beach huts. I think he might be staying in one.'

'Cool. I think your beach huts are so cute. Why doesn't everyone stay in them?'

'I don't think you're allowed to. There's probably a by-law to stop you. There are by-laws to stop you doing most things you want to do, I seem to remember as a kid.'

'Well, good luck. How are things back in Camley?'

Stella realized, with a pang of guilt, that she hadn't checked yet today.

'Don't worry,' Debora reassured her. 'I'll make sure everything's on course. Following Cameron around isn't a full-time job. As a matter of fact, he seems to be behaving.'

'You still love him, don't you?'

'Well, you know,' Debora replied calmly, 'me and Tammy Wynette seem to be one-man women.'

Debora waved her goodbye.

Stella jumped on the first bus that came along and got off as soon as she glimpsed a row of beach huts. There were rows and rows as far as the eye could see with doors in orange, turquoise, lemon, hot-pink, purple and sea-green. As it was a Thursday and very early, most of the huts were still closed up. The open ones seemed to be occupied by oldies in bathing costumes with skin like pickled walnuts or young mums with babies or toddlers too young for school. It struck Stella that there were more dogs than people at this hour, scampering along the edge of the shingle where the tide had left strands of seaweed and patches of greyish sand to explore.

She felt the kick of excitement as she started her search. Maybe at last she was going to discover her missing grandson.

An hour later, the excitement was beginning to ebb with the receding tide. She had shown the photograph to all the people she came across, an ice-cream man and the owner of a cafe-kiosk which sold everything from bacon sandwiches to fragrant French crêpes, but no one seemed to have seen either the boy or the dog. Stella bought herself a latte and resumed the search.

After an hour of searching, she was beginning to feel desperate. A man with a dog a bit like Jesse's lurcher stopped for a moment to use his phone and she made one last attempt to show him the photograph and explain the story.

He shook his head. 'You should ask the Beach Hut Man. He knows everyone down here.'

'The Beach Hut Man?'

'I'm afraid I don't know his name or where he lives, but he's usually around here somewhere. He mends beach huts. Like a public service. Doesn't charge anyone except materials. Bit eccentric, really, but a nice bloke. I don't know what he lives off. Certainly not mending beach huts.'

Stella thanked him, feeling a tiny bit better. For what seemed like miles she wandered up and down the beach huts in search of a character who seemed to be more elusive than the Scarlet Pimpernel. Eventually, exhausted, she went back to The Old Galleon. Wondering if maybe she should say sorry, she went up and knocked on Cameron's door, but it was Duncan who appeared on the landing.

'Too early for Cam, I'm afraid.'

Still a little embarrassed about last night, Stella shrugged and made for the stairs. Duncan came with her. The lobby was empty. Outside the sun shone invitingly. Stella said goodbye and crossed the road, darting between cars, and stood on the seafront, breathing in the salt air. To her surprise Duncan was still at her side.

Life in Brighton started slowly and they had the whole of

the prom to themselves. 'I can see why people love it here,' she announced, more wistfully than she had intended.

'Not missing Camley, then?'

Stella looked at him, wondering if the question were loaded. After all, it was true she wasn't missing Camley.

Out of nowhere a group of grizzled but frighteningly fit rollerbladers swooped past and almost knocked them down so that Duncan had to grab her and pull her out of the way. 'They're not taking any prisoners. I hope I'm that fit at seventy. Have you ever tried it?'

'What?' she asked, momentarily confused.

'Rollerblading,' he laughed.

'I'm not the physical type.' Stella shook her head.

'Me neither. Always the last to be picked for football.' He stood looking at the pier for a moment, the breeze ruffling his hair and bringing a sparkle to his grey-blue eyes. He was still a good-looking man. Success and America had given him a laid-back image that suited him. 'Funny, I don't think I'm a physical coward but there's one thing I've always hated the idea of.'

'What's that?'

He pointed to the pier which was just opening up for business. 'Rollercoasters! It's ridiculous because the odds of being killed are far greater crossing the road but they scare the hell out of me.'

Stella laughed. 'Me too. I could never go on them with Emma and I felt a real wuss. I used to fantasize that I'd go to a theme park on my own and have a go.'

'Let's do it.' He grabbed her hand before she had time to protest and announced in the kind of pompous voice they had on newsreels: 'Together they conquered their fear and faced the uncertain future.'

Then they were running along the prom, Stella shaking her head and trying to protest that this was nuts.

'Turbo Coaster or Crazy Mouse?' Duncan asked, as they went through the entrance.

Stella glanced at the girl in the booth enquiringly. 'The Crazy Mouse is famous for its negative vertical G forces,' she announced in a voice devoid of interest.

'What the hell does that mean?' Stella demanded.

The girl winked. 'It means it's pretty fucking scary.'

'C'mon, let's go for it.' Duncan took her hand again and they headed along the pier past the Twister and the Wild River and the terrifying Turbo Coaster. Stella glanced back with longing at the dodgems and the Waltzer.

'Do we really have to?'

But they were already climbing up towards the start of the Crazy Mouse.

'We're only just opening, mate,' the attendant greeted them. 'Only two of you?' You'll be flung together, then, won't you?'

And then they were secured and the bar was coming down on the car, and before Stella had time for further protests they started off.

They headed towards the first bend quite slowly, with the sea beyond, forty feet down. This wasn't so bad.

Another bend.

And another.

With the town behind them and the sea below, the car began to swirl dizzyingly and drop, drop, drop, swooping downwards so fast that the air was knocked from her lungs and she opened her mouth and screamed before the whole thing began again.

'Holy shit!' Stella shouted inelegantly. 'Whose crazy idea was this?'

And down they swooped again.

She realized she was hanging on to Duncan with one hand and the bar with the other. The words 'white-knuckle ride' popped into her consciousness.

And then some miracle took place.

She actually began to enjoy it! She turned to him, laughing, and found that he was laughing too. By some trick of the light or the wind, he looked thirty years younger. What a great smile he had, somehow she hadn't noticed. *All that American dentistry*, she told herself firmly.

At last they slowed down and arrived back at the beginning. 'Well,' Stella grinned, 'that was the longest one minute and twenty seconds of my life!'

For answer, Duncan leaned over and kissed her lightly on the lips.

It was so sudden and unexpected that Stella almost wondered if she'd imagined it.

She stared back at him, trying to interpret what he meant by it.

'Right, folks,' the operator reassured her she hadn't gone mad. 'Break it up now. Don't forget to get your picture.' He grinned broadly. 'Unless you're married to other people.'

He turned away, laughing at his own joke.

Duncan dragged her to the booth where their photo was already available.

In the photograph they both had their heads thrown back and were looking surprisingly happy.

'We're not buying that!' she insisted, but Duncan was already handing over the money. 'Come on,' he stuffed the photograph into his coat pocket, 'let's go and get a doughnut. You haven't lived till you've had a doughnut on Brighton Pier. They're the food of the gods.'

They were cooked on the spot and only came in packets of three or six. 'Six, obviously,' Duncan insisted. 'We deserve it.'

The doughnuts were hot, amazingly light and melted in the mouth, quite unlike the usual stodgy, doughy things that stuck to the roof of your mouth.

'There you go. Two new experiences in one morning. Not bad for a pair of sexagenarians.'

Three new experiences, Stella almost added, but Duncan was already looking at his phone. 'Some minor crisis at the Dome. I'm afraid I'll have to go. At least it isn't the star being out cold this time. Yet. You are coming to the show, aren't you?'

'With Debora, I expect.'

'Great. There'll be some kind of do afterwards for family and friends.'

It was on the tip of Stella's tongue to ask: 'Is Amber going to be there?' but she realized how presumptuous it would sound. Quite probably it had meant nothing, a happy gesture on a happy day. What was the matter with her? She wasn't some silly seventeen-year-old. So Duncan had kissed her. It must have been the exhilaration of the moment, nothing more.

Duncan turned left out of The Old Galleon and cut through the Lanes towards the Dome. A *Big Issue* seller brandished a copy at him. 'Help the homeless, mate!' He had a gaunt junkie's face with long, lank hair and most of his teeth missing. Duncan glanced at the magazine. It featured a huge photograph of Cameron on the cover. Laughing, Duncan held out his money.

'Poor bloke, eh?' was the seller's surprising response. 'I may be down on my luck but at least I haven't got gout. I thought gout was something only that old bloke who built the Pavilion would have . . . what's 'is name? Prince somebody.'

'The Prince Regent?'

'That's the one! I suppose it's all the drugs these stars take.' He winked knowingly at Duncan.

Duncan walked on, looking for the nearest news-stand. He saw one on the corner of the Old Steine. There was Cameron's face again, this time taking up the entire front page of the *Daily Post*, with the headline: A Pain in the Toe for Ageing Rock God. Great. How the hell had they got hold of that story? Virtually no one knew about Cam's condition.

He walked briskly north, picking up a takeaway coffee from the little Italian stall. 'Don't worry, mate,' counselled the coffee seller. 'It might never happen.'

Duncan grinned ruefully. 'It just did.'

Feeling Groovy was on Kensington Gardens, one of the narrow streets he'd walked down with Stella. He smiled again at the name above the shop. How happy must they have been to come up with Feeling Groovy for a second-hand record shop?

The place was almost empty apart from a lugubrious lurcher and a bored-looking assistant. 'Anything I could help you with?' asked the bearded assistant.

'Thanks,' Duncan replied. 'I wondered if Jesse was about?'

The bearded youth glanced behind him.

'Who wants him?' asked a voice from behind a beaded 1950s curtain. Then Jesse stepped out. 'Duncan!' Jesse looked suddenly hunted. 'I wasn't expecting you!'

'Could we go and grab a coffee or something?' Duncan enquired.

'You've already got one,' pointed out Jesse.

'Take the dog for a walk, then?'

'OK?' he asked the assistant.

'Fine.' The beard nodded. 'The Vinyl Appreciation Society don't seem to be early risers. All those years of smoking dope seem to have slowed down their body clocks.'

Duncan glanced at Jesse as they walked together, the dog on the lead between them. He looked fine. A little thin perhaps, but remarkably cheerful for a runaway.

'How've you been?'

'OK. You?'

Duncan laughed. 'I haven't run away from home. Though occasionally I'd quite like to when Cameron gets particularly irritating.' He paused, his eyes on Jesse. 'Your gran's here. She's been looking everywhere for you.'

'I'm glad someone has. Not my mum and dad, you note.' The bitterness in his voice made Duncan reach out and put an arm round him. 'Your mum was here too. Then Ruby got chicken pox.'

'Not my dad, though. His diary is too full of convicts on death row to save. What's a moody teenager compared to that?'

'Look, Jesse. Can I go and find Stella? Will you stay at the shop till she comes? Not run off or anything?'

'OK. Scout's honour. Actually, I wasn't allowed to join the Scouts. Too militaristic, according to Dad. It was the poncy Woodcraft Folk for me.' Jesse sat down on a low wall and picked up Licorice. It touched Duncan to the core to see how the dog seemed to be his only source of affection.

'How did you find me?' Jesse asked.

'Dora told Stella she'd heard from you. She really didn't want to, Stella says, but she's worried about you too. Then they tracked down your friend Kirsty.'

'Kirsty warned me they'd been round.'

'Your gran suggested you might work in a record shop.' He grinned at Jesse. 'Given your propensity for terrible Sixties music. So she and I went round them all looking for you. Do you realize there are six in Brighton? You couldn't have chosen a place that only went for downloading? By the way, were you sleeping in Kirsty's beach hut?'

'Did she tell you?'

'Stella worked it out from a photo she saw at Kirsty's. All the hostels and homeless shelters had drawn a blank.'

'You really did all look for me, then?'

Jesse pretended to wipe his nose on his sleeve but Duncan guessed he was hiding his tears. 'But we didn't think you were allowed to.'

'You're not. Someone called the cops once. The Beach Hut Man knew about me, though. He caught me once and I thought that was it. But he's OK. As soon as he saw I wasn't vandalizing the place he let me help him with his jobs. He said it could be a kind of apprenticeship. So Gran's been looking all over for me. She really does care, doesn't she?'

'I'm sure your mum and dad do too.'

'Yeah, like they really show it.'

'Do you have Stella's mobile number?'

Jesse laughed. 'I do but she's an old person, remember, no matter what she looks like. She'll have her phone switched off.'

Jesse was right. Stella would have been mortified, since she considered herself pretty phone-savvy. Duncan rang Debora instead and asked if she knew where Stella was.

'Going to look at beach huts for some reason. She said she wanted to take some photographs.'

'I'll see you a bit later,' Duncan instructed Jesse. 'Don't go away. Do you need money for anything?'

Jesse grinned. 'I'm earning, remember.'

Duncan spotted a passing taxi and waved it down.

Stella began walking along the strip of tarmac next to the shingle beach. As the time passed more beach-hut owners seemed to be in evidence but no one who fitted the description of the Beach Hut Man.

A mile on she came across a man up a ladder, wearing only dungarees and a baseball cap, with a mahogany tan browner than the Cuprinol he was using to touch up a decaying rafter, and realized she'd struck gold. Everyone who passed seemed to know him and called out a greeting or request that he might drop by and look at some damp or a leaking bit of clapboard. 'You seem very popular,' Stella called up to him.

He came down the ladder and held out his hand.

'That's why they call me the Beach Hut Man.'

She decided to let him talk a little and to win his trust before wading in with any requests about Jesse. 'Are beach huts your hobby?'

He grinned. 'Obsession, my missus'd say. I love 'em. Can't bear to see them fall into rack and ruin so I help repair them. For free.'

'No wonder you're popular. Are they all the same, the huts?'

He laughed as if she'd cracked some uproarious joke. 'As different as Buckingham Palace is to a budgie cage. Some folks do them up to the nines with shelves and nick-nacks and bunches of flowers and shells, other folks just use them as storage for their windbreaker and deck chairs.'

Stella suddenly remembered the days they'd come to the seaside when she was a child, with a proper caravanserai of mother, father, aunties and uncles all carrying chairs, tables, cool bags, cushions, picnic baskets and, of course, the inevitable British windbreaker. The stripey windbreaker was as much a tradition of British holidaymaking as the towels your mum would hold up for your dad to protect his modesty.

Stella took the photograph of Jesse out of her bag. 'I just wondered if you'd seen this boy down here? He's my grandson.

I thought he might have been staying in a pale-blue and lime-green hut owned by some friends.'

'Don't the owners know?'

'Their daughter might, but she isn't saying.'

'Teenagers, eh? Nice-looking lad,' he said cagily.

'Yes, but have you seen him?'

He studied her intently, then decided to trust her. 'I might have. A lad who looks a bit like that helps me sometimes.'

'Do you know his name?'

'He never said. I saw him down here late one night. Almost called the police. Then he came right up to me and held out a hand. Well, I couldn't call the police after that, could I?' He seemed to be giving something his deepest consideration.

'Are you a friend of that other chap?'

Stella looked gobsmacked. 'What other chap?'

'Night before last. Tall and grey-haired. Fancy dresser. Tanned skin like he's been on holiday. It was his shoes I noticed. They made me laugh. Blue suede shoes. He asked about the boy too.'

'Blue suede shoes?' Stella realized she was sounding like a parrot.

'Yeah, you know,' he suddenly warbled, wiggling his hips: *'You can do anything but don't step on my blue suede shoes . . .'*

Stella felt a stab of fear. What did this man want with her grandson? The thought of all the terrible things that could happen to an innocent and good-looking boy flooded into her mind.

'Could you give him a message?'

'What, the man with the blue suede shoes?'

'No. Jesse. My grandson. If you see him again, could you ask him to call me?' She wrote down the number in case somehow Jesse had lost it. 'Tell him I've been looking everywhere for him and I won't make him come home. I just want to talk to him.'

'Will do.' The Beach Hut Man nodded. 'At least, I will if I see him.'

'Thanks a lot.' Stella squeezed his hand. He smiled back. She was an attractive woman. For her age. 'You're doing a great job here.'

She turned back towards the town. Now all she had to do was find the man with the blue suede shoes. And discover what the hell he was doing looking for her grandson. And hope to goodness that Jesse would ring her.

Seventeen

—————

The bus she jumped on only went as far as the pier, so Stella was soon deposited among a crowd of laughing holiday-makers, some of whom had caught the sun and were glowing a fiery pink which would give them sleepless nights later.

She debated whether to wait for another bus or walk the half-mile to her hotel. On a whim she decided to walk along the pier and grab some lunch. Strolling along with the wind blowing in her hair she came to the booth showing the photographs from the Crazy Mouse. Duncan had taken a copy but the original was still there.

Stella smiled to herself ruefully, admitting it was no accident she found herself on the pier again. She wanted a copy too. She paid the rip-off cost of £7.50 while they printed one up and then placed it carefully in the front pocket of her handbag. Then she ordered fish and chips and ate them sitting on a bench watching a group of mothers with their toddlers on the beach below run in and out of the sea screaming with delight. Soon Ruby would be old enough to do that. She hoped desperately that Emma and Stuart could sort themselves out and persuade

Jesse that they had done so, so that their family could be healed. Somehow it was worse when your child's marriage failed than it was when your own did, because you experienced their sadness and sense of failure, plus the guilt of wondering if you also held some responsibility. Had you not loved them enough, failed to make them feel sufficiently secure so that they could give love, or had you not given them the right example of what a stable, loving family ought to be?

She finished her lunch and set off back down the pier. What would she do if she hadn't found Jesse by tomorrow? She would have to go back to her real life and take up the reins of normality. The thought depressed her.

In front of her a couple were posing for a seaside photographer who was saying something funny that was making them laugh. She saw him take photographs of other couples and families, just on spec, as they strolled along the pier. Could he have taken a photo of Duncan and her without them even knowing?

Feeling sixteen again she looked at the board, plastered with photos of happy holidaying people. There, right in the bottom corner, was a photograph of Duncan and her. Stella glanced round guiltily as if someone might come up and accuse her of unforgivably foolish behaviour, then ordered a copy from the photographer.

Duncan was leaning over her and whispering something in her ear. She had no idea what it was but she had her head down, looking almost shy. She wondered if she looked like that in photographs with Matthew. Young, eager, almost hesitant.

And Matthew. Wasn't he totally different with Fabia to how he had been with her?

As she pondered these questions she suddenly noticed what

Duncan was wearing. A dark bomber jacket over a white tee shirt, faded blue jeans and blue suede shoes. That meant that it had been Duncan who had been on the beach looking for Jesse. Duncan had known that Jesse was hiding out in Kirsty's parents' beach hut and even though she had been eaten up with worry he hadn't told her!

She felt herself going white with anger. What the hell did he think he was up to? She half ran back down the pier, glad she was wearing trainers, and crossed the road to The Old Galleon.

Debora was sitting sunning herself on the terrace.

'Stella! Duncan's been hunting high and low for you. He's looking like a kid at Christmas. I don't know what you two are hatching. I thought it was Cameron you'd wanted to see.'

At that moment Duncan spilled out of the bar, looking so relieved to see her that she forgot about the Beach Hut Man's revelation.

'Is it Jesse?'

Duncan just smiled. 'Come on. I've got a cab waiting.'

In five minutes they were outside the record shop.

She had hardly opened the door when a lanky figure shot out and flung himself into her arms, half dragging her down the street so that his comrades wouldn't witness the tears he was trying so hard to disguise.

Stella almost wept as well, with love and relief, and delight that he so clearly wanted to be found.

Before she could speak a dog tore out of the shop and barked at them jealously, jumping up between them, outraged at having a rival for the object of her adoration.

'Down, Licky!' Jesse grinned.

But the dog was having none of it. She continued to bark furiously until Jesse bent down and picked her up in his arms.

'Do you think Mum and Dad will let me keep her? You'll have her if they don't, won't you, please, Gran?'

'I will,' intervened Duncan.

They both looked at him in surprise. 'But you live in California,' Stella reminded him.

'I'm thinking of moving back. It's no place for the old.'

'I thought it was where the old all went. For the heat.'

'That's Florida. Anyway they're Americans. Oddly enough you get to miss the old country.'

'But what about Cameron?'

'Cameron'll survive. Are you thinking of going with him?' She knew he was only teasing, that he knew perfectly well that the suggestion was ludicrous.

'Duncan,' Stella remembered she was furious with him, 'don't be so bloody ridiculous!'

Jesse watched them both, smiling to himself.

'Gran, do you know what?' Jesse asked, his eyes shining. 'Duncan's asked if I want to play guitar with Cameron to-morrow. He says he put some mad offer about it on their website.'

'Stupid of me,' Duncan admitted. 'A hip brat like you would never have looked at our website anyway.'

She saw the grin that flashed between them. Duncan seemed to have a way with Jesse which was all the more surprising as he had no kids of his own.

'That's very generous of Duncan.' Stella smiled her thanks.

'How else do you think he persuaded me to give myself in?' Jesse's mischievous tone reassured Stella that he had clearly survived his adventure without too much damage.

'Don't forget, you troublesome youth, we've got to OK it with Cameron first.'

'You've got to ring your mum and dad. Now!' Stella got out her phone and handed it to him.

'Jesse!' shouted Emma when she realized it was her son. 'Oh God, Jess, you idiot, you darling, are you all right?'

'Jess, my God!' This time it was Stuart. 'I'm coming to get you. Now, this minute!'

'Dad, Dad, calm down! I can't leave till Saturday lunchtime. I promised the people I work for.'

'The people you work for? But surely we matter more than they do?' He realized his mistake, that he was treating Jesse like a child again, riding roughshod over Jesse's needs, even. 'OK, OK, whatever you say, but Jess? You promise you won't do a runner?'

Jesse laughed. 'Gran's here. She's not going to let me out of her sight, are you, Gran?'

Stella suddenly realized the import of Jesse's words. If he wouldn't leave Brighton till lunchtime on Saturday she wouldn't be back in time for the concert in her own garden! Biting back her disappointment, Stella realized that staying with Jesse mattered more to her than the concert.

'Jess, we've been so worried about you,' Stuart continued, his voice raw with anguish. 'We love you, Jess. You do know that? There's been a big hole in the family without you.'

'Yes, Dad. I know that.'

'Things will be different. We'll all sit down and talk about it together. As a family.'

'Even Ruby?'

Stuart laughed. 'Even Ruby. She's missed you too. And Izzy keeps laying a place for you at supper.'

Jesse brushed a tear off his face roughly. 'Give her a hug from me.'

'Mum wants to speak to Gran.'

Jesse handed the phone to Stella. 'Are you sure he's going to come home?' Emma asked her.

'I'll bring him, don't worry.'

'But you've got the concert in your garden. You can't stay there till lunch on Saturday. The doors open at one-thirty. I'll come down and get him.'

'Your mum says she'll come and get you today.'

With all the self-centredness of youth, Jesse shook his head vehemently.

'It's all right. I'll stay.'

Jesse smiled at her gratefully. That was worth the sacrifice. Besides, there were plenty of others who could hold the fort. Suze. Debora. Matthew and Fabia.

With a jolt she realized that she had mentally bracketed them together. She wouldn't think about that now. She'd found her grandson!

'Why don't we all go and find some food?' Duncan suggested. 'Now that we've found the selfish runaway I've realized how starving I am.'

Stella glanced anxiously at her grandson to see how he would take this, but he was smiling happily. 'Some of us have jobs.'

Duncan cracked with appreciative laughter. 'Touché. Yes, I do realize I am a parasite on the world of nine-to-five. Stella?'

Stella shook her head. Her feelings about Duncan were too complicated already. Besides, she'd told Debora she'd be back.

They walked back to The Old Galleon.

'Why didn't you tell me you thought you'd found him? The Beach Hut Man said you'd already been down there looking for him. I came here wanting to murder you.'

'I didn't know if it was really Jesse at the beach hut.' He stopped for a moment, looking at her intently. 'I know you're

333

a strong woman, Stella. But even strong people can be fragile sometimes. Jesse has no idea of the stress he's put you under, the little beast. I was worried what it would be like for you if it was all a blind alley.'

They were almost back at the hotel. They stood outside for a moment feeling the power of the sunshine on their faces. 'Thank you, Duncan, for all the trouble you've been to.'

'I like Jesse. I think he's got a lot of potential.'

'I wish his parents could see it.'

'He's shown he can survive without them. At his age that takes a lot of nerve. And I'm pretty sure underneath the bluster his parents are shit scared that he's managed to do that. Maybe they'll try harder now they know he's capable of walking away from them. And strong enough to do it.'

Stella sighed. 'I really do hope so.'

For a moment it looked as if he wanted to say something else but Cameron burst out of the door, the first five buttons of his shirt undone, revealing thick grey hair that wouldn't have shamed a yak. 'Hello, Dunc, old mate. You're for it, I can tell you. You'd better come in and face the damage.' He smiled at Stella as if she had never wounded his tender pride. 'Stella, the very woman I wanted to see. I gather there's something particular you wanted to ask me.' He flicked Duncan away as if he were an annoying fly and pushed him into the revolving doors. 'Now what was it you wanted me to do?'

Stella explained her plan to rid them all of Amber, while Cameron listened, sipping his Krug and nodding wisely. 'Not bad, not bad. It might work. Let's bloody hope so, eh?'

'So what's Duncan in disgrace for now?'

'What do you think, my lovely? Spending too much time with you, of course. Despite your ageing womb.'

'Cameron, please, or I might have to assault you in public which wouldn't be at all good for your image.'

'Her words, not mine. Tell you what, though, I happen to know it was Amber who planted the gout story, and I don't think Duncan will appreciate that, do you?'

'How on earth do you know that?'

'The rock critic on the *Post*'s a mate of mine. We were in rehab together.'

Stella looked stunned that Cameron had ever been in rehab.

Cameron read her thoughts and grinned. 'His worked better than mine.'

'You know what, Cameron Keene?' Stella realized that she was speaking no less than the truth. 'You are a disgraceful individual, but for some reason I'm incredibly fond of you.'

'I know you are,' Cameron replied, unmoved, and patted her hand. 'It's because I'm lovable. As long as you're not married to me.'

Stella leaned forward. 'On the subject of marriage, I've got a suggestion to make to you.'

He looked at her doubtfully. 'I thought you were still married to Matthew.'

Stella giggled. 'I'm not talking about me. I'm talking about Debora.'

Cameron sighed. 'Deb was the best wife I've ever had.'

'Why don't you remarry her, then? You and Roxy don't seem to even live together.'

'Roxy's a good girl. She wouldn't even ask for maintenance if we split. Fabia'd be livid with her. She'd say this generation has no moral standards. Besides, she lives off Roxy.'

'Maybe not for much longer.'

He looked at her meaningfully. 'Shall I go and break the news to Dunc about who shopped my gout to the *Post*?'

Stella walked back to her hotel and started to pack her bag. Soon reality would be returning and she wasn't sure she was ready for it.

Brighton had taken on its own wild and wonderful allure, like the parallel universe in a movie. Would she be able to simply step through the membrane of fantasy and rejoin her previous life? Tomorrow was the last day she'd be here. After that she would be returning to Camley.

And then she would find out.

Stella picked Jesse up from the record shop as soon as he finished work at six the next day. His workmates were standing around to wish him luck. She hadn't seen him so excited since his sixth birthday party. He was so full of anticipation that he forgot his rucksack and one of the beards had to chase down the street after them.

They hurried past Brighton Pavilion, through the Pavilion Gardens, which was filled with Cam fans sitting on rugs picnicking as if they were going to Glyndebourne, past the carved stone arches with the big gold 'D' for the Dome above them, and headed for the stage door. A few last-minute returns were being sold and Stella had to laugh that even the ticket sales booths were carved in wood like Eastern fantasies.

The girl sitting in the small reception area backstage treated them as if they were proper artists. Jesse could hardly believe it when she handed them both a badge that said: Access All Areas. He looked down at it as he slotted his badge into its plastic casing as if it were an Olympic Gold.

Jesse stood beside her, enthralled, staring at the photographs of bands and singers who had played at the Dome. The receptionist followed his gaze. 'Pink Floyd debuted *Dark Side of the Moon* here in 1972,' she announced proudly. 'Bowie,

Hendrix and Tangerine Dream have all played here. But we think our finest hour,' she looked at Stella as someone likely to appreciate this triumph, 'was Abba winning the Eurovision Song Contest here with "Waterloo"!'

The joys of Abba were lost on Jesse. He was gawping as if he'd seen an apparition. 'Look, Gran, there!' On the wall behind the girl's head was an enlarged ticket for 8 November 1969 to see The Incredible String Band.

'Can I take a photo with my phone?'

'Course you can. Do you want me to take one of both of you with it?'

Jesse looked embarrassed but Stella had no such compunction. 'Yes!' she announced. 'We do!'

As they went backstage to look for Duncan, Jesse was mesmerized by everything he saw, from the harassed runner Cameron kept busy before every show with some new and exotic demand – tonight it was a Pinball machine – to the guys on the lighting and sound desks, and the roadies testing out the instruments and doing the sound checks. 'Cam's planning a little surprise tonight with the confetti canons,' Laurie informed them. 'Since it's the last official show in the tour.' He grinned at Stella. 'Not forgetting yours, of course.'

Stella could quite see why people in bands saw each other and their entourages as family, right down to the squabbles. They were beginning to feel like her family too.

They found Cameron and Duncan in the Band Room having a pre-show bite of smoked salmon and scrambled egg on bagels.

'I've been keeping an eye on him.' Debora appeared from one of the dressing rooms and joined them. 'He's surprisingly sober.'

'Plenty of time yet,' Cameron goaded her, his mouth full of salmon.

'And by the way,' she whispered to Stella, 'all is not well with Duncan and Amber. He can't believe she could have shopped Cam's gout to the newspapers!'

'So, how is the new rock star?' Cameron indicated Jesse. Stella breathed a sigh of relief. Cameron had obviously agreed to Jesse's debut. 'Come on, then, young 'un, let's go through a few chords, shall we?'

Jesse smiled. 'Actually, I downloaded them from the Internet and I've been practising all night.' He grinned at Cameron. 'Didn't want to look like a complete dick.'

He played them to Cameron.

Cameron clapped and shook his head in amazement. 'Wonderful thing, the Internet. Pity it's killing the recording business.'

'Just as well you own all those golf courses and hotels,' reminded Duncan with a wink.

'I wasn't actually thinking of myself,' was the pompous rejoinder.

'That's a first,' Debora murmured and congratulated Jesse, who was looking unashamedly proud to have impressed Cameron with his chord sequences.

'So what happens next?' Stella was almost as excited as Jesse.

'We smoke a few spliffs, drop the odd pill and crack open the Jack Daniel's,' Cameron informed her.

'You wish.' Duncan grinned. 'Mostly we play Grand Theft Auto.'

'Duncan,' Cameron tutted, 'we have an image to keep up here.'

Jesse laughed delightedly. 'I'm pretty good at Grand Theft Auto.'

'Thank God for that,' Duncan congratulated. 'You can take over minding Cameron.'

'What about the instruments?' Jesse asked shyly. 'Don't you have to check them yourselves?' Stella could tell that he was in teenage-boy heaven.

'Laurie will have done all that,' Cameron shrugged, 'that's why we pay him vast amounts of money. Besides which, I'm getting deaf. It's all that playing next to giant amps in dingy dives when we were young.'

'As well as the gout?' Jesse asked daringly. Stella couldn't believe this was the same troubled kid who'd run away from home.

'Watch it, cock,' Cameron snapped. 'You could be off the bill, you know.'

'I'm sorry,' Jesse stammered, 'I didn't mean to cause offence.'

Cameron ruffled his hair, suddenly affectionate. 'None taken, lad, none taken. You remind me of my kid, actually. Which one is it, Deb?'

'Karl,' replied Debora without looking up from her copy of *Vogue*.

'That's the one. Karl. He's in a band of his own. Wouldn't join ours. Had to make his own way. Silly little bugger.'

'Actually,' Debora pointed out, 'Cold Heart are quite well known.'

'Your son's in Cold Heart?' blurted Jesse, impressed. 'They're amazing.'

'As a matter of fact,' Duncan decided it would be politic to interrupt, 'Jesse's a big fan of The Incredible String Band.'

'They played here in 1969,' Jesse announced. 'Would you like to see a photo of the ticket?'

If Cameron had been wearing glasses he would have looked

over the top of them. 'I'd keep that to yourself, if I was you, son.'

'Nonsense,' supported Duncan staunchly. 'They were true artists. Remember that thirteen-minute reflection on life, love and amoebas? Who else had that purity and innocence? Not to mention complete lack of commercialism? Even the Archbishop of Canterbury said they were miraculous.'

'I rest my case.' Cameron grinned. 'Besides,' he glanced at Stella with an anything-but-pure expression, 'I had another source of purity and innocence.'

'Don't you have to get changed or something?' Stella quickly intervened.

Cameron looked down at his blue jeans and denim shirt. 'What's wrong with this?' he demanded in hurt tones. 'We're not fucking Queen, you know.'

Debora jumped up. 'You look gorgeous. Just like James Taylor when he looked like James Taylor.' She winked at Stella.

'He's bald as a billiard ball now.' Cameron tossed his shoulder-length locks proudly.

Laurie appeared at just the right time, announcing that he'd checked the line-up and it was time for Cam to come and do his own sound check.

'Come on, then, you weird kid,' Cameron put his arm round Jesse, 'come and hear some real music.' He headed for the stage with Duncan.

Jesse laughed and said he just needed to get his guitar.

'I like Cam, don't you?' he whispered to Stella as he picked it up. 'Not as much as Duncan, obviously.'

'How do you all actually live like this?' Stella asked Debora when they'd gone.

Debora closed her magazine. 'Crazy, isn't it? Real life has a habit of seeming a bit dull afterwards. Going to the super-market. Doing the laundry.'

Stella could well imagine. She was certainly finding it hard to picture herself painting pets and putting up with Matthew. On the other hand, this clearly wasn't real life or anything approximating it.

'And we don't tour that much, thanks to Dunc's financial wizardry. We wouldn't have come this time if it hadn't been for Cam wanting to re-master "Don't Leave Me". We're going to do that next week after your concert. Speaking of which, I'm heading off to Camley tonight after the show. Gotta make sure my canapés are all there!'

The fact that the concert in her garden was tomorrow seemed quite unreal. In fact, Camley seemed unreal and even the cause they were fundraising for. She felt as if she'd landed in this alien universe and she was enjoying herself quite inor-dinately much. Tomorrow all that would end.

Maybe it wasn't before time.

'Debora,' she got up and gave Debora an unexpected hug. 'I'm so glad you came. I'm so glad we've become friends.'

Debora hugged her back. 'Me too, Stella. I feel like I've known you forever. Now let's go and keep an eye on Cameron and make sure he was only kidding about those pills and spliffs.'

Stella was longing to see every single aspect of the backstage experience but now that Jesse was happily found, real life was beginning to seep back in. And with it a big dollop of guilt that she'd left everything in Camley to Suze to supervise.

'I won't be a moment.' She waved Debora off. 'I've had six missed calls from Suze. I'd better just check that everything's OK for tomorrow.'

'*Stella!*' was Suze's reply when she picked up the phone. '*Why haven't you been returning my messages?*'

'I'm really sorry. Jesse and I are backstage at Cameron's last concert. It's all so exciting I forgot to check my phone.'

'Even though the effing concert tomorrow is *in your garden*?' Suze was boiling with righteous indignation.

'I'm so sorry, Suze, after all the work you've all done.'

'I should bloody well think so. We can't all swan off on backstage fantasies imagining we're sixteen again.'

'How's it all going, anyway?' she asked contritely, knowing Suze was right.

'As a matter of fact, pretty well. The marquee's up, chairs arrived, fizz cooling away nicely, though I did have a bit of a barney with the champagne people. They object to us cooling it in dustbins full of ice. Apparently, it makes the labels come off so people can't tell whose free champagne they're drinking. On the other hand, as I said, no one'll appreciate their champagne anyway unless it's cold.'

Stella could just imagine the champagne PR having to confront the force that was Suze and needing to go home and lie down.

'The auction prizes are here, including Amber's womb, of course . . .'

Where *was* Amber? Stella suddenly thought. Not like her to stay out of the limelight.

'. . . Bernie may be eighty but he's still offering a day of DIY, bless him; the garden centre's given us a pergola, or was it an arbour? The thing that looks like a sentry box without the sentry; The Glebe's thrown in a free three-course lunch; you're painting a pet, oh, and someone donated the most adorable old English sheepdog puppy, you won't believe how cute, all black and white and fluffy like a mini Dulux dog. It almost made *me* a dog lover and you know how I can't stand animals.'

'That all sounds wonderful. Oh, by the way, I invited that young man Hal.'

'Stella! I thought he'd be the last person you wanted, what with your Emma.'

'I have a plan for Hal,' Stella announced mysteriously.

'That sounds ominous. Does it involve inscribing Adulterer on his tummy like that guy had Pervert in *The Girl with the Dragon Tattoo*?'

'Not quite. Worse, I think.'

'Oh, goody. We also had a call from a girl calling herself Dolours – you gave her the number – could that really be right? Doesn't it mean pain or something?'

'I think it's more like Sorrow. I think Dolours is named after the Virgin Mary and her seven sorrows.'

'Good God! Have I ever told you I'm glad I'm an atheist?'

'Frequently.'

'Well, here's another reason, so I can't go calling my unfortunate offspring weird religious names.'

'Anyway, what did Dolours have to say?'

'That she's got a ticket and she's coming tomorrow.'

'Wonderful. Tomorrow is shaping up really promisingly.'

'Why?' Suze asked suspiciously. 'Stella, what are you up to?'

'You'll have to wait and see. I just hope I get there, that's all.'

'*What?!* What do you mean, you hope you'll get here?'

'Jesse isn't free till one p.m., and I'm not letting him out of my sight till he's back with his mum and dad.'

'Stella, have I told you that sometimes I would like to kill you?'

'I know, I'm a stubborn old bag, but I have to do it.' She realized she'd left the most important question till last. 'What about Matthew and Fabia?'

'Hasn't he been in touch? Even about Jesse?'

'No, not once since I left.'

'You're kidding!'

'Matthew is not good at imagining realities other than his own.'

'I can see that. As a matter of fact, they've been skipping around holding hands like Romeo and Juliet. And stop pretending you don't care.'

'I do care.' The trouble was, while she was here, in this strange alternative reality, she couldn't bring herself to come to a decision. And she knew that when she came home and had to face his betrayal, she would care very much indeed. But what she wanted to do about it, she had no idea.

'Good. You're going to have to get off your cloud, to coin a phrase, and deal with this, you know.'

'I know.'

'Roxy's been livid with her. And Bernie's been equally livid with him.'

The fact that other people were involved, feeling sorry for her, fighting her corner, did penetrate her armour. Tomorrow, she told herself, like Scarlett O'Hara, I'll deal with it all tomorrow.

'Cameron's down to play at two-thirty. We'll push it back as much as we can, but two hundred people have paid good money to see him.'

'I know.'

'Well, you're certainly a good grandmother.'

Stella said goodbye. The question she didn't want to face was – was she really doing it all for Jesse? Or did she want to keep Duncan in her life just a little bit longer?

*

The roar from the waiting audience in the Dome told Stella that Cameron must have just appeared on stage.

She ran to the VIP viewing area just in time. Debora handed her a glass of champagne and pointed out Jesse, who was standing shyly at the back. Cameron walked to the front of the stage, unhooked the microphone and began to stride back and forwards right up to the lip of the stage.

'Hello, Brighton!' he shouted.

'Hello, Cameron!' they shouted back.

'We don't care if we baby boomers get a bad press just because we were young in the Sixties, do we?'

'No, we don't!'

'Was it our fault if we lived through the best time to be young in the whole of history?'

'No!' they returned with one voice.

Stella surveyed the crowd. There were two thousand of them, most of them about Stella's own age. They'd come in their blue jeans and their cowboy boots, their maxi dresses and their denim shirts.

'Did we ask for cheap houses and good pensions?'

'No!'

'Who, here, went to rock festivals?'

Loads of hands went up.

'Who wore flowers in their hair?'

Not so many hands this time. 'Good for you!'

'Lit their matches for Bob Dylan?'

'Yeah!' roared the crowd.

'Did anyone come to the Floyd concert here on this hallowed stage in 1972?'

When fifty or so put up their hands Cameron bowed elaborately down to them. 'Respect!'

'We don't care if we spend our kids' inheritance, do we? Buy that Lamborghini! Ride round the States on that Harley!'

'Yeah!'

'Let's hear it for Grey Power, you bunch of sad old hippies!'

The response could probably be heard ten miles away in dull, respectable Worthing.

'Scary, aren't they?' whispered a voice. She turned to find Duncan next to her. 'I predict a white riot.'

Cameron wasn't finished yet. 'I'd like to introduce the members of my band to you.' He named the drummer, bass player and his rhythm guitarist. 'And tonight, for one night only, we are joined by a very special guest, Mr Jesse Cope. Step forward, Jesse!'

Stella fumbled for her phone. She'd have to capture this or the family would kill her.

A cheer went up from a small group at the back. Jesse's colleagues from Feeling Groovy brought the age range down by about fifty years.

After that they launched into their set, the familiar feel-good music bringing everyone to their feet. And as at the previous concert, there was puzzled disappointment that Cameron, despite constant shouts for it, hadn't played 'Don't Leave Me in the Morning'.

Then came the tidal wave of relief as he came back on stage for his encore and launched straight into his best-known song. All over the auditorium couples caught each other's eyes, held hands and swayed lovingly. It was strange, marvelled Stella again, that a song so full of raw pain and unfulfilled longing could be 'our song' to so many people, instantly taking them back to their still-remembered youth.

On the final note, the confetti canons were fired, showering the entire audience in multi-coloured heart shapes.

'He's amazing with the audience, isn't he?' whispered Debora as they made their way backstage again.

'He's turning into an old softie,' commented Duncan. 'He'd have been a laughing stock if he'd done that forty years ago. By the way, Jesse was terrific.'

Stella smiled at him gratefully. It had really been down to him that Jesse had had this amazing chance.

They edged along the corridors past the caterers' plastic cases, piled high, which had contained the food and drink for the after-show party. The Band Room was already crowded with record-company executives, sponsors, local bigwigs, and members of the band and their families and friends. Staff from the caterers in black trousers and white tee shirts saying CREW CATERING handed round drinks and snacks to the hungry hordes.

Finally, Cameron himself arrived, Jesse in tow.

'He did all right, the lad,' Cameron congratulated, 'but I've told him he doesn't want to be a musician. Life on the road, drink and drugs all around you, your arse licked by useless toadies . . .' He looked straight at Duncan who started to laugh. 'Get a proper job. Choose a three-piece suite like that Scotch guy said. Right, now mine's a double Bell's, if anyone's asking.'

Debora went off to get him one.

'Shit,' Jesse suddenly announced, 'I forgot!' He ran off, leaving Stella anxiously wondering what was happening. In five minutes he was back clutching his rucksack. He deposited it on a table and started to decant an old Coke can, a pair of trainers and his headphones. At last he produced a battered vinyl album and handed it triumphantly to Stella. 'Robbie from the shop found it.'

Cameron grabbed it. 'Fuckin' hell, I've never even seen this myself. It must be some German bloody bootleg!'

347

The album was covered in blurry now-faded photographs that purported to capture moments in the rock star's real life. There was Cameron leapfrogging over another band member.

'I never did that in my life!' he protested. Then, looking at one showing him drinking from a bottle of Southern Comfort, he added, 'I loathe the stuff, I'm not Janis fucking Joplin!' There was another showing Cameron lying asleep in the back of a bus, completely zonked out. 'That's more like it! Probably been tripping!'

And, finally, there was a small photograph of a young girl with long blonde hair and huge, luminous eyes looking straight at the camera.

'My God,' Stella could hardly believe what she was seeing. 'It's me!'

They all stared at it. The girl was definitely her.

'Have you never seen it before either?'

Stella shook her head.

'How did they get the photograph?'

'From me.'

They all looked at Duncan.

'I was quite into photography then. A real backstage Bailey. It was for some limited edition. They probably only printed about a thousand copies. Could be worth a fortune now.'

Cameron studied the photograph with fascination. 'You haven't changed a bit, Stell. You've still got that Marianne Faithfull look that drove us all wild.'

Stella laughed out loud at the outrageous flattery. 'Except that I'm over sixty!'

'It doesn't matter, Gran,' Jesse informed her, 'you're still a ledge!'

'What's a ledge?' Stella asked, now laughing and crying at the same time.

'A legend, of course,' Duncan interpreted. 'And Jesse's absolutely right. You are a legend.'

A strange hush seemed to fall on the room. People began to stand back and make way for a late arrival.

Stella turned to find Amber walking towards them, dressed like a latter-day Goth from head to foot in tight black satin, her hair loose about her shoulders and her impressive breasts drawing the eye of every man in the room.

'So, what's all the excitement, then?' she asked, a tolerant smile pinned to her face.

'A brilliant surprise from Jesse,' Duncan explained. Stella noticed how he made sure Jesse got the credit. 'He found an old album of Cam's at the record shop where he works. It has a photograph of Stella, the perfect Sixties girl.'

'Taken by Duncan,' added Cameron, delighted to get the chance to stick the knife in. 'Isn't she gorgeous?' He held out the album for Amber to see.

Amber ignored it. 'Seeing as it's such a big night for surprises . . .' she let the words rest tantalizingly in the air until she had all their attention. 'I've got a surprise of my own. I've just found out I'm three months pregnant.' She glanced around the room, savouring the shock on all the different faces, from Cameron's to Laurie's, the roadie's. And, most of all, on Duncan's. 'Isn't that great now?'

Eighteen

In the stunned silence that followed, Amber looked not at Duncan but at Stella, with a smile of such superiority that Stella would have loved to slap her silly self-satisfied face. Amber's message was almost laughably clear: the triumph of the young womb over the old.

And Stella might indeed have been wounded and humiliated but for one thing. The vivid memory of Dolours telling her that Amber had been so turned off by having to look after her little brothers and sisters that, despite unanimous opposition, she had conned her way into getting herself sterilized. So unless Amber was the subject of a genuine miracle or had somehow had that process reversed, the happy announcement she'd just shared had to be a bluff.

Stella could just imagine the scenario Amber had in mind. She would persuade decent, honourable Duncan to stand by her, and then, when Stella was safely off the scene, she would wake up one day and have a convenient miscarriage.

She glanced at Duncan. His face was blank. She guessed he was genuinely shocked, horrified, even, but that his code of honour would not let him show it. She saw him drag his features into a smile of congratulation.

But she wasn't going to let the ghastly Amber get away with this stunt and inflict herself on Duncan and the people Stella had come to care for so much: Cameron, Debora, even Laurie the roadie.

And she had a pretty good idea how she was going to go about it.

'So, Duncan, me lad,' Cameron was the first to fill the shocked silence. 'You're going to be a father. I can highly recommend it. I have four wonderful children.'

'Five,' corrected Debora.

'Five wonderful children.' Cameron laughed. And then, in a discreet undertone while Amber let herself be congratulated, he added, 'Shall we crack open the champagne or start wearing black?'

'The weirdest thing is,' Debora pointed out softly, as soon as Duncan had walked away, 'she was looking straight at you when she told him the good news. Does she think you two are falling in love or something?'

Debora suddenly stared at Stella as if she had been struck by a bolt of lightning. 'You *are* falling in love!'

Stella shook her head. 'We're far too old and it's much too complicated. Maybe forty years ago we might have.'

'He says forty years ago the beautiful Stella hardly knew he existed.'

Stella flushed and looked away. Except for that one embarrassing night so long ago that both had tried to forget as soon as possible and never mentioned again. How different he was now, his shyness mellowed into sophistication, his inexperience into witty worldliness. Now it was Cameron who was a lovable buffoon and Duncan who had become the attractive one.

'But, Jeez, Stella,' now the shock had worn off, her mind was working furiously, 'remember what her sister told us? We can't let her get away with this! She picks the one decent man on the planet who'd stand by her and pulls the oldest trick in the book!'

'I know. Duncan's beginning to see through her and wham! Suddenly she's having his baby. But don't worry, as a matter of fact, I have a few tricks up my sleeve too. Shh! Duncan's coming back.'

Stella found that, for once in her life, she had no idea what to say and was grateful to Debora for speaking first. 'Gosh, Duncan, that was quite a surprise.'

Duncan just smiled. There were lines of anxiety in his tanned forehead she hadn't seen before but it was typical of him that he said nothing to suggest that he'd been as shocked as they were. 'The thing is,' Duncan glanced across at Amber who was revelling in her apparent status as mother-to-be, 'I've always hated the sight of an old man boasting about his babies. Fathers should be young and optimistic and able to roll on the floor. Not some old guy with a lovely young woman.'

'I'm sure you'd be able to roll on the floor,' was all Stella managed to say.

Debora, sensing she might be in the way, slipped off to fill the glasses.

Duncan's eyes fixed on hers for an instant. 'I'm sorry, Stella.'

Neither of them made any attempt to discuss or deny the obvious.

'Don't be,' and as she spoke she realized it was the painful truth, 'Amber's done me a favour. I think Brighton went to my head. I obviously still think I'm a rock chick and there's nothing sadder than that. Real life beckons for both of us.' She almost added that it had been the most memorable week of her life, but knew somehow that she didn't need to.

Outrageous and dishonest though Amber's action was, it was also a wake-up call, a reminder to Stella that ever since she had come home and found Cameron Keene's silver Airstream parked in her driveway, she had been living a fantasy.

Time to wake up. Time to decide if she was going to fight to save her marriage. Time to go home.

'So,' Cameron attempted to chase away the gloom that had descended on everyone but Amber and keep the party going, 'who's coming with me to the karaoke bar next door? I thought it'd be quite a laugh if I got up and sang my own songs.'

Stella shook her head, though she had to admit it sounded entertaining.

Duncan made his excuses and went to look for Amber.

'What's the betting she'd be one of those loathsome mums-to-be who renounce everything except kale smoothies?' Debora murmured. 'And make everyone else have them too. Poor old Duncan. Men really should learn to keep their trousers on. Speaking of which, I guess I'd better go and stop Cameron bringing back the waitress.'

'Do you really have to?' Stella wondered if life with Cameron would be worth the effort.

'Of course I don't. But he'll behave if I'm there and I'll feel powerful. Besides,' she winked at Stella, 'you should see me do "Like a Virgin"!'

Outside the Dome, they stood on the pavement for a moment. 'Are you really all right? About Duncan, I mean?'

'Of course, I am. It's a timely reminder. And don't worry.' Stella tapped the side of her nose. 'I'm not going to let her get away with it.'

'How intriguing. I wouldn't miss this for the world. So, the big day's here at last. I'm going early to dump my stuff at The Glebe and to make sure those canapés are cookin'. Is everything under control back there in commuter-land?'

'Suze will be on top of it, she's remarkably efficient under her disorganized exterior.'

Neither of them mentioned Matthew or Fabia but Debora sensed that some painful choices had been made tonight that Stella was going to keep to herself. She held out her arms to Stella. 'I love you, Stella Ainsworth. I can't think how I've lived without you all my life!'

'I know. I feel the same. Will you go back to the States? You know you're welcome to stay with us as long as you like.' As she made the offer she realized that she was talking as if life would be the same as it had ever been. Yet would it?

'I'm not sure. Maybe it's time for a change. Maybe I'll stay in London and try Internet dating.'

They looked at each other and laughed at this fate worse than death. 'I hear there's a site called Hot Grannies.'

'I hope that isn't what it sounds like. See you tomorrow, lovely Debora.'

'Ditto, lovely Stella. What have you done with Jesse, by the way?'

'Duncan has given him a room at The Old Galleon. I expect he'll go karaoke-ing with the band now he's a temporary member. Maybe I should have gone after all.'

'Don't worry, I'll look after him.'

Stella walked towards the seafront. The stars were amazing, like glitter scattered on a velvet cloth. To think, she told herself, I was just living my life, measuring it out in spaghetti Bolognese. She thought of Emma and Stuart, and Izzy and Ruby and Jesse. Of Suze and Bernie. And Matthew. Maybe on Sunday, when it was all over, she would invite them round, make an extra-large bowl and take up the reins of her life again.

She slept surprisingly well and didn't wake till nine, when the phone buzzed next to her.

'Good morning, Starshine,' Suze's earth-shattering warble of the words from the musical *Hair* greeted her.

Through her half-asleep consciousness Stella sat up in bed and answered with the next line. 'My God,' Stella demanded, 'did I just sing you the chorus from *Hair*? I must be going positively senile. I didn't even know I knew it! What's the news from the fundraising front? How goes Rock for Regeneration?'

'It would go a lot better if we knew when you'd be here. But fortunately you have an extraordinarily able second-in-command. *Moi.*'

'I'm no longer captain of that ship.' Stella sensed that Suze didn't want to mention Matthew and Fabia. That wasn't good. Usually she couldn't wait to give Stella an earful.

'I am due to pick Jesse up at one-thirty. The train leaves at one-fifty and gets into Camley at two-twenty. I have already purchased the tickets. We will get a taxi from there and I estimate being with you by two-thirty.'

'God, Stella, that's cutting it a bit fine, isn't it? Cameron's billed to sing then and the auction is after that.'

'Would it be possible to reverse them? Talk to Debora. She could swap heaven and hell through a little negotiation with God and the Devil. It'd be nothing after a life spent with Cameron.'

'See you later, Alligator.'

'In a while, Crocodile.'

Shut up, she told herself, climbing out of bed, any more

historical rock references and they could start their own Wiki-pedia.

She packed up her things and decided to have a last wander around Brighton. But before she did she called home. There was no answer. Everyone must be in the garden getting ready. So she left a message which Matthew probably wouldn't get, telling him of her arrival details and wishing them all good luck.

Then she paid her bill.

Without actually intending to she found herself in the street she had wandered around with Duncan. There were spaces on the first-floor balcony of an inviting-looking cafe and she decided to have breakfast there. On the way in she picked up a local free-sheet from a pile on the ground. She wanted to savour this last morning feeling part of this unique place.

Her cappuccino arrived and she opened the paper. On the front page was a huge review of Cameron's concert, and in the photo, right at the back, was Jesse. He even got a mention as a promising newcomer who brought a breath of fresh energy to this venerable institution.

Stella laughed out loud. How Cameron would hate being called a venerable institution! 'Although there is a revival in heritage brands like Cameron Keene, Status Quo and the Who taking to the road,' continued the review, no doubt written by someone aged ten, 'they can't just rely on endlessly belting out nothing but the old stuff to a younger audience. One way to keep fresh is to inject new blood into the line-up. The inclusion of Jesse Cope was inspired.'

Stella finished her coffee and picked up another three papers on her way out.

She spent the next couple of hours wandering around. She bought a dream catcher for Ruby, a psychedelic phone cover for Izzy and a pastel silk scarf for Emma which would blend with the muted shades she loved so much.

At last it was time to go and pick up Jesse. He would be thrilled with the review in the paper.

For once the shop was quite full. A bespectacled man in a beret and dark glasses was looking through the vinyl LPs while his son of about eight played with his phone. A young woman with amazing dreadlocks leaned on the counter looking through a book of poems by Patti Smith, while two grey-haired men called out jazz titles to each other to check if they already had that version in their collection.

Jesse was dealing with a customer.

Beginning to get jumpy about the time, Stella pointed to her watch. They only had half an hour to catch their train.

Jesse nodded and tried to hurry the man up. Suddenly, from behind the curtain, Robbie, one of the bearded assistants, appeared with a cupcake with a J-shaped candle stuck in it.

'There you go, mate,' he teased, 'don't forget us when you're a big rock star!'

Jesse was almost overcome as he blew out the candle, especially when Robbie produced an upended tin of dog food with another candle in it for Licorice.

By now Stella was frantically gesturing at the door.

When they produced their phone footage of last night's concert with Jesse's moment in the limelight, Stella knew when she was beaten. This was an amazing moment for her grandson, the introverted solitary boy who'd felt so unvalued that he'd run away from home, finding himself suddenly the centre of attention and clearly valued by the people he'd worked with.

She texted Suze that they had missed the train and to just go ahead without her.

At long last, Jesse tore himself away, with the dog on a nice red lead someone had produced as a parting gift. 'Sorry, Gran. I'm really, really sorry, but I couldn't just walk out, could I?'

'Of course you couldn't. Don't worry, there'll be other trains.'

Stella put her arm round her grandson, biting back her disappointment. You couldn't have everything you wanted in life; how often had she been telling herself that lately?

They waved goodbye to Jesse's workmates. Stella held his guitar while he shouldered his rucksack.

'Excuse me?' asked a voice behind them. 'Are you Mrs Ainsworth and Mr Jesse Cope?' They both swivelled round to find a taxi driver in an immaculate black suit holding open the door of a grey Mercedes. 'Please hop in. I will see to the bags. Then I am to drive you to Camley double quick.'

Stella definitely wasn't going to argue. She didn't know which good angel was responsible for sending it, but it was definitely a lifesaver. Instead of dashing to the station and finding that there was no train for an hour, they could lie back against the Mercedes' beige leather seating and leave the whole thing in the lap of the gods, or in this case, the friendly Nigerian driver.

They'd both forgotten Licorice, who leaped up onto the seat between them and settled down happily with her nose on Jesse's thigh.

'I hope Licky isn't car sick,' Stella commented.

For reply, the dog yawned dangerously as if she might indeed throw up, then closed her mouth and went to sleep.

'You know,' Stella shook her head, 'that dog would have winked if it knew how.'

She looked at her watch again then leaned forward to speak to the driver. 'What's the traffic like between here and Camley?'

'Very bad on the A23. Do not worry. I will take you round

the highways and byways. We will put our trust in God. He will get us there in the wink of an eye.'

'I'd rather Cameron had sent a helicopter,' whispered Jesse.

'Jesse Cope, you are being corrupted by rock royalty.'

'Perhaps you would like to join me in prayer?' offered the driver as he overtook a white van on the wrong side of the road going into Caterham.

'How about a hymn instead?' Stella suggested diplomatically. 'Guide Me O Thou Great Redeemer' seemed appropriate, rather like appealing to the Almighty for divine satnav, so they opted for that.

They both sang all they could remember of that venerable hymn and any others they could recall from school assemblies and unwillingly attended church services while the driver, content that he was carrying two Christian souls, though slightly disappointed that he was too late to convert them, drove at frightening speed through several red lights and even more amber ones, safe in the knowledge that the Lord would protect him from accident, prosecution or fixed penalties, until they reached the outskirts of Camley.

At last they were near home and it was almost 2.15 p.m. They passed The King's Arms with its garden where they'd had the tango lessons, Fabia's retro shop, looking bustling and busy, the plot where they hadn't yet managed to have the open-air cinema, even the site by the canal where Stella hoped the council would build offices out of old sea containers. This was real life, this was what she'd been fighting for.

The last week had been an idyll, an interlude, a moment out of time. And like all moments out of time, it had to end.

The Mercedes turned down their road. There were cars everywhere, parked on both sides and on the grass verges. She could imagine Mr and Mrs Husky hopping about irately.

'Here you are,' announced the driver, coming to a stop, 'delivered to you by the Almighty . . . and also ABC Cars of Croydon.' He handed them his card with a flourish.

'Do you know who booked the car?' Stella asked, suddenly curious, yet not sure she really wanted to know.

'Madam,' announced their smiling driver, 'I am only the messenger. For that you must ask further up the chain.'

He came round and opened the door. Stella stepped out. For a moment the house looked unfamiliar to her, as if it weren't the home she had lived in for most of her married life. And then she caught sight of the Airstream parked slap bang in her driveway, with Bernie leaning out of its window, happy as a pig in clover, checking tickets.

'Stella, Stella, thank God!' Suze ran down the drive. 'We've held off as long as we possibly can but the locals are getting restless!'

Jesse followed her with the bags, down the garden path at the side of the house.

The garden had been utterly transformed. Stella's painting studio was invisible behind the open-sided marquee which contained a bar, flowing with free champagne, and the small stage. Just like in Brighton, Laurie had obviously been busy banking up the amps and testing the guitars and microphones. But that was the only similarity. The whole garden was decked with bunting made out of squares of coloured cloth rivalling the pink and yellow of her riotous rose garden. Hollyhocks in every colour nodded engagingly, surrounded by Delft-blue delphiniums, scented stocks, snapdragons, and bright red geraniums. All around the edge of the garden people sat in chairs, nibbling their canapés and drinking champagne from the real glasses Fabia had insisted on. In the background a string quartet, commandeered by someone or other, entertained them with discreet chamber music.

Stella glanced round. Cameron was over by the bar, predictably knocking back free fizz – not by the glass but the bottle, which he held by its gold-topped neck like an Elizabethan lady in her ruff heading for the executioner. Roxy was there too, managing to look hip and modern in some kind of retro tea dress. And, oh my God, next to her was the French bulldog owner, complete with his dog in its socks.

When he caught sight of Stella he broke away from the group, Roxy in tow. She hadn't realized how very handsome he was. Clearly Roxy thought so too.

'Mrs Ainsworth,' he protested, 'I thought it was funny at first but my life's been made a misery by everyone wanting my dog. I can't get on with my work.'

'Come off it,' interrupted Roxy, 'I bet you've been loving every minute!'

Stella watched her, fascinated.

'So your dog's famous. Get over it. And she doesn't have to wear the socks, does she?' She leaned down and took them off. The dog looked at her gratefully.

'Hang on,' he protested, 'it's my bloody dog!' He studied her intently for a moment. 'You're Foxy Roxy!' he accused as if she had been deliberately concealing her identity.

'Yes.' She grinned. 'I'm nearly as famous as your dog!' She linked arms with him and picked up the dog at the same time. 'And now, sexy bulldog owner, we're going to get ourselves another glass of champagne.'

On the other side of the crowded lawn Stella saw Emma and Stuart arriving. Izzy spotted her brother and ran whooping towards him. 'Jess . . . eeee!' She threw herself into his arms.

Her daughter and son-in-law, holding Ruby, followed almost shyly.

Stella held her breath, hoping they had the good sense not to be angry.

'Mum, Dad, I can't tell you what an incredible time I've had!' Jesse stopped, realizing how this must sound to them when they'd been worrying about him so much.

'Jesse, darling,' Emma flung herself at him. 'As long as you're home safely none of it matters.'

Then Stuart was hugging him too and Ruby made a grab for his shirt collar. Stuart was the first to speak. 'Stella sent us the recording of last night. You were amazing!'

'I'm sorry, Dad,' Stella realized he was choking back the tears, 'I didn't mean to cause you all that worry. It's just that I couldn't go on as I was.'

Emma touched his cheek with her hand, tears streaming down her own face. 'Dad and I are going to have proper counselling, not with that silly woman.' She looked appealingly at Jesse. 'We could do it as a family, if you like, then you'd really get the chance to say what you thought of us.'

'No way.' Jesse shook his head. 'I'm quite happy to give it to you straight. I don't need the Nuremberg Trials.'

Stuart looked at him, amazed, hardly able to believe this was the same inarticulate boy who had disappeared such a short time ago.

'Oh,' Izzy said, disappointed. 'I thought it might be like when we tried to go to church as a family. We got Crunchies after that.'

Jesse grinned at her and turned back to his parents. 'You might not like it when I do.'

'Anything's better than what we've been through while you were gone. We love you, Jess.'

Jesse stood up straight and looked his father in the eye. 'Then you'll forget wanting me to read Law at university and let me go to music college.' He looked over towards Cameron, who was still quaffing free champagne at the bar. 'I might even get a celebrity reference to put on my CV and how many kids my age can claim that!'

Stuart grinned. 'I'm proud of you, Jess.'

'I know, Dad, but we need you at home more. You're an amazing lawyer, the way you stick up for the underprivileged, but I'm quite deserving too. I could teach you the guitar! Two months, maybe three and you'd be playing "Stairway to Heaven".'

'That's right, Jesse!' Roxy was passing, Phil the bulldog owner in tow. 'Get it in writing while you've got the power. Knowing parents, I give it a week at the most!'

'Thanks, Roxy,' Jesse replied. 'Gran says it was your tweet that helped her find me.'

'As long as you wanted to be found. I wasn't sure about that.'

Jesse looked at his mum and dad. 'I think maybe it was about time.'

Stella felt tears blur her eyes and turned away. She had to admire the fact that Emma and Stuart hadn't even mentioned the exams he had missed.

Where the hell was Matthew? Buried in the middle of the crowd somewhere?

And then she saw his car draw up and park behind the Airstream. She ran across the lawn greeting people as she went.

Fabia and he were emptying the boot of what looked like crates of wine.

'Stella, hello!' There was no delight in his voice, not even the stirrings of affection. 'These buggers are drinking us dry.

We've just been to Aldi to replenish the champagne.' He put the last case down on the pavement.

'Stella . . .' at last there was some emotion . . . 'we really need to talk.'

And with those words, standing like Ruth amid the alien fizz, Stella realized her marriage was over.

Nineteen

The extraordinary thing was, she felt only a lack.

She ought to feel something, she knew; fury, sorrow, resentment, loss, even emptiness, and yet she felt none of these things. And then she realized she did feel something: relief. Then, suddenly, other things too, fear uppermost, the terrifying question of what she was going to do now, how she would survive financially, the fear of loneliness, or perhaps even dying alone, but there was another feeling. That if she could conquer the fears, as she had the rollercoaster, perhaps there would be something better waiting for her on the other side.

But she hadn't been alone when she'd conquered the fear of the rollercoaster. She'd been with Duncan.

Fabia had had the tact for once to go and look for someone to help with the wine and left Matthew and Stella to face each other in the deserted driveway. Even Bernie had abandoned his post and joined the happy crowd.

'I'm sorry, Stella, I didn't mean to fall for Fabia. I expect you think it's pretty ridiculous, a stuffy accountant like me falling for someone so glamorous. You probably think it's pathetic, an old man suddenly wanting to dance and play the saxophone and feel young again.'

'No, Matthew, I don't think it's pathetic at all. I've watched you coming back to life since Fabia appeared. It was she who did it, not me.' She couldn't have been this generous, Stella knew, if Duncan hadn't come back into her own life. Yet soon he would be leaving again.

'Are you and Pappy going to get divorced?'

Stella swung round to find Izzy standing behind her, small and anxious, seeing another of the pillars of her own insecure life tumble before her eyes.

'I don't know, darling.' Stella opened her arms and pulled her granddaughter to her. 'But I'll always be here whatever happens, I promise you that.'

Izzy buried her face in Stella's familiar-smelling flowery shirt. 'I came to tell you, Cameron's going to be on soon. Jesse doesn't want you to miss it.'

The clapping started behind them. The auction was beginning. Stella tried to shake off the sensation that she was under anaesthetic, that when she came round her life would somehow be exactly as it had been before Jesse ran away, before Cameron's Airstream appeared, before she'd met Duncan again.

She wondered who would be conducting it. The usual charity auctioneer from the last remaining cattle auction in the South East?

'I'd better go,' Matthew told them both, 'I'm afraid it's me.' He started to walk towards the stage. 'Hello, everybody!'

When there was rather a feeble response, he repeated, louder, 'Hello, everybody!'

This time the response was less feeble. 'Hello, Matthew!'

'Thank you for supporting this wonderful venture, which, thanks to the incredible generosity of Cameron Keene –' he paused for the loud cheer as Cameron raised his bottle of fizz – 'we have been able to call Rock for Regeneration. And I want all of you to remember, as you reach for your wallets, what we've got to save here. In Camley we're near the city, but not in the city. We have the smell of mown lawns, while they have the smell of rubbish. The suburbs may be laughed at and yet this is where a lot of people live and a lot of people LOVE living. Let's show them how good Camley is, let's show Shoreditch and Chelsea that Camley is great, Camley is hip! And with your help, proud suburbanites, let's raise some money to save the places we love!'

The auction started, as many auctions do, with the generous offer of the hire of a country cottage in Cornwall. Stella smiled to see the husbands and wives debate that it was a five hour journey, versus the number of people they could fit in the cottage for the price. Then the bidding started, closing at £1,100.

Next up was Stella's offer of a pet painting. Maybe the presence of the French bulldog, plus Licorice in her red bandana and the sheepdog puppy, melted pet lovers' hearts because this went for a respectable £600.

A day with Roxy took them all by surprise by raising £1,500.

Debora's cookery course at The Glebe went for a modest £400, but Debora clearly didn't give a toss.

The adorable old English puppy went to Bernie for £300, to replace his dead black Lab. Everyone who knew him roared their delight as he tucked the wriggling bundle under his arm.

Then came the star attraction, Amber's giant technicolour womb.

Stella couldn't stop herself glancing around to see if Duncan had arrived and looked quickly away. He was standing under her weeping willow, between Amber, hateful Hal and the hideous dog, Donleavy. For a moment she wondered what had happened to Dolours.

And then the bidding began.

It was slow at first. Stella imagined this was what always happened when the item was genuinely valuable. And then it began to hot up. Stella could see that after five minutes it was between only two people, an earnest-looking man in spectacles and Hal.

It was already at five thousand pounds. Five thousand pounds! At a little unofficial auction in a suburban garden. She could see the doubt begin to settle on the face of the man in specs. His wife was already elbowing and tutting. Soon he would drop out.

To Matthew's utter amazement, Stella stepped in, telling Izzy she wouldn't be a minute.

She had a score to settle with Hal, and though she had no intention of owning the hideous geometric uterus, she thought he deserved to pay the maximum possible for it. This, she knew, was a dangerous game.

She was spurred on by the oohs and aahs of the audience and the announcement that wafted clearly across the crowd from Amber, 'Oh look, Duncan, Stella wants my womb!'

Hal, she knew, saw her simply as Emma's disapproving mother, a granny, and part of the pre-digital generation, whom everyone knew were simply a joke.

But, living in Camley, Stella was a regular at various small local auction houses. A life with Matthew had meant that they were forever bidding for works by the master, no matter how humble, that hopefully no one else had recognized.

Matthew watched as Stella bid, teased, drew back till the last possible moment, then bid again. When the spectacled bidder finally dropped out it became a duel between her and Hal. A game of poker.

And unlike Hal, Stella was good at reading reactions, which was why she managed to leave him hanging on, via her teasingly provocative tactics like coitus interruptus, at seven and a half thousand pounds.

The whole audience clapped as a slightly dazed Hal made the accidental final bid against himself of eight grand.

Amber ran towards him and planted a kiss on his lips in front of the whole gathering.

She then took a bow as if she were a Covent Garden diva, and she and Hal progressed through the admiring audience like Antony and Cleopatra.

Stella glanced at her daughter to see what she made of this but Emma simply shrugged at such mad extravagance and went on talking to Stuart.

Stella walked up to Amber and congratulated her. 'And of course on your pregnancy. Will you live in America?' She took a deep breath. 'I suppose you can choose wherever you want now that Cameron's getting a new business manager.'

She could see the shock registering on Amber's face. She wasn't to know it was something Stella had cooked up with Cameron to put the fear of God into her. Amber, like so many others, had assumed that Cameron was the one with the money and Duncan simply worked for him. Amber might do quite well from her painting but she hadn't expected to have to live off it.

Behind them, Cameron raised his glass wickedly as if in endorsement.

Stella glanced around the garden to make sure that Duncan was nowhere near and saw that Dolours, this time a vision in purple velvet, had arrived and was looking around her, shy for once, because she didn't know anyone.

Stella almost ran across the crowded lawn towards her. 'I'm so glad you're here.' She grabbed a glass from a passing helper and handed it to Amber's sister.

'Not really my scene.' Dolours grinned. 'I'm usually the one serving behind the bar.'

'I just thought I'd warn you,' Stella announced with a conspiratorial smile, 'your sister's just announced she's pregnant.'

'Jesus, Mary and Joseph! Now that really would be a miracle!'

On the other side of the garden Cameron had decided to abandon the bar and start making for the stage where he was about to be announced.

Laurie intercepted him, waving the free paper Stella had brought with her from Brighton. 'Cameron, old son, did you know you were a venerable institution?'

Cam stopped in his tracks and looked penetratingly at his roadie. 'What did I hear you say, minion?'

Laurie smiled blissfully. 'Not just a venerable institution, you're a heritage brand, mate, like the National Trust and HP Sauce!' Laurie fell about laughing just at the moment that Amber O'Riordan, emerging artist and mother-to-be, noticed her younger sister Dolours standing next to Stella at the bar.

The triumphal smile vanished from her face as she strode towards them, shaking off Hal's supportive arm. 'What the fuck are you doing here?' she demanded.

'Well, now, Bernie, that's not a very nice greeting, is it?' replied her sister. 'I thought seeing as you couldn't make it to my hen party, I'd catch up with you here.'

'Your sister and I got quite friendly in Brighton, didn't we, Lou?' Stella smiled.

Duncan was standing just behind them, talking to Cameron.

'Duncan,' Stella raised her voice, drawing them both into the conversation,

'I don't think you've ever met Amber's sister, Dolours, have you?'

Duncan shook his head in astonishment at the moment Dolours met Amber's horrified gaze.

'So, Bernie – sorry, Amber,' Dolours addressed her sister with a wicked glint in her eye. 'I hear I've to congratulate you. Stella tells me there's going to be a happy event. I hope you'll be inviting the whole family to the baptism.'

Amber turned to her new benefactor, Hal, with a beseeching look worthy of a Puccini heroine and fainted into his arms. Since Amber was generously built and Hal a fashionably skinny nerd, the poor man staggered under his newly acquired burden.

Stella and Dolours exchanged a satisfied smile. 'Hal,' Stella suggested, 'why don't you take Amber inside. I think she needs a little lie-down.'

'I really ought to go with her,' Duncan began to protest before Dolours gripped his arm. 'Duncan,' she insisted firmly, 'I think there're one or two things you ought to know about my sister . . .'

Dolours led a bemused Duncan back towards the bar just as Matthew, by now relishing his role as Master of Ceremonies, began to announce the highlight of the afternoon.

Cameron came to the microphone. Stella could see that Jesse was longing to be on stage but was hanging back, his old shy self now that he was on home ground.

'Right, you lot of rich shits,' Cameron announced, dispensing with the more usual 'ladies and gentlemen'. 'Personally, I loathed Camley and couldn't get out quick enough.' The audience roared with laughter. Being insulted by Cameron Keene was clearly a rare treat. 'But now I see the place isn't as bad as I thought. That must be a sign of ageing.' Another laugh. 'So, thank you for paying good money to see this venerable institution.' He grinned and waved his copy of the Brighton paper. 'Apparently, what we "heritage brands" need is a bit of youthful energy, so would Mr Jesse Cope step up onto the stage and join us for the first number, please!'

Jesse ran through the crowd as his delighted parents applauded and hugged each other.

'Now, before I start, I'd just like to say that I'd like my wife to come up on stage.'

'Which one?' heckled someone in the audience.

At the back of the crowd Roxy looked at Debora and said, 'He means you, Debora. He always meant you. Me and Halle, we were just distractions.'

'But you're married to him!' Debora pointed out.

'Yeah, well, he's asked me for a Haitian divorce. It's a reference to some song by Steely Dan, whoever they are. I said fine but I'd prefer one from England.' She pushed Debora through the crowd until she was climbing onto the stage.

'I am one helluva bad bet, Debora, but will you have me back?'

Debora looked at the audience of nice middle-class people from the suburbs. 'Shall we make him beg, ladies and gentlemen?'

'Yes!' roared the audience.

Cameron got down on his knees.

'Mind the gout!' shouted someone from the back.

'Will you have me back, Debora?'

'Shall I take him back, ladies and gentlemen?'

This time the roar was even louder. It seemed to Stella that it was more like the roar from a stadium than two hundred genteel people from Camley.

In front of a thrilled and delighted audience who would have paid their thirty pounds just for this moment, Cameron and Debora kissed, then she stepped back into the wings as Cameron dispensed with his usual routine and stunned the band by going straight into his first and most famous song.

The whole audience stood, entranced.

At the back of the garden, hidden by the shadow of her studio, Stella found Duncan was back by her side.

'I'm sorry you had to find out about Amber.'

'I'm not.'

And then Cameron's smoky, pain-shredded voice rang out through the still afternoon air:

Don't leave me in the morning,
Baby, I don't want to let you go;
Don't leave me in the morning,
Baby, I know our love could grow . . .

'Do you really think he wrote it about me?' Stella asked, still not quite convinced.

'I know he didn't.'

The sudden edge in Duncan's voice made her look in his direction. 'What do you mean?'

'Because Cameron didn't write it.'

Stella turned to him, a bewildered expression on her face. 'What do you mean?'

'I wrote it.'

Stella shook her head. 'Sorry? Are you saying you wrote Cameron Keene's greatest hit?'

'Yes. I wrote it. About you.'

It was as if they were completely alone in the middle of the noisy, crowded garden.

'It was after we spent that night together. You'd just told Cameron you wouldn't go with him and he took off, just like that, and left us both behind without a word. I was as upset as you were. I think you did it because you felt sorry for me. I knew it was a mercy fuck but you were the beautiful Stella Scott and I didn't care why you did it. I just didn't want the night to ever end. I didn't want you to get up in the morning and leave me. When you did I wrote the words to the song.'

He held up a dog-eared notebook.

'You hardly ever spoke to me again after that night and I thought I'd die.'

Stella felt the shame rise in her at the cruelty of youth. 'I'm so sorry, Duncan, I can't believe I behaved like that.' She hesitated, then added haltingly, hardly able to face him, 'But that song has made millions and millions for Cameron.'

'So what? I've loved you for forty years.' His eyes fixed on hers. 'I didn't begrudge Cameron his success because he hasn't loved anyone like I've loved you. I still love you, Stella. And I think you love me.'

Before she had a chance to answer, three dogs raced past them. Amber's horrible boxer, Donleavy, about to commit rapine on the gentle Licorice, followed by the sheepdog puppy.

Stella picked up a dustbin that had held ice for the champagne and poured it over the disgraceful Donleavy.

As he slunk off, she heard the sound of clapping and turned to find Izzy and Jesse ranged in defence of Licorice in case Donleavy decided on another attempt.

'Gran,' asked Izzy, trying to keep up with the mysterious speed of adult developments. 'If you and Granddad do get divorced, are you going to marry Duncan?'

Stella found something quite fundamental had happened to her voice.

'I probably shouldn't say this,' Izzy held tight onto Jesse's hand, 'but Duncan's a lot more fun than Granddad. And don't worry about Mum and Dad. They've been expecting it, haven't they, Jess?'

'Too right,' endorsed Jesse with a grin. 'Mum guessed when she saw you and Duncan together in Brighton. She thinks it's a really good idea because you won't be able to lecture her any more.'

Stella avoided Duncan's eye, still overwhelmed by the situation she found herself in.

Donleavy suddenly shook the water from his fur, soaking them all.

'Jesse, can you take that awful dog back to Amber?' Stella picked up the cowering Licorice. 'I'll bring her with me in a minute.'

Her two grandchildren dragged the disgusting dog in the direction of its owner.

Despite her protests, Duncan removed Licorice from Stella's grasp and placed the dog on the ground.

'I hope I'm not for the dustbin treatment too,' he announced as he pulled Stella into his arms.

The kiss that followed left Stella in no doubt of his intentions.

'Next time, when we go to bed together, I'd better make it a little more memorable.'

'But, Duncan,' Stella was beginning to come to her senses. 'We can't possibly get together, even if Matthew does go off with Fabia.'

'You're not going to tell me we're too old?'

'You live in America. I couldn't just up sticks and leave my grandchildren.'

'Who said you'd need to? Has it never crossed your mind, my long-lost inspiration, that Matthew has never been that interested in his grandchildren, whereas I like them and, as you've just heard, I think they quite like me? So I'm obviously going to have to move here. Especially now that I'm no longer Cameron's manager. Or so Amber tells me.' He smiled at Stella's look of embarrassment. 'I suppose you're pairing her off with the unfortunate tech millionaire?'

As Stella appeared to be lost for words, he kissed her again. This time Licorice seemed to be quite resigned to the situation and made no protest. 'And let's face it, Fabia isn't going to be exactly a hands-on step-grandmother. I think you'll have to have me whether you like it or not. Though I do have one more question.' He looked at her with a decidedly un-grandparental glint in his eye.

'*Are* you going to leave me in the morning?'

'I suppose that depends,' Stella replied, pulling him towards her again, 'on who gets up to make the tea.'

If you enjoyed *What Became of You, My Love?* you'll love
The Time of Their Lives. Read on for an extract

The Time of Their Lives

by

MAEVE HARAN

OUT NOW

The must-read novel for anyone who wasn't born yesterday

Sal had spent a lifetime building a career as a magazine editor
but she hadn't banked on a nasty surprise from the one area of
her life over which she had no control.

Claudia loved her urban existence – the thought of the
country sent shivers down her spine. But, as many women will
know, other people's needs always seem to come first . . .

Ella is ready to try something different. But she hadn't
bargained on quite such a radical change . . .

Laura succumbed to the oldest cliché in the book. But it
didn't make it any easier to accept.

Outside of the supportive world of their friendships,
they find their lives are far from what they expected – the
generation that wanted to change the world didn't bargain
on getting old.

CHAPTER 1

'OK, girls,' Claudia looked round at her three closest friends who were gathered for their usual night out in The Grecian Grove, a basement wine bar sporting badly drawn murals of lecherous shepherds chasing nymphs who didn't look as if they were trying that hard to get away, 'does anyone know what date it is today?'

To call them girls, Claudia knew, was pushing it. They weren't girls, as a matter of fact, they were women. Late middle-aged women. Once they would have been called old, but now, since sixty was the new forty, that had all changed.

Sal, Ella and Laura shrugged and exchanged mystified glances. 'It's not your birthday? No, that's in February and you'll be—' Ella ventured.

'Don't say it out loud!' cut in Sal, ever the most age-conscious of them. 'Someone might hear you!'

'What, some snake-hipped potential young lover?' Laura teased. 'I would feel I owed him the truth.'

'It's the thirtieth of September,' Claudia announced as if pulling a rabbit from a hat.

'So?' They all looked bemused.

'It was on the thirtieth of September that we all first met.' Claudia pulled a faded photograph from her bag. 'The first day of term at university. Over forty years ago!'

Sal looked as if she might pass out. The others scrambled

to see. There they were. Four hopeful eighteen-year-olds with long fringes, short skirts and knee-length boots, optimism and hope shining out of their fresh young faces.

'I must admit,' Ella said proudly, 'we look pretty good. Why do the young never believe they're beautiful? All I remember thinking was that my skin was shit and I ought to lose a stone.'

Claudia looked from her friends to the photo. At first glance Sal had worn best, with her chic clothes and fashionable haircut, but then she'd never had a husband or children to wear her out. Besides, there was something a little overdone about Sal's look that spoke of trying too hard. Laura had always been the most conventionally pretty, given to pastel sweaters and single strings of pearls. You knew, looking at Laura, that as a child she had probably owned a jewellery-box with a ballerina on top which revolved to the music. This ballerina had remained Laura's fashion icon. Next there was Ella. She had always been the elfin one. Then, three years ago, tragedy had struck out of a blue sky and had taken its toll, but she was finally looking like the old Ella. Oddly, she looked younger, not older, because she didn't try to alter her age.

Then there was Claudia herself with her carefully coloured hair in the same shade of nut-brown she always chose, not because it was her actual colour, she couldn't even recall what that was, but because Claudia believed it looked more natural. She wore her usual baggy beige jumper with the inevitable camisole underneath, jeans and boots.

'It can't be as long ago as that,' Sal wailed, looking as if she could see a bus coming towards her and couldn't get out of its path.

'They were good times, weren't they?' sighed Ella. She knew her two daughters judged things differently. They saw their parents' generation as selfish, not to mention promiscuous and probably druggy. The baby boomers had been the lucky ones, they moaned, inheritors of full employment, generous pensions and cheap property prices while their children had to face insecure jobs, extortionate housing costs and working till they were seventy.

Ella thought about it. They were right about the promiscuous bit. She would never dare confess to her daughters that at the age of twenty she'd prevented a man from telling her his name as they made love, preferring instead the excitement of erotic anonymity. How awful. Had she really done that? Not to mention slept with more men than she could remember the names of. Ah, the heady days after the Pill and before Aids.

Ella found herself smiling.

It had been an amazing moment. The music, the festivals, the sense that the young suddenly had the power and that times really were a-changing. But it was all a very long while ago.

Claudia put the photograph carefully back in her bag. 'I have a question to ask.' She poured them another glass of wine. 'The question is, seeing as we may have another thirty years to live, what the hell are we going to do with the rest of our lives?'

'Won't you go on teaching?' Ella asked, surprised. Claudia was so dedicated to her profession and had been teaching French practically since they left university. 'I thought you could go on forever nowadays.'

'I'm not sure I want to,' Claudia replied.

They stared at her, shocked. 'But you love teaching. You say it keeps you in touch with the young!' Laura protested.

'Not enough in touch, apparently.' Claudia tried to keep the bitterness out of her voice. 'I'm out of tune with technology, it seems. My favourite year group has been reassigned to a younger teacher who gets them to learn slang on YouTube.

It's having an energizing effect on even the slowest pupils according to the deputy head.'

Claudia tried not to remember the deputy head's patron-izing tone yesterday, when she had explained, as if talking to a very old person, that Peter Dooley, a squirt of thirty known by the rest of the staff as Drooly Dooley because of his habit of showering you with spit when he talked, would be taking over her favourite pupils.

'Mr Dooley!' Claudia had replied furiously. 'He has no experience of the real France! He looks everything up on the Internet!'

Too late she realized her mistake.

'Exactly!' the deputy head insisted; she was only thirty herself, with an MBA, not even a teaching degree, from a uni-versity in the North East – an ex-poly at that, Claudia had thought bitchily.

'But you've always been amazing with your pupils!' Sal defended indignantly. 'Do you remember, years before the Internet, you made tapes up with you and Gaby speaking French to one another? Your pupils loved them!'

Claudia blanched. The deputy head had actually produced one of these twenty-year-old anachronisms during their inter-view and had had the gall to hold it up and ask in a sugary tone, 'Of course you probably think the old ways are best, don't you, Claudia?'

Claudia had wanted to snap that she was perfectly au fait with modern teaching methods, thank you very much. But the truth was she was beginning to feel defeated. For the first time, since those heady days of the photograph, she had started to feel old. And it wasn't the fault of memory loss or the war with grey hair.

It was technology.

Jean-Paul Sartre might say hell was other people, but he'd

never been to an Apple store on a busy Saturday, only to be told you needed an appointment to talk to a 'genius', one of a thousand identikit geeky youths, before you could ask a simple question.

Nor had he to contend with the horrors of the 'managed learning environment' where pupils and even their parents could go online and access their school work from home. Even the tech-savviest staff found it a nightmare to operate. As if that weren't enough, now teachers were expected to identify their pupils' weaknesses using some hideous software developed by a ten-year-old!

'Snotty cow,' Ella's angry voice echoed through The Grecian Grove in Claudia's defence. 'You're far better at technology than I am. I still think an iPad is something made by Optrex. What are you going to do about it?'

'Actually,' Claudia realized the truth for the first time herself, 'I might even resign.'

'Claudia, no!' Laura was shocked. 'But you love teaching and you're really good at it!'

'Am I? Seriously, girls, the bastards think we're has-beens. Drooly Dooley even said, "If it's any consolation, Claudia, a lot of the older teachers are struggling with the system."'

'Bollocks!' protested Sal, emptying her glass.

'Anyway, another school would snap you up!' Laura, always the positive one in the group, happily married for twenty-five years and a great believer in the virtues of the institution, was attempting to answer Claudia's question. 'You're a wonderful teacher. You'd find something else useful to do. Funny, it only seems the blink of an eye since we first met. We should just keep calm and carry on. It'll only be another blink till we're ninety.'

'Except that this blink will be punctuated by arthritis, memory loss and absence of bladder control,' Sal pointed out laconically. 'And anyway, you should fight back! Don't take ageism lying down. We're not old yet. Not even middle-aged.'

Maybe because she was the one who most needed to earn her living, Sal was fighting ageing the hardest. She had declared war on body fat, laughter lines and any clothing in baggy linen. The dress she wore today was black gabardine, strictly sculpted and teamed with high heels. Ella had given up on anything but flatties years ago, and Claudia was wearing trainers so that she could walk to the tube.

She liked to walk to work on school days. But would there be any more school to walk to? Claudia asked herself glumly, as she poured out the last of the resin-flavoured Greek wine into their glasses.

'You'd definitely find another teaching job,' Laura comforted, with all the encouraging optimism of someone who didn't really need to work.

'Would I?' Despite the jeans, Claudia felt suddenly old. Who would want to employ a teacher on a high pay-scale who wouldn't see sixty again?

'Come on, Clo,' Ella encouraged. 'You're the dangerous radical in our midst. You were in Paris in 'sixty-eight throwing paving stones! You can't just give up because some snotty jobsworth is trying to sideline you!'

Claudia sipped her wine and winced. The trouble was she wasn't sure she wanted to fight back. She was beginning to feel tired. She looked around at her friends. 'A toast.' Claudia raised her glass. 'To us. It was bloody amazing while it lasted.'

'I'll drink to that,' Sal seconded. 'But it isn't over yet!'

'Oh, come on, Sal, admit it.' Ella shook her head. 'We're not middle-aged, we're ancient.'

'No we're not. There's no such thing as old any more. We're YAHs – Young At Hearts. Or maybe we're SWATS.'

'I thought that was a valley in Pakistan,' Claudia giggled.

'Or some kind of police unit,' seconded Ella.

Sal ignored them. 'Still Working At Sixty.'

'If we *are* still working,' Claudia sighed. 'Or in your case, Sal, maybe it's SOTS. Still Out There at Sixty.'

'That makes me sound like an ageing cougar with a drink problem!'

'And your point is . . . ?' Ella teased.

'Now, now,' Laura admonished. 'Don't gang up on Sal.'

'The thing is, we're just not old like people have been old in the past,' persisted Sal. 'At my age my mother looked like the Queen – with a curly perm and twinsets. I wear jeans and shop at H&M!'

'It's true we all look nothing like our mothers did,' Laura conceded. 'The only way you can tell a woman's age these days is to look at her husband!'

'The thing is we may *be* old but we don't *feel* old,' Sal insisted, 'that's what makes us different. We're the baby boomers, the Me Generation. We've always ripped up the rules and done it our way. Ageing isn't inevitable any more, it's a choice! And I, for one, am not choosing it.'

'I don't know.' Ella stretched out the arm in which she got occasional twinges of rheumatism. 'Sometimes I do feel old.'

'Nonsense! We'll never be old. We're the Woodstock generation! What was that Joni Mitchell song?' Sal delved into the recesses of her memory. 'You know, the one about being stardust and needing to get back to the Garden?'

'Yes,' Ella raised her glass. 'Let's just hope the Garden's wheelchair accessible.'

On the tube home Claudia got out her phone and set it to calculator. Yes, she was tech-savvy enough to do that, thank you, even though her daughter Gaby said she only used her phone to send nags-by-text. She roughly added up their major outgoings. If she gave up now it would damage her pension. She couldn't help smiling at Ella's jibe about her throwing paving stones in 1968, when here she was agonizing about pensions. What would the young Claudia have thought of that?

But then she'd only been an accidental anarchist. In fact, she'd really been an au pair, only seventeen, trying to improve her French before A levels, staying with a well-heeled family in the smart sixteenth arrondissement. That's when she met Thierry, best friend of the family's son. It had been Thierry, darkly good-looking with black horn-rimmed specs and an intellectual air, who had persuaded her, on her rare day off, to come and see what the students were doing.

Claudia, from safe suburban Surrey, had been entranced by the heady air of revolution, the witty graffiti daubed on the elegant buildings: *Be realistic, demand the impossible*, *I am a Marxist, Groucho Tendency*, and even more by the alluringly radical Thierry himself.

It had all been so daring and exciting. She had joined hands with Thierry and his clean-cut friends in their corduroy jackets and short haircuts, not at all the standard image of revolting students, to block the Paris streets so that the hated *flics* couldn't pass. She had ridden on his shoulders – like girls now did at music festivals – in the Latin Quarter with hundreds of thousands of others demanding sexual liberation and an end to paternalism.

It all seemed a far cry from today.

She went back to her calculations. How would they survive without her salary? Badly. At this rate, if she gave up teaching, she'd have to get a job in B&Q like all the other oldies! The most infuriating thing was that Claudia knew she was good at her job. She could enthuse her students and she was popular too. But it was true that she didn't use new technology as much as Peter Dooley did. She wondered if she was being a Luddite. *No,* she reminded herself, *I'm bloody good at what I do.* And what if she did give up? She could always coach pupils at a crammer.

But what Ella had said was true; she was still a bit of a boat-rocker and she hated privilege that could be bought by rich parents. *If I give up, I'm bound to pick up some work*, she told herself. But, deep down, Claudia knew that no matter how good she was, her age was beginning to tell against her.

By the time she got home, the brief respite from her problems brought on by wine and friendship had evaporated. She walked up their garden path, noticing that the light was on in the sitting room and that, unusually, her husband Don – also a teacher, in his case of politics – was sitting at the computer underneath the cheese plant, another feisty survivor from the Sixties. The height of fashion in 1969, cheese plants were as quaint as aspidistras now, but Claudia felt an inexplicable loyalty to it and refused to chuck it out.

She had spent most of last night moaning to him about the deputy head. In contrast to her own gloomy mood, Don seemed unusually cheery, which amazed her since recently he had been depressed about his own job. Tonight he seemed a different person.

'Hello, love.' He grinned at her, suddenly boyish. 'I think I may have found the answer to our problems!'

Somewhere deep inside, alarm bells rang. This wasn't like Don. She was always the one who got things organized, made the decisions, rang the changes. Don had always been impractical, disorganized, totally disinterested in anything remotely useful. He was usually far more caught up with how to make the electoral system come alive to bored and phone-fixated teenagers than whether the roof was leaking or where they could get a better rate of interest on their modest savings. These things he left to 'Clever Claudia'.

Their daughter Gaby had followed his example and always turned to her mother, not her father, for loans, advice and late-night lifts.

'OK,' Claudia took off her coat and hung it in the hall cupboard. 'So what *is* the answer to our problems?'

'We'll look into retiring. It'll only be a couple of years early. They always used to be asking for volunteers among the older teachers. We cost more. They can easily replace us with some kid straight out of teacher training, then we can sell this place and downsize to Surrey, near your parents, and live on the income from our investment.' His eyes shone like an early-day evangelist with a new parable to preach. 'You could keep chickens!'

Claudia shuddered. She'd always said retiring was something you did before going to bed, not with the rest of your life. On the other hand, could she stomach Drooly Dooley easing her out of her own department?

She could think of a number of extremely rude French slang expressions to describe the little toad, much ruder than those on the Internet, of which *pauvre mec* was by some way the tamest. What if she protested to Stephen, the head teacher? He was almost her own age. Would that mean he would support her or take his deputy's part? Claudia knew she had a bit of a reputation for arguing. No doubt Stephen would remember it. Besides, the days of mass early retirement for teachers was long gone. Too expensive and too many teachers, worn out by classroom confrontation, had already opted for it. Still, they might be open to negotiation . . .

She'd have to make herself more troublesome.

One thing she knew. She didn't feel ready to bury herself in the sticks. 'But I don't want to keep bloody chickens! And I don't want to move to bloody Surrey!'

'It's only twenty miles down the motorway,' Don placated, his eyes still shining dangerously and his missionary zeal undimmed. 'Half an hour on the train, max.'

'What about me?' demanded a voice quivering with outrage. 'Surrey is the home of the living dead.' Gaby, their daughter, stood in the doorway, her face ashen at the prospect of a rural retreat.

Claudia, who'd grown up there, quite agreed.

Gaby, at twenty-eight, still lived at home. Claudia loved having her. Her daughter was terrific fun and often filled the kitchen with her friends. But she also worried that Gaby really ought to be finding a job that paid enough for her to be able to move out. Gaby's response was that due to the greedy depredations of the generation above she was too broke, but Claudia sometimes feared it was because she wasn't a sticker. She had a perfectly good degree in geography but had thrown herself, in swift succession, into being an actress, a waitress, the receptionist for a vet, a call-centre operative, a circus performer (only two weeks at that), and an art gallery assistant. Recently she had decided she wanted to be an architect. Claudia and Don had exchanged glances and not mentioned the extremely lengthy training. Currently, she was at least working for one, albeit in a very junior capacity.

'We could help you with the rent on a flat,' her father announced, as if the solution were obvious.

Gaby brightened perceptibly while Claudia wondered if Don had lost his mind. 'Somewhere in Shoreditch, maybe? Or Hoxton?' Gaby named perhaps the two hippest areas in the now-fashionable East End.

'I'm not sure about that,' Don began.

'Neither am I,' Claudia agreed waspishly. 'More like in Penge on what our income will be if I leave. But that's because this whole idea of moving is ludicrous.'

'Why?' Don stood his ground for once.

'My job is here. I like London.'

'But as you say yourself, you may not want to go on with your job. What happens if Dooley gets Head of Department?'

Claudia ignored this hideous prospect. 'What about the culture on our doorstep?' she protested. 'Theatres, galleries, restaurants?'

'You never consume the culture. You're always saying theatre tickets are priced so only Russian oligarchs can afford them.'

'Art galleries, then.'

'When did you last go to an art gallery?'

Claudia moved guiltily onwards, conscious that, living in the middle of one of the world's great cities, she rarely consumed its cultural delights. 'And then there're my friends! I couldn't move twenty miles from The Grecian Grove!'

'Don't you think you're being a little selfish?' Don demanded.

'Don't you think *you* are?' Claudia flashed back. 'You've never even mentioned moving before and now it's all *my* fault because I don't want to live in the fake country.'

'Surrey isn't the fake country. Anyway, we could move to the real country. It'd probably be cheaper.'

'And even further from my friends!'

'Yes,' Don was getting uncharacteristically angry now, 'it's always about the coven, isn't it? The most important thing in your life.'

'How dare you call them the coven?'

'Hubble bubble, gossip, gossip. Sal bitching about her colleagues. Ella moaning about the son-in-law from hell, Laura judging every man by whether he's left his wife yet.'

Despite herself, Claudia giggled at the accuracy of his description.

'Thank God for that,' Gaby breathed. 'I thought you two

were heading for the divorce court rather than the far reaches of the M25. You never fight.'

'Anyway, what about *your* friends?' Claudia asked Don. 'You'd miss your Wednesdays at the Bull as much as I'd pine for my wine bar.' Each Wednesday Don met up with his three buddies to moan about their head teachers, Ofsted and the state of British education. But friendship, it seemed, wasn't hard-wired into men as it was into women.

'Cup of tea?' offered Don as if it might provide the healing power of the Holy Grail. 'Redbush?'

Claudia nodded. 'The vanilla one.'

'I know, the vanilla one.'

She kissed Gaby and went upstairs. He knew her so well, all her likes and dislikes over thirty years. They were bonded by all the tiny choices they'd made, each a brick in the citadel of their marriage. But citadels could lock you in as well as repel invaders.

Claudia undressed quickly and slipped into bed, her nerves still on edge.

Don appeared bearing tea, then disappeared into the bathroom.

Two minutes later he slipped naked into bed, the usual signal for their lovemaking. 'I'm sorry. I shouldn't have sprung it on you like that. It was really unfair.'

'Telling me.'

He began to kiss her breast. Claudia stiffened, and not with sexual anticipation. How could men think you could use sex to say sorry, when women needed you to say sorry, and mean it, before they could even consider wanting sex?

Ella got off the bus and walked along the towpath where the Grand Union Canal met up with the Thames. It was a moonlit night and a wide path of silver illuminated the water, vaguely swathed in mist, which reminded her of one of the holy pictures she had collected as a child at her convent school. These holy pictures often featured the effect of light on water as a symbol of supernatural peace. But Ella didn't feel peaceful tonight. It was one of those nights when she missed Laurence.

Any religious faith she'd had had long deserted her. It might have been a help, she supposed, when Laurence had died so suddenly, without her even being able to say goodbye, a random statistic on the News, an unlucky victim of a rare train crash. The safest form of travel. Ha. Or maybe, if she'd had faith, she might have lost it at the unfair nature of his death, away on a day's business, standing in for a colleague, not even his own client.

She thought of Claudia, and Claudia's question. What were they all going to do with the rest of their lives? It was a good question. Work, she knew, had saved her then.

It had only been her job that had got her through the grief when Laurence died. Without work to go to she would have pulled the duvet over her head and never got out of bed again.

Of course, she'd had to be strong for her daughters, but they were grown-up now, thirty-two and thirty, no longer living at home. In fact, another reason Ella had had to be strong was to prevent Julia, her eldest and bossiest daughter, swooping down on her and treating her like a small child incapable of deciding anything for itself.

Cory, her younger daughter, had been harder to console because the last time she'd seen her dad they'd quarrelled over some silly matter, and she couldn't believe she'd never see him again so they could make it up.

That had been three years ago; Ella almost had to pinch herself. The imprint of his head on the pillow next to hers had hardly disappeared. The bed felt crazily wide and every single morning she woke, she heard the empty silence of the house and had to put the radio on instantly. Jim Naughtie had proved no substitute for Laurence but he was better than nothing.

A tactless colleague, whose own husband had left her, insisted that death was better than divorce because at least you had the memories.

But sometimes the memories were the problem. She could still walk into the house, put her keys on the hall table next to the bunch of flowers she'd picked from the garden, and listen, expecting to hear the sound of sport on the television.

Her job as a lawyer had been doubly useful. She had fought the train company for an admission of guilt, not just for her but for the others. And then, when she got the admission, the fight had gone out of her. As soon as she'd hit sixty, she'd retired, just like that. Everyone had been stunned. Perhaps herself most of all.

Now she was crossing the square in front of her house. Even though it was in London it had once been a village green where a market was held, and archery contests. Now it was gravelled over but still felt more a part of the eighteenth century than the present day.

Ella stopped to look at her house, the house on which she had lavished so much care and love, the house where she had spent all her married life.

It was a handsome four-storey building of red brick with square twelve-paned windows and large stone steps going up to the front door. It was this entrance she loved the most, with its elegant portico and delicate fluted columns. Once it had been lived in by weavers, now only the substantial middle class could afford to live here.

She stopped for a moment as she put her key in the door and looked upwards. A jumbo jet was just above her, on its descent into Heathrow. It seemed so close she could reach out and catch it in her hand. Incongruously, these triumphs of Queen Anne elegance were right beneath the flight path. The area where she lived was a tiny enclosure of history surrounded on all sides by towering office blocks benefiting from their nearness to the profitable M4 corridor. The square was one of those little unexpected revelations that made people love London.

Inside the front door she could hear a radio playing and stood stock still, frozen in memory. But it wasn't Laurence, Laurence was dead. It was probably Cory, who had the disconcerting habit of turning up and staying the night if she happened to be nearby. In fact, once she'd got over the shock, Ella was delighted to have her younger daughter there.

'Cory!' she called out. 'Cory, is that you?'

Footsteps thundered up the wooden stairs from the basement and a coltish figure flung itself at her. Cory was a striking girl, slender, with skin pale as wax against a waterfall of dark brown hair. But it was her eyes that arrested you. They were a quite extraordinary bright dark blue. Sometimes they were dancing with light, yet, more often, Ella saw a sadness in their depths that worried her. Cory had so much to feel confident about – an ethereal beauty, quick intelligence, and a job she enjoyed as a museum administrator – but it had only been Laurence who had the capacity to make her believe in herself. When Ella tried to praise her daughter she somehow got it wrong, and Cory would shrug off the compliment – whether to her good taste in clothes, or an acute observation she had made – with a little angry shake, like a duckling that is eager to leave the nest but can't quite fly unaided. Today, at least, she seemed in an effervescent mood.

'Hey, Ma, how are you? I was at a boring meeting in Uxbridge and thought you might love to see me.'

'Did you now?' laughed Ella, taking in the glass of wine in her daughter's hand. She was about to ask, playfully, 'And how is that Sauvignon I was saving?' But she knew Cory would look immediately stricken, so she bit the comment back. 'Don't worry,' Ella shrugged, 'I'd join you but I've been out with the girls already.'

'Speaking of girls, your next-door neighbour is popping back in a mo. She's got something to ask you.'

'Ah. She and Angelo probably want me to water the cat or something.'

'Are they going away?'

'They're *always* going away.' Her neighbours, Viv and Angelo, shared the disconcerting energy of the prosperous early retired. They were both over sixty but had arrested their image at about twenty-six. Viv had the look of the young Mary Quant, all miniskirts, sharp bob, and big necklaces. Angelo had well-cut grey hair, almost shoulder-length, and was given to wearing hoodies in pale apricot. They drove around in an open-topped Mini with loud Sixties music blaring. If there was a line between eternally youthful and weird and creepy, they were just the right side of it. Though, looking at them, Ella sometimes wondered if anyone admitted to their age any more.

It was a constant source of surprise to Ella that Viv and Angelo also had an allotment. And this, it transpired, was the source of the favour Viv wanted to ask when she rang the doorbell half an hour later.

'Sorry it's so late. Cory said you'd be back. It's just that we're off at the crack of dawn. And I just wondered, Ella love, if you could cast an occasional eye over the allotment for us. Once a week will do, twice at the most.'

'How long are you away for?'

'Only three weeks. Diving in the Isla Mujeres.'

'Where on earth is that?'

'Mexico, I think. Angelo booked it.' Viv and Angelo went on so many holidays even they lost count. Their pastimes always made Ella feel slightly exhausted. Paragliding, hill walking, white-water rafting, cycling round vineyards – there was no end to activities for the fit and adventurous well-heeled retiree.

'And what would I have to do?'

'Just keep it looking tidyish. The allotment police are a nightmare. Keep threatening to banish anyone who doesn't keep their plot looking like Kew Gardens.'

'There aren't really allotment police, are there?' Cory demanded.

'No,' Viv admitted. 'That's what we call the committee. They used to be old boys in braces and straw hats. Now Angelo suspects they're all LGBT.'

'What is LGBT?' Ella asked.

'Mu-um!' Cory corrected, looking mock-offended. 'Lesbian Gay Bisexual Transgender.'

'Good Heavens!' Ella didn't often feel old but she did now. 'Well, that's pretty comprehensive.' In fact it probably said more about Angelo than the allotment holders.

'You just need to do a bit of deadheading, sweep the leaves, look busy. We're always being reminded of what a long waiting list there is – of far more deserving people than we are. Here's the key.'

Viv kissed her three times. 'Oh, and by the way, we've had a burglar alarm fitted next door. Angelo insisted.' She handed Ella a piece of paper. 'Here's the code if it goes off. You've got our keys anyway, haven't you?'

'Yes,' agreed Ella, beginning to feel like an unpaid concierge.

Viv was already down the garden path. 'Off at six. Angelo hates wasting a whole day travelling so we have to get the first flight out.'

'You have to admit,' marvelled Cory, 'they've got a lot of get up and go for oldies.'

'Too bloody much, if you ask me. They're trying to prove there's nothing they're too old for.'

Ella double-locked the door and dragged the bolt across, then began drawing the heavy silk curtains, undoing the fringed tiebacks with their gold gesso moulding. This was a job she especially liked. The old house with its wooden floors and oak panelling always seemed to emanate a sigh of satisfaction and embrace the peacefulness of night-time.

'You know, Mum,' Cory's thoughts broke in, 'you really ought to do the same.'

'What? Deep-sea diving? Or paragliding?'

Cory smiled ruefully, laughing at the unlikely idea of Ella throwing herself out of anything. 'Get a burglar alarm.'

'I hate burglar alarms,' Ella replied. She almost added: 'You can't forestall the unexpected, look at what happened to Dad', but it would have been too cruel. 'You're beginning to sound like your big sister Julia. Come on, time for bed. Do you want a hottie?'

Cory shook her head. 'I think I'll stay up and watch telly for a bit.'

Ella went down to the basement kitchen and made tea, thinking of Laurence. It was the little habits that she missed most, the comforting routines that knit together your couple-dom. And here she was still doing it without him. Now all she had to look forward to was babysitting her neighbours' allot-ment while they swanned off living the life of people thirty years younger. Except that people who were actually thirty years younger couldn't afford to do it.

Ella turned off the light, listening for a moment to the big old house's silence. It had been a wreck when they'd bought it, with a tree growing in the waterlogged basement. She had coaxed the house back to life with love and devotion, steeping herself in the history of the period, studying the other houses in the square so that theirs would be just as lovely.

'Good night, house,' she whispered so that Cory didn't think she'd finally lost it. 'We're all each other has these days. Too much to hope anything exciting is going to happen to me.'

She shook herself metaphorically as she went upstairs to bed. She'd tried so hard to resist self-pity during the dark days after Laurence's death, she was damned if she was going to give in to it now.

Sal stood in the wastes of Eagleton Road hoping a taxi would come past. She shouldn't get a cab, she knew. It was unnecessary and not even something she could charge to expenses, as one could in the heyday of magazines, when staff just charged everything they liked and The Great Provider, aka *Euston Magazine*, paid up without a whimper. Now the publishing landscape was getting as bleak as Siberia.

Sal began walking desultorily towards the tube station, playing one of her favourite games which decreed that if a cab went past before she got there, fate intended her to jump into it, and who could argue with fate? Sal realized she was stacking the odds by walking particularly slowly in her unsuitable high heels. The thing was, these shoes were made for taxi travel and no one, especially their designer, had envisaged a customer schlepping down the uneven pavement of Eagleton Road.

Fate was on her side and a lone cab hove into view with its light on.

Sal hailed it with all the joy and relief of a refugee getting the last berth on a transport ship out of some war-torn hotspot.

'Middlebridge Crescent, please.' They headed off for the rather sleazy enclave in North Kensington, on the borders of upmarket Notting Hill Gate, where Sal had managed to find an unfurnished flat thirty years ago, settling for four somewhat uninviting rooms in an unappealing road in exchange for the nearness of its glamorous big sister.

The truth was, although Sal gave every appearance of being the career woman on top of life, there were aspects of living she was hopeless at: mortgages, pensions, savings plans. None of these had ever caught her imagination like sample sales, freebies to exotic spas, London Fashion Week – these were what made Sal's heart beat faster.

She paid the cab driver, and was touched that he waited till she had safely descended the steps to her front door, in case any marauding mugger should be concealed there. 'Good night, miss,' he called, although he knew and she knew that this description, though technically true, was an entirely generous gesture.

'Good night,' she responded, opening her grey-painted front door. Funny how grey front doors had suddenly become *de rigueur* on brick-fronted houses, and any other colour suddenly seemed strange and somehow wrong. That was how fashion worked, of course. Grey wasn't simply the new black, as far as front doors went; it was the new red, green and blue.

She shivered as she turned her key, grateful for the warm embrace of central heating, which might not be as enticing as a waiting lover, but was a lot cheaper to run and far less temperamental.

October already. Incredible. She smiled at the memory of the photograph of the four of them and then recoiled at the thought of how many years ago it was. She had never imagined that here she would be, more than forty years later, living alone, paying her way, dependent for her standard of living on the whim of Maurice Euston and his daughter Marian, who had just been elevated to Managing Director.

It struck her as she sat down on her aubergine velvet sofa and shucked off her agonizing heels that the all-important Christmas issue would be out by the end of the month. Of course, the whole thing had been put to bed months ago. All those children simpering round the Christmas tree in cute pyjamas had actually been sweating in a heat-wave. All the same, she – Sal – still believed in the fantasy. It didn't matter if they had to cheat a little to make the fantasy work. She had never felt cynical and bored, never wanted to shout: 'Oh for God's sake, I've heard that idea four hundred times before!' at some hapless young journalist.

Sal loved magazines. When she was growing up on her Carlisle council estate, she hadn't been able to afford them and had devoured as many as she could at the hairdresser when her mum had her Tuesday afternoon cheap-rate shampoo and set. They remained a gorgeous parcel of me-time. Gift-wrapped with glossiness and sprinkled with celebrity stardust, they brought pleasure to millions. Well, maybe not quite millions, that was half the problem, but thousands anyway. To Sal, a magazine was still something you held in your hand, savouring the thrill of flicking through the first pages, not something you summoned on your iPad or furtively consulted online during your lunch break. She knew you had to keep up, though, and had worked hard to make sure these options were there, and as inviting as any offered by *Modern Style*'s rivals.

Sal made herself a cup of green tea. She mustn't let the magazine take up her entire waking life. She was no workaholic. She had other interests and passions.

Didn't she?

Laura parked in the driveway of her solid suburban house. She had been careful only to have two small glasses so that she would be below the limit. Laura preferred driving to taking the bus or tube. Somehow it meant she didn't have to leave the protective cocoon of home, and that was how she liked it. You could argue that the tube was more interesting. All those different nationalities. People reading books, e-readers, free newspapers, playing games on their phones. And the fashions. She liked seeing all the ways young women put their clothes together. But there were also beggars, stringing you some story, the noisy drunks talking out loud to themselves, and the exhausted, worn-out workers who made Laura feel faintly guilty about her easy life.

Tonight, though she knew it was awful, she also felt slightly smug. It was amazing that, out of the four of them, she was the only one who was truly happy with her life. Ella had had that tragedy, so utterly unfair, out of the blue like that; Sal never thought about anyone but Sal, which was why she'd ended up on her own; and Claudia had been married a long time, but she was always moaning about Don's head being in the clouds, and they never seemed to be soulmates. Not like she and Simon were.

It was an object of pride to Laura that Simon loved her and his home as much as he did, that they were perfectly happy in each other's company. Of course she loved her friends, but Simon came first.

And she knew he felt the same about her. In fact, the only source of friction between them was their children. When Bella had become a Goth, Simon was appalled. Laura, on the other hand, rather admired her for it. She knew that she herself was a boringly conservative dresser and partly blamed this for Bella needing to express her individuality by clothing herself like the heroine of a Hammer horror film in a silk top hat, veil and Victorian riding gear. When Bella had dyed her silky blonde hair inky black, Simon had almost cried.

And she knew that their son, Sam, quiet, heavy-metal loving Sam, who loathed all sports, was a disappointment to Simon too. Simon had been so thrilled at having a son that he had plonked him in front of the TV for *Match of the Day* from the moment he was born. And the only result had been that Sam hated football until he was at least twelve.

Even though it could be stressful at times, Laura was still grateful that both her children lived at home. Home and family were the same thing in her book. And, Laura had to admit, their children were especially precious after all the fertility problems they'd had. There had been times when Laura had almost given up. Simon had argued the whole thing was taking too much of a toll on her, though she'd felt that he was referring to himself. He had hated all the rollercoaster of hope and disappointment of assisted conception even more than she had. And then, finally, at forty, to find that she was pregnant with Bella! She would never forget that positive pregnancy test as long as she lived. And to make their world complete, Sam had come along two years later.

Ever since their arrival, she had wanted to be here for them, not out at work, but providing a safe and happy environment. She relished being home when they came back from school and shouted, 'Hi, Mum, I'm back.'

Still hugging herself at how much she loved them she went up to bed. The sight of her bedroom always made her happy. It was so exactly what she'd wanted. Soft carpets, crisp white linen, roses in a vase. The air in the room was cold since Simon, the product of boarding school, liked the window wide open. It was one of the few things besides the children that they argued about. Fortunately, he slept like a corpse so she could get away with closing it as soon as he nodded off. If she remembered, she would guiltily open it a few inches in the morning before he woke.

As she slipped into bed he murmured and turned. She thought perhaps he was feeling amorous and experienced a wave of guilt as he shifted back to the wall, eyes closed.

The sheets had been clean this morning, which always gave her a dilemma. There was something seductive about clean sheets, but, equally, did one want to spoil them with the messiness of making love? Not that they had much of that these days. Simon seemed perfectly affectionate yet rarely pushed for sex. Laura had even wondered about Viagra.

'With my husband we had to wait forever for it to work,' warned Susie, her tennis partner. 'Not to mention me having to wank him like a Thai hooker all the time unless he did it himself. And then, just as you're nodding off, there it'll be, poking into your bum. And once it's up, it's up for hours.'

Laura had giggled, imagining an erotic puppet show with Mr Punch using his willy instead of the usual stick and chanting, 'That's the way to do it!'

On the whole she was glad Simon was sound asleep.

extracts reading groups

competitions books new

discounts extracts extracts

competitions reading groups

books new discounts

reading groups new extracts events

events books reading groups

extracts books new titles reading groups

interviews

books events extracts extracts events new

discounts events interviews books

new books events events new books extracts

events new

discounts extracts discounts books

www.panmacmillan.com

extracts events reading groups

competitions books extracts new books